PENGUIN CLASSICS

THE WITHERED ARM
AND OTHER STORIES 1874–1888

THOMAS HARDY was born in a cottage in Higher Bockhampton, near Dorchester, on 1 June 1940. He was educated locally and at sixteen was articled to a Dorchester architect, John Hicks. In 1862 he moved to London and found employment with another architect, Arthur Blomfield. He now began to write poetry and published an essay. By 1867 he had returned to Dorset to work as Hicks's assistant and began his first (unpublished) novel, *The Poor Man and the Lady*.

On an architectural visit to St Juliot in Cornwall in 1870 he met his first wife, Emma Gifford. Before their marraige in 1874 he had published four novels and was earning his living as a writer. More novels followed and in 1878 the Hardys moved from Dorset to the London literary scene. But in 1885, after building his house at Max Gate near Dorchester, Hardy again returned to Dorset. He then produced most of his major novels: *The Mayor of Casterbridge* (1886), *The Woodlanders* (1887), *Tess of the D'Urbervilles* (1891), *The Pursuit of the Well-Beloved* (1892) and *Jude the Obscure* (1895). During the same period he published three volumes of short stories: *Wessex Tales* (1888), *A Group of Noble Dames* (1891) and *Life's Little Ironies* (1894). Amidst the controversy caused by *Jude the Obscure*, he turned to the poetry he had been writing all his life. In the next thirty years he published over nine hundred poems and his epic drama in verse, *The Dynasts*.

After a long and bitter estrangement, Emma Hardy died at Max Gate in 1912. Paradoxically, the event triggered some of Hardy's finest love poetry. In 1914, however, he married Florence Dugdale, a close friend for several years. In 1910 he had been awarded the Order of Merit and was recognized, even revered, as the major literary figure of the time. He died on 11 January 1928. His ashes were buried in Westminster Abbey and his heart at Stinsford in Dorset.

KRISTIN BRADY is the author of *The Short Stories of Thomas Hardy: Tales of Past and Present* (1982) and of *George Eliot* (1992), as well as numerous articles on Hardy, Eliot, Nathaniel Hawthorne and feminist theory. Educated at the University of Toronto, she was Professor of English at the University of Western Ontario, where she taught in the Department of English and in the Centre for Women's Studies and Feminist Research. Kristin Brady died in 1998.

PATRICIA INGHAM is General Editor of all Hardy's fiction in the Penguin Classics Edition. She is a Fellow of St Anne's College, Reader in English and *The Times* Lecturer in English Language, the University of Oxford. She has written extensively on the Victorian novel and on Hardy in particular. Her most recent publications include *Dickens, Women and Language* (1992) and *The Language of Gender and Class: Transformation in the Victorian Novel* (1996). She has also edited Elizabeth Gaskell's *North and South* and Thomas Hardy's *The Pursuit of the Well-Beloved and The Well-Beloved* and *The Woodlanders* for Penguin Classics.

THOMAS HARDY

The Withered Arm and Other Stories

1874–1888

Edited with an Introduction and Notes by
KRISTIN BRADY

PENGUIN BOOKS

PENGUIN BOOKS

Published by the Penguin Group
Penguin Books Ltd, 27 Wrights Lane, London w8 5tz, England
Penguin Putnam Inc., 375 Hudson Street, New York, New York 10014, USA
Penguin Books Australia Ltd, Ringwood, Victoria, Australia
Penguin Books Canada Ltd, 10 Alcorn Avenue, Toronto, Ontario, Canada m4v 3b2
Penguin Books (NZ) Ltd, Private Bag 102902, NSMC, Auckland, New Zealand

Penguin Books Ltd, Registered Offices: Harmondsworth, Middlesex, England

Published in Penguin Classic Books 1999
3 5 7 9 10 8 6 4 2

Editorial matter copyright © Kristin Brady, 1999
General Editor's Preface and Chronology copyright © Patricia Ingham, 1996
All rights reserved

The moral right of the editor has been asserted

Set in 10/12.5pt Monotype Baskerville
Typeset by Rowland Phototypesetting Ltd, Bury St Edmunds, Suffolk
Printed in England by Clays Ltd, St Ives plc

Except in the United States of America, this book is sold subject
to the condition that it shall not, by way of trade or otherwise, be lent,
re-sold, hired out, or otherwise circulated without the publisher's
prior consent in any form of binding or cover other than that in
which it is published and without a similar condition including this
condition being imposed on the subsequent purchaser

CONTENTS

ACKNOWLEDGEMENTS

I am happy to offer formal thanks to the staffs of several libraries for access to research materials and various incarnations of Hardy's stories: the British Library; the Bodleian Library; the University of Toronto Library; the University of British Columbia Library; the Toronto Metropolitan Library; and the D. B. Weldon Library at the University of Western Ontario, especially David Murphy in the Department of Interlibrary Loans and David Newman in Special Collections.

My work was greatly aided by a grant from the University of Western Ontario (funded by the Social Sciences and Humanities Research Council of Canada), which supplied travel funds and an expert Research Assistant, Professor Grace Kehler. The Department of English also provided careful and energetic Research Assistants, Jacqueline Mottl (with the help of Joan Mottl) and Tina Tasikas, who spent many hours collating the stories. Several generous colleagues offered their advice and erudition: Dr Judith Williams and Professors D. M. R. Bentley, Cecily Devereux, Richard F. Green, Donald Hair, Thomas J. Lennon, John Leonard, Antony Littlewood, Corinne Mandel, Leslie Murison, R. J. Shroyer, Leon Surette and Keith Wilson. Professor Patricia Ingham was a supremely knowledgeable, patient and helpful General Editor; and Lindeth Vasey, more than a copy editor, offered useful information and checked sources in the British Library.

Support of all kinds (including last-minute trips to the library) came as always from Professor Richard Hillman. And Malcolm, who still likes his stories to be shorter than Hardy's, made sure that there was time to play.

GENERAL EDITOR'S PREFACE

This edition uses, with one exception, the first edition in *volume* form of each of Hardy's novels and therefore offers something not generally available. Their dates range from 1871 to 1897. The purpose behind this choice is to present each novel as the creation of its own period and without revisions of later times, since these versions have an integrity and value of their own. The outline of textual history that follows is designed to expand on this statement.

All of Hardy's fourteen novels, except *Jude the Obscure* (1895) which first appeared as a volume in the Wessex Novels, were published individually as he wrote them (from 1871 onwards). Apart from *Desperate Remedies* (1871) and *Under the Greenwood Tree* (1872), all were published first as serials in periodicals, where they were subjected to varying degrees of editorial interference and censorship. *Desperate Remedies* and *Under the Greenwood Tree* appeared directly in volume form from Tinsley Brothers. By 1895 ten more novels had been published in volumes by six different publishers.

By 1895 Hardy was sufficiently well-established to negotiate with Osgood, McIlvaine a collected edition of all earlier novels and short story collections plus the volume edition of *Jude the Obscure*. *The Well-Beloved* (radically changed from its serialized version) was added in 1897, completing the appearance of all Hardy's novels in volume form. Significantly this collection was called the 'Wessex Novels' and contained a map of 'The Wessex of the Novels' and authorial prefaces, as well as frontispieces by Macbeth-Raeburn of a scene from the novel sketched 'on the spot'. The texts were heavily revised by Hardy, amongst other things, in relation to topography, to strengthen the 'Wessex' element so as to suggest that this half-real half-imagined location had been coherently conceived from the beginning, though of course he knew that this was not so. In practice 'Wessex' had an uncertain and ambiguous development in the earlier editions. To trace the growth of Wessex in the novels as they appeared it is necessary to read them in their original pre-1895 form. For the 1895–6 edition represents a substantial layer of reworking.

Similarly, in the last fully revised and collected edition of 1912–13, the Wessex Edition, further alterations were made to topographical detail and photographs of Dorset were included. In the more open climate of opinion then prevailing, sexual and religious references were sometimes (though not always) made bolder. In both collected editions there were also many changes of other kinds. In addition, novels and short story volumes were grouped thematically as 'Novels of Character and Environment', 'Romances and Fantasies' and 'Novels of Ingenuity' in a way suggesting a unifying master plan underlying all texts. A few revisions were made for the Mellstock Edition of 1919–20, but to only some texts.

It is various versions of the 1912–13 edition which are generally available today, incorporating these layers of alteration and shaped in part by the critical climate when the alterations were made. Therefore the present edition offers the texts as Hardy's readers first encountered them, in a form of which he in general approved, the version that his early critics reacted to. It reveals Hardy as he first dawned upon the public and shows how his writing (including the creation of Wessex) developed, partly in response to differing climates of opinion in the 1870s, 1880s and early 1890s. In keeping with these general aims, the edition will reproduce all contemporary illustrations where the originals were line drawings. In addition for all texts which were illustrated, individual volumes will provide an appendix discussing the artist and the illustrations.

The exception to the use of the first volume editions is *Far From the Madding Crowd*, for which Hardy's holograph manuscript will be used. That edition will demonstrate in detail just how the text is 'the creation of its own period': by relating the manuscript to the serial version and to the first volume edition. The heavy editorial censoring by Leslie Stephen for the serial and the subsequent revision for the volume provide an extreme example of the processes that in many cases precede and produce the first book versions. In addition, the complete serial version (1892) of *The Well-Beloved* will be printed alongside the volume edition, since it is arguably a different novel from the latter.

To complete the picture of how the texts developed later, editors trace in their Notes on the History of the Text the major changes in 1895–6 and 1912–13. They quote significant alterations in their explanatory notes and include the authorial prefaces of 1895–6 and 1912–13. They also indicate something of the pre-history of the texts in manuscripts where these are available. The editing of the short stories will be separately dealt with in the two volumes containing them.

Patricia Ingham
St Anne's College, Oxford

1840 2 June: Thomas Hardy born, Higher Bockhampton, Dorset, eldest child of a builder, Thomas Hardy, and Jemima Hand, who had been married for less than six months. Younger siblings: Mary, Henry, Katharine (Kate), to whom he remained close.

1848–56 Schooling in Dorset.

1856 Hardy watched the hanging of Martha Browne for the murder of her husband. (Thought to be remembered in the death of Tess Durbeyfield.)

1856–60 Articled to Dorchester architect, John Hicks; later his assistant.

late 1850s Important friendship with Horace Moule (eight years older, middle-class and well-educated), who became his intellectual mentor and encouraged his self-education.

1862 London architect, Arthur Blomfield, employed him as a draughtsman. Self-education continued.

1867 Returned to Dorset as a jobbing architect. He worked for Hicks on church restoration.

1868 Completed his first novel *The Poor Man and the Lady* but it was rejected for publication (see 1878).

1869 Worked for the architect Crickmay in Weymouth, again on church restoration.

1870 After many youthful infatuations thought to be referred to in early poems, met his first wife, Emma Lavinia Gifford, on a professional visit to St Juliot in north Cornwall.

1871 *Desperate Remedies* published in volume form by Tinsley Brothers.

1872 *Under the Greenwood Tree* published in volume form by Tinsley Brothers.

1873 *A Pair of Blue Eyes* (previously serialized in *Tinsleys' Magazine*). Horace Moule committed suicide.

1874 *Far from the Madding Crowd* (previously serialized in the *Cornhill*

Magazine). Hardy married Emma and set up house in London (Surbiton). They had no children, to Hardy's regret; and she never got on with his family.

1875 The Hardys returned to Dorset (Swanage).

1876 *The Hand of Ethelberta* (previously serialized in the *Cornhill Magazine*).

1878 *The Return of the Native* (previously serialized in *Belgravia*). The Hardys moved back to London (Tooting). Serialized version of part of first unpublished novel appeared in *Harper's Weekly* in New York as *An Indiscretion in the Life of an Heiress*. It was never included in his collected works.

1880 *The Trumpet-Major* (previously serialized in *Good Words*). Hardy ill for many months.

1881 *A Laodicean* (previously serialized in *Harper's New Monthly Magazine*). The Hardys returned to Dorset.

1882 *Two on a Tower* (previously serialized in the *Atlantic Monthly*).

1885 The Hardys moved for the last time to a house, Max Gate, outside Dorchester, designed by Hardy and built by his brother.

1886 *The Mayor of Casterbridge* (previously serialized in the *Graphic*).

1887 *The Woodlanders* (previously serialized in *Macmillan's Magazine*).

1888 *Wessex Tales*.

1891 *A Group of Noble Dames* (tales). *Tess of the D'Urbervilles* (previously serialized in censored form in the *Graphic*). It simultaneously enhanced his reputation as a novelist and caused a scandal because of its advanced views on sexual conduct.

1892 Hardy's father, Thomas, died. Serialized version of *The Well-Beloved*, entitled *The Pursuit of the Well-Beloved*, in the *Illustrated London News*. Growing estrangement from Emma.

1892–3 *Our Exploits at West Poley*, a long tale for boys, published in an American periodical, the *Household*.

1893 Met Florence Henniker, one of several society women with whom he had intense friendships. Collaborated with her on *The Spectre of the Real* (published 1894).

1894 *Life's Little Ironies* (tales).

1895 *Jude the Obscure*, a savage attack on marriage which worsened relations with Emma. Serialized previously in *Harper's New Monthly Magazine*. It received both eulogistic and vitriolic reviews. The latter were a factor in his ceasing to write novels.

1895–6   First Collected Edition of novels: Wessex Novels (16 volumes), published by Osgood, McIlvaine. This included the first book edition of *Jude the Obscure*.

1897   *The Well-Beloved* (rewritten) published as a book; added to the Wessex Novels as vol. XVII. From now on he published only the poetry he had been writing since the 1860s. **No more novels**.

1898   *Wessex Poems and Other Verses*. Hardy and Emma continued to live at Max Gate but were now estranged and 'kept separate'.

1901   *Poems of the Past and the Present*.

1902   Macmillan became his publishers.

1904   Part 1 of *The Dynasts* (epic-drama in verse on Napoleon). Hardy's mother, Jemima, 'the single most important influence in his life', died.

1905   Met Florence Emily Dugdale, his future second wife, then aged 26. Soon a friend and secretary.

1906   Part 2 of *The Dynasts*.

1908   Part 3 of *The Dynasts*.

1909   *Time's Laughingstocks and Other Verses*.

1910   Awarded Order of Merit, having previously refused a knighthood.

1912–13   Major collected edition of novels and verse, revised by Hardy: The Wessex Edition (24 volumes). 27 November: Emma died still estranged. This triggered the writing of Hardy's finest love-lyrics about their early time in Cornwall.

1913   *A Changed Man and Other Tales*.

1914   10 February: married Florence Dugdale (already hurt by his poetic reaction to Emma's death). *Satires of Circumstance. The Dynasts: Prologue and Epilogue*.

1915   Mary, Hardy's sister, died. His distant young cousin, Frank, killed at Gallipoli.

1916   *Selected Poems*.

1917   *Moments of Vision and Miscellaneous Verses*.

1919–20 Mellstock Edition of novels and verse (37 volumes).

1922 *Late Lyrics and Earlier with Many Other Verses.*

1923 *The Famous Tragedy of the Queen of Cornwall* (drama).

1924 Dramatized *Tess* performed at Dorchester. Hardy infatuated with the local woman, Gertrude Bugler, who played Tess.

1925 *Human Shows, Far Phantasies, Songs and Trifles.*

1928 Hardy died on 11 January. His heart was buried in Emma's grave at Stinsford, his ashes in Westminster Abbey. *Winter Words in Various Moods and Metres* published posthumously. Hardy's brother, Henry, died.

1928–30 Hardy's autobiography published (on his instructions) under his second wife's name.

1937 Florence Hardy (his second wife) died.

1940 Hardy's last sibling, Kate, died.

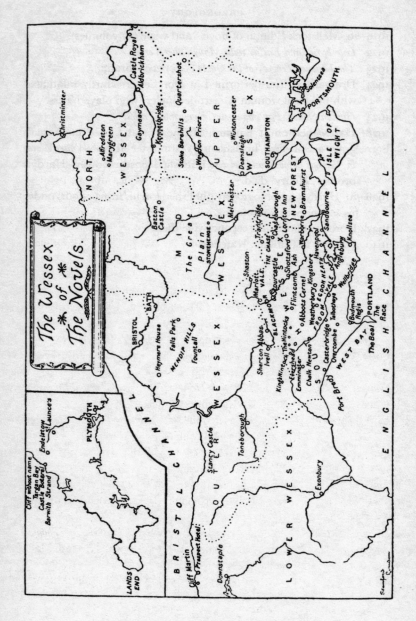

This map is from the Wessex Novels Edition, 1895–6

BIBLIOGRAPHICAL NOTE

The following abbreviations are used for frequently cited sources:

Barnes — William Barnes, *A Glossary of the Dorset Dialect with a Grammar of its Word Shapening and Wording*, 2nd edn (1886; rpt. Guernsey: Toucan Press, 1970)

Biography — Michael Millgate, *Thomas Hardy: A Biography* (Oxford: Oxford University Press, 1982)

Brady — Kristin Brady, *The Short Stories of Thomas Hardy: Tales of Past and Present* (Basingstoke: Macmillan, 1982)

Collected Letters — Thomas Hardy, *The Collected Letters of Thomas Hardy*, ed. Richard Little Purdy and Michael Millgate, 7 vols. (Oxford: Oxford University Press, 1978–88)

DNB — *Dictionary of National Biography*, ed. Leslie Stephen, 63 vols. (London: Smith, Elder, 1885–1900)

Firor — Ruth Firor, *Folkways in Thomas Hardy* (1931; New York: Barnes, 1962)

Gatrell — Simon Gatrell, *Hardy the Creator: A Textual Biography* (Oxford: Clarendon, 1988)

Kay-Robinson — Denys Kay-Robinson, *The Landscape of Thomas Hardy* (Exeter: Webb & Bower, 1984)

Lea — Hermann Lea, *Thomas Hardy's Wessex* (1913; rpt. Basingstoke: Macmillan, 1977)

Life — Thomas Hardy, *The Life and Work of Thomas Hardy*, ed. Michael Millgate (Basingstoke: Macmillan, 1984)

Literary Notebooks — Thomas Hardy, *The Literary Notebooks of Thomas Hardy*, ed. Lennart A. Björk, 2 vols. (London: Macmillan, 1985)

Mitchell — *Victorian Britain: An Encyclopedia*, ed. Sally Mitchell (New York: Garland, 1988)

OED 2	*Oxford English Dictionary*, prepared by J. A. Simpson and E. S. C. Weiner, 2nd edn., 20 vols. (Oxford: Clarendon, 1989)
Personal Notebooks	Thomas Hardy, *The Personal Notebooks of Thomas Hardy*, ed. Richard H. Taylor (Basingstoke: Macmillan, 1979)
Personal Writings	Thomas Hardy, *Thomas Hardy's Personal Writings: Prefaces, Literary Opinions, Reminiscences*, ed. Harold Orel (1966; Lawrence: University Press of Kansas, 1969)
Poetical Works	Thomas Hardy, *The Complete Poetical Works of Thomas Hardy*, ed. Samuel Hynes, 5 vols. (Oxford: Clarendon, 1982–95)
Purdy	Richard Little Purdy, *Thomas Hardy: A Bibliographical Study* (1954; Oxford: Clarendon, 1968)
Ray	Martin Ray, *Thomas Hardy: A Textual Study of the Short Stories* (Aldershot: Ashgate, 1997)
Smith	J. B. Smith, 'Dialect in Hardy's Short Stories', *Thomas Hardy Annual* 3 (1985), 79–92
Studies	Thomas Hardy, *Thomas Hardy's 'Studies, Specimens &c.' Notebook*, ed. Pamela Dalziel and Michael Millgate (Oxford: Clarendon, 1994)
Udal	John Symonds Udal, *Dorsetshire Folk-Lore*, 2nd edn. (1922; rpt. Guernsey: Toucan Press, 1970)
Wilson	Keith Wilson, *Thomas Hardy on Stage* (Basingstoke: Macmillan, 1995)
Wright	J. Wright, *English Dialect Dictionary*, 6 vols. (1898–1905; rpt. Oxford: Oxford University Press, 1970)

The following abbreviations are used for particular printings of Hardy's stories:

1879 *HW*	1879 printing of 'The Distracted Preacher' in *Harper's Weekly*
1879 *NQM*	1879 printing of 'The Distracted Preacher' in *New Quarterly Magazine*

1880 *HW* 1880 printing of 'Fellow-Townsmen' in *Harper's Weekly*

1880 *NQM* 1880 printing of 'Fellow-Townsmen' in *New Quarterly Magazine*

1883 *LM* 1883 printing of 'The Three Strangers' in *Longman's Magazine*

1883a *HW* 1883 printing of 'The Three Strangers' in *Harper's Weekly*

1883 *G* 1883 printing of 'The Romantic Adventures of a Milkmaid' in the *Graphic*

1883b *HW* 1883 printing of 'The Romantic Adventures of a Milkmaid' in *Harper's Weekly*

1884 *EIM* 1884 printing of 'Interlopers at the Knap' in *English Illustrated Magazine*

1888 *MM* 1888 printing of 'The Waiting Supper' in *Murray's Magazine*

1888 *BM* 1888 printing of 'The Withered Arm' in *Blackwood's Edinburgh Magazine*

1888 *WT* *Wessex Tales: Strange, Lively, and Commonplace* (London: Macmillan, 1888)

1896 *WT* *Wessex Tales: Strange, Lively, and Commonplace* (London: Osgood, McIlvaine, 1896)

1912 *WT* *Wessex Tales: Strange, Lively, and Commonplace* (London: Macmillan, 1912)

1913 *CM* *A Changed Man, The Waiting Supper, and Other Tales, Concluding With The Romantic Adventures of a Milkmaid* (London: Macmillan, 1913)

INTRODUCTION

The narratives collected in this first and in the second Penguin volume
of the short fiction of Thomas Hardy number slightly above a third
of the more than fifty stories he published between 1874 and 1900.
When making the difficult decisions about what to include, I have
attempted to draw together stories that are both engaging for readers
and representative of different phases in Hardy's career as a writer of
short narrative. I have also chosen two early uncollected stories that
are not widely available. And in keeping with the aim of this Penguin
series to convey a sense of each work as 'the creation of its own period',
I have ordered the stories chronologically, based on the time of their
first publication.[1] The texts in this volume date from 1874, when
Hardy's first prose narrative appeared (I am bypassing his 1865 sketch,
'How I Built Myself a House'), to 1888, the year in which he published
his first collection of short fiction, *Wessex Tales*. During this period,
when his name became associated with such major novels as *Far From
the Madding Crowd*, *The Return of the Native*, *The Mayor of Casterbridge*,
and *The Woodlanders*, Hardy was simultaneously in the process of
establishing himself as a writer of first-rate short fiction. For in spite
of his cynicism about the poor market for stories – he told his friend
Florence Henniker that 'publishers are as a rule shy of them, except
those that are written by people who cannot write long ones successfully'[2] – Hardy came gradually to use them as important vehicles for
experimenting with new ideas and techniques: since no single story
would receive the extended attention from reviewers that was given
to a novel, Hardy could take extra risks with the short narratives, and
he sometimes did.

'Destiny and a Blue Cloak', Hardy's first story and a relatively
minor one, is still a revealing starting point for an examination of the
short fiction. Hardy mailed it to *The New York Times* five days before
his first marriage in September 1874, at a time when he was working

hard to make a living in London by his writing alone.[3] 'Destiny' does not aspire, however, to the technical sophistication of *Far From the Madding Crowd*, which had just been published in England with great success, and instead looks backward to the melodramatic plotting and stereotypical characterizations of *Desperate Remedies* (1871), the book Hardy wrote deliberately in the mould of the sensation novel, a popular genre during the 1860s. Indeed, the story's emphasis on Agatha Pollin's moments of shuddering and shivering suggests a self-conscious use of that genre's conventions, which included titillating sexual details inadmissible in a standard romance plot. In this relatively simple story, we see Hardy rehearsing a technique he would use habitually in his later stories, that of foregrounding bodily feelings in order to explore the complicated dynamics of a sexual relationship. In 'Destiny', Hardy uses this device, not to depict the courtship of the two romance protagonists, which is quintessentially conventional, but to dramatize the repulsion felt by young Agatha Pollin toward the sexual overtures of the 'aged youth' Farmer Lovill. Most grotesque is the scene in which Agatha's white chemise is a representation of her nascent sexuality, while Lovill's walking-stick is the phallic embodiment of his unwanted sexual desire for her. His rescue of her chemise when it is being swept toward her uncle's mill-wheel, as he is seen 'hooking and crooking [his stick] with all his might', becomes emblematic of his ultimate possession of her person, for it is in response to this incident that he begins to think of her in sexual terms: in another passage full of *double entendre*, we are told that 'Farmer Lovill retired [from this scene], lifting his fingers privately, to express amazement on a small scale, and murmuring, "What a nice young thing! Well, to be sure. Yes, a nice child – young woman rather, indeed, a marriageable woman, come to that; of course she is." '[4] This play on literal and figural representations of sexuality is crude and obvious, but it also looks forward to the more symbolically charged use of strawberries and roses in Alec D'Urberville's harrassment of Tess – not to mention the notorious assault with a pig's pizzle in Arabella's first encounter with Jude. 'Destiny' anticipates, indeed, several prominent scenarios and ideas in Hardy's later work. Most obviously, Lovill is a dry run for Lord Mountclere, the ancient bridegroom in *The Hand of Ethelberta*, published a year after 'Destiny' (this similarity may be a reason why the story was never collected in volume form). In addition, the wheel-of-fortune-like revolving fates of Agatha and Frances Lovill look forward to similar structural elements in the plotting of 'Fellow-Townsmen' and 'The Withered Arm' – as well as in *The Mayor of Casterbridge* (1886) – and the possibility of becoming infatuated with a stranger is more thoroughly explored in 'An Imaginative Woman' (1894). The idea of Oswald being attracted to the 'name' of Frances while seeing the 'face' of 'Agatha' is likewise a simpler version of the splitting in 'On the Western Circuit' (1891) between the passionate language of Edith Harnham and the youthful body of her illiterate servant Anna.

As all these comparisons suggest, 'Destiny and a Blue Cloak' serves as an early testing ground for Hardy's interest in the sexual politics of the romance plot. Pamela Dalziel has suggested that the story is 'a statement on the social marginalization of women', for '[i]n no other work of Hardy's is the paucity of options for women more bleakly presented than in "Destiny" '[5] Yet the story must also be seen as disturbingly contradictory, for it does not contain even indirect criticism of the attitudes that create such marginalization, typified in Oswald's initial greeting to Agatha 'in the free manner usual with him toward pretty and inexperienced country girls'. Hardy's distinctly male narrator is no different from Oswald in this respect, for he too, though sympathetic with the individual, condescends toward women as a group: when Agatha is parted from Oswald, the narrator describes her as wandering about, 'weav[ing] thoughts of him that young women understand so well', and after her engagement to Lovill, she secretly writes to Oswald 'with all the womanly strategy she [is] capable of'. This assumption of an essential female instinct or mode of behaviour, also characteristic of Hardy's later narrations, may be linked to ideas about female sexuality proposed in 1871 by Charles Darwin (whom Hardy admired) in *The Descent of Man*.

Following 'Destiny', Hardy did not publish another story until two years after the 1875 appearance of *The Hand of Ethelberta*, perhaps because he spent the intervening time travelling in Europe, moving house to several different places in Dorset and beginning the massive project of self-education that was to take palpable form in the *Literary Notebooks*. In any case, 'The Thieves Who Couldn't Help Sneezing', published while Hardy was living at Sturminster Newton in 1877, obviously did not require much of Hardy's creative energy or concentration, and its interest lies more in its modest charm than in any close connections to his later work – except, perhaps, in its preoccupation with class. A children's story, 'Thieves' adapts the fairy-tale figure of the boy who outwits evil or powerful forces in the adult world. Thus fourteen-year-old Hubert defends his yeoman class by triumphing over both the common thieves who steal his horse and a wealthy Baronet, whose family subject him to a series of indignities. When they mockingly offer him snuff, a stimulant used chiefly by upper-class men and associated with social niceties of which Hubert has no knowledge,[6] he responds in whimsical retaliation by using it simultaneously to reveal the hiding place of the thieves and to prove his cleverness and honesty. With this double focus on issues of morality and class, the story portrays a rite of passage that links virility, not with snuff and noble birth, but with the yeoman's integrity and resourcefulness – characteristics that link Hubert with several of Hardy's heroes, especially Diggory Venn of *The Return of the Native*, the novel that began its serialization only a month after the publication of 'Thieves'.

While *Return* was appearing during most of 1878, Hardy also published two more short stories: 'The Impulsive Lady of Croome Castle', which was later to be collected in *A Group of Noble Dames* as 'The Duchess of Hamptonshire', and 'An Indiscretion in the Life of an Heiress', revised from the manuscript of Hardy's unpublished first novel, *The Poor Man and the Lady*. After his move back to London in March, however, Hardy devoted most of his energies to research for *The Trumpet-Major*, set on the Dorset coast during the Napoleonic period, and this location may have reminded him of the lively stories he had heard about smuggling along the same coastline during the 1830s. For 'The Distracted Preacher', first published in April 1879, is adapted from several oral sources, including some from Hardy's family. In 1871, he had written a personal note about his grandfather's smuggling:

The spirits often smelt all over the house, being proof, & had to be lowered for drinking. The tubs . . . were brought at night by men on horseback, 'slung,' or in carts. A whiplash across the window pane would awake my grandfather at 2 or 3 in the morning, & he would dress & go down. Not a soul was there, but a heap of tubs loomed up in front of the door. He would set to work & stow them away in the dark closet aforesaid, & nothing more would happen till dusk the following evening, when groups of dark long-bearded fellows would arrive, & carry off the tubs in two & fours slung over their shoulders.[7]

This attention paid to evocative particulars from oral accounts – note the word 'slung', a dialect term for the way in which the barrels were placed on the horse's flanks – can be found as well in 'The Distracted Preacher', which lists the places where the preventive-men searched for the contraband liquor and carefully initiates the reader into a complex vocabulary of smuggling.

Not coincidentally, this narrative – Hardy's first full-scale effort in the short story and the earliest work collected in *Wessex Tales* (the version reprinted here) – is also the first of the short narratives to contain the kind of regional content that was later associated with his 'Novels of Character and Environment' and with his fictional microcosm of 'Wessex'. Indeed, the story's courtship plot dramatizes the moral and political differences, not only between the Methodist chapel and the Church of England, but also between an urban middle class and a rural artisan class. Told chiefly from the perspective of a Methodist minister from the Midlands, the story depends for its interest and humour on his naïveté and on his simultaneous attraction to and repudiation of the illegal activities carried out by Lizzy Newberry and her fellow south-coast smugglers. A tension between the values of the characters' two contrasting worlds never leaves the story, a fact that is reflected even in its textual history: while revisions between 1879 and 1888 made Lizzy's marriage with the minister more plausible,[8] Hardy added a note to the 1912 Wessex edition of *Wessex Tales* that offers what was, for him, the more historically accurate and the preferable ending: marriage to her cousin Owlett and emigration to America. Hardy had previously yielded, he explained, to the narrow requirements for fiction in magazine publication, but was later willing to offer his generally urban readers – at least in a note – an ending that challenged unquestioning acceptance of middle-class respectability. Even in the pre-1912 version, moreover, Lizzie's final negation of her former self (it is hard to imagine her living in the Midlands and writing a tract against her own past) cannot help but disappoint the reader and so calls the story's conventional ending into question: satisfaction of Stockdale's desire suppresses the vitality of Lizzy, so appealing both to himself and to the reader. Stockdale's fulfilment also runs parallel with, as John Goode has pointed out, 'the decline of the livelihood of the smuggling community brought about by the increasing violence of the state'.[9] In both versions, then, the story has a metafictional dimension: given the social and moral tensions it provokes, there is no easily satisfying closure, no romance formula that will reconcile the shallow and moralistic values of Stockdale with the economic, political and cultural differences that mark Lizzy Newberry's fragile rural community.

In April 1880, when Hardy was still living in London and while the serialization of *The Trumpet-Major* continued, he published 'Fellow-Townsmen', another story that takes place on the south coast of England, but in emphasis and tone it is radically different from 'The Distracted Preacher', whose remote setting in time and place served as a distancing framework that was both nostalgic and ironic. 'Fellow-Townsmen' takes place during 1845–66, when the extension of the railway to southern England was completed, and in the only town on the south coast of England where the chief livelihood was manufacturing. In keeping with this shift to what is, for Wessex, an urban or 'town' setting, the protagonist Barnet is a figure of sophistication and alienation, and his story is the frustrated pursuit by a middle-aged man of a lost past. Much more internalized than 'The Distracted Preacher', 'Fellow-Townsmen' dwells on the continuing misery of its hero and finally dramatizes the extent to which he himself has created his unhappy predicament. For although events sometimes seem to work against Barnet, he ultimately fails to secure what he desires because he withdraws too readily from complicated situations. Crucial to such a reading is the story's closure, which shows him subverting the conventional 'happy ending' of the romance plot: Barnet proposes to Lucy within minutes of seeing her after a twenty-one-year gap and then just as impulsively leaves her without a trace.

Changes made to the beginning of the story for 1888 *Wessex Tales* (the copy-text used here) emphasize Barnet's neurotic tendencies. The periodical version, instead of showing the two men in a phaeton comparing their lives, had opened with Barnet slamming the door on his wife after making a nasty discovery about her; he then had made his way to the apartment of his friend Downe. The revised version presents the argument between Barnet and his wife as part of a steady deterioration in their marriage, rather than the result of a single discovery, and increases the explicitness in the first dialogue between Barnet and Lucy Savile about the sexual nature of their past relationship. Thus the later Barnet is a victim as much of his own self-conscious indecisiveness as of circumstances – a fact that led J. Hillis Miller to align him with many of 'Hardy's most important characters', for whom there always comes a moment when 'lucid detachment' replaces the desire for sexual fulfilment.[10] It is perhaps not coincidental that 'Fellow-Townsmen' was written at a time when Hardy's own marriage was becoming stressful and that Lucy has strong affinities with Eliza Bright Nicholls, whom Hardy had courted before he met his first wife. In any case, Hardy had a special affection for 'Fellow-Townsmen', which he told Florence Henniker in 1904 was preferable to the enormously popular 'The Three Strangers' because 'there is more human nature in it'.[11]

When 'Fellow-Townsmen' appeared, Hardy was beginning his next novel, *A Laodicean*, but this work was interrupted by disruptions in his personal life: another trip to Europe; the decision, much against Emma's inclination, to return to Dorset; and the serious and painful ailment, beginning in October 1880, that kept him in bed for several months. Early in his confinement, however, Hardy received a letter from the eminent critic Leslie Stephen suggesting that he 'write an exceedingly pleasant series of stories upon your special topic. I mean prose idyls of country life – short sketches of Hodge & his ways, wh. might be made very attractive & would have a certain continuity so as to make a volume or more at some future date'.[12] Perhaps in response to these encouraging words, Hardy began to produce stories with increasing rapidity: in December 1881, after he had moved to Wimborne in Dorset, he published 'Benighted Travellers' ('The Honourable Laura' in *A Group of Noble Dames*) and 'What the Shepherd Saw', followed in December 1882 by 'A Legend of Eighteen Hundred and Four' (called 'A Tradition of Eighteen Hundred and Four' in the 1894 *Life's Little Ironies*). Like the novels of this period (*A Laodicean* in 1881 and *Two on a Tower* in 1882), these stories are not the best Hardy wrote, but their melodramatic settings display an interest in theatrical effects that dates back at least to his 1879 stage adaptation of *Far From the Madding Crowd*, and they may have prepared Hardy for the impressive accomplishment of 'The Three Strangers', published in March 1883. This much anthologized story has always attracted readers by its ingenious shaping and its attention to dramatic irony – attributes that also made it readily adaptable for the stage. Indeed, Hardy's comment of 1911 to J. M. Barrie about *The Three Wayfarers*, his 1893 one-act play based on the story – he called it 'that little melodramatic thing of mine'[13] – may well have been an instance of false modesty. For Hardy involved himself in its productions even during the last few years of his life, and he strategically placed the story at the beginning of *Wessex Tales*, where it stood as a point of entry into the fictional world of Wessex, a place that would receive increasingly precise and complex definition in Hardy's subsequent work.

This regional appeal in 'The Three Strangers' derived from its detailed attention to language, rituals and music that even in 1883 marked a lost way of life. The christening feast in the remote cottage of Shepherd and Shepherdess Fennel offers a vivid impression of Dorset country life, and the story's narrative voice, both elegiac and instructional in its tone, draws the reader into the 1820s, a period of severe economic depression, when a man could still be hanged for stealing a sheep in order to feed his hungry family and where in a few places – including Bere Regis, not far from the Fennel cottage – there was serious unrest. This local history stands as a backdrop to the story's events, as do Hardy's personal memories, some based on anecdotes he heard from his parents and grandparents. To the end of his life, Hardy told stories of the hangings that he and his relatives had witnessed – Timothy Sommers's predicament must be seen in this context – and he often lamented the loss of a whole class of village artisans, who were forced by economic circumstances to move to cities or to emigrate.[14] Though Sommers is not hanged, it must be remembered, he is forced permanently to leave his native place and way of life. Like Lizzy Newberry in 'The Distracted Preacher' – staged in 1911 along with *The Three Wayfarers*[15] – Sommers must forsake the familial and social world that made him so resourceful and resilient. Thus Hardy's obsessive concern with dialect and social rituals in these two stories – as well as in their dramatic productions – is a reflection of his interest, historical and personal, in a rural culture that was slipping away even before he was born. In both narratives, the comic and dramatic elements are enabled and modified by this elegiac framework.

'The Romantic Adventures of a Milkmaid', written at Wimborne during roughly the same time as 'The Three Strangers' and published in summer 1883, is a story that Hardy considered for dramatic adaptation,[16] but in plot structure and style it is more closely allied with the fairy-tale qualities found in 'Thieves' than with the regional specificity of the two early stories staged in Hardy's lifetime. For in spite of precise details about Margery Tucker's life and class-standing as a milkmaid during the 1840s, the story's impact does not depend on historical circumstances (its setting was changed from Dorset to Devon for the 1913 *A Changed Man*, with little effect on the plot). Indeed, this text – which combines elements from 'Red Riding Hood', 'Cinderella' and the ballad of 'The Daemon Lover' – has strangely mythic overtones and does not easily satisfy the requirements of a reader looking for realistic narrative (this may be the reason why the story was more popular in the United States, where 'romance' was a respected genre, than in Britain). Yet it is precisely the incongruous combination of varied plots that gives the story its complexity: in the characterization of Baron von Xanten, the wicked wolf whom Red Riding Hood meets in the woods is also the Prince Charming who dances with Cinderella at the ball, and these opposing roles are brought together by his affinities with the suicidal, self-obsessed Byronic hero and with the figure of the daemon lover, who entices the vain and ambitious wife away from her domestic world.[17] In conflating these characterizations, the story exposes hidden elements in the structure of many romances: sexual attraction involves imaginative projection on the beloved, and class barriers can make such desire both more tempting and more tenuous. So the characters cannot be said to 'fall in love', but rather are caught up in fantasies that are 'romantic', with all the accompanying connotations of self-delusion. In this context, it should be remembered that the chapter in *Far From the Madding Crowd* describing Sergeant Troy's self-dramatizing attentions to the tomb of Fanny Robin – whom, when alive, he had exploited and neglected – is called 'Troy's Romanticism'. Though the title 'Romantic Adventures of a Milkmaid' may have led some readers to expect a titillating story, the narrative cynically uncovers some of the psychic mechanisms underlying sexual attraction, and it does so for both the female and the male characters: anticipating the destructive dynamic in the courtship of Tess Durbeyfield and Angel Clare, it shows how a rural milkmaid might make a 'demi-god' of a suitor above her in class, while he might see her, equally falsely, as a figure of pastoral simplicity and naturalness.

In contrast to *Tess*, however, the story places greater emphasis on female weakness, and the instability of its sexual politics is most apparent in the changes Hardy made for publication in 1913 *A Changed Man*. In the 1883 version (the copy-text for this volume), Margery staunchly refuses to go with the baron on his yacht because she wants to remain loyal to Jim, and she shares responsibility with von Xanten for ending their relationship, though her strength afterwards seems to come only from the competing erotic focus of the baby: at least superficially, the marriage plot has subsumed the romance plot. In the 1913 version, however, Margery is made more ambivalent, even at the end of the story, in her feelings about Jim Hayward; the baron is made both more explicit about his sexual interest in Margery and more daemonic; and in the conclusion, which makes his death a certainty rather than a possibility, Margery confesses to Jim that she was disappointed by von Xanten's failure finally to take her on his yacht. These changes move the story in the direction of an alternative ending that Hardy described, the year before his death, in the margin of his copy of *A Changed Man*:

the foregoing finish of the Milkmaid's Adventures by a re-union with her husband was adopted to suit the requirements of the summer number of a periodical in which the story was first printed. But it is well to inform readers that the ending originally sketched was a different one, Margery, instead of returning to Jim, disappearing with the Baron in his yacht at Idmouth after his final proposal to her, & being no more heard of in England.[18]

This ending conforms with the plot of 'The Daemon Lover' and anticipates Hardy's 1893 story, 'The Fiddler of the Reels', where the mysterious Gypsy's diabolical control over the sexuality of the heroine is absolute. It is also significant that in both 'Romantic Adventures' and 'Fiddler' the enchanting powers of the seducer are linked to his racial or cultural otherness. Baron von Xanten's foreignness may be a Gothic touch, but it also allies this story, so often read only in terms of pastoral contrasts between simple and sophisticated, with a xenophobic discourse, pervasive at the end of the nineteenth century, that linked the sexually dangerous with the alien. At another level, however, the Baron is not antithetical to Margery's world, for crucial to both endings is the intense homosocial bond formed between him and Jim Hayward. Thus while Margery's marriage is the fulfilment of a commonplace contract into which she has been coerced, the baron willingly makes his promise to Jim in a ceremony of mystical import: the milkmaid may have 'adventures' (note the ironic attribution to her experience of a word usually applied to male heroic quests), but it is the men who together decide her sexual fate. In both versions, then, an allusion by Hayward to his bond with the baron closes the narrative: 'however he might move ye ['ee in the 1913 version], he'll never come. He swore it to me: and he was a man of his word.'

Masculine fulfilment is the main focus of 'Our Exploits at West Poley', a children's story completed after Hardy moved to Dorchester in 1883, but not published until ten years later. In this fairy-tale propounding middle-class virtues, the young protagonist learns to balance caution and energy, thus becoming a prosperous farmer. The same maturity and happy fate, however, are not granted to the heroes of the next few narratives Hardy wrote, including the magnificently tragic Michael Henchard of *The Mayor of Casterbridge*, the novel begun early in 1884, and the pathetically self-defeating Charles Darton of 'Interlopers at the Knap', a story published in May of the same year and collected in 1888 *Wessex Tales* (the copy-text for this edition).[19] The story begins, significantly at Christmas, with Darton's quest for a wife as he finds his way, like the wise men, through an unknown landscape. Yet neither the appealing Sally Hall, who nervously awaits him, nor the beautiful Helena Hall, who had earlier rejected him and who appears to him in Sally's dress as though a figure from a dream, finally brings him happiness. For after choosing the newly widowed Helena over the self-protective and magnanimous Sally, Darton, like Mr Barnet of 'Fellow-Townsmen', then regrets losing the woman he had rejected. Sally, however, is a different figure from Lucy Savile and elects never to marry. Having discovered that Darton is not the hero she thought him to be, she settles into a satisfying life in her old home on her prosperous farm; thus she, not Darton, enjoys the happy fate of the protagonist in 'Exploits'.

In this secure and comfortable position, Sally feels no need to accept other marriage proposals either, including that of Japheth Johns, who seems in many respects to be the ideal opposite of his friend Darton (he is not unlike Diggory Venn). From the beginning, he appreciates Sally in ways that Darton does not, and with his neighbouring farm he is in a social and economic position to marry her. Even the biblical antecedents invoked by the names of Japheth (the son of Noah who received his father's blessing to bear much fruit) and Sally (the diminutive for Sarah, the wife of Abraham who became the mother of patriarchs) suggest that a union between them would be appropriate and satisfying. What the story exposes, however, is the persistent reliance of the romance plot on the desire for such artificial symmetry and fulfilment: leading the reader in the direction of Barnet's own 'purely formal' reasoning, which assumes first that anniversaries are propitious and then that they are unpropitious, the narrative finally refuses to demonstrate that such forms of magical thinking have any truth. Flying in the face of its own romance structure, the story ends with no marriage at all, and spinsterhood, conventionally presented as an image of failure and as the quintessentially unhappy closure, is the way of life elected by the heroine to preserve her sense of contentment.[20] This post-biblical Sarah aggressively determines not to be the wife, or the mother, of a patriarch.

In the years following the appearance of 'Interlopers', which included the publication of *Mayor* (1886) and *The Woodlanders* (1887), as well as the move into Max Gate just outside Dorchester, Hardy experimented, with varying success, in several types of story. In March 1885, he published in the *Detroit Post* 'Ancient Earthworks and What Two Enthusiastic Scientists Found Therein', a mood piece set at Maiden Castle which he didn't present to the British public until 1893 (as 'Ancient Earthworks at Casterbridge') because of its caricature of Edward Cunnington, a local antiquary.[21] 'A Mere Interlude' and 'Alicia's Diary', which appeared, respectively, in October 1885 and 1887, explore the kinds of extreme plot devices that would become typical of more successful stories written during the 1890s. The most sustained experiment of this period, however, was 'The Waiting Supper', a novella-length work published in *Murray's Magazine* during January and February 1888 (the copy-text for this edition), but not collected until 1913 in *A Changed Man* – perhaps because of its similarities in plot to many other works: *A Pair of Blue Eyes* (1872), *Far From the Madding Crowd* and *Two on a Tower*, plus two major stories, 'A Tragedy of Two Ambitions' (1888) and 'Barbara of the House of Grebe' (1891). Like 'Romantic Adventures', 'The Waiting Supper' has a different closure in each of its two versions, neither of them a standard happy resolution. Indeed, with thirty and twenty-five years between versions for 'Romantic Adventures' and 'The Waiting Supper', these stories – given prominence in the title of the 1913 *A Changed Man, The Waiting Supper, and Other Tales, Concluding with the Romantic Adventures of a Milkmaid* – draw attention to the tenuousness of all endings, happy or otherwise.

'The Waiting Supper' echoes several texts about unconsummated love – George Crabbe's 'The Parting Hour' and 'Procrastination' in his 1812 *Tales*, Matthew Arnold's 'Too Late' (1852), Robert Browning's 'The Statue and the Bust' (1855) – and presents a romance plot that fails, like that of 'Fellow-Townsmen', both because circumstances work against the lovers and because they are indecisive or passive. In the first version, Christine Bellston, finally given the opportunity to marry Nicholas Long after her long absent husband has been found drowned, argues with characteristic equivocation that in their old age such a move would not be 'worth while', and Nic, also repeating his own past pattern of melancholy withdrawal, '[falls] in with these views of hers to some extent'. Christine is certain that her husband is dead, and her reluctance to marry Nic is thus attributable to her customary complacency – as well as to a legitimate recognition that they are 'perhaps happier than we should be in any other relation, seeing what old people we have grown'. The implication is that both partners have outlived the romance plot, making irrelevant its expectations for consummation and fulfilment. In the 1913 version, however, Hardy introduced substantive changes: the social differences originally dividing Christine and Nic were somewhat reduced; Nic was made less despairing after the news of Bellston's return; and the only sign of Bellston's arrival on the night of the prenuptial supper was the delivery of his portmanteau, not his actual appearance at the house. The evidence for Bellston's death was also made uncertain: in the 1888 version, the watch found on the corpse has engraved on it 'J. Bellston: 1838', but in 1913 the inscription was changed to 'the name of the maker of her husband's watch, which she well remembered', and the following exchange was added to the final dialogue between Christine and Nic:

'I have strange fancies,' she said. 'I suppose it *must* have been my husband who came back, and not some other man.'

Nicholas felt that there was little doubt. 'Besides – the skeleton,' he said.

'Yes . . . If it could not have been another person's — but no, of course it was he.'

The 1913 version thus introduces the possibility, however remote, that Bellston is still alive. In the earlier version, Christine's tendency toward retreat and procrastination seems the chief motivation for her actions; in the later version, however, the plot might be seen either as offering her some basis for her rationalization or as foregrounding her tendency to find reasons for her irrational position. 'The Waiting Supper' of 1913 thus adds an indeterminacy that puts the reader in an intriguing quandary, not knowing whether Christine or Nic is right. In either case, the narrative calls the standard romance plot into question. Love between these partners continues only because consummation – the consuming of the waiting supper – has been once again postponed, this time until death.

'The Withered Arm' – first published, like 'The Waiting Supper', in January 1888 – also interrogates the romance plot, this time by passing over its expected focus on events leading up to the conventional closure of marriage. Concentrating instead on the disastrous aftermaths of two courtships (in one case abandonment and an illegitimate child, in the other an unhappy childless marriage), the work forcefully condemns both the sexual double standard and economic exploitation of the labouring classes. Rhoda Brook, its betrayed milkmaid, is thus significantly different from Margery (or from Tess Durbeyfield in the novel which Hardy was to publish three years later) because she is portrayed more than twelve years following a sexual encounter. Her story, then, is at least as much about her relationship with her child and with the wife of her child's father as it is about her connection with the man himself; and the dynamic in this complex network of domestic and extra-domestic relationships is so intense that the story exceeds the boundaries of realism. As Suzanne R. Johnson has argued, 'Hardy uses the fantastic as a means of avoiding the domestic, and essentially bourgeois ideology of social realism.'[22] This 'fantastic' element was controversial even before the story was published. Four days after it was rejected by *Longman's Magazine* in September 1887 for its grimness and its perceived inappropriateness for magazine-reading girls,[23] Hardy sent it to William Blackwood, trying this time to make the grimness marketable. Alluding in one letter to its 'Blackwood flavour', he suggested in another that 'It is of rather a weird nature – but as the taste of readers seems to run in that direction just now perhaps its character is no disqualification.'[24] After its publication in *Blackwood's Edinburgh Magazine*, and before its appearance a few months later in 1888 *Wessex Tales* (the copy-text for this edition), Hardy recommended 'The Withered Arm' to friends for its 'creepy' or 'weird' qualities, which he insisted were linked to the story's origin in 'fact'.[25] As he explained in his 1896 preface to *Wessex Tales*,

Since writing this story some years ago I have been reminded by an aged friend [his grandmother] of 'Rhoda Brook' that, in relating her dream, my forgetfulness has weakened the facts out of which the tale grew. In reality it was while lying down on a hot afternoon that the incubus oppressed her and she flung it off, with the results upon the body of the original as described. To my mind the occurrence of such a vision in the daytime is more impressive than if it had happened in a midnight dream. Readers are therefore asked to correct the misrelation, which affords an instance of how our imperfect memories insensibly formalize the fresh originality of living fact – from whose shape they slowly depart, as machine-made castings depart by degrees from the sharp hand-work of the mould.

This notion of 'fact', it should be noted, is diametrically opposed to conventions of realism, for when Leslie Stephen, whom Hardy greatly admired, criticized the story's ambivalent shifting between supernatural and naturalistic elements, Hardy made only perfunctory changes to its wording and later commented that Stephen's letter was 'a dull and unimaginative example of gratuitous criticism'.[26] Important for Hardy is an overlapping of the commonplace and the weird, figured in the story's contrast between prosaic settings (the dairy, the road, the Lodge home, Casterbridge) and the eerie places associated with the heath (Rhoda's home, Conjuror Trendle's cottage). As Romey T. Keys has argued, the use of Egdon Heath, already established in Hardy's fiction as a 'special domain' of the Uncanny, locates the story precisely 'at the intersection of reason and reverie'.[27]

Yet these extravagant details also have strong connections with the actualities of Dorset history, for an important aspect of this narrative is its setting in the late 1820s or early 1830s, and it continually establishes parallels between the exploited situations of its fallen woman and of its rural workers. Rhoda is not only the mother of Farmer Lodge's illegitimate son, but also a milker on a farm whose dairyman must pay Lodge nine pounds a year for the use of each of its eighty animals. In a sense, Lodge owns all of the female bodies in the story: Rhoda, the labouring woman whom he violated, made pregnant and abandoned; Gertrude, the genteel woman whom he married and neglects; the other milkmaids, both 'regular and supernumerary', who milk his cows for small wages; and the cows, which reproduce and lactate for his profit. The narrator's concluding focus, therefore – which takes the form of a speculation on Rhoda's 'sombre thoughts . . . beating inside that impassive, wrinkled brow, to the rhythm of the alternating milk-streams' – stands as a succinct allusion to the triple conflation of Rhoda's sexual, maternal and economic roles. Rhoda's unnamed child, moreover, is an extension of his mother's exploitation: in order to eat, he breaks laws that protect the property of farmers like his father, and he dies – significantly, he is the age his mother was when she bore him – wearing the smockfrock that is emblematic of his oppressed class.[28]

The distinctive and confident use of regional and oral history in 'The Withered Arm' coincides with an important stage in Hardy's development as a writer of short fiction. For at roughly this point he began to think of his stories, not only as cash-yielding, ephemeral works for the popular periodical press, but also as parts of bound volumes which, like his novels, would be reviewed in prestigious journals. He was also beginning to think about 'Wessex' as a consistent and overarching setting for all of his fiction, and both concerns seem to have contributed to Hardy's decision, less than two months after the publication of 'The Withered Arm', to collect his best stories in a volume. On 29 February 1888, Hardy sent to Macmillan 'The Three Strangers', 'The Withered Arm', 'Fellow-Townsmen', 'Interlopers at the Knap' and 'The Distracted Preacher' to discover if the company 'would be willing to publish them as collected', noting that '[s]ome well-known critics have often advised me to reprint them, informing me that they are as good as anything I have ever written (however good that may be)'. This query, which cautiously but definitively put the stories at the level of the widely recognized novels, received a positive response within a week,[29] and *Wessex Tales* (in two volumes) was published in early May. From this point onward, Hardy wrote most of his stories with an eye to book publication and, as will be demonstrated by the selections in the second volume of this Penguin edition, he increasingly made short fiction the vehicle for an exploration of controversial techniques and ideas. The publication of *Wessex Tales* was thus a watershed in Hardy's fiction-writing career: the volume that established him as a writer of serious short fiction also announced, for the first time in a published title, the official name of his fictional microcosm. *Wessex Tales*, in sum, proclaimed the importance of 'Wessex' for Hardy's stories and the centrality of the stories in Hardy's imaginative world.

Notes

1. All of the texts I have chosen were completed shortly before magazine publication; see Note on the History of the Texts for my justification of copy-text choices.

2. *Collected Letters*, II, 37.

3. The date of composition for 'Destiny' is not clear. It is possible that Hardy wrote it in about a month after he sent off the corrected manuscript of *Far From the Madding Crowd* in early August 1874 (see Brady, 161 and Pamela Dalziel, 'Hapless "Destiny": an uncollected story of marginalized lives', *Thomas Hardy Journal* 8 (1992), 41–2). The story could also be a completed version of the short-story manuscript Hardy described to William Tinsley in December 1873 as 'only one quarter finished' (*Collected Letters*, I, 25), in which case it was begun before the completion of *Far From the Madding Crowd*.

4. Pamela Dalziel notes that this description 'is almost a direct quotation of Henery Fray's response to Bathsheba's unexpected gift of ten shillings' in *Far From the Madding Crowd* when he 'lifted his eyebrows and fingers to express amazement on a small scale' (Thomas Hardy, *The Excluded and Collaborative Stories*, ed. Pamela Dalziel (Oxford: Clarendon, 1992), p. 26). This use of the image, with its different context, its focus on the fingers with the exclusion of the eyebrows, and its addition of the word 'privately', has strongly sexual connotations.

5. Dalziel, 'Hapless "Destiny" ', pp. 47, 46.

6. On snuff see V. G. Kiernan, *Tobacco: A History* (London: Hutchinson Radius, 1991), pp. 27 and 34.

7. *Personal Notebooks*, 9.

8. Hardy introduced a number of details that intensify the sexual suggestiveness in the characterization of Lizzy Newberry, while reducing her use of local dialect, thus increasing her acceptability for a middle-class Methodist preacher from the Midlands. Lizzy's feelings about Stockdale were also made less ambivalent, and Jim Owlett, Lizzy's cousin and fellow smuggler, was made to seem less a sexual threat.

9. John Goode, *Thomas Hardy: The Offensive Truth* (Oxford: Basil Blackwell, 1988), p. 74.

10. J. Hillis Miller, *Thomas Hardy: Distance and Desire* (Cambridge: Harvard University Press, 1970), pp. 186–7.

11. *Collected Letters*, III, 151.

12. Leslie Stephen to Hardy, 19 Nov. 1880 (Dorset County Museum), quoted in Brady, 180.

13. *Collected Letters*, IV, 193.

14. See 'The Dorsetshire Labourer', *Personal Writings*, 168–90.

15. The stage adaptation was written by A. H. Evans, but Hardy contributed a programme note for it and offered advice about the production (Wilson, 76).

16. See Wilson, 118–19.

17. For elements from 'The Daemon Lover', see Michael Benazon, ' "The Romantic Adventures of a Milkmaid": Hardy's modern romance', *English Studies in Canada* 5 (1979), 61–2; Geoffrey Doel, 'The supernatural background to "The Romantic Adventures of a Milkmaid" by Thomas Hardy', *Somerset and Dorset Notes & Queries* 30 (1978), 324–35; and Ray, pp. 330–31.

18. Quoted in Michael Millgate, *Thomas Hardy: His Career as a Novelist* (New York: Random House, 1971), p. 283. The typewritten notes for a stage version give still another pair of endings: in one, Margery runs off with the baron, but Jim expresses the hope that she will return after the baron's expected death, and an inserted handwritten addition gives Jim a note of certainty and triumph; in the alternative version, which has a line drawn through it and a comment that it is not a very satisfactory ending, Margery returns to Jim (f. 3).

19. There were few substantive changes for 1888 *WT*, except that the tension in the conversation between Mrs Hall and her son Philip was heightened; dialect was removed from her speech – making her even more respectable in her manner – and Japheth Johns was made to seem less sophisticated, a change that was emphasized further in later versions of the story. In 1912 *WT*, Sally Hall's self-confidence in her final rejection of Darton was also intensified.

20. This reading of 'Interlopers' contradicts my own earlier interpretation, which argues that in her refusal of Japheth Sally is too recalcitrant (Brady, 33–7).

21. See *Biography*, 244–5.

22. Suzanne R. Johnson, 'Metamorphosis, desire, and the fantastic in Thomas Hardy's "The Withered Arm" ', *Modern Language Studies* 23 (1993), 131.

23. *Collected Letters*, VII, 106.

24. *Collected Letters*, I, 168–9.

25. *Collected Letters*, I, 172–3.

26. S. M. Ellis, 'Thomas Hardy: some personal recollections', *Fortnightly Review* ns 123 (1928), 397; the chief alteration was to substitute in 1888 *WT* – for the speculative 'if' in the statement from 1888 *BM*, 'Rhoda Brook dreamed, *if* her assertion that she really saw, before falling asleep, was not to be believed' – the definite word 'since'. At the same stage of revision (perhaps because 1888 *BM* had been published anonymously, but 1888 *WT* was not), Hardy moved the story's setting from Stickleford, a place closely linked with his past, to Holmstoke, a location without previous Wessex associations.

27. Romey T. Keys, 'Hardy's uncanny narrative: a reading of "The Withered Arm" ', *Texas Studies in Literature and Language* 27 (1985), 116.

28. Anne Alexander (*Thomas Hardy: The 'Dream-Country' of His Fiction* (London: Barnes & Noble, 1987), pp. 169–70) was the first to note this correlation in age. For fuller discussions of the story's historical elements, see John Rabbett, *From Hardy to Faulkner: Wessex to Yoknapatawpha* (New York: St Martin's Press, 1989), pp. 14–15, 20–21 and 138; and Roger Ebbatson, ' "The Withered Arm" and history', *Critical Survey* 5 (1993), 131–5.

29. *Collected Letters*, I, 174–5.

Only two books have been devoted exclusively to Thomas Hardy's short fiction: Kristin Brady, *The Short Stories of Thomas Hardy: Tales of Past and Present* (London: Macmillan, 1982), a close reading of the four story collections, and Martin Ray, *Thomas Hardy: A Textual Study of the Short Stories* (Aldershot: Ashgate, 1997), a detailed history of the collected narratives. Many books on Hardy's fiction omit significant mention of the stories, but the following are valuable exceptions: J. Hillis Miller, *Thomas Hardy: Distance and Desire* (Cambridge: Harvard University Press, 1970); Michael Millgate, *Thomas Hardy: His Career as a Novelist* (New York: Random House, 1971); Simon Gatrell, *Hardy the Creator: A Textual Biography* (Oxford: Clarendon, 1988); John Goode, *Thomas Hardy: The Offensive Truth* (Oxford: Basil Blackwell, 1988); John Rabbett, *From Hardy to Faulkner: Wessex to Yoknapatawpha* (New York: St Martin's Press, 1989); T. R. Wright, *Hardy and the Erotic* (New York: St Martin's Press, 1989); Roger Ebbatson, *Hardy: The Margin of the Unexpressed* (Sheffield: Sheffield Academic Press, 1993); Gayla R. Steel, *Sexual Tyranny in Wessex: Hardy's Witches and Demons of Folklore* (New York: Peter Lang, 1993); and Keith Wilson, *Thomas Hardy on Stage* (Basingstoke: Macmillan, 1995).

A few general essays on the stories have appeared: Irving Howe, 'A note on Hardy's stories', *Hudson Review* 19 (1966), 259–66; Alexander Fischler, 'Theatrical techniques in Thomas Hardy's short stories', *Studies in Short Fiction* 3 (1966), 435–45; Norman Page, 'Hardy's short stories: a reconsideration', *Studies in Short Fiction* 11 (1974), 75–84; A. F. Cassis, 'A note on the structure of Hardy's short stories', *Colby Library Quarterly*, 10th ser. (1974), 287–96; Maire A. Quinn, 'Thomas Hardy and the short story' in *Budmouth Essays on Thomas Hardy: Papers Presented at the 1975 Summer School*, ed. F. B. Pinion (Dorchester: Thomas Hardy Society, 1976), pp. 74–85; J. B. Smith, 'Dialect in Hardy's short stories', *Thomas Hardy Annual* 3 (1985), 79–92; and Norman D. Prentiss, 'The poetics of interruption in Hardy's poetry and short stories', *Victorian Poetry* 31 (1993), 41–60.

A few other essays deal prominently with the short fiction: James F. Scott, 'Thomas Hardy's use of the gothic: an examination of five representative works', *Nineteenth-Century Fiction* 17 (1963), 363–80; Simon Gatrell, 'The early stages of Hardy's fiction', *Thomas Hardy Annual*, no. 2, ed. Norman Page (London: Macmillan, 1984), pp. 3–29; and Michael Rabiger, 'Hardy's fictional process and his emotional life', *Alternative Hardy*, ed. Lance St John Butler (New York: St Martin's Press, 1989), pp. 88–109.

There is also a selection of essays about some individual stories from this edition. On 'Destiny and a Blue Cloak', see Pamela Dalziel, 'Hapless "Destiny": an uncollected story of marginalized lives', *Thomas Hardy Journal* 8 (1992), 41–9. On 'Fellow-Townsmen', see Toby C. Herzog, 'Hardy's "Fellow-Townsmen": a primer for the novels', *Colby Library Quarterly* 18 (1982), 231–40. On 'The Three Strangers', see William Van O'Connor, 'Cosmic irony in Hardy's "The Three Strangers"', *English Journal* 47 (1958), 248–54 and 262; James L. Roberts, 'Legend and symbol in Hardy's "The Three Strangers"', *Nineteenth-Century Fiction* 17 (1962), 191–4; Keith Wilson, 'Hardy and the hangman: the dramatic appeal of "The Three Strangers"', *English Literature in Transition* 24 (1981), 155–60; and Francesco Marroni, ' "The Three Strangers" and the verbal representation of Wessex', *Thomas Hardy Journal* 8 (1992), 26–39. On 'The Romantic Adventures of a Milkmaid', see George Wing, 'Tess and the romantic milkmaid', *Review of English Literature* 3 (1962), 22–30; Geoffrey Doel, 'The supernatural background to "The Romantic Adventures of a Milkmaid" by Thomas Hardy', *Somerset and Dorset Notes & Queries* 30 (1978), 324–35; Michael Benazon, ' "The Romantic Adventures of a Milkmaid": Hardy's modern romance', *English Studies in Canada* 5 (1979), 56–65; and Simon Gatrell, 'Topography in "The Romantic Adventures of a Milkmaid"', *Thomas Hardy Journal* 3 (1987), 38–45. On 'The Waiting Supper', see Annie Escuret, 'Une nouvelle de T. Hardy: "The Waiting Supper"', *Cahiers victoriens et édouardiens*, No. 8 (1979), 39–52. On 'The Withered Arm', see Romey T. Keys, 'Hardy's uncanny narrative: a reading of "The Withered Arm"', *Texas Studies in Literature and Language* 27 (1985),

106–23; Roger Ebbatson, ' "The Withered Arm" and history', *Critical Survey* 5 (1993), 131–5; and Suzanne R. Johnson, 'Metamorphosis, desire, and the fantastic in Thomas Hardy's "The Withered Arm" ', *Modern Language Studies* 23 (1993), 131–41.

Hardy's own perspectives on the stories or on ideas and images within them can be found in several published sources: *The Collected Letters of Thomas Hardy*, ed. Richard Little Purdy and Michael Millgate, 7 vols. (Oxford: Oxford University Press, 1978–88); *The Life and Work of Thomas Hardy*, ed. Michael Millgate (Basingstoke: Macmillan, 1984); *The Literary Notebooks of Thomas Hardy*, ed. Lennart A. Björk, 2 vols. (London: Macmillan, 1985); *The Personal Notebooks of Thomas Hardy*, ed. Richard H. Taylor (Basingstoke: Macmillan, 1979); *Thomas Hardy's Personal Writings: Prefaces, Literary Opinions, Reminiscences*, ed. Harold Orel (1966; Lawrence: University Press of Kansas, 1969); *Thomas Hardy's 'Studies, Specimens &c.' Notebook*, ed. Pamela Dalziel and Michael Millgate (Oxford: Clarendon Press, 1994). The definitive biography of Hardy remains Michael Millgate's *Thomas Hardy: A Biography* (Oxford: Oxford University Press, 1982).

A NOTE ON THE HISTORY OF THE TEXTS

In a series that aims to offer the fictional texts of Thomas Hardy 'as [his] readers first encountered them, in a form of which he in general approved, the version that his early critics reacted to' (General Editor's Preface), no simple or single decision about choice of copy-text can be made to cover all of the short fiction. For unlike most of the novels, many of Hardy's stories did not achieve book publication immediately after their appearance in magazines, and there was sometimes a considerable gap (up to thirty-two years) between the periodical printing of a story (the version first encountered by Hardy's readers) and its appearance in book form (the version of which he generally approved and to which the early critics responded); neither choice, in short, necessarily fulfils all three requirements. Given this difficulty, I have decided in principle to privilege the first texts Hardy approved for reviewers (for the history of Hardy's collections of short stories, see Appendix I) over those that first appeared to the public eye and so to use as copy-text the first volume edition rather than the magazine publication. For the book printings often included the insertion (or restoration) of details and passages that were too adventurous for periodicals and thus might be considered, if not the texts that are closest to Hardy's original intentions (a concept that has been questioned by recent textual critics), at least the versions he preferred at the point when they would receive their first formal reviews. Before the appearance of *Wessex Tales* in 1888, there was no documented critical reception of most of the stories.

The exceptions to my general rule will be the stories that were not collected until 1913 in *A Changed Man* or not at all in Hardy's lifetime. For the former, I have reprinted the magazine version because a considerable gap in time (and substantive textual changes) intervened between magazine and volume publication, and to assimilate the revisions of 1913 would necessitate – in opposition to this edition's offering the stories 'as Hardy's readers *first* encountered them' (my emphasis) – an inclusion of details that came only in association with the 1912 Wessex Edition. For the uncollected stories, 'Destiny and a Blue Cloak' and 'The Thieves Who Couldn't Help Sneezing', the magazine printing is the only version. 'Destiny' first appeared in *The New York Times* on 4 October 1874, pp. 2–3 , under the heading 'CURRENT LITERATURE'. 'Thieves' was published in the 1877 *Father Christmas: Our Little Ones' Budget*, edited, under the pseudonym of 'Miss N. D'Anvers', by Nancy R. E. Meugens. This Christmas annual for children was published under the auspices of the *Illustrated London News*.

The copy-text for 'The Distracted Preacher' is 1888 *Wessex Tales*, published by Macmillan on 4 May. The story had first appeared as 'The Distracted Young Preacher' in the *New Quarterly Magazine* for April 1879, and, in five instalments from 19 April to 17 May 1879, in the American periodical *Harper's Weekly*. Martin Ray speculates that the American serialization 'is an earlier version . . . , perhaps set from proofs, which Hardy later further emended before the story appeared in the *New Quarterly Magazine*'.[1] The textual history of 'Fellow-Townsmen' runs parallel to that of 'The Distracted Preacher': it appeared in the *New Quarterly Magazine* (April 1880) and *Harper's Weekly* (five instalments from 17 April to 15 May 1880), and its American publication seems to have represented an earlier version. Harper & Brothers also published it in book form. The story was then revised and collected in 1888 *Wessex Tales*, the copy-text for this edition. 'The Three Strangers' first appeared in the March 1883 *Longman's Magazine* and an almost identical version was published in two instalments (3 and 10 March 1883) in *Harper's Weekly*; it then was collected in 1888 *Wessex Tales* (the copy-text used here). 'The Romantic Adventures of a Milkmaid' first appeared in the special Summer number of the 1883 *Graphic* (the copy-text for this volume), which marked the beginning of Hardy's association with a journal that published some of his most controversial works, including the short-story collection *A Group of Noble Dames*, and *Tess of the D'Urbervilles*. Simon Gatrell notes that the extra Summer and Christmas numbers of the *Graphic* 'were more substantial than the normal weekly copies, and Hardy showed his professional versatility in meeting happily the demand for a tale of a length somewhere between the usual short story and the novel'.[2] The novella-length 'Romantic Adventures' appeared almost simultaneously in seven instalments from 23 June to 4 August in *Harper's Weekly*, and Harper & Brothers also published it, before the serialization was completed, in volume form. Richard Little Purdy notes that 'Romantic Adventures' was 'widely pirated . . . and more frequently and cheaply reprinted in America through many years than perhaps any other work of Hardy's'.[3] Hardy did not collect 'Romantic Adventures' in volume form until the 1913 Macmillan printing of *A Changed Man*, in which he placed 'a dozen minor novels that have been published in the periodical press at various dates in the past' (Prefatory Note). 'Interlopers at the Knap' first appeared in the May 1884 *English Illustrated Magazine* and then was collected in the 1888 first printing of *Wessex Tales*, which serves as the copy-text for this volume. 'The Waiting Supper' appeared in the January and February numbers of *Murray's Magazine* for 1888, which provides the copy-text for this volume, and in *Harper's Weekly* for 31 December 1887 and 7 January 1888. On Christmas Day 1890, Hardy then published in the *Dorset County Chronicle*, without acknowledging the source, a conflation of the closing scenes from 'The Waiting Supper', which he entitled 'The Intruder, A Legend of the "Chronicle" Office'. After that, 'The Waiting Supper' did not appear again – perhaps because of its similarities to other Hardy stories and novels – until *A Changed Man*. For 'The Withered Arm', a period of only about four months intervened between its periodical publication in the January 1888 *Blackwood's Edinburgh Magazine* and the 1888 *Wessex Tales*, used here as copy-text.[4]

This edition follows exactly the chosen copy-texts, with minor exceptions. First, because the stories come from a variety of sources, I have standardized in the following instances: words with 'ise' and 'or' spellings have become 'ize' and 'our', respectively (e.g. 'recognize' and 'honour'); single quotation marks have been used, and punctuation at the end of a quotation has been moved outside the quotation marks, except in dialogue; M-dashes have become N-dashes, and 2M-dashes have become M-dashes; hyphens have been removed from such words and phrases as 'today', 'tomorrow', 'tonight', 'goodbye' (or 'goodby'), 'good morning', 'good afternoon', 'good evening' and 'good night', as well as from place names (e.g. Maiden Newton); in order to remove inconsistencies, hyphens have been added where necessary to 'turnpike-road', 'broad-arrows' 'harbour-road', 'lime-burner', 'country-road', and 'new-comer', but removed from the first part of 'master-lime-burner' and from 'mantelpiece', 'dairymaid' and 'bedroom'; there is no full stop after titles such as 'Mr'; punctuation appears in roman type after a word in italic, but remains in italic within a phrase or sentence in italic; ellipses have been standardized to three periods; and 'gray' has become 'grey'. I have also silently corrected typographical errors. In 'The Romantic Adventures of a Milkmaid', the word 'Chapter' has been deleted (as it is from 1913 *CM*) from each numbered heading. Other typographical features of a particular publication (such as the use of 'THE END') have also been removed from all the stories.

Notes

1. Ray, p. 58.
2. Gatrell, 71.
3. Purdy, 48–9.
4. Three of the stories in this volume have been produced for the BBC: 'The Distracted Preacher' (John Hale, 1969), 'Fellow-Townsmen' (Douglas Livingstone, 1973) and 'The Withered Arm' (Rhys Adrian, 1973).

The Withered Arm and Other Stories

1874–1888

DESTINY AND A BLUE CLOAK

I

'Good morning, Miss Lovill!' said the young man, in the free manner usual with him toward pretty and inexperienced country girls.

Agatha Pollin – the maiden addressed – instantly perceived how the mistake had arisen. Miss Lovill was the owner of a blue autumn wrapper, exceptionally gay for a village; and Agatha, in a spirit of emulation rather than originality, had purchased a similarly enviable article for herself, which she wore today for the first time. It may be mentioned that the two young women had ridden together from their homes to Maiden Newton on this foggy September morning, Agatha prolonging her journey thence to Weymouth by train,[1] and leaving her acquaintance at the former place. The remark was made to her on Weymouth esplanade.

Agatha was now about to reply very naturally, 'I am not Miss Lovill,' and she went so far as to turn up her face to him for the purpose, when he added, 'I've been hoping to meet you. I have heard of your – well, I must say it – beauty, long ago, though I only came to Beaminster[2] yesterday.'

Agatha bowed – her contradiction hung back – and they walked slowly along the esplanade together without speaking another word after the above point-blank remark of his. It was evident that her new friend could never have seen either herself or Miss Lovill except from a distance.

And Agatha trembled as well as bowed. This Miss Lovill – Frances Lovill – was of great and long renown as the beauty of Cloton village,[3] near Beaminster. She was five and twenty and fully developed, while Agatha was only the niece of the miller of the same place, just nineteen, and of no repute as yet for comeliness, though she undoubtedly could boast of much. Now, were the speaker, Oswald Winwood, to be told that he had not lighted upon the true Helen,[4] he would instantly apologize for his mistake and leave her side, a contingency of no great matter but for one curious emotional circumstance – Agatha had already lost her heart to him. Only in secret had she acquired this interest in Winwood – by hearing much report of his talent and by watching him several times from a window; but she loved none the less in that she had discovered that Miss Lovill's desire to meet and talk with the same intellectual luminary was in a fair way of approaching the intensity of her own. We are never unbiased appraisers, even in love, and rivalry usually operates as a stimulant to esteem even while it is acting as an obstacle to opportunity. So it had been with Agatha in her talk to Miss Lovill that morning concerning Oswald Winwood.

The Weymouth season was almost at an end, and but few loungers were to be seen on the parades, particularly at this early hour. Agatha looked over the iridescent sea, from which the veil of mist was slowly rising, at the white cliffs on the left, now just beginning to gleam in a weak sunlight, at the one solitary yacht in the midst, and still delayed her explanation. Her companion went on:

'The mist is vanishing, look, and I think it will be fine, after all. Shall you stay in Weymouth the whole day?'

'No. I am going to Portland[5] by the twelve o'clock steam-boat. But I return here again at six to go home by the seven o'clock train.'

'I go to Maiden Newton by the same train, and then to Beaminster by the carrier.'

'So do I.'

'Not, I suppose, to walk from Beaminster to Cloton at that time in the evening?'

'I shall be met by somebody – but it is only a mile, you know.'

That is how it all began; the continuation it is not necessary to detail at length. Both being somewhat young and impulsive, social forms were not scrupulously attended to. She discovered him to be on board the steamer as it plowed the emerald waves of Weymouth Bay, although he had wished her a formal goodbye at the pier. He had altered his mind, he said, and thought that he would come to Portland, too. They returned by the same boat, walked the velvet sands till the train started, and entered a carriage together.

All this time, in the midst of her happiness, Agatha's conscience was sombre with guiltiness at not having yet told him of his mistake. It was true that he had not more than once or twice called her by Miss Lovill's name since the first greeting in the morning; but he certainly was still under the impression that she was Frances Lovill. Yet she perceived that though he had been led to her by another's name, it was her own proper person that he was so rapidly getting to love, and Agatha's feminine insight suggested blissfully to her that the face belonging to the name would after this encounter have no power to drag him away from the face of the day's romance.

They reached Maiden Newton at dusk, and went to the inn door, where stood the old-fashioned hooded van which was to take them to Beaminster. It was on the point of starting, and when they had mounted in front the old man at once drove up the long hill leading out of the village.

'This has been a charming experience to me, Miss Lovill,' Oswald said, as they sat side by side. 'Accidental meetings have a way of making themselves pleasant when contrived ones quite fail to do it.'

It was absolutely necessary to confess this time, though all her bliss were at once destroyed.

'I am not really Miss Lovill!' she faltered.

'What! not the young lady – and are you really not Frances Lovill?' he exclaimed, in surprise.

'O forgive me, Mr Winwood! I have wanted so to tell you of your mistake; indeed I have, all day – but I couldn't – and it is so wicked and wrong of me! I am only poor Agatha Pollin, at the mill.'

'But why couldn't you tell me?'

'Because I was afraid that if I did you would go away from me and not care for me any more, and I l-l-love you so dearly!'

The carrier being on foot beside the horse, the van being so dark, and Oswald's feelings being rather warm, he could not for his life avoid kissing her there and then.

'Well,' he said, 'it doesn't matter; you are yourself anyhow. It is you I like, and nobody else in the world – not the name. But, you know, I was really looking for Miss Lovill this morning. I saw the back of her head yesterday, and I have often heard how very good-looking she is. Ah! suppose you had been she. I wonder —'

He did not complete the sentence. The driver mounted again, touched the horse with the whip, and they jogged on.

'You forgive me?' she said.

'Entirely – absolutely – the reason justified everything. How strange that you should have been caring deeply for me, and I ignorant of it all the time!'

They descended into Beaminster and alighted, Oswald handing her down. They had not moved from the spot when another female figure also alighted, dropped her fare into the carrier's hand, and glided away.

'Who is that?' said Oswald to the carrier. 'Why, I thought we were the only passengers!'

'What?' said the carrier, who was rather stupid.

'Who is that woman?'

'Miss Lovill, of Cloton. She altered her mind about staying at Beaminster,[6] and is come home again.'

'Oh!' said Agatha, almost sinking to the earth. 'She has heard it all. What shall I do, what shall I do?'

'Never mind it a bit,' said Oswald.

II

The mill stood beside the village high-road, from which it was separated by the stream, the latter forming also the boundary of the mill garden, orchard, and paddock on that side. A visitor crossed a little wood bridge imbedded in oozy, aquatic growths, and found himself in a space where usually stood a wagon laden with sacks, surrounded by a number of bright-feathered fowls.

It was now, however, just dusk, but the mill was not closed, a stripe of light stretching as usual from the open door across the front, across the river, across the road, into the hedge beyond. On the bridge, which was aside from the line of light, a young man and girl stood talking together. Soon they moved a little way apart, and then it was apparent that their right hands were joined. In receding one from the other they began to swing their arms gently backward and forward between them.

'Come a little way up the lane, Agatha, since it is the last time,' he said. 'I don't like parting here. You know your uncle does not object.'

'He doesn't object because he knows nothing to object to,' she whispered. And they both then contemplated the fine, stalwart figure of the said uncle, who could be seen moving about inside the mill, illuminated by the candle, and circumscribed by a faint halo of flour, and hindered by the whirr of the mill from hearing anything so gentle as lovers' talk.

Oswald had not relinquished her hand, and, submitting herself to a bondage she appeared to love better than freedom, Agatha followed him across the bridge, and they went down the lane engaged in the low, sad talk common to all such cases, interspersed with remarks peculiar to their own.

'It is nothing so fearful to contemplate,' he said. 'Many live there for years in a state of rude health, and return home in the same happy condition. So shall I.'

'I hope you will.'

'But aren't you glad I am going? It is better to do well in India than badly here. Say you are glad, dearest; it will fortify me when I am gone.'

'I am glad,' she murmured faintly. 'I mean I am glad in my mind. I don't think that in my heart I am glad.'

'Thanks to Macaulay,[7] of honoured memory, I have as good a chance as the best of them!' he said, with ardour. 'What a great thing competitive examination is; it will put good men in good places, and make inferior men move lower down; all bureaucratic jobbery will be swept away.'

'What's bureaucratic, Oswald?'

'Oh! that's what they call it, you know. It is – well, I don't exactly know what it is. I know this, that it is the name of what I hate, and that it isn't competitive examination.'

'At any rate it is a very bad thing,' she said, conclusively.

'Very bad, indeed; you may take my word for that.'

Then the parting scene began, in the dark, under the heavy-headed trees which shut out sky and stars. 'And since I shall be in London till the Spring,' he remarked, 'the parting doesn't seem so bad – so all at once. Perhaps you may come to London before the Spring, Agatha.'

'I may; but I don't think I shall.'

'We must hope on all the same. Then there will be the examination, and then I shall know my fate.'

'I hope you'll fail! – there, I've said it; I couldn't help it, Oswald!' she exclaimed, bursting out crying. 'You would come home again then!'

'How can you be so disheartening and wicked, Agatha! I – I didn't expect —'

'No, no; I don't wish it; I wish you to be best, top, very very best!' she said. 'I didn't mean the other; indeed, dear Oswald, I didn't. And will you be sure to come to me when you are rich? Sure to come?'

'If I'm on this earth I'll come home and marry you.'

And then followed the goodbye.

III

In the Spring came the examination. One morning a newspaper directed by Oswald was placed in her hands, and she opened it to find it was a copy of the *Times*. In the middle of the sheet, in the most conspicuous place, in the excellent neighbourhood of the leading articles, was a list of names, and the first on the list was Oswald Winwood. Attached to his name, as showing where he was educated, was the simple title of some obscure little academy, while underneath came public school and college men in shoals. Such a case occurs sometimes, and it occurred then.[8]

How Agatha clapped her hands! for her selfish wish to have him in England at any price, even that of failure, had been but a paroxysm of the wretched parting, and was now quite extinct. Circumstances combined to hinder another meeting between them before his departure, and, accordingly, making up her mind to the inevitable in a way which would have done honour to an older head, she fixed her mental vision on that sunlit future – far away, yet always nearing – and contemplated its probabilities with a firm hope.

At length he had arrived in India, and now Agatha had only to work and wait; and the former made the latter more easy. In her spare hours she would wander about the river brinks and into the coppices, and there weave thoughts of him by processes that young women understand so well. She kept a diary, and in this, since there were few events to chronicle in her daily life, she sketched the changes of the landscape, noted the arrival and departure of birds of passage, the times of storms and foul weather – all which information, being mixed up with her life and taking colour from it, she sent as scraps in her letters to him, deriving most of her enjoyment in contemplating his.

Oswald, on his part, corresponded very regularly. Knowing the days of the Indian mail, she would go at such times to meet the post-man in early morning, and to her unvarying inquiry, 'A letter for me?' it was seldom, indeed, that there came a disappointing answer. Thus the season passed, and Oswald told her he should be a judge some day, with many other details, which, in her mind, were viewed chiefly in their bearing on the grand consummation – that he was to come home and marry her.

Meanwhile, as the girl grew older and more womanly, the woman whose name she had once stolen for a day grew more of an old maid, and showed symptoms of fading. One day Agatha's uncle, who, though still a handsome man in the prime of life, was a widower with four children, to whom she acted the part of eldest sister, told Agatha that Frances Lovill was about to become his second wife.

'Well!' said Agatha, and thought, 'What an end for a beauty!'

And yet it was all reasonable enough, notwithstanding that Miss Lovill might have looked a little higher. Agatha knew that this step would produce great alterations in the small household of Cloton Mill, and the idea of having as aunt and ruler the woman to whom she was in some sense indebted for a lover, affected Agatha with a slight thrill of dread. Yet nothing had ever been spoken between the two women to show that Frances had heard, much less resented, the explanation in the van on that night of the return from Weymouth.

IV

On a certain day old farmer Lovill called. He was of the same family as Frances, though their relationship was distant. A considerable business in corn had been done from time to time between miller and farmer, but the latter had seldom called at Pollin's house. He was a bachelor, or he would probably never have appeared in this history, and he was mostly full of a boyish merriment rare in one of his years. Today his business with the miller had been so imperative as to bring him in person, and it was evident from their talk in the mill that the matter was payment. Perhaps ten minutes had been spent in serious converse when the old farmer turned away from the door, and, without saying good morning, went toward the bridge. This was unusual for a man of his temperament.

He was an old man – really and fairly old – sixty-five years of age at least. He was not exactly feeble, but he found a stick useful when walking in a high wind. His eyes were not yet bleared, but in their corners was occasionally a moisture like majolica glaze – entirely absent in youth. His face was not shriveled, but there were unmistakable puckers in some places. And hence the old gentleman, unmarried, substantial, and cheery as he was, was not doted on by the young girls of Cloton as he had been by their mothers in former time. Each year his breast impended a little further over his toes, and his chin a little further over his breast, and in proportion as he turned down his nose to earth did pretty females turn up theirs at him. They might have liked him as a friend had he not shown the abnormal wish to be regarded as a lover. To Agatha Pollin this aged youth was positively distasteful.

It happened that at the hour of Mr Lovill's visit Agatha was bending over the pool at the mill head, sousing some white fabric in the water. She was quite unconscious of the farmer's presence near her, and continued dipping and rinsing in the idlest phase possible to industry, until she remained quite still, holding the article under the water, and looking at her own reflection within it. The river, though gliding slowly, was yet so smooth that to the old man on the bridge she existed in duplicate – the pouting mouth, the little nose, the frizzed hair, the bit of blue ribbon, as they existed over the surface, being but a degree more distinct than the same features beneath.

'What a pretty maid!' said the old man to himself. He walked up the margin of the stream, and stood beside her.

'Oh!' said Agatha, starting with surprise. In her flurry she relinquished the article she had been rinsing, which slowly turned over and sank deeper, and made toward the hatch of the mill-wheel.

'There – it will get into the wheel, and be torn to pieces!' she exclaimed.

'I'll fish it out with my stick, my dear,' said Farmer Lovill, and kneeling cautiously down he began hooking and crooking with all his might. 'What thing is it – of much value?'

'Yes; it is my best one!' she said involuntarily.

'It – what is the it?'

'Only something – a piece of linen.' Just then the farmer hooked the endangered article, and dragging it out, held it high on his walking-stick – dripping, but safe.

'Why, it is a chemise!' he said.

The girl looked red, and instead of taking it from the end of the stick, turned away.

'Hee-hee!' laughed the ancient man. 'Well, my dear, there's nothing to be ashamed of that I can see in owning to such a necessary and innocent article of clothing. There, I'll put in on the grass for you, and you shall take it when I am gone.'

Then Farmer Lovill retired, lifting his fingers privately, to express amazement on a small scale, and murmuring, 'What a nice young thing! Well, to be sure. Yes, a nice child – young woman rather; indeed, a marriageable woman, come to that; of course she is.'

The doting old person thought of the young one all this day in a way that the young one did not think of him. He thought so much about her, that in the evening, instead of going to bed, he hobbled privately out by the back door into the moonlight, crossed a field or two, and stood in the lane, looking at the mill – not more in the hope of getting a glimpse of the attractive girl inside than for the pleasure of realizing that she was there.

A light moved within, came nearer, and ascended. The staircase window was large, and he saw his goddess going up with a candle in her hand. This was indeed worth coming for. He feared he was seen by her as well, yet hoped otherwise in the interests of his passion, for she came and drew down the window blind, completely shutting out his gaze. The light vanished from this part, and reappeared in a window a little further on.

The lover drew nearer; this, then, was her bedroom. He rested vigorously upon his stick, and straightening his back nearly to a perpendicular, turned up his amorous face.

She came to the window, paused, then opened it.

'Bess its deary-eary heart! it is going to speak to me!'⁹ said the old man, moistening his lips, resting still more desperately upon his stick, and straightening himself yet an inch taller. 'She saw me then!'

Agatha, however, made no sign; she was bent on a far different purpose. In a box on her window-sill was a row of mignonette, which had been sadly neglected since her lover's departure, and she began to water it, as if inspired by a sudden recollection of its condition. She poured from her water-jug slowly along the plants, and then, to her astonishment, discerned her elderly friend below.

'A rude old thing!' she murmured.

Directing the spout of the jug over the edge of the box, and looking in another direction that it might appear to be an accident, she allowed the stream to spatter down upon her admirer's face, neck, and shoulders, causing him to beat a quick retreat. Then Agatha serenely closed the window, and drew down that blind also.

'Ah! she did not see me; it was evident she did not, and I was mistaken!' said the trembling farmer, hastily wiping his face, and mopping out the rills trickling down within his shirt-collar as far as he could get at them, which was by no means to their termination. 'A pretty creature, and so innocent, too! Watering her flowers; how I like a girl who is fond of flowers! I wish she had spoken, and I wish I was younger. Yes, I know what I'd do with the little mouse!' And the old gentleman tapped emotionally upon the ground with his stick.

V

'Agatha, I suppose you have heard the news from somebody else by this time?' said her Uncle Humphrey some two or three weeks later. 'I mean what Farmer Lovill has been talking to me about.'

'No, indeed,' said Agatha.

'He wants to marry ye if you be willing.'

'O, I never!' said Agatha with dismay. 'That old man!'

'Old? He's hale and hearty; and, what's more, a man very well to do. He'll make you a comfortable home, and dress ye up like a doll, and I'm sure you'll like that, or you baint a woman of woman born.'

'But it *can't be*, uncle! – other reasons –'

'What reasons?'

'Why, I've promised Oswald Winwood – years ago!'

'Promised Oswald Winwood years ago, have you?'

'Yes; surely you know it, Uncle Humphrey. And we write to one another regularly.'

'Well, I can just call to mind that ye are always scribbling and getting letters from somewhere. Let me see – where is he now? I quite forget.'

'In India still. Is it possible that you don't know about him, and what a great man he's getting? There are paragraphs about him in our paper very often. The last was about some translation from Hindostani that he'd been making. And he's coming home for me.'

'I very much question it. Lovill will marry you at once, he says.'

'Indeed, he will not.'

'Well, I don't want to force you to do anything against your will, Agatha, but this is how the matter stands. You know I am a little behindhand in my dealings with Lovill – nothing serious, you know, if he gives me time – but I want to be free of him quite in order to go to Australia.'[10]

'Australia!'

'Yes. There's nothing to be done here. I don't know what business is coming to – can't think. But never mind that; this is the point: if you will marry Farmer Lovill, he offers to clear off the debt, and there will no longer be any delay about my own marriage; in short, away I can go. I mean to, and there's an end on't.'

'What, and leave me at home alone?'

'Yes, but a married woman, of course. You see the children are getting big now. John is twelve and Nathaniel ten, and the girls are growing fast, and when I am married again I shall hardly want you to keep house for me – in fact, I must reduce our family as much as possible. So that if you could bring your mind to think of Farmer Lovill as a husband, why, 'twould be a great relief to me after having the trouble and expense of bringing you up. If I can in that way edge out of Lovill's debt I shall have a nice bit of money in hand.'

'But Oswald will be richer even than Mr Lovill,' said Agatha, through her tears.

'Yes, yes. But Oswald is not here, nor is he likely to be. How silly you be.'

'But he will come, and soon, with his eleven hundred a year and all.'

'I wish to Heaven he would. I'm sure he might have you.'

'Now, you promise that, uncle, don't you?' she said, brightening. 'If he comes with plenty of money before you want to leave, he shall marry me, and nobody else.'

'Ay, if he comes. But, Agatha, no nonsense. Just think of what I've been telling you. And at any rate be civil to Farmer Lovill. If this man Winwood were here and asked for ye, and married ye, that would be a very different thing. I do mind now that I saw something about him and his doings in the papers; but he's a fine gentleman by this time, and won't think of stooping to a girl like you. So you'd better take the one who is ready; old men's darlings fare very well as the world goes. We shall be off in nine months, mind, that I've settled. And you must be a married woman afore that time, and wish us goodbye upon your husband's arm.'

'That old arm couldn't support me.'

'And if you don't agree to have him, you'll take a couple of hundred pounds out of my pocket; you'll ruin my chances altogether – that's the long and the short of it.'

Saying which the gloury man turned his back upon her, and his footsteps became drowned in the rumble of the mill.

VI

Nothing so definite was said to her again on the matter for some time. The old yeoman hovered round her, but, knowing the result of the interview between Agatha and her uncle, he forbore to endanger his suit by precipitancy. But one afternoon he could not avoid saying, 'Aggie, when may I speak to you upon a serious subject?'

'Next week,' she replied, instantly.

He had not been prepared for such a ready answer, and it startled him almost as much as it pleased him. Had he known the cause of it his emotions might have been different. Agatha, with all the womanly strategy she was capable of, had written post-haste to Oswald after the conversation with her uncle, and told him of the dilemma. At the end of the present week his answer, if he replied with his customary punctuality, would be sure to come. Fortified with his letter she thought she could meet the old man. Oswald she did not doubt.

Nor had she any reason to. The letter came prompt to the day. It was short, tender, and to the point. Events had shaped themselves so fortunately that he was able to say he would return and marry her before the time named for the family's departure for Queensland.

She danced about for joy. But there was a postscript to the effect that she might as well keep this promise a secret for the present, if she conveniently could, that his intention might not become a public talk in Cloton. Agatha knew that he was a rising and aristocratic young man, and saw at once how proper this was.

So she met Mr Lovill with a simple flat refusal, at which her uncle was extremely angry, and her disclosure to him afterward of the arrival of the letter went but a little way in pacifying him. Farmer Lovill would put in upon him for the debt, he said, unless she could manage to please him for a short time.

'I don't want to please him,' said Agatha. 'It is wrong to encourage him if I don't mean it.'

'Will you behave toward him as the Parson advises you?'

The Parson! That was a new idea, and, from her uncle, unexpected.

'I will agree to what Mr Davids[11] advises about my mere daily behaviour before Oswald comes, but nothing more,' she said. 'That is, I will if you know for certain that he's a good man, who fears God and keeps the commandments.'[12]

'Mr Davids fears God, for sartin, for he never ventures to name Him outside the pulpit; and as for the commandments, 'tis knowed how he swore at the church-restorers for taking them away from the chancel.'

'Uncle, you always jest when I am serious.'

'Well, well! at any rate his advice on a matter of this sort is good.'

'How is it you think of referring me to him?' she asked, in perplexity; 'you so often speak slightingly of him.'

'Oh – well,' said Humphrey, with a faintly perceptible desire to parry the question, 'I have spoken roughly about him once now and then; but perhaps I was wrong. Will ye go?'

'Yes, I don't mind,' she said, languidly.

When she reached the Vicar's study Agatha began her story with reserve, and said nothing about the correspondence with Oswald; yet an intense longing to find a friend and confidant led her to indulge in more feeling than she had intended, and as a finale she wept. The genial incumbent, however, remained quite cool, the secret being that his heart was involved a little in another direction – one, perhaps, not quite in harmony with Agatha's interests – of which more anon.

'So the difficulty is,' he said to her, 'how to behave in this trying time of waiting for Mr Winwood, that you may please parties all round and give offense to none.'

'Yes, Sir, that's it,' sobbed Agatha, wondering how he could have realized her position so readily. 'And uncle wants to go to Australia.'

'One thing is certain,' said the Vicar; 'you must not hurt the feelings of Mr Lovill. Wonderfully sensitive man – a man I respect much as a godly doer.'

'Do you, Sir?'

'I do. His earnestness is remarkable.'

'Yes, in courting.'

'The cue is: treat Mr Lovill gently – gently as a babe! Love opposed, especially an old man's, gets all the stronger. It is your policy to give him seeming encouragement, and so let his feelings expend themselves and die away.'

'How am I to? To advise is so easy.'

'Not by acting untruthfully, of course. You say your lover is sure to come back before your uncle leaves England.'

'I know he will.'

'Then pacify old Mr Lovill in this way: Tell him you'll marry him when your uncle wants to go, if Winwood doesn't come for you before that time.[13] That will quite content Mr Lovill, for he doesn't in the least expect Oswald to return, and you'll see that his persecution will cease at once.'

'Yes; I'll agree to it,' said Agatha promptly.

Mr Davids had refrained from adding that neither did he expect Oswald to come, and hence his advice. Agatha on her part too refrained from stating the good reasons she had for the contrary expectation, and hence her assent. Without the last letter perhaps even her faith would hardly have been bold enough to allow this palpable driving of her into a corner.

'It would be as well to write Mr Lovill a little note, saying you agree to what I have advised,' said the Parson evasively.

'I don't like writing.'

'There's no harm. "If Mr Winwood doesn't come I'll marry you," &c. Poor Mr Lovill will be content, thinking Oswald will not come; you will be content, knowing he will come; your uncle will be content, being indifferent which of two rich men has you and relieves him of his difficulties. Then, if it's the will of Providence, you'll be left in peace. Here's a pen and ink; you can do it at once.'

Thus tempted, Agatha wrote the note with a trembling hand. It really did seem upon the whole a nicely strategic thing to do in her present environed situation. Mr Davids took the note with the air of a man who did not wish to take it in the least, and placed it on the mantelpiece.

'I'll send it down to him by one of the children,' said Aggy, looking wistfully at her note with a little feeling that she should like to have it back again.

'Oh, no, it is not necessary,' said her pleasant adviser. He had rung the bell; the servant now came, and the note was sent off in a trice.

When Agatha got into the open air again her confidence returned, and it was with a mischievous sense of enjoyment that she considered how she was duping her persecutors by keeping secret Oswald's intention of a speedy return. If they only knew what a firm foundation she had for her belief in what they all deemed but an improbable contingency, what a life they would lead her; how the old man would worry her uncle for payment, and what general confusion there would be. Mr Davids' advice was very shrewd, she thought, and she was glad she had called upon him.

Old Lovill came that very afternoon. He was delighted, and danced a few bars of a hornpipe[14] in entering the room. So lively was the antique boy that Agatha was rather alarmed at her own temerity when she considered what was the basis of his gaiety; wishing she could get from him some such writing as he had got from her, that the words of her promise might not in any way be tampered with, or the conditions ignored.

'I only accept you conditionally, mind,' she anxiously said. 'That is distinctly understood.'

'Yes, yes,' said the yeoman. 'I am not so young as I was, little dear, and beggars musn't be choosers. With my ra-ta-ta – say, dear, shall it be the first of November?'

'It will really never be.'

'But if he doesn't come, it shall be the first of November?'

She slightly nodded her head.

'Clk! – I think she likes me!' said the old man aside to Aggy's uncle, which aside was distinctly heard by Aggy.

One of the younger children was in the room, drawing idly on a slate. Agatha at this moment took the slate from the child, and scribbled something on it.

'Now you must please me by just writing your name here,' she said in a voice of playful indifference.

'What is it?' said Lovill, looking over and reading. ' "If Oswald

Winwood comes to marry Agatha Pollin before November, I agree to give her up to him without objection." Well, that is cool for a young lady under six feet, upon my word – hee-hee!' He passed the slate to the miller, who read the writing and passed it back again.

'Sign – just in courtesy,' she coaxed.

'I don't see why –'

'I do it to test your faith in me; and now I find you have none. Don't you think I should have rubbed it out instantly? Ah, perhaps I can be obstinate too!'

He wrote his name then. 'Now I have done it, and shown my faith,' he said, and at once raised his fingers as if to rub it out again. But with hands that moved like lightning she snatched up the slate, flew up stairs, locked it in her box, and came down again.

'Souls of men – that's sharp practice,' said the old gentleman.

'Oh, it is only a whim – a mere memorandum,' said she. 'You had my promise, but I had not yours.'

'Ise wants my slate,' cried the child.

'I'll buy you a new one, dear,' said Agatha, and soothed her.

When she had left the room old Lovill spoke to her uncle somewhat uneasily of the event, which, childish as it had been, discomposed him for the moment.

'Oh, that's nothing,' said Miller Pollin assuringly; 'only play – only play. She's a mere child in nater, even now, and she did it only to tease ye. Why, she overheard your whisper that you thought she liked ye, and that was her playful way of punishing ye for your confidence. You'll have to put up with these worries, farmer. Considering the difference in your ages, she is sure to play pranks. You'll get to like 'em in time.'

'Ay, ay, faith, so I shall! I was always a Turk for sprees! – eh, Pollin? hee-hee!' And the suitor was merry again.

VII

Her life was certainly much pleasanter now. The old man treated her well, and was almost silent on the subject nearest his heart. She was obliged to be very stealthy in receiving letters from Oswald, and on this account was bound to meet the post-man, let the weather be what it would. These transactions were easily kept secret from people out of the house, but it was a most difficult task to hide her movements from her uncle. And one day brought utter failure.

'How's this – out already, Agatha?' he said, meeting her in the lane at dawn on a foggy morning. She was actually reading a letter just received, and there was no disguising the truth.

'I've been for a letter from Oswald.'

'Well, but that won't do. Since he don't come for ye, ye must think no more about him.'

'But he's coming in six weeks. He tells me all about it in this very letter.'

'What – really to marry you?' said her uncle incredulously.

'Yes, certainly.'

'But I hear that he's wonderfully well off.'

'Of course he is; that's why he's coming. He'll agree in a moment to be your surety for the debt to Mr Lovill.'

'Has he said so?'

'Not yet; but he will.'

'I'll believe it when I see him and he tells me so. It is very odd, if he means so much, that he hev never wrote a line to me.'

'We thought – you would force me to have the other at once if he wrote to you,' she murmured.

'Not I, if he comes rich. But it is rather a cock-and-bull story, and since he didn't make up his mind before now, I can't say I be much in his favour. Agatha, you had better not say a word to Mr Lovill about these letters; it will make things deuced unpleasant if he hears of such goings on. You are to reckon yourself bound by your word. Oswald won't hold water, I'm afeard. But I'll be fair. If he do come, proves his income, marries ye willy-nilly, I'll let it be, and the old man and I must do as we can. But barring that – you keep your promise to the letter.'

'That's what it will be, uncle. Oswald will come.'

'Write you must not. Lovill will smell it out, and he'll be sharper than you will like. 'Tis not to be supposed that you are to send love-letters to one man as if nothing was going to happen between ye and another man. The first of November is drawing nearer every day. And be sure and keep this a secret from Lovill for your own sake.'

The more clearly that Agatha began to perceive the entire contrast of expectation as to issue between herself and the other party to the covenant, the more alarmed she became. She had not anticipated such a narrowing of courses as had occurred. A malign influence seemed to be at work without any visible human agency. The critical time drew nearer, and, though no ostensible preparation for the wedding was made, it was evident to all that Lovill was painting and papering his house for somebody's reception. He made a lawn where there had existed a nook of refuse; he bought furniture for a woman's room. The greatest horror was that he insisted upon her taking his arm one day, and there being no help for it she assented, though her distaste was unutterable. She felt the skinny arm through his sleeve, saw over the wry shoulders, looked upon the knobby feet, and shuddered. What if Oswald should not come; the time for her uncle's departure was really getting near. When she reached home she ran up to her bedroom.

On recovering from her dreads a little, Agatha looked from the window. The deaf lad John, who assisted in the mill, was quietly glancing toward her, and a gleam of friendship passed over his kindly face as he caught sight of her form. This reminded her that she had, after all, some sort of friend close at hand. The lad knew pretty well how events stood in Agatha's life, and he was always ready to do on her part whatever lay in his power. Agatha felt stronger, and resolved to bear up.

VIII

Heavens! how anxious she was! It actually wanted only ten days to the first of November, and no new letter had come from Oswald.

Her uncle was married, and Frances was in the house, and the preliminary steps for emigration to Queensland had been taken. Agatha surreptitiously obtained newspapers, scanned the Indian shipping news till her eyes ached, but all to no purpose, for she knew nothing either of route or vessel by which Oswald would return. He had mentioned nothing more than the month of his coming, and she had no way of making that single scrap of information the vehicle for obtaining more.

'In ten days, Agatha,' said the old farmer. 'There is to be no show or fuss of any kind; the wedding will be quite private, in consideration of your feelings and wishes. We'll go to church as if we were taking a morning walk, and nobody will be there to disturb you. Tweedledee!' He held up his arm and crossed it with his walking-stick, as if he were playing the fiddle, at the same time cutting a caper.

'He will come, and then I shan't be able to marry you, even th-th-though I may wish to ever so much,' she faltered, shivering. 'I have promised him, and I *must* have him, you know, and you have agreed to let me.'

'Yes, yes,' said Farmer Lovill, pleasantly. 'But that's a misfortune you need not fear at all, my dear; he won't come at this late day and compel you to marry him in spite of your attachment to me. But, ah – it is only a joke to tease me, you little rogue! Your uncle says so.'

'Agatha, come, cheer up, and think no more of that fellow,' said her uncle when they chanced to be alone together. ' 'Tis ridiculous, you know. We always knew he wouldn't come.'

The day passed. The sixth morning came, the noon, the evening. The fifth day came and vanished. Still no sound of Oswald. His friends now lived in London, and there was not a soul in the parish, save herself, that he corresponded with, or one to whom she could apply in such a delicate matter as this.

It was the evening before her wedding-day, and she was standing alone in the gloom of her bedchamber looking out on the plot in front of the mill. She saw a white figure moving below, and knew him to be the deaf miller lad, her friend. A sudden impulse animated Agatha. She had been making desperate attempts during the last two days to like the old man, and, since Oswald did not come, to marry him without further resistance, for the sheer good of the family of her uncle, to whom she was indeed indebted for much; but had only got so far in her efforts as not to positively hate him. Now rebelliousness came unsought. The lad knew her case, and upon this fact she acted.

Gliding down stairs, she beckoned to him, and, as they stood together in the stream of light from the open mill door, she communicated her directions, partly by signs, partly by writing, for it was difficult to speak to him without being heard all over the premises.

He looked in her face with a glance of confederacy, and said that he understood it all. Upon this they parted.

The old man was at her house that evening, and when she withdrew wished her goodbye 'for the present' with a dozen smiles of meaning. Agatha had retired early, leaving him still there, and when she reached her room, instead of looking at the new dress she was supposed to be going to wear on the morrow, busied herself in making up a small bundle of ordinary articles of clothing. Then she extinguished her light, lay down upon the bed without undressing, and waited for a preconcerted time.

In what seemed to her the dead of night, but which she concluded must be the time agreed upon – half-past five – there was a slight noise as of gravel being thrown against her window. Agatha jumped up, put on her bonnet and cloak, took up her bundle, and went down stairs without a light. At the bottom she slipped on her boots, and passed amid the chirping crickets to the door. It was unbarred. Her uncle, then, had risen, as she had half expected, and it necessitated a little more caution. The morning was dark as a cavern, not a star being visible; but knowing the bearings well, she went cautiously and in silence to the mill door. A faint light shone from inside, and the form of the mill-cart appeared without, the horse ready harnessed to it. Agatha did not see John for the moment, but concluded that he was in the mill with her uncle, who had just at this minute started the wheel for the day. She at once slipped into the vehicle and under the tilt, pulling some empty sacks over, as it had been previously agreed that she should do, to avoid the risk of discovery. After a few minutes of suspense she heard John coming from under the wall, where he had apparently been standing and watching her safely in, and mounting in front, away he drove at a walking pace.

Her scheme had been based upon the following particulars of mill business: Thrice a week it was the regular custom for John and another young man to start early in the morning, each with a horse and covered cart, and go in different directions to customers a few miles off, the carts being laden overnight. All that she had asked John to do this morning was to take her with him to a railway station about ten miles distant, where she might safely wait for an up train.

How will John act on returning – what will he say – how will he excuse himself? she thought as they jogged along. 'John!' she said, meaning to ask him about these things; but he did not hear, and she was too confused and weary after her wakeful night to be able to think consecutively on any subject. But the relief of finding that her uncle did not look into the cart caused a delicious lull in her, and while listlessly watching the dark grey sky through the triangular opening between the curtains at the fore part of the tilt, and John's elbow projecting from the folds of one of them, showing where he was sitting on the outside, she fell asleep.

She awoke after a short interval – everything was just the same – jog, jog, on they went; there was the dim slit between the curtains in front, and, after slightly wondering that John had not troubled himself to see that she was comfortable, she dozed again. Thus Agatha remained until she had a clear consciousness of the stopping of the cart. It aroused her, and looking at once through a small opening at the back, she perceived in the dim dawn that they were turning right about; in another moment the horse was proceeding on the way back again.

'John, what are you doing?' she exclaimed, jumping up, and pulling aside the curtain which parted them.

John did not turn.

'How fearfully deaf he is!' she thought, 'and how odd he looks behind, and he hangs forward as if he were asleep. His hair is snow-white with flour; does he never clean it, then?' She crept across the sacks, and slapped him on the shoulder. John turned then.

'Hee-hee, my dear!' said the blithe old gentleman; and the moisture of his aged eye glistened in the dawning light, as he turned and looked into her horrified face. 'It is all right; I am John, and I have given ye a nice morning's airing to refresh ye for the uncommon duties of today; and now we are going back for the ceremony – hee-hee!'

He wore a miller's smock-frock on this interesting occasion, and had been enabled to play the part of John in the episode by taking the second cart and horse and anticipating by an hour the real John in calling her.

Agatha sank backward. How on earth had he discovered the scheme of escape so readily; he, an old and by no means suspicious man? But what mattered a solution! Hope was crushed, and her rebellion was at an end. Agatha was awakened from thought by another stopping of the horse, and they were again at the mill-door.

She dimly recognized her uncle's voice speaking in anger to her when the old farmer handed her out of the vehicle, and heard the farmer reply, merrily, that girls would be girls and have their freaks, that it didn't matter, and that it was a pleasant jest on this auspicious morn. For himself, there was nothing he had enjoyed all his life so much as a practical joke which did no harm. Then she had a sensation of being told to go into the house, have some food, and dress for her marriage with Mr Lovill, as she had promised to do on that day.

All this she did, and at eleven o'clock became the wife of the old man.

When Agatha was putting on her bonnet in the dusk that evening, for she would not illuminate her ghastly face by a candle, a rustling came against the door. Agatha turned. Her uncle's wife, Frances, was looking into the room, and Agatha could just discern upon her aunt's form the blue cloak which had ruled her destiny.

The sight was almost more than she could bear. If, as seemed likely, this effect was intended, the trick was certainly successful. Frances did not speak a world.

Then Agatha said in quiet irony, and with no evidence whatever of regret, sadness, or surprise at what the act revealed: 'And so you told Mr Lovill of my flight this morning, and set him on the track? It would be amusing to know how you found out my plan, for he never could have done it by himself, poor old darling.'

'Oh, I was a witness of your arrangement with John last night – that was all, my dear,' said her aunt pleasantly. 'I mentioned it then to Mr Lovill, and helped him to his joke of hindering you . . . . . . You remember the van, Agatha, and how you made use of my name on that occasion, years ago, now?'

'Yes, and did you hear our talk that night? I always fancied otherwise.'

'I heard it all. It was fun to you; what do you think it was to me – fun, too? – to lose the man I longed for, and to become the wife of a man I care not an atom about?'

'Ah, no. And how you struggled to get him away from me, dear aunt!'

'And have done it, too.'

'Not you, exactly. The Parson and fate.'

'Parson Davids kindly persuaded you, because I kindly persuaded him, and persuaded your uncle to send you to him. Mr Davids is an old admirer of mine. Now do you see a wheel within a wheel, Agatha?'

Calmness was almost insupportable by Agatha now, but she managed to say: 'Of course you have kept back letters from Oswald to me?'

'No, I have not done that,' said Frances. 'But I told Oswald, who landed at Southampton last night, and called here in great haste at seven this morning, that you had gone out for an early drive with the man you were to marry today, and that it might cause confusion if he remained. He looked very pale, and went away again at once to catch the next London train, saying something about having been prevented by a severe illness from sailing at the time he had promised and intended for the last twelvemonth.'

The bride, though nearly slain by the news, would not flinch in the presence of her adversary. Stilling her quivering flesh, she said smiling: 'That information is deeply interesting, but does not concern me at all, for I am my husband's darling now, you know, and I wouldn't make the dear man jealous for the world.' And she glided down stairs to the chaise.

THE THIEVES WHO COULDN'T
HELP SNEEZING

Many years ago, when oak-trees now past their prime were about as large as elderly gentlemen's walking-sticks, there lived in Wessex a yeoman's son, whose name was Hubert. He was about fourteen years of age, and was as remarkable for his candour and lightness of heart as for his physical courage, of which, indeed, he was a little vain.

One cold Christmas Eve his father, having no other help at hand, sent him on an important errand to a small town several miles from home. He travelled on horseback, and was detained by the business till a late hour of the evening. At last, however, it was completed; he returned to the inn, the horse was saddled, and he started on his way. His journey homeward lay through the Vale of Blackmore,[1] a fertile but somewhat lonely district, with heavy clay roads and crooked lanes. In those days, too, a great part of it was thickly wooded.

It must have been about nine o'clock when, riding along amid the overhanging trees upon his stout-legged cob Jerry, and singing a Christmas carol, to be in harmony with the season, Hubert fancied that he heard a noise among the boughs. This recalled to his mind that the spot he was traversing bore an evil name. Men had been waylaid there. He looked at Jerry, and wished he had been of any other colour than light grey; for on this account the docile animal's form was visible even here in the dense shade. 'What do I care?' he said aloud, after a few minutes of reflection. 'Jerry's legs are too nimble to allow any highwayman to come near me.'

'Ha! ha! indeed,' was said in a deep voice; and the next moment a man darted from the thicket on his right hand, another man from the thicket on his left hand, and another from a tree-trunk a few yards ahead. Hubert's bridle was seized, he was pulled from his horse, and although he struck out with all his might, as a brave boy would naturally do, he was overpowered. His arms were tied behind him, his legs bound tightly together, and he was thrown into the ditch. The

27

robbers, whose faces he could now dimly perceive to be artificially blackened, at once departed, leading off the horse.

As soon as Hubert had a little recovered himself, he found that by great exertion he was able to extricate his legs from the cord; but, in spite of every endeavour, his arms remained bound as fast as before. All, therefore, that he could do was to rise to his feet and proceed on his way with his arms behind him, and trust to chance for getting them unfastened. He knew that it would be impossible to reach home on foot that night, and in such a condition; but he walked on. Owing to the confusion which this attack caused in his brain, he lost his way, and would have been inclined to lie down and rest till morning among the dead leaves had he not known the danger of sleeping without wrappers in a frost so severe. So he wandered further onwards, his arms wrung and numbed by the cord which pinioned him and his heart aching for the loss of poor Jerry, who never had been known to kick, or bite, or show a single vicious habit. He was not a little glad when he discerned through the trees a distant light. Towards this he made his way, and presently found himself in front of a large mansion with flanking wings, gables, and towers, the battlements and chimneys showing their shapes against the stars.

All was silent; but the door stood wide open, it being from this door that the light shone which had attracted him. On entering he found himself in a vast apartment arranged as a dining-hall, and brilliantly illuminated. The walls were covered with a great deal of dark wainscoting, formed into moulded panels, carvings, closet-doors, and the usual fittings of a house of that kind. But what drew his attention most was the large table in the midst of the hall, upon which was spread a sumptuous supper, as yet untouched. Chairs were placed around, and it appeared as if something had occurred to interrupt the meal just at the time when all were ready to begin.

Even had Hubert been so inclined, he could not have eaten in his helpless state, unless by dipping his mouth in the dishes, like a pig or cow. He wished first to obtain assistance; and was about to penetrate further into the house for that purpose when he heard hasty footsteps in the porch and the words, 'Be quick!' uttered in the deep voice which had reached him when he was dragged from the horse. There was only just time for him to dart under the table before three men entered the dining-hall. Peeping from beneath the hanging edges of the tablecloth, he perceived that their faces, too, were blackened, which at once removed any remaining doubts he may have felt that these were the same thieves.

'Now, then,' said the first – the man with the deep voice – 'let us hide ourselves. They will all be back again in a minute. That was a good trick to get them out of the house – eh?'

'Yes. You well imitated the cries of a man in distress,' said the second.

'Excellently,' said the third.

'But they will soon find out that it was a false alarm. Come, where shall we hide? It must be some place we can stay in for two or three hours, till all are in bed and asleep. Ah! I have it. Come this way! I have learnt that the further closet is not opened once in a twelvemonth; it will serve our purpose exactly.'

The speaker advanced into a corridor which led from the hall. Creeping a little farther forward, Hubert could discern that the closet stood at the end, facing the dining-hall. The thieves entered it, and closed the door. Hardly breathing, Hubert glided forward, to learn a little more of their intention, if possible; and, coming close, he could hear the robbers whispering about the different rooms where the jewels, plate, and other valuables of the house were kept, which they plainly meant to steal.

They had not been long in hiding when a gay chattering of ladies and gentlemen was audible on the terrace without. Hubert felt that it would not do to be caught prowling about the house, unless he wished to be taken for a robber himself; and he slipped softly back to the hall, out at the door, and stood in a dark corner of the porch, where he could see everything without being himself seen. In a moment or two a whole troop of personages came gliding past him into the house. There were an elderly gentleman and lady, eight or nine young ladies, as many young men, besides half-a-dozen men-servants and maids. The mansion had apparently been quite emptied of its occupants.

'Now, children and young people, we will resume our meal,' said the old gentleman. 'What the noise could have been I cannot understand. I never felt so certain in my life that there was a person being murdered outside my door.'

Then the ladies began saying how frightened they had been, and how they had expected an adventure, and how it had ended in nothing after all.

'Wait a while,' said Hubert to himself. 'You'll have adventure enough by-and-by, ladies.'

It appeared that the young men and women were married sons and daughters of the old couple, who had come that day to spend Christmas with their parents.

The door was then closed, Hubert being left outside in the porch. He thought this a proper moment for asking their assistance; and, since he was unable to knock with his hands, began boldly to kick the door.

'Hullo! What disturbance are you making here?' said a footman who opened it; and seizing Hubert by the shoulder, he pulled him into the dining-hall. 'Here's a strange boy I have found making a noise in the porch, Sir Simon.'

Everybody turned.

'Bring him forward,' said Sir Simon, the old gentleman before mentioned. 'What were you doing there, my boy?'

'Why, his arms are tied!' said one of the ladies.

'Poor fellow!' said another.

Hubert at once began to explain that he had been waylaid on his journey home, robbed of his horse, and mercilessly left in this condition by the thieves.

'Only to think of it!' exclaimed Sir Simon.

'That's a likely story,' said one of the gentleman-guests, incredulously.

'Doubtful, hey?' asked Sir Simon.

'Perhaps he's a robber himself,' suggested a lady.

'There is a curiously wild wicked look about him, certainly, now that I examine him closely,' said the old mother.

Hubert blushed with shame; and, instead of continuing his story, and relating that the robbers were concealed in the house, he doggedly held his tongue, and half resolved to let them find out their danger for themselves.

'Well, untie him,' said Sir Simon. 'Come, since it is Christmas Eve, we'll treat him well. Here, my lad; sit down in that empty seat at the bottom of the table, and make as good a meal as you can. When you have had your fill we will listen to more particulars of your story.'

The feast then proceeded; and Hubert, now at liberty, was not at all sorry to join in. The more they ate and drank the merrier did the company become; the wine flowed freely, the logs flared up the chimney, the ladies laughed at the gentlemen's stories; in short, all went as noisily and as happily as a Christmas gathering in old times possibly could do.

Hubert, in spite of his hurt feelings at their doubts of his honesty, could not help being warmed both in mind and in body by the good cheer, the scene, and the example of hilarity set by his neighbours. At last he laughed as heartily at their stories and repartees as the old Baronet, Sir Simon, himself. When the meal was almost over one of the sons, who had drunk a little too much wine, after the manner of men in that century, said to Hubert, 'Well, my boy, how are you? Can you take a pinch of snuff?' He held out one of the snuff-boxes which were then becoming common among young and old throughout the country.

'Thank you,' said Hubert, accepting a pinch.

'Tell the ladies who you are, what you are made of, and what you can do,' the young man continued, slapping Hubert upon the shoulder.

'Certainly,' said our hero, drawing himself up, and thinking it best to put a bold face on the matter. 'I am a travelling magician.'

'Indeed!'

'What shall we hear next?'

'Can you call up spirits from the vasty deep, young wizard?'[2]

'I can conjure up a tempest in a cupboard,' Hubert replied.

'Ha-ha!' said the old Baronet, pleasantly rubbing his hands. 'We must see this performance. Girls, don't go away: here's something to be seen.'

'Not dangerous, I hope?' said the old lady.

Hubert rose from the table. 'Hand me your snuff-box, please,' he said to the young man who had made free with him. 'And now,' he continued, 'without the least noise, follow me. If any of you speak it will break the spell.'

They promised obedience. He entered the corridor, and, taking off his shoes, went on tiptoe to the closet door, the guests advancing in a silent group at a little distance behind him. Hubert next placed a stool in front of the door, and, by standing upon it, was tall enough to reach to the top. He then, just as noiselessly, poured all the snuff from the box along the upper edge of the door, and, with a few short puffs of breath, blew the snuff through the chink into the interior of the closet. He held up his finger to the assembly, that they might be silent.

'Dear me, what's that?' said the old lady, after a minute or two had elapsed.

A suppressed sneeze had come from inside the closet.

Hubert held up his finger again.

'How very singular,' whispered Sir Simon. 'This is most interesting.'

Hubert took advantage of the moment to gently slide the bolt of the closet door into its place. 'More snuff,' he said, calmly.

'More snuff,' said Sir Simon. Two or three gentlemen passed their boxes, and the contents were blown in at that top of the closet. Another sneeze, not quite so well suppressed as the first, was heard: then another, which seemed to say that it would not be suppressed under any circumstances whatever. At length there arose a perfect storm of sneezes.

'Excellent, excellent for one so young!' said Sir Simon. 'I am much interested in this trick of throwing the voice – called, I believe, ventriloquism.'[3]

'More snuff,' said Hubert.

'More snuff,' said Sir Simon. Sir Simon's man brought a large jar of the best scented Scotch.[4]

Hubert once more charged the upper chink of the closet, and blew the snuff into the interior, as before. Again he charged, and again, emptying the whole contents of the jar. The tumults of sneezes became really extraordinary to listen to – there was no cessation. It was like wind, rain, and sea, battling in a hurricane.

'I believe there are men inside, and that it is no trick at all!' exclaimed Sir Simon, the truth flashing on him.

'There are,' said Hubert. 'They are come to rob the house; and they are the same who stole my horse.'

The sneezes changed to spasmodic groans. One of the thieves, hearing Hubert's voice, cried, 'Oh! mercy! mercy! let us out of this!'

'Where's my horse?' said Hubert.

'Tied to the tree in the hollow behind Short's Gibbet. Mercy! mercy! let us out, or we shall die of suffocation!'

All the Christmas guests now perceived that this was no longer sport, but serious earnest. Guns and cudgels were procured; all the men-servants were called in, and arranged in position outside the closet. At a signal Hubert withdrew the bolt, and stood on the defensive. But the three robbers, far from attacking them, were found crouching in the corner, gasping for breath. They made no resistance; and, being pinioned, were placed in an out-house till the morning.

Hubert now gave the remainder of his story to the assembled company, and was profusely thanked for the services he had rendered. Sir Simon pressed him to stay over the night, and accept the use of the best bed-room the house afforded, which had been occupied by Queen Elizabeth and King Charles successively[5] when on their visits to this part of the country. But Hubert declined, being anxious to find his horse Jerry, and to test the truth of the robbers' statements concerning him.

Several of the guests accompanied Hubert to the spot behind the gibbet, alluded to by the thieves as where Jerry was hidden. When they reached the knoll and looked over, behold! there the horse stood, uninjured, and quite unconcerned. At sight of Hubert he neighed joyfully; and nothing could exceed Hubert's gladness at finding him. He mounted, wished his friends 'Good night!' and cantered off in the direction they pointed out as his nearest way, reaching home safely about four o'clock in the morning.

THE DISTRACTED PREACHER[1]

I

How his cold was cured

Something delayed the arrival of the Wesleyan minister,[2] and a young man came temporarily in his stead. It was on the thirteenth of January 183–[3] that Mr Stockdale, the young man in question, made his humble entry into the village, unknown, and almost unseen. But when those of the inhabitants who styled themselves of his connection became acquainted with him, they were rather pleased with the substitute than otherwise, though he had scarcely as yet acquired ballast of character sufficient to steady the consciences of the hundred-and-forty Methodists of pure blood who, at this time, lived in Nether Mynton,[4] and to give in addition supplementary support to the mixed race which went to church in the morning and chapel in the evening, or when there was a tea[5] – as many as a hundred-and-ten people more, all told, and including the parish-clerk in the winter-time, when it was too dark for the vicar to observe who passed up the street at seven o'clock – which, to be just to him, he was never anxious to do.

It was owing to this overlapping of creeds that the celebrated population-puzzle arose among the denser gentry of the district around Nether Mynton: how could it be that a parish containing fifteen score of strong, full-grown Episcopalians, and nearly thirteen score of well-matured Dissenters, numbered barely two-and-twenty score adults in all?

The young man being personally interesting, those with whom he came in contact were content to waive for a while the graver question of his sufficiency. It is said that at this time of his life his eyes were affectionate, though without a ray of levity; that his hair was curly, and his figure tall; that he was, in short, a very lovable youth, who won upon his female hearers as soon as they saw and heard him, and caused them to say, 'Why didn't we know of this before he came, that we might have gied him a warmer welcome!'

The fact was that, knowing him to be only provisionally selected, and expecting nothing remarkable in his person or doctrine, they and the rest of his flock in Nether Mynton had felt almost as indifferent about his advent as if they had been the soundest church-going parishioners in the country, and he their true and appointed parson. Thus when Stockdale set foot in the place nobody had secured a lodging for him, and though his journey had given him a bad cold in the head, he was forced to attend to that business himself. On inquiry he found that the only possible accommodation in the village would be found at the house of one Mrs Lizzy Newberry, at the upper end of the street.

It was a youth who gave this information, and Stockdale asked him who Mrs Newberry might be.

The boy said that she was a widow-woman, who had got no husband, because he was dead. Mr Newberry, he added, had been a well-to-do man enough, as the saying was, and a farmer; but he had gone off in a decline. As regarded Mrs Newberry's serious side, Stockdale gathered that she was one of the trimmers who went to church and chapel both.

'I'll go there,' said Stockdale, feeling that, in the absence of purely sectarian lodgings, he could do no better.

'She's a little particular, and won't hae gover'ment folks, or curates, or the pa'son's friends, or such like,' said the lad dubiously.

'Ah, that may be a promising sign: I'll call. Or no; just you go up and ask first if she can find room for me. I have to see one or two persons on another matter. You will find me down at the carrier's.'

In a quarter of an hour the lad came back, and said that Mrs Newberry would have no objection to accommodate him, whereupon Stockdale called at the house. It stood within a garden-hedge, and seemed to be roomy and comfortable. He saw an elderly woman, with whom he made arrangements to come the same night, since there was no inn in the place, and he wished to house himself as soon as possible; the village being a local centre from which he was to radiate at once to the different small chapels in the neighbourhood. He forthwith sent his luggage to Mrs Newberry's from the carrier's, where he had taken shelter, and in the evening walked up to his temporary home.

As he now lived there, Stockdale felt it unnecessary to knock at the door; and entering quietly he had the pleasure of hearing footsteps scudding away like mice into the back quarters. He advanced to the parlour, as the front room was called, though its stone floor was scarcely disguised by the carpet, which only overlaid the trodden areas, leaving sandy deserts under the furniture. But the room looked snug and cheerful. The firelight shone out brightly, trembling on the bulging mouldings of the table-legs, playing with brass knobs and handles, and lurking in great strength on the under surface of the chimney-piece. A deep arm-chair, covered with horsehair, and studded with a countless throng of brass nails, was pulled up on one side of the fireplace. The tea-things were on the table, the teapot cover was open, and a little hand-bell had been laid at that precise point towards which a person seated in the great chair might be expected instinctively to stretch his hand.

Stockdale sat down, not objecting to his experience of the room thus far, and began his residence by tinkling the bell. A little girl crept in at the summons, and made tea for him. Her name, she said, was Marther Sarer, and she lived out there, nodding towards the road and village generally. Before Stockdale had got far with his meal, a tap sounded on the door behind him, and on his telling the inquirer to come in, a rustle of garments caused him to turn his head. He saw before him a fine and extremely well-made young woman, with dark hair, a wide, sensible, beautiful forehead, eyes that warmed him before he knew it, and a mouth that was in itself a picture to all appreciative souls.

'Can I get you anything else for tea?' she said, coming forward a step or two, an expression of liveliness on her features, and her hand waving the door by its edge.

'Nothing, thank you,' said Stockdale, thinking less of what he replied than of what might be her relation to the household.

'You are quite sure?' said the young woman, apparently aware that he had not considered his answer.

He conscientiously examined the tea-things, and found them all there. 'Quite sure, Miss Newberry,' he said.

'It is Mrs Newberry,' said she. 'Lizzy Newberry. I used to be Lizzy Simpkins.'

'Oh, I beg your pardon, Mrs Newberry.' And before he had occasion to say more she left the room.

Stockdale remained in some doubt till Martha Sarah came to clear the table. 'Whose house is this, my little woman?' said he.

'Mrs Lizzy Newberry's, sir.'

'Then Mrs Newberry is not the old lady I saw this afternoon?'

'No. That's Mrs Newberry's mother. It was Mrs Newberry who comed in to you just by now, because she wanted to see if you was good-looking.'

Later in the evening, when Stockdale was about to begin supper, she came again. 'I have come myself, Mr Stockdale,' she said. The minister stood up in acknowledgment of the honour. 'I am afraid little Marther might not make you understand. What will you have for supper? – there's cold rabbit, and there's a ham uncut.'

Stockdale said he could get on nicely with those viands, and supper was laid. He had no more than cut a slice when tap-tap came to the door again. The minister had already learnt that this particular rhythm in taps denoted the fingers of his enkindling landlady, and the doomed young fellow buried his first mouthful under a look of receptive blandness.

'We have a chicken in the house, Mr Stockdale – I quite forgot to mention it just now. Perhaps you would like Marther Sarer to bring it up?'

Stockdale had advanced far enough in the art of being a young man to say that he did not want the chicken, unless she brought it up herself; but when it was uttered he blushed at the daring gallantry of the speech, perhaps a shade too strong for a serious man and a minister. In three minutes the chicken appeared, but, to his great surprise, only in the hands of Martha Sarah. Stockdale was disappointed, which perhaps it was intended that he should be.

He had finished supper, and was not in the least anticipating Mrs Newberry again that night, when she tapped and entered as before.

Stockdale's gratified look told that she had lost nothing by not appearing when expected. It happened that the cold in the head from which the young man suffered had increased with the approach of night, and before she had spoken he was seized with a violent fit of sneezing which he could not anyhow repress.

Mrs Newberry looked full of pity. 'Your cold is very bad tonight, Mr Stockdale.'

Stockdale replied that it was rather troublesome.

'And I've a good mind' – she added archly, looking at the cheerless glass of water on the table, which the abstemious young minister was going to drink.

'Yes, Mrs Newberry?'

'I've a good mind that you should have something more likely to cure it than that cold stuff.'

'Well,' said Stockdale, looking down at the glass, 'as there is no inn here, and nothing better to be got in the village, of course it will do.'

To this she replied, 'There is something better, not far off, though not in the house. I really think you must try it, or you may be ill. Yes, Mr Stockdale, you shall.' She held up her finger, seeing that he was about to speak. 'Don't ask what it is; wait, and you shall see.'

Lizzy went away, and Stockdale waited in a pleasant mood. Presently she returned with her bonnet and cloak on, saying, 'I am so sorry, but you must help me to get it. Mother has gone to bed. Will you wrap yourself up, and come this way, and please bring that cup with you.'

Stockdale, a lonely young fellow, who had for weeks felt a great craving for somebody on whom to throw away superfluous interest, and even tenderness, was not sorry to join her; and followed his guide through the back door, across the garden, to the bottom, where the boundary was a wall. This wall was low, and beyond it Stockdale discerned in the night shades several grey headstones, and the outlines of the church roof or tower.

'It is easy to get up this way,' she said, stepping upon a bank which abutted on the wall; then putting her foot on the top of the stonework, and descending by a spring inside, where the ground was much higher, as is the manner of graveyards to be. Stockdale did the same, and followed her in the dusk across the irregular ground till they came to the tower door, which, when they had entered, she softly closed behind them.

'You can keep a secret?' she said in a musical voice.

'Like an iron chest!' said he fervently.

Then from under her cloak she produced a small lighted lantern, which the minister had not noticed that she carried at all. The light showed them to be close to the singing-gallery stairs, under which lay a heap of lumber of all sorts, but consisting mostly of decayed framework, pews, panels, and pieces of flooring, that from time to time had been removed from their original fixings in the body of the edifice and replaced by new.

'Perhaps you will drag some of those boards aside?' she said, holding the lantern over her head to light him better. 'Or will you take the lantern while I move them?'

'I can manage it,' said the young man, and acting as she ordered, he uncovered, to his surprise, a row of little barrels bound with wood hoops, each barrel being about as large as the nave of a common waggon-wheel. When they were laid open Lizzy fixed her eyes on him, as if she wondered what he would say.

'You know what they are?' she asked, finding that he did not speak.

'Yes, barrels,' said Stockdale simply. He was an inland man, the son of highly respectable parents, and brought up with a single eye to the ministry, and the sight suggested nothing beyond the fact that such articles were there.

'You are quite right, they are barrels,' she said, in an emphatic tone of candour that was not without a touch of irony.

Stockdale looked at her with an eye of sudden misgiving. 'Not smugglers' liquor?' he said.

'Yes,' said she. 'They are tubs of spirit that have accidentally come[6] over in the dark from France.'

In Nether Mynton and its vicinity at this date people always smiled at the sort of sin called in the outside world illicit trading; and these little tubs of gin and brandy were as well known to the inhabitants as turnips. So that Stockdale's innocent ignorance, and his look of alarm when he guessed the sinister mystery, seemed to strike Lizzy first as ludicrous, and then as very awkward for the good impression that she wished to produce upon him.

'Smuggling is carried on here by some of the people,' she said in a gentle, apologetic voice. 'It has been their practice for generations, and they think it no harm. Now, will you roll out one of the tubs?'

'What to do with it?' said the minister.

'To draw a little from it to cure your cold,' she answered. 'It is so burning strong⁷ that it drives away that sort of thing in a jiffy. Oh, it is all right about our taking it. I may have what I like; the owner of the tubs says so. I ought to have had some in the house, and then I shouldn't ha' been put to this trouble; but I drink none myself, and so I often forget to keep it indoors.'

'You are allowed to help yourself, I suppose, that you may not inform where their hiding-place is?'

'Well, no; not that particularly; but I may take any if I want it. So help yourself.'

'I will, to oblige you, since you have a right to it,' murmured the minister; and though he was not quite satisfied with his part in the performance, he rolled one of the tubs out from the corner into the middle of the tower floor. 'How do you wish me to get it out – with a gimlet, I suppose?'

'No, I'll show you,' said his interesting companion; and she held up with her other hand a shoemaker's awl and a hammer. 'You must never do these things with a gimlet, because the wood-dust gets in; and when the buyers pour out the brandy that would tell them that the tub had been broached. An awl makes no dust, and the hole nearly closes up again. Now tap one of the hoops forward.'

Stockdale took the hammer and did so.

'Now make the hole in the part that was covered by the hoop.'

He made the hole as directed. 'It won't run out,' he said.

'Oh yes it will,' said she. 'Take the tub between your knees, and squeeze the heads; and I'll hold the cup.'

Stockdale obeyed; and the pressure taking effect upon the tub, which seemed to be thin, the spirit spirted out in a stream. When the cup was full he ceased pressing, and the flow immediately stopped.

'Now we must fill up the keg with water,' said Lizzy, 'or it will cluck like forty hens when it is handled, and show that 'tis not full.'

'But they tell you you may take it?'

'Yes, the *smugglers*; but the *buyers* must not know that the smugglers have been kind to me at their expense.'

'I see,' said Stockdale doubtfully. 'I much question the honesty of this proceeding.'

By her direction he held the tub with the hole upwards, and while he went through the process of alternately pressing and ceasing to press, she produced a bottle of water, from which she took mouthfuls, conveying each to the keg by putting her pretty lips to the hole,[8] where it was sucked in at each recovery of the cask from pressure. When it was again full he plugged the hole, knocked the hoop down to its place, and buried the tub in the lumber as before.

'Aren't the smugglers afraid that you will tell?' he asked as they recrossed the churchyard.

'Oh no; they are not afraid of that. I couldn't do such a thing.'

'They have put you into a very awkward corner,' said Stockdale emphatically. 'You must, of course, as an honest person, sometimes feel that it is your duty to inform – really you must.'

'Well, I have never particularly felt it as a duty; and, besides, my first husband —' She stopped, and there was some confusion in her voice. Stockdale was so honest and unsophisticated that he did not at once discern why she paused; but at last he did perceive that the words were a slip, and that no woman would have uttered 'first husband' by accident unless she had thought pretty frequently of a second. He felt for her confusion, and allowed her time to recover and proceed. 'My husband,' she said, in a self-corrected tone, 'used to know of their doings, and so did my father, and kept the secret. I cannot inform, in fact, against anybody.'

'I see the hardness of it,' he continued, like a man who looked far into the moral of things. 'And it is very cruel that you should be tossed and tantalized between your memories and your conscience. I do hope, Mrs Newberry, that you will soon see your way out of this unpleasant position.'

'Well, I don't just now,' she murmured.

By this time they had passed over the wall and entered the house, where she brought him a glass and hot water, and left him to his own reflections. He looked after her vanishing form, asking himself whether he, as a respectable man, and a minister, and a shining light, even though as yet only of the halfpenny-candle sort, were quite justified in doing this thing. A sneeze settled the question; and he found that when the fiery liquor was lowered by the addition of twice or thrice the quantity of water, it was one of the prettiest cures for a cold in the head that he had ever known, particularly at this chilly time of the year.

Stockdale sat in the deep chair about twenty minutes sipping and meditating, till he at length took warmer views of things, and longed for the morrow, when he would see Mrs Newberry again. He then felt that, though chronologically at a short distance, it would in an emotional sense be very long before tomorrow came, and walked restlessly round the room. His eye was attracted by a framed and glazed sampler in which a running ornament of fir-trees and peacocks surrounded the following pretty bit of sentiment: –

'Rose-leaves smell when roses thrive,
Here's my work while I'm alive;
Rose-leaves smell when shrunk and shed,
Here's my work when I am dead.

'Lizzy Simpkins. Fear God. Honour the King.
'Aged 11 years.'

' 'Tis hers,' he said to himself. 'Heavens, how I like that name!'

Before he had done thinking that no other name from Abigail to Zenobia would have suited his young landlady so well, tap-tap came again upon the door; and the minister started as her face appeared yet another time, looking so disinterested that the most ingenious would have refrained from asserting that she had come to affect his feelings by her seductive eyes.

'Would you like a fire in your room, Mr Stockdale, on account of your cold?'

The minister, being still a little pricked in the conscience for countenancing her in watering the spirits, saw here a way to self-chastisement. 'No, I thank you,' he said firmly; 'it is not necessary. I have never been used to one in my life, and it would be giving way to luxury too far.'

'Then I won't insist,' she said, and disconcerted him by vanishing instantly.

Wondering if she was vexed by his refusal, he wished that he had chosen to have a fire, even though it should have scorched him out of bed and endangered his self-discipline for a dozen days. However, he consoled himself with what was in truth a rare consolation for a budding lover, that he was under the same roof with Lizzy; her guest, in fact, to take a poetical view of the term lodger; and that he would certainly see her on the morrow.

The morrow came, and Stockdale rose early, his cold quite gone. He had never in his life so longed for the breakfast hour as he did that day, and punctually at eight o'clock, after a short walk, to reconnoitre the premises, he re-entered the door of his dwelling. Breakfast passed, and Martha Sarah attended, but nobody came voluntarily as on the night before to inquire if there were other wants which he had not mentioned, and which she would attempt to gratify. He was disappointed, and went out, hoping to see her at dinner. Dinner-time came; he sat down to the meal, finished it, lingered on for a whole hour, although two new teachers were at that moment waiting at the chapel-door to speak to him by appointment. It was useless to wait longer, and he slowly went his way down the lane, cheered by the thought that, after all, he would see her in the evening, and perhaps engage again in the delightful tub-broaching in the neighbouring church tower, which proceeding he resolved to render more moral by steadfastly insisting that no water should be introduced to fill up, though the tub should cluck like all the hens in Christendom. But nothing could disguise the fact that it was a queer business; and his countenance fell when he thought how much more his mind was interested in that matter than in his serious duties.

However, compunction vanished with the decline of day. Night came, and his tea and supper; but no Lizzy Newberry, and no sweet temptations. At last the minister could bear it no longer, and said to his quaint little attendant, 'Where is Mrs Newberry today?' judiciously handing a penny as he spoke.

'She's busy,' said Martha.

'Anything serious happened?' he asked, handing another penny, and revealing yet additional pennies in the background.

'Oh no – nothing at all!' said she, with breathless confidence. 'Nothing ever happens to her. She's only biding upstairs in bed because 'tis her way sometimes.'

Being a young man of some honour, he would not question further, and assuming that Lizzy must have a bad headache, or other slight ailment, in spite of what the girl had said, he went to bed dissatisfied, not even setting eyes on old Mrs Simpkins. 'I said last night that I should see her tomorrow,' he reflected; 'but that was not to be!'

Next day he had better fortune, or worse, meeting her at the foot of the stairs in the morning, and being favoured by a visit or two from her during the day – once for the purpose of making kindly inquiries about his comfort, as on the first evening, and at another time to place a bunch of winter-violets on his table, with a promise to renew them when they drooped. On these occasions there was something in her smile which showed how conscious she was of the effect she produced, though it must be said that it was rather a humorous than a designing consciousness, and savoured more of pride than of vanity.

As for Stockdale, he clearly perceived that he possessed unlimited capacity for backsliding, and wished that tutelary saints were not denied to Dissenters. He set a watch upon his tongue and eyes for the space of one hour and a half, after which he found it was useless to struggle further, and gave himself up to the situation. 'The other minister will be here in a month,' he said to himself when sitting over the fire. 'Then I shall be off, and she will distract my mind no more! . . . And then, shall I go on living by myself for ever? No; when my two years of probation are finished, I shall have a furnished house to live in, with a varnished door and a brass knocker; and I'll march straight back to her, and ask her flat, as soon as the last plate is on the dresser!'

Thus a titillating fortnight was passed by young Stockdale, during which time things proceeded much as such matters have done ever since the beginning of history. He saw the object of attachment several times one day, did not see her at all the next, met her when he least expected to do so, missed her when hints and signs as to where she should be at a given hour almost amounted to an appointment. This mild coquetry was perhaps fair enough under the circumstances of their being so closely lodged, and Stockdale put up with it as philosophically as he was able. Being in her own house, she could, after vexing or disappointing him of her presence, easily win him back by suddenly surrounding him with those little attentions which her position as his landlady put it in her power to bestow. When he had waited indoors half the day to see her, and on finding that she would not be seen, had gone off in a huff to the dreariest and dampest walk he could discover, she would restore equilibrium in the evening with 'Mr Stockdale, I have fancied you must feel draught o' nights from your bedroom window, and so I have been putting up thicker curtains this afternoon while you were out'; or, 'I noticed that you sneezed twice again this morning, Mr Stockdale. Depend upon it that cold is hanging about you yet; I am sure it is – I have thought of it continually; and you must let me make a posset for you.'

Sometimes in coming home he found his sitting-room rearranged, chairs placed where the table had stood, and the table ornamented with the few fresh flowers and leaves that could be obtained at this season, so as to add a novelty to the room. At times she would be standing on a chair outside the house, trying to nail up a branch of the monthly rose which the winter wind had blown down; and of course he stepped forward to assist her, when their hands got mixed in passing the shreds and nails. Thus they became friends again after a disagreement. She would utter on these occasions some pretty and deprecatory remark on the necessity of her troubling him anew; and he would straightway say that he would do a hundred times as much for her if she should so require.

II

How he saw two other men

Matters being in this advanced state, Stockdale was rather surprised one cloudy evening, while sitting in his room, at hearing her speak in low tones of expostulation to some one at the door. It was nearly dark, but the shutters were not yet closed, nor the candles lighted; and Stockdale was tempted to stretch his head towards the window. He saw outside the door a young man in clothes of a whitish colour, and upon reflection judged their wearer to be the well-built and rather handsome miller who lived below. The miller's voice was alternately low and firm, and sometimes it reached the level of positive entreaty; but what the words were Stockdale could in no way hear.

Before the colloquy had ended, the minister's attention was attracted by a second incident. Opposite Lizzy's home grew a clump of laurels, forming a thick and permanent shade. One of the laurel boughs now quivered against the light background of sky, and in a moment the head of a man peered out, and remained still. He seemed to be also much interested in the conversation at the door, and was plainly lingering there to watch and listen. Had Stockdale stood in any other relation to Lizzy than that of a lover, he might have gone out and examined into the meaning of this; but being as yet but an unprivileged ally, he did nothing more than stand up and show himself against the firelight, whereupon the listener disappeared, and Lizzy and the miller spoke in lower tones.

Stockdale was made so uneasy by the circumstance, that as soon as the miller was gone, he said, 'Mrs Newberry, are you aware that you were watched just now, and your conversation heard?'

'When?' she said.

'When you were talking to that miller. A man was looking from the laurel-tree as jealously as if he could have eaten you.'

She showed more concern than the trifling event seemed to demand, and he added, 'Perhaps you were talking of things you did not wish to be overheard?'

'I was talking only on business,' she said.

'Lizzy, be frank!' said the young man. 'If it was only on business, why should anybody wish to listen to you?'

She looked curiously at him. 'What else do you think it could be, then?'

'Well – the only talk between a young woman and man that is likely to amuse an eavesdropper.'

'Ah yes,' she said, smiling in spite of her preoccupation. 'Well, my cousin Owlett[9] has spoken to me about matrimony, every now and then, that's true; but he was not speaking of it then. I wish he had been speaking of it, with all my heart. It would have been much less serious for me.'

'O Mrs Newberry!'

'It would. Not that I should ha' chimed in with him, of course. I wish it for other reasons. I am glad, Mr Stockdale, that you have told me of that listener. It is a timely warning, and I must see my cousin again.'

'But don't go away till I have spoken,' said the minister. 'I'll out with it at once, and make no more ado. Let it be Yes or No between us, Lizzy; please do!' And he held out his hand, in which she freely allowed her own to rest, but without speaking.

'You mean Yes by that?' he asked, after waiting a while.

'You may be my sweetheart, if you will.'

'Why not say at once you will wait for me until I have a house and can come back to marry you?'

'Because I am thinking – thinking of something else,' she said with embarrassment. 'It all comes upon me at once, and I must settle one thing at a time.'

'At any rate, dear Lizzy, you can assure me that the miller shall not be allowed to speak to you except on business? You have never directly encouraged him?'

She parried the question by saying, 'You see, he and his party have been in the habit of leaving things on my premises sometimes, and as I have not denied him, it makes him rather forward.'

'Things – what things?'

'Tubs – they are called Things here.'

'But why don't you deny him, my dear Lizzy?'

'I cannot well.'

'You are too timid. It is unfair of him to impose so upon you, and get your good name into danger by his smuggling tricks. Promise me that the next time he wants to leave his tubs here you will let me roll them into the street?'

She shook her head. 'I would not venture to offend the neighbours so much as that,' said she, 'or do anything that would be so likely to put poor Owlett into the hands of the exciseman.'[10]

Stockdale sighed, and said that he thought hers a mistaken generosity when it extended to assisting those who cheated the king of his dues. 'At any rate, you will let me make him keep his distance as your lover, and tell him flatly that you are not for him?'

'Please not, at present,' she said. 'I don't wish to offend my old neighbours. It is not only Owlett who is concerned.'

'This is too bad,' said Stockdale impatiently.

'On my honour, I won't encourage him as my lover,' Lizzy answered earnestly. 'A reasonable man will be satisfied with that.'

'Well, so I am,' said Stockdale, his countenance clearing.

III

The mysterious greatcoat

Stockdale now began to notice more particularly a feature in the life of his fair landlady, which he had casually observed, but scarcely ever thought of before. It was that she was markedly irregular in her hours of rising. For a week or two she would be tolerably punctual, reaching the ground-floor within a few minutes of half-past seven. Then suddenly she would not be visible till twelve at noon, perhaps for three or four days in succession; and twice he had certain proof that she did not leave her room till half-past three in the afternoon. The second time that this extreme lateness came under his notice was on a day when he had particularly wished to consult with her about his future movements; and he concluded, as he always had done, that she had a cold, headache, or other ailment, unless she had kept herself invisible to avoid meeting and talking to him, which he could hardly believe. The former supposition was disproved, however, by her innocently saying, some days later, when they were speaking on a question of health, that she had never had a moment's heaviness, headache, or illness of any kind since the previous January twelvemonth.

'I am glad to hear it,' said he. 'I thought quite otherwise.'

'What, do I look sickly?' she asked, turning up her face to show the impossibility of his gazing on it and holding such a belief for a moment.

'Not at all; I merely thought so from your being sometimes obliged to keep your room through the best part of the day.'

'Oh, as for that – it means nothing,' she murmured, with a look which some might have called cold, and which was the worst look that he liked to see upon her. 'It is pure sleepiness, Mr Stockdale.'

'Never!'

'It is, I tell you. When I stay in my room till half-past three in the afternoon, you may always be sure that I slept soundly till three, or I shouldn't have stayed there.'

'It is dreadful,' said Stockdale, thinking of the disastrous effects of such indulgence upon the household of a minister, should it become a habit of everyday occurrence.

'But then,' she said, divining his good and prescient thoughts, 'it only happens when I stay awake all night. I don't go to sleep till five or six in the morning sometimes.'

'Ah, that's another matter,' said Stockdale. 'Sleeplessness to such an alarming extent is real illness. Have you spoken to a doctor?'

'Oh no – there is no need for doing that – it is all natural to me.' And she went away without further remark.

Stockdale might have waited a long time to know the real cause of her sleeplessness, had it not happened that one dark night he was sitting in his bedroom jotting down notes for a sermon, which unintentionally occupied him for a considerable time after the other members of the household had retired. He did not get to bed till one o'clock. Before he had fallen asleep he heard a knocking at the door, first rather timidly performed, and then louder. Nobody answered it, and the person knocked again. As the house still remained undisturbed,

Stockdale got out of bed, went to his window, which overlooked the door, and opening it, asked who was there.

A young woman's voice replied that Susan Wallis was there, and that she had come to ask if Mrs Newberry could give her some mustard to make a plaster with, as her father was taken very ill on the chest.

The minister, having neither bell nor servant, was compelled to act in person. 'I will call Mrs Newberry,' he said. Partly dressing himself, he went along the passage and tapped at Lizzy's door. She did not answer, and, thinking of her erratic habits in the matter of sleep, he thumped the door persistently, when he discovered, by its moving ajar under his knocking, that it had only been gently pushed to. As there was now a sufficient entry for the voice, he knocked no longer, but said in firm tones, 'Mrs Newberry, you are wanted.'

The room was quite silent; not a breathing, not a rustle, came from any part of it. Stockdale now sent a positive shout through the open space of the door: 'Mrs Newberry!' – still no answer, or movement of any kind within. Then he heard sounds from the opposite room, that of Lizzy's mother, as if she had been aroused by his uproar though Lizzy had not, and was dressing herself hastily. Stockdale softly closed the younger woman's door and went on to the other, which was opened by Mrs Simpkins before he could reach it. She was in her ordinary clothes, and had a light in her hand.

'What's the person calling about?' she said in alarm.

Stockdale told the girl's errand, adding seriously, 'I cannot wake Mrs Newberry.'

'It is no matter,' said her mother. 'I can let the girl have what she wants as well as my daughter.' And she came out of the room and went downstairs.

Stockdale retired towards his own apartment, saying, however, to Mrs Simpkins from the landing, as if on second thoughts, 'I suppose there is nothing the matter with Mrs Newberry, that I could not wake her?'

'Oh no,' said the old lady hastily. 'Nothing at all.'

Still the minister was not satisfied. 'Will you go in and see?' he said. 'I should be much more at ease.'

Mrs Simpkins returned up the staircase, went to her daughter's room, and came out again almost instantly. 'There is nothing at all the matter with Lizzy,' she said; and descended again to attend to the applicant, who, having seen the light, had remained quiet during this interval.

Stockdale went into his room and lay down as before. He heard Lizzy's mother open the front door, admit the girl, and then the murmured discourse of both as they went to the store-cupboard for the medicament required. The girl departed, the door was fastened, Mrs Simpkins came upstairs, and the house was again in silence. Still the minister did not fall asleep. He could not get rid of a singular suspicion, which was all the more harassing, in being, if true, the most unaccountable thing within his experience. That Lizzy Newberry was in her bedroom when he made such a clamour at the door he could not possibly convince himself, notwithstanding that he had heard her come upstairs at the usual time, go into her chamber, and shut herself up in the usual way. Yet all reason was so much against her being elsewhere, that he was constrained to go back again to the unlikely theory of a heavy sleep, though he had heard neither breath nor movement during a shouting and knocking loud enough to rouse the Seven Sleepers.[11]

Before coming to any positive conclusion he fell asleep himself, and did not awake till day. He saw nothing of Mrs Newberry in the morning, before he went out to meet the rising sun, as he liked to do when the weather was fine; but as this was by no means unusual, he took no notice of it. At breakfast-time he knew that she was not far off by hearing her in the kitchen, and though he saw nothing of her person, that back apartment being rigorously closed against his eyes, she seemed to be talking, ordering, and bustling about among the pots and skimmers in so ordinary a manner, that there was no reason for his wasting more time in fruitless surmise.

The minister suffered from these distractions, and his extemporized sermons were not improved thereby. Already he often said Romans for Corinthians in the pulpit,[12] and gave out hymns in strange cramped metres, that hitherto had always been skipped, because the congregation could not raise a tune to fit them. He fully resolved that as soon as his few weeks of stay approached their end he would cut the matter short, and commit himself by proposing a definite engagement, repenting at leisure if necessary.

With this end in view, he suggested to her on the evening after her mysterious sleep that they should take a walk together just before dark, the latter part of the proposition being introduced that they might return home unseen. She consented to go; and away they went over a stile, to a shrouded footpath suited for the occasion. But, in spite of attempts on both sides, they were unable to infuse much spirit into the ramble. She looked rather paler than usual, and sometimes turned her head away.

'Lizzy,' said Stockdale reproachfully, when they had walked in silence a long distance.

'Yes,' said she.

'You yawned – much my company is to you!' He put it in that way, but he was really wondering whether her yawn could possibly have more to do with physical weariness from the night before than mental weariness of that present moment. Lizzy apologized, and owned that she was rather tired, which gave him an opening for a direct question on the point; but his modesty would not allow him to put it to her; and he uncomfortably resolved to wait.

The month of February passed with alternations of mud and frost, rain and sleet, east winds and north-westerly gales. The hollow places in the ploughed fields showed themselves as pools of water, which had settled there from the higher levels, and had not yet found time to soak away. The birds began to get lively, and a single thrush came just before sunset each evening, and sang hopefully on the large elm-tree which stood nearest to Mrs Newberry's house. Cold blasts and brittle earth had given place to an oozing dampness more unpleasant in itself than frost; but it suggested coming spring, and its unpleasantness was of a bearable kind.

Stockdale had been going to bring about a practical understanding with Lizzy at least half-a-dozen times; but, what with the mystery of her apparent absence on the night of the neighbour's call, and her curious way of lying in bed at unaccountable times, he felt a check within him whenever he wanted to speak out. Thus they still lived on as indefinitely affianced lovers, each of whom hardly acknowledged the other's claim to the name of chosen one. Stockdale persuaded himself that his hesitation was owing to the postponement of the ordained minister's arrival, and the consequent delay in his own departure, which did away with all necessity for haste in his courtship; but perhaps it was only that his discretion was reasserting itself, and telling him that he had better get clearer ideas of Lizzy before arranging for the grand contract of his life with her. She, on her part, always seemed ready to be urged further on that question than he had hitherto attempted to go; but she was none the less independent, and to a degree which would have kept from flagging the passion of a far more mutable man.

On the evening of the 1st of March he went casually into his bedroom about dusk, and noticed lying on a chair a greatcoat, hat, and breeches.[13] Having no recollection of leaving any clothes of his own in that spot, he went and examined them as well as he could in the twilight, and found that they did not belong to him. He paused for a moment to consider how they might have got there. He was the only man living in the house; and yet these were not his garments, unless he had made a mistake. No, they were not his. He called up Martha Sarah.

'How did these things come in my room?' he said, flinging the objectionable articles to the floor.

Martha said that Mrs Newberry had given them to her to brush, and that she had brought them up there thinking they must be Mr Stockdale's, as there was no other gentleman a-lodging there.

'Of course you did,' said Stockdale. 'Now take them down to your mis'ess, and say they are some clothes I have found here and know nothing about.'

As the door was left open he heard the conversation downstairs. 'How stupid!' said Mrs Newberry, in a tone of confusion. 'Why, Marther Sarer, I did not tell you to take 'em to Mr Stockdale's room?'

'I thought they must be his as they was so muddy,' said Martha humbly.

'You should have left 'em on the clothes-horse,' said the young mistress severely; and she came upstairs with the garments on her arm, quickly passed Stockdale's room, and threw them forcibly into a closet at the end of a passage. With this the incident ended, and the house was silent again.

There would have been nothing remarkable in finding such clothes in a widow's house had they been clean; or moth-eaten, or creased, or mouldy from long lying by; but that they should be splashed with recent mud bothered Stockdale a good deal. When a young pastor is in the aspen stage of attachment, and open to agitation at the merest trifles, a really substantial incongruity of this complexion is a disturbing thing. However, nothing further occurred at that time; but he became watchful, and given to conjecture, and was unable to forget the circumstance.

One morning, on looking from his window, he saw Mrs Newberry herself brushing the tails of a long drab greatcoat, which, if he mistook not, was the very same garment as the one that had adorned the chair of his room. It was densely splashed up to the hollow of the back with neighbouring Nether Mynton mud, to judge by its colour, the spots being distinctly visible to him in the sunlight. The previous day or two having been wet, the inference was irresistible that the wearer had quite recently been walking some considerable distance about the lanes and fields. Stockdale opened the window and looked out, and Mrs Newberry turned her head. Her face became slowly red; she never had looked prettier, or more incomprehensible. He waved his hand affectionately and said good morning; she answered with embarrassment, having ceased her occupation on the instant that she saw him, and rolled up the coat half-cleaned.

Stockdale shut the window. Some simple explanation of her proceeding was doubtless within the bounds of possibility; but he himself could not think of one; and he wished that she had placed the matter beyond conjecture by voluntarily saying something about it there and then.

But, though Lizzy had not offered an explanation at the moment, the subject was brought forward by her at the next time of their meeting. She was chatting to him concerning some other event, and remarked that it happened about the time when she was dusting some old clothes that had belonged to her poor husband.

'You keep them clean out of respect to his memory?' said Stockdale tentatively.

'I air and dust them sometimes,' she said, with the most charming innocence in the world.

'Do dead men come out of their graves and walk in mud?' murmured the minister, in a cold sweat at the deception that she was practising.

'What did you say?' asked Lizzy.

'Nothing, nothing,' said he mournfully. 'Mere words – a phrase that will do for my sermon next Sunday.' It was too plain that Lizzy was unaware that he had seen actual pedestrian splashes upon the skirts of the tell-tale overcoat, and that she imagined him to believe it had come direct from some chest or drawer.

The aspect of the case was now considerably darker. Stockdale was so much depressed by it that he did not challenge her explanation, or threaten to go off as a missionary to benighted islanders, or reproach her in any way whatever. He simply parted from her when she had done talking, and lived on in perplexity, till by degrees his natural manner became sad and constrained.

IV

At the time of the new moon

The following Thursday was changeable, damp, and gloomy; and the night threatened to be windy and unpleasant. Stockdale had gone away to Knollsea[14] in the morning, to be present at some commemoration service there, and on his return he was met by the attractive Lizzy in the passage. Whether influenced by the tide of cheerfulness which had attended him that day, or by the drive through the open air, or whether from a natural disposition to let bygones alone, he allowed himself to be fascinated into forgetfulness of the greatcoat incident, and upon the whole passed a pleasant evening; not so much in her society as within sound of her voice, as she sat talking in the back parlour to her mother, till the latter went to bed. Shortly after this Mrs Newberry retired, and then Stockdale prepared to go upstairs himself. But before he left the room he remained standing by the dying embers awhile, thinking long of one thing and another; and was only aroused by the flickering of his candle in the socket as it suddenly declined and went out. Knowing that there were a tinder-box, matches, and another candle in his bedroom, he felt his way upstairs without a light. On reaching his chamber he laid his hand on every possible ledge and corner for the tinder-box, but for a long time in vain. Discovering it at length, Stockdale produced a spark, and was kindling the brimstone, when he fancied that he heard a movement in the passage. He blew harder at the lint, the match flared up, and looking by aid of the blue light through the door, which had been standing open all this time, he was surprised to see a male figure vanishing round the top of the staircase with the evident intention of escaping unobserved. The personage wore the clothes which Lizzy had been brushing, and something in the outline and gait suggested to the minister that the wearer was Lizzy herself.

But he was not sure of this; and, greatly excited, Stockdale determined to investigate the mystery, and to adopt his own way for doing it. He blew out the match without lighting the candle, went into the passage, and proceeded on tiptoe towards Lizzy's room. A faint grey square of light in the direction of the chamber-window as he approached told him that the door was open, and at once suggested that the occupant was gone. He turned and brought down his fist upon the handrail of the staircase: 'It was she; in her late husband's coat and hat!'

Somewhat relieved to find that there was no intruder in the case, yet none the less surprised, the minister crept down the stairs, softly put on his boots, overcoat, and hat, and tried the front door. It was fastened as usual: he went to the back door, found this unlocked, and emerged into the garden. The night was mild and moonless, and rain had lately been falling, though for the present it had ceased. There was a sudden dropping from the trees and bushes every now and then, as each passing wind shook their boughs. Among these sounds Stockdale heard the faint fall of feet upon the road outside, and he guessed from the step that it was Lizzy's. He followed the sound, and, helped by the circumstance of the wind blowing from the direction in which the pedestrian moved, he got nearly close to her, and kept there, without risk of being overheard. While he thus followed her up

the street or lane, as it might indifferently be called, there being more
hedge than houses on either side, a figure came forward to her from
one of the cottage doors. Lizzy stopped; the minister stepped upon
the grass and stopped also.

'Is that Mrs Newberry?' said the man who had come out, whose
voice Stockdale recognized as that of one of the most devout members
of his congregation.

'It is,' said Lizzy.

'I be quite ready – I've been here this quarter-hour.'

'Ah, John,' said she, 'I have bad news; there is danger tonight for
our venture.'

'And d'ye tell o't! I dreamed there might be.'

'Yes,' she said hurriedly; 'and you must go at once round to where
the chaps are waiting, and tell them they will not be wanted till
tomorrow night at the same time. I go to burn the lugger off.'

'I will,' he said; and instantly went off through a gate, Lizzy continuing her way.

On she tripped at a quickening pace till the lane turned into
the turnpike-road, which she crossed, and got into the track for
Ringsworth. Here she ascended the hill without the least hesitation,
passed the lonely hamlet of Holworth,[15] and went down the vale on
the other side. Stockdale had never taken any extensive walks in this
direction, but he was aware that if she persisted in her course much
longer she would draw near to the coast, which was here between two
and three miles distant from Nether Mynton; and as it had been about
a quarter-past eleven o'clock when they set out, her intention seemed
to be to reach the shore about midnight.

Lizzy soon ascended a small mound, which Stockdale at the same
time adroitly skirted on the left; and a dull monotonous roar burst
upon his ear. The hillock was about fifty yards from the top of the
cliffs, and by day it apparently commanded a full view of the bay.
There was light enough in the sky to show her disguised figure against
it when she reached the top, where she paused, and afterwards sat
down. Stockdale, not wishing on any account to alarm her at this
moment, yet desirous of being near her, sank upon his hands and
knees, crept a little higher up, and there stayed still.

The wind was chilly, the ground damp, and his position one in which he did not care to remain long. However, before he had decided to leave it, the young man heard voices behind him. What they signified he did not know; but, fearing that Lizzy was in danger, he was about to run forward and warn her that she might be seen, when she crept to the shelter of a little bush which maintained a precarious existence in that exposed spot; and her form was absorbed in its dark and stunted outline as if she had become part of it. She had evidently heard the men as well as he. They passed near him, talking in loud and careless tones, which could be heard above the uninterrupted washings of the sea, and which suggested that they were not engaged in any business at their own risk. This proved to be the fact: some of their words floated across to him, and caused him to forget at once the coldness of his situation.

'What's the vessel?'

'A lugger, about fifty tons.'

'From Cherbourg,[16] I suppose?'

'Yes, 'a b'lieve.'

'But it don't all belong to Owlett?'

'Oh no. He's only got a share. There's another or two in it – a farmer and such like, but the names I don't know.'

The voices died away, and the heads and shoulders of the men diminished towards the cliff, and dropped out of sight.

'My darling has been tempted to buy a share by that unbeliever Owlett,' groaned the minister, his honest affection for Lizzy having quickened to its intensest point during these moments of risk to her person and name. 'That's why she's here,' he said to himself. 'Oh, it will be the ruin of her!'

His perturbation was interrupted by the sudden bursting out of a bright and increasing light from the spot where Lizzy was in hiding. A few seconds later, and before it had reached the height of a blaze, he heard her rush past him down the hollow like a stone from a sling, in the direction of home. The light now flared high and wide, and showed its position clearly. She had kindled a bough of furze and stuck it into the bush under which she had been crouching; the wind fanned the flame, which crackled fiercely, and threatened to consume the bush as well as the bough. Stockdale paused just long enough to notice thus much, and then followed rapidly the route taken by the young woman. His intention was to overtake her, and reveal himself as a friend; but run as he would he could see nothing of her. Thus he flew across the open country about Holworth, twisting his legs and ankles in unexpected fissures and descents, till, on coming to the gate between the downs and the road, he was forced to pause to get breath. There was no audible movement either in front or behind him, and he now concluded that she had not outrun him, but that, hearing him at her heels, and believing him one of the excise party, she had hidden herself somewhere on the way, and let him pass by.

He went on at a more leisurely pace towards the village. On reaching the house he found his surmise to be correct, for the gate was on the latch, and the door unfastened, just as he had left them. Stockdale closed the door behind him, and waited silently in the passage. In about ten minutes he heard the same light footstep that he had heard in going out; it paused at the gate, which opened and shut softly, and then the door-latch was lifted, and Lizzy came in.

Stockdale went forward and said at once, 'Lizzy, don't be frightened. I have been waiting up for you.'

She started, though she had recognized the voice. 'It is Mr Stockdale, isn't it?' she said.

'Yes,' he answered, becoming angry now that she was safe indoors, and not alarmed. 'And a nice game I've found you out in tonight. You are in man's clothes, and I am ashamed of you!'

Lizzy could hardly find a voice to answer this unexpected reproach.

'I am only partly in man's clothes,' she faltered, shrinking back to the wall. 'It is only his greatcoat and hat and breeches that I've got on, which is no harm, as he was my own husband; and I do it only because a cloak blows about so, and you can't use your arms. I have got my own dress under just the same – it is only tucked in! Will you go away upstairs and let me pass? I didn't want you to see me at such a time as this.'

'But I have a right to see you. How do you think there can be anything between us now?' Lizzy was silent. 'You are a smuggler,' he continued sadly.

'I have only a share in the run,' she said.

'That makes no difference. Whatever did you engage in such a trade as that for, and keep it such a secret from me all this time?'

'I don't do it always. I only do it in winter-time when 'tis new moon.'

'Well, I suppose that's because it can't be done anywhen else . . . You have regularly upset me, Lizzy.'

'I am sorry for that,' Lizzy meekly replied.

'Well now,' said he more tenderly, 'no harm is done as yet. Won't you for the sake of me give up this blamable and dangerous practice altogether?'

'I must do my best to save this run,' said she, getting rather husky in the throat. 'I don't want to give you up – you know that; but I don't want to lose my venture. I don't know what to do now! Why I have kept it so secret from you is that I was afraid you would be angry if you knew.'

'I should think so. I suppose if I had married you without finding this out you'd have gone on with it just the same?'

'I don't know. I did not think so far ahead. I only went tonight to burn the folks off, because we found that the excisemen knew where the tubs were to be landed.'

'It is a pretty mess to be in altogether, is this,' said the distracted young minister. 'Well, what will you do now?'

Lizzy slowly murmured the particulars of their plan, the chief of which were that they meant to try their luck at some other point of the shore the next night; that three landing-places were always[17] agreed upon before the run was attempted, with the understanding that, if the vessel was burnt off from the first point, which was Ringsworth, as it had been by her tonight, the crew should attempt to make the second, which was Lullstead,[18] on the second night; and if there, too, danger threatened, they should on the third night try the third place, which was behind a headland farther west.

'Suppose the officers hinder them landing there too?' he said, his attention to this interesting programme displacing for a moment his concern at her share in it.

'Then we shan't try anywhere else all this dark – that's what we call the time between moon and moon – and perhaps they'll string the tubs to a stray-line, and sink 'em a little-ways from shore, and take the bearings; and then when they have a chance they'll go to creep for 'em.'

'What's that?'

'Oh, they'll go out in a boat and drag a creeper – that's a grapnel – along the bottom till it catch hold of the stray-line.'

The minister stood thinking; and there was no sound within doors but the tick of the clock on the stairs, and the quick breathing of Lizzy, partly from her walk and partly from agitation, as she stood close to the wall, not in such complete darkness but that he could discern against its whitewashed surface the greatcoat and broad hat which covered her.

'Lizzy, all this is very wrong,' he said. 'Don't you remember the lesson of the tribute-money? "Render unto Caesar the things that are Caesar's."[19] Surely you have heard that read times enough in your growing up?'

'He's dead,' she pouted.

'But the spirit of the text is in force just the same.'

'My father did it, and so did my grandfather, and almost everybody in Nether Mynton lives by it, and life would be so dull if it wasn't for that, that I should not care to live at all.'

'I am nothing to live for, of course,' he replied bitterly. 'You would not think it worth while to give up this wild business and live for me alone?'

'I have never looked at it like that.'

'And you won't promise, and wait till I am ready?'

'I cannot give you my word tonight.' And, looking thoughtfully down, she gradually moved and moved away, going into the adjoining room, and closing the door between them. She remained there in the dark till he was tired of waiting, and had gone up to his own chamber.

Poor Stockdale was dreadfully depressed all the next day by the discoveries of the night before. Lizzy was unmistakably a fascinating young woman, but as a minister's wife she was hardly to be contemplated. 'If I had only stuck to father's little grocery business, instead of going in for the ministry,[20] she would have suited me beautifully!' he said sadly, until he remembered that in that case he would never have come from his distant home to Nether Mynton, and never have known her.

The estrangement between them was not complete, but it was sufficient to keep them out of each other's company. Once during the day he met her in the garden-path, and said, turning a reproachful eye upon her, 'Do you promise, Lizzy?' But she did not reply. The evening drew on, and he knew well enough that Lizzy would repeat her excursion at night – her half-offended manner had shown that she had not the slightest intention of altering her plans at present. He did not wish to repeat his own share of the adventure; but, act as he would, his uneasiness on her account increased with the decline of day. Supposing that an accident should befall her, he would never forgive himself for not being there to help, much as he disliked the idea of seeming to countenance such unlawful escapades.

V

How they went to Lullstead and back

As he had expected, she left the house at the same hour at night, this time passing his door without stealth, as if she knew very well that he would be watching, and were resolved to brave his displeasure. He was quite ready, opened the door quickly, and reached the back door almost as soon as she.

'Then you will go, Lizzy?' he said as he stood on the step beside her, who now again appeared as a little man with a face altogether unsuited to his clothes.

'I must,' she said, repressed by his stern manner.

'Then I shall go too,' said he.

'And I am sure you will enjoy it!' she exclaimed in more buoyant tones. 'Everybody does who tries it.'[21]

'God forbid that I should!' he said. 'But I must look after you.'

They opened the wicket and went up the road abreast of each other, but at some distance apart, scarcely a word passing between them. The evening was rather less favourable to smuggling enterprise than the last had been, the wind being lower, and the sky somewhat clear towards the north.

'It is rather lighter,' said Stockdale.

' 'Tis, unfortunately,' said she. 'But it is only from those few stars over there. The moon was new today at four o'clock, and I expected clouds. I hope we shall be able to do it this dark, for when we have to sink 'em for long it makes the stuff taste bleachy, and folks don't like it so well.'

Her course was different from that of the preceding night, branching off to the left over Lord's Barrow as soon as they had got out of the lane and crossed the highway. By the time they reached Chaldon Down,[22] Stockdale, who had been in perplexed thought as to what he should say to her, decided that he would not attempt expostulation now, while she was excited by the adventure, but wait till it was over, and endeavour to keep her from such practices in future. It occurred to him once or twice, as they rambled on, that should they be surprised by the excisemen, his situation would be more awkward than hers, for it would be difficult to prove his true motive in coming to the spot; but the risk was a slight consideration beside his wish to be with her.

They now arrived at a ravine which lay on the outskirts of Chaldon, a village two miles on their way towards the point of the shore they sought. Lizzy broke the silence this time: 'I have to wait here to meet the carriers. I don't know if they have come yet. As I told you, we go to Lullstead tonight, and it is two miles farther than Ringsworth.'

It turned out that the men had already come; for while she spoke two or three dozen heads broke the line of the slope, and a company of men at once descended from the bushes where they had been lying in wait. These carriers were men whom Lizzy and other proprietors regularly employed to bring the tubs from the boat to a hiding-place inland. They were all young fellows of Nether Mynton, Chaldon, and the neighbourhood, quiet and inoffensive persons,[23] who simply engaged to carry the cargo for Lizzy and her cousin Owlett, as they would have engaged in any other labour for which they were fairly well paid.

At a word from her they closed in together. 'You had better take it now,' she said to them; and handed to each a packet. It contained

six shillings, their remuneration for the night's undertaking, which
was paid beforehand without reference to success or failure; but,
besides this, they had the privilege of selling as agents when the run
was successfully made. As soon as it was done, she said to them, 'The
place is the old one at Lullstead'; the men till that moment not having
been told whither they were bound, for obvious reasons. 'Owlett will
meet you there,' added Lizzy. 'I shall follow behind, to see that we
are not watched.'

The carriers went on, and Stockdale and Mrs Newberry followed
at the distance of a stone's-throw. 'What do these men do by day?'
he said.

'Twelve or fourteen of them are labouring men. Some are brick-
makers, some carpenters, some masons,[24] some thatchers. They
are all known to me very well. Nine of 'em are of your own congregation.'

'I can't help that,' said Stockdale.

'Oh, I know you can't. I only told you. The others are more
church-inclined, because they supply the pa'son with all the spirits he
requires, and they don't wish to show unfriendliness to a customer.'

'How do you choose 'em?' said Stockdale.

'We choose 'em for their closeness, and because they are strong
and surefooted, and able to carry a heavy load a long way without
being tired.'

Stockdale sighed as she enumerated each particular, for it proved
how far involved in the business a woman must be who was so well
acquainted with its conditions and needs. And yet he felt more tenderly
towards her at this moment than he had felt all the foregoing day.
Perhaps it was that her experienced manner and bold indifference
stirred his admiration in spite of himself.

'Take my arm, Lizzy,' he murmured.

'I don't want it,' she said. 'Besides, we may never be to each other
again what we once have been.'

'That depends upon you,' said he, and they went on again as before.

The hired carriers paced along over Chaldon Down with as little
hesitation as if it had been day, avoiding the cart-way, and leaving
the village of East Chaldon on the left, so as to reach the crest of the

hill at a lonely trackless place not far from the ancient earthwork called Round Pound. An hour's brisk walking brought them within sound of the sea, not many hundred yards from Lullstead Cove. Here they paused, and Lizzy and Stockdale came up with them, when they went on together to the verge of the cliff. One of the men now produced an iron bar, which he drove firmly into the soil[25] a yard from the edge, and attached to it a rope that he had uncoiled from his body. They all began to descend, partly stepping, partly sliding down the incline, as the rope slipped through their hands.

'You will not go to the bottom, Lizzy?' said Stockdale anxiously.

'No. I stay here to watch,' she said. 'Owlett is down there.'

The men remained quite silent when they reached the shore; and the next thing audible to the two at the top was the dip of heavy oars, and the dashing of waves against a boat's bow. In a moment the keel gently touched the shingle, and Stockdale heard the footsteps of the thirty-six carriers running forwards over the pebbles towards the point of landing.

There was a sousing in the water as of a brood of ducks plunging in, showing that the men had not been particular about keeping their legs, or even their waists, dry from the brine; but it was impossible to see what they were doing, and in a few minutes the shingle was trampled again. The iron bar sustaining the rope, on which Stockdale's hand rested, began to swerve a little, and the carriers one by one appeared climbing up the sloping cliff, dripping audibly as they came, and sustaining themselves by the guide-rope. Each man on reaching the top was seen to be carrying a pair of tubs, one on his back and one on his chest,[26] the two being slung together by cords passing round the chine hoops, and resting on the carrier's shoulders. Some of the stronger men carried three by putting an extra one on the top behind, but the customary load was a pair, these being quite weighty enough to give their bearer the sensation of having chest and backbone in contact after a walk of four or five miles.

'Where is Owlett?' said Lizzy to one of them.

'He will not come up this way,' said the carrier. 'He's to bide on shore till we be safe off.' Then, without waiting for the rest, the foremost men plunged across the down; and, when the last had ascended, Lizzy pulled up the rope, wound it round her arm, wriggled the bar from the sod, and turned to follow the carriers.

'You are very anxious about Owlett's safety,' said the minister.

'Was there ever such a man!' said Lizzy. 'Why, isn't he my cousin?'

'Yes. Well, it is a bad night's work,' said Stockdale heavily. 'But I'll carry the bar and rope for you.'

'Thank God, the tubs have got so far all right,' said she.

Stockdale shook his head, and, taking the bar, walked by her side towards the downs; and the moan of the sea was heard no more.

'Is this what you meant the other day when you spoke of having business with Owlett?' the young man asked.

'This is it,' she replied. 'I never see him on any other matter.'

'A partnership of that kind with a young man is very odd.'

'It was begun by my father and his, who were brother-laws.'

Her companion could not blind himself to the fact that where tastes and pursuits were so akin as Lizzy's and Owlett's, and where risks were shared, as with them, in every undertaking, there would be a peculiar appropriateness in her answering Owlett's standing question on matrimony in the affirmative. This did not soothe Stockdale, its tendency being rather to stimulate in him an effort to make the pair as inappropriate as possible, and win her away from this nocturnal crew to correctness of conduct and a minister's parlour in some far-removed inland county.

They had been walking near enough to the file of carriers for Stockdale to perceive that, when they got into the road to the village, they split up into two companies of unequal size, each of which made off in a direction of its own. One company, the smaller of the two, went towards the church, and by the time that Lizzy and Stockdale reached their own house these men had scaled the churchyard wall, and were proceeding noiselessly over the grass within.

'I see that Owlett has arranged for one batch to be put in the church again,' observed Lizzy. 'Do you remember my taking you there the first night you came?'

'Yes, of course,' said Stockdale. 'No wonder you had permission to broach the tubs – they were his, I suppose?'

'No, they were not – they were mine; I had permission from myself.

The day after that they went several miles inland in a waggon-load of manure, and sold very well.'

At this moment the group of men who had made off to the left some time before began leaping one by one from the hedge opposite Lizzy's house, and the first man, who had no tubs upon his shoulders, came forward.

'Mrs Newberry, isn't it?' he said hastily.

'Yes, Jim,' said she. 'What's the matter?'

'I find that we can't put any in Badger's Clump tonight, Lizzy,' said Owlett. 'The place is watched. We must sling the apple-tree in the orchet if there's time. We can't put any more under the church lumber than I have sent on there, and my mixen hev already more in en than is safe.'

'Very well,' she said. 'Be quick about it – that's all. What can I do?'

'Nothing at all, please. Ah, it is the minister! – you two that can't do anything had better get indoors and not be seed.'[27]

While Owlett thus conversed, in a tone so full of contraband anxiety and so free from lover's jealousy, the men who followed him had been descending one by one from the hedge; and it unfortunately happened that when the hindmost took his leap, the cord slipped which sustained his tubs: the result was that both the kegs fell into the road, one of them being stove in by the blow.

' 'Od drown it all!' said Owlett, rushing back.

'It is worth a good deal, I suppose?' said Stockdale.

'Oh no – about two guineas and half to us now,' said Lizzy excitedly. 'It isn't that – it is the smell! It is so blazing strong before it has been lowered by water, that it smells dreadfully when spilt in the road like that! I do hope Latimer[28] won't pass by till it is gone off.'

Owlett and one or two others picked up the burst tub and began to scrape and trample over the spot, to disperse the liquor as much as possible; and then they all entered the gate of Owlett's orchard, which adjoined Lizzy's garden on the right. Stockdale did not care to follow them, for several on recognizing him had looked wonderingly at his presence, though they said nothing. Lizzy left his side and went to the bottom of the garden, looking over the hedge into the orchard, where the men could be dimly seen bustling about, and apparently hiding the tubs. All was done noiselessly, and without a light; and when it was over they dispersed in different directions, those who had taken their cargoes to the church having already gone off to their homes.

Lizzy returned to the garden-gate, over which Stockdale was still abstractedly leaning. 'It is all finished: I am going indoors now,' she said gently. 'I will leave the door ajar for you.'

'Oh no – you needn't,' said Stockdale; 'I am coming too.'

But before either of them had moved, the faint clatter of horses' hoofs broke upon the ear, and it seemed to come from the point where the track across the down joined the hard road.

'They are just too late!' cried Lizzy exultingly.

'Who?' said Stockdale.

'Latimer, the riding-officer, and some assistant of his. We had better go indoors.'

They entered the house, and Lizzy bolted the door. 'Please don't get a light, Mr Stockdale,' she said.

'Of course I will not,' said he.

'I thought you might be on the side of the king,' said Lizzy, with faintest sarcasm.

'I am,' said Stockdale. 'But, Lizzy Newberry, I love you, and you know it perfectly well; and you ought to know, if you do not, what I have suffered in my conscience on your account these last few days!'

'I guess very well,' she said hurriedly. 'Yet I don't see why. Ah, you are better than I!'

The trotting of the horses seemed to have again died away, and the pair of listeners touched each other's fingers in the cold 'Good night' of those whom something seriously divided. They were on the landing, but before they had taken three steps apart, the tramp of the horsemen suddenly revived, almost close to the house. Lizzy turned to the staircase window, opened the casement about an inch, and put her face close to the aperture. 'Yes, one of 'em is Latimer,' she whispered. 'He always rides a white horse. One would think it was the last colour for a man in that line.'

Stockdale looked, and saw the white shape of the animal as it passed by; but before the riders had gone another ten yards, Latimer reined in his horse, and said something to his companion which neither Stockdale nor Lizzy could hear. Its drift was, however, soon made evident, for the other man stopped also; and sharply turning the horses' heads they cautiously retraced their steps. When they were again opposite Mrs Newberry's garden, Latimer dismounted, and the man on the dark horse did the same.

Lizzy and Stockdale, intently listening and observing the proceedings, naturally put their heads as close as possible to the slit formed by the slightly opened casement; and thus it occurred that at last their cheeks came positively into contact. They went on listening, as if they did not know of the singular circumstance which had happened to their faces, and the pressure of each to each rather increased than lessened with the lapse of time.

They could hear the excisemen sniffing the air like hounds as they paced slowly along. When they reached the spot where the tub had burst, both stopped on the instant.

'Ay, ay, 'tis quite strong here,' said the second officer. 'Shall we knock at the door?'

'Well, no,' said Latimer. 'Maybe this is only a trick to put us off the scent. They wouldn't kick up this stink anywhere near their hiding-place. I have known such things before.'

'Anyhow, the things, or some of 'em, must have been brought this way,' said the other.

'Yes,' said Latimer musingly. 'Unless 'tis all done to tole us the wrong way. I have a mind that we go home for tonight without saying a word, and come the first thing in the morning with more hands. I know they have storages about here, but we can do nothing by this owl's light. We will look round the parish and see if everybody is in bed, John; and if all is quiet, we will do as I say.'

They went on, and the two inside the window could hear them passing leisurely through the whole village, the street of which curved round at the bottom and entered the turnpike-road at another junction. This way the excisemen followed, and the amble of their horses died quite away.

'What will you do?' said Stockdale, withdrawing from his position.

She knew that he alluded to the coming search by the officers, to divert her attention from their own tender incident by the casement, which he wished to be passed over as a thing rather dreamt of than done. 'Oh, nothing,' she replied, with as much coolness as she could command under her disappointment at his manner. 'We often have such storms as this. You would not be frightened if you knew what fools they are. Fancy riding o' horseback through the place: of course they will hear and see nobody while they make that noise; but they are always afraid to get off, in case some of our fellows should burst out upon 'em, and tie them up to the gate-post, as they have done before now. Good night, Mr Stockdale.'

She closed the window and went to her room, where a tear fell from her eyes; and that not because of the alertness of the riding-officers.

VI

The great search at Nether Mynton

Stockdale was so excited by the events of the evening, and the dilemma that he was placed in between conscience and love, that he did not sleep, or even doze, but remained as broadly awake as at noonday. As soon as the grey light began to touch ever so faintly the whiter objects in his bedroom he arose, dressed himself, and went downstairs into the road.

The village was already astir. Several of the carriers had heard the well-known tramp of Latimer's horse while they were undressing in the dark that night, and had already communicated with each other and Owlett on the subject. The only doubt seemed to be about the safety of those tubs which had been left under the church gallery-stairs, and after a short discussion at the corner of the mill, it was agreed that these should be removed before it got lighter, and hidden in the middle of a double hedge bordering the adjoining field. However, before anything could be carried into effect, the footsteps of many men were heard coming down the lane from the highway.

'Damn it, here they be,' said Owlett, who, having already drawn the hatch and started his mill for the day, stood stolidly at the mill-door covered with flour, as if the interest of his whole soul was bound up in the shaking walls around him.

The two or three with whom he had been talking dispersed to their usual work, and when the excise officers, and the formidable body of men they had hired, reached the village cross, between the mill and Mrs Newberry's house, the village wore the natural aspect of a place beginning its morning labours.

'Now,' said Latimer to his associates, who numbered thirteen men in all, 'what I know is that the things are somewhere in this here place. We have got the day before us, and 'tis hard if we can't light upon 'em and get 'em to Budmouth Custom-house before night. First we will try the fuel-houses, and then we'll work our way into the chimmers, and then to the ricks and stables, and so creep round. You have nothing but your noses to guide ye, mind, so use 'em today if you never did in your lives before.'

Then the search began. Owlett, during the early part, watched from his mill-window, Lizzy from the door of her house, with the greatest self-possession. A farmer down below, who also had a share in the run, rode about with one eye on his fields and the other on Latimer and his myrmidons, prepared to put them off the scent if he should be asked a question. Stockdale, who was no smuggler at all, felt more anxiety than the worst of them, and went about his studies with a heavy heart, coming frequently to the door to ask Lizzy some question or other on the consequences to her of the tubs being found.

'The consequences,' she said quietly, 'are simply that I shall lose 'em. As I have none in the house or garden, they can't touch me personally.'

'But you have some in the orchard?'

'Owlett rents that of me, and he lends it to others. So it will be hard to say who put any tubs there if they should be found.'

There was never such a tremendous sniffing known as that which took place in Nether Mynton parish and its vicinity this day. All was done methodically, and mostly on hands and knees. At different hours of the day they had different plans. From daybreak to breakfast-time the officers used their sense of smell in a direct and straightforward manner only, pausing nowhere but at such places as the tubs might be supposed to be secreted in at that very moment, pending their removal on the following night. Among the places tested and examined were: —

Hollow trees	Cupboards	Culverts
Potato-graves	Clock-cases	Hedgerows
Fuel-houses	Chimney-flues	Faggot-ricks
Bedrooms	Rainwater-butts	Haystacks
Apple-lofts	Pigsties	Coppers and ovens.

After breakfast they recommenced with renewed vigour, taking a new line; that is to say, directing their attention to clothes that might be supposed to have come in contact with the tubs in their removal from the shore, such garments being usually tainted with the spirit, owing to its oozing between the staves. They now sniffed at —

Smock-frocks	Smiths' and shoemakers' aprons
Old shirts and waistcoats	Knee-naps and hedging-gloves
Coats and hats	Tarpaulins
Breeches and leggings	Market-cloaks
Women's shawls and gowns	Scarecrows.

And, as soon as the mid-day meal was over, they pushed their search into places where the spirits might have been thrown away in alarm: —

Horse-ponds	Mixens	Sinks in yards
Stable-drains	Wet ditches	Road-scrapings, and
Cinder-heaps	Cesspools	Back-door gutters.

But still these indefatigable excisemen discovered nothing more than the original tell-tale smell in the road opposite Lizzy's house, which even yet had not passed off.

'I'll tell ye what it is, men,' said Latimer, about three o'clock in the afternoon, 'we must begin over again. Find them tubs I will.'

The men, who had been hired for the day, looked at their hands and knees, muddy with creeping on all fours so frequently, and rubbed their noses, as if they had almost had enough of it; for the quantity of bad air which had passed into each one's nostril had rendered it nearly as insensible as a flue. However, after a moment's hesitation, they prepared to start anew, except three, whose power of smell had quite succumbed under the excessive wear and tear of the day.

By this time not a male villager was to be seen in the parish. Owlett was not at his mill, the farmers were not in their fields, the parson was not in his garden, the smith had left his forge, and the wheelwright's shop was silent.

'Where the divil are the folk gone?' said Latimer, waking up to the fact of their absence, and looking round. 'I'll have 'em up for this! Why don't they come and help us? There's not a man about the place but the Methodist parson, and he's an old woman. I demand assistance in the king's name!'

'We must find the jineral public afore we can demand that,' said his lieutenant.

'Well, well, we shall do better without 'em,' said Latimer, who changed his moods at a moment's notice. 'But there's great cause of suspicion in this silence and this keeping out of sight, and I'll bear it in mind. Now we will go across to Owlett's orchard, and see what we can find there.'

Stockdale, who heard this discussion from the garden-gate, over which he had been leaning, was rather alarmed, and thought it a mistake of the villagers to keep so completely out of the way. He himself, like the excisemen, had been wondering for the last half-hour what could have become of them. Some labourers were of necessity engaged in distant fields, but the master-workmen should have been at home; though one and all, after just showing themselves at their shops, had apparently gone off for the day. He went in to Lizzy, who sat at a back window sewing, and said, 'Lizzy, where are the men?'

Lizzy laughed. 'Where they mostly are when they're run so hard as this.' She cast her eyes to heaven. 'Up there,' she said.

Stockdale looked up. 'What – on the top of the church tower?' he asked, seeing the direction of her glance.

'Yes.'

'Well, I expect they will soon have to come down,' said he gravely. 'I have been listening to the officers, and they are going to search the orchard over again, and then every nook in the church.'

Lizzy looked alarmed for the first time. 'Will you go and tell our folk?' she said. 'They ought to be let know.' Seeing his conscience struggling within him like a boiling pot, she added, 'No, never mind, I'll go myself.'

She went out, descended the garden, and climbed over the church-yard wall at the same time that the preventive-men were ascending the road to the orchard. Stockdale could do no less than follow her. By the time that she reached the tower entrance he was at her side, and they entered together.

Nether Mynton church-tower was, as in many villages, without a turret, and the only way to the top was by going up to the singers' gallery, and thence ascending by a ladder to a square trap-door in the floor of the bell-loft, above which a permanent ladder was fixed, passing through the bells to a hole in the roof. When Lizzy and Stockdale reached the gallery and looked up, nothing but the trap-door and the five holes for the bell-ropes appeared. The ladder was gone.

'There's no getting up,' said Stockdale.

'Oh yes, there is,' said she. 'There's an eye looking at us at this moment through a knot-hole in that trap-door.'

And as she spoke the trap opened, and the dark line of the ladder was seen descending against the whitewashed wall. When it touched the bottom Lizzy dragged it to its place, and said, 'If you'll go up, I'll follow.'

The young man ascended, and presently found himself among consecrated bells[29] for the first time in his life, nonconformity having been in the Stockdale blood for some generations. He eyed them uneasily, and looked round for Lizzy. Owlett stood here, holding the top of the ladder.

'What, be you really one of us?' said the miller.

'It seems so,' said Stockdale sadly.

'He's not,' said Lizzy, who overheard. 'He's neither for nor against us. He'll do us no harm.'

She stepped up beside them, and then they went on to the next stage, which, when they had clambered over the dusty bell-carriages, was of easy ascent, leading towards the hole through which the pale sky appeared, and into the open air. Owlett remained behind for a moment, to pull up the lower ladder.

'Keep down your heads,' said a voice, as soon as they set foot on the flat.

Stockdale here beheld all the missing parishioners, lying on their stomachs on the tower roof, except a few who, elevated on their hands and knees, were peeping through the embrasures of the parapet. Stockdale did the same, and saw the village lying like a map below him, over which moved the figures of the excisemen, each foreshortened to a crablike object, the crown of his hat forming a circular disc in the centre of him. Some of the men had turned their heads when the young preacher's figure arose among them.

'What, Mr Stockdale?' said Matt Grey, in a tone of surprise.

'I'd as lief that it hadn't been,' said Jim Clarke. 'If the pa'son should see him a trespassing here in his tower, 'twould be none the better for we, seeing how 'a do hate chapel-members. He'd never buy a tub of us again, and he's as good a customer as we have got this side o' Warm'll.'[30]

'Where is the pa'son?' said Lizzy.

'In his house, to be sure, that he may see nothing of what's going on – where all good folks ought to be, and this young man likewise.'

'Well, he has brought some news,' said Lizzy. 'They are going to search the orchet and church; can we do anything if they should find?'

'Yes,' said her cousin Owlett. 'That's what we've been talking o', and we have settled our line. Well, be dazed!'

The exclamation was caused by his perceiving that some of the searchers, having got into the orchard, and begun stooping and creeping hither and thither, were pausing in the middle, where a tree smaller than the rest was growing. They drew closer, and bent lower than ever upon the ground.

'Oh, my tubs!' said Lizzy faintly, as she peered through the parapet at them.

'They have got 'em, 'a b'lieve,' said Owlett.

The interest in the movements of the officers was so keen that not a single eye was looking in any other direction; but at that moment a shout from the church beneath them attracted the attention of the smugglers, as it did also of the party in the orchard, who sprang to their feet and went towards the churchyard wall. At the same time those of the Government men who had entered the church unperceived by the smugglers cried aloud, 'Here be some of 'em at last.'

The smugglers remained in a blank silence, uncertain whether 'some of 'em' meant tubs or men; but again peeping cautiously over the edge of the tower they learnt that tubs were the things descried; and soon these fated articles were brought one by one into the middle of the churchyard from their hiding-place under the gallery-stairs.

'They are going to put 'em on Hinton's vault till they find the rest,' said Lizzy hopelessly. The excisemen had, in fact, begun to pile up the tubs on a large stone slab which was fixed there; and when all were brought out from the tower, two or three of the men were left standing by them, the rest of the party again proceeding to the orchard.

The interest of the smugglers in the next manoeuvres of their enemies became painfully intense. Only about thirty tubs had been secreted in the lumber of the tower, but seventy were hidden in the orchard, making up all that they had brought ashore as yet, the remainder of the cargo having been tied to a sinker and dropped overboard for another night's operations. The excisemen, having re-entered the orchard, acted as if they were positive that here lay hidden the rest of the tubs, which they were determined to find before nightfall. They spread themselves out round the field, and advancing on all fours as before, went anew round every apple-tree in the enclosure. The young tree in the middle again led them to pause, and at length the whole company gathered there in a way which signified that a second chain of reasoning had led to the same results as the first.

When they had examined the sod hereabouts for some minutes, one of the men rose, ran to a disused porch of the church where tools were kept, and returned with the sexton's pickaxe and shovel, with which they set to work.

'Are they really buried there?' said the minister, for the grass was so green and uninjured that it was difficult to believe it had been disturbed. The smugglers were too interested to reply, and presently they saw, to their chagrin, the officers stand two on each side of the tree; and, stooping and applying their hands to the soil, they bodily lifted the tree and the turf around it. The apple-tree now showed itself to be growing in a shallow box, with handles for lifting at each of the four sides. Under the site of the tree a square hole was revealed, and an exciseman went and looked down.

'It is all up now,' said Owlett quietly. 'And now all of ye get down before they notice we are here; and be ready for our next move. I had better bide here till dark, or they may take me on suspicion, as 'tis on my ground. I'll be with ye as soon as daylight begins to pink in.'

'And I?' said Lizzy.

'You please look to the linch-pins and screws; then go indoors and know nothing at all. The chaps will do the rest.'

The ladder was replaced, and all but Owlett descended, the men passing off one by one at the back of the church, and vanishing on their respective errands. Lizzy walked boldly along the street, followed closely by the minister.

'You are going indoors, Mrs Newberry?' he said.

She knew from the words 'Mrs Newberry' that the division between them had widened yet another degree.

'I am not going home,' she said. 'I have a little thing to do before I go in. Martha Sarah will get your tea.'

'Oh, I don't mean on that account,' said Stockdale. 'What *can* you have to do further in this unhallowed affair?'

'Only a little,' she said.

'What is that? I'll go with you.'

'No, I shall go by myself. Will you please go indoors? I shall be there in less than an hour.'

'You are not going to run any danger, Lizzy?' said the young man, his tenderness reasserting itself.

'None whatever – worth mentioning,' answered she, and went down towards the Cross.

Stockdale entered the garden-gate, and stood behind it looking on. The excisemen were still busy in the orchard, and at last he was tempted to enter, and watch their proceedings. When he came closer he found that the secret cellar, of whose existence he had been totally unaware, was formed by timbers placed across from side to side about a foot under the ground, and grassed over.

The excisemen looked up at Stockdale's fair and downy countenance, and evidently thinking him above suspicion, went on with their work again. As soon as all the tubs were taken out, they began tearing up the turf, pulling out the timbers, and breaking in the sides, till the cellar was wholly dismantled and shapeless, the apple-tree lying with its roots high to the air. But the hole which had in its time held so much contraband merchandise was never completely filled up, either then or afterwards, a depression in the greensward marking the spot to this day.

VII

The walk to Warm'ell Cross; and afterwards

As the goods had all to be carried to Budmouth that night, the excisemen's next object was to find horses and carts for the journey, and they went about the village for that purpose. Latimer strode hither and thither with a lump of chalk in his hand, marking broad-arrows so vigorously on every vehicle and set of harness that he came across, that it seemed as if he would chalk broad-arrows on the very hedges and roads. The owner of every conveyance so marked was bound to give it up for Government purposes. Stockdale, who had had enough of the scene, turned indoors thoughtful and depressed. Lizzy was already there, having come in at the back, though she had not yet taken off her bonnet. She looked tired, and her mood was not much brighter than his own. They had but little to say to each other; and the minister went away and attempted to read; but at this he could not succeed, and he shook the little bell for tea.

Lizzy herself brought in the tray, the girl having run off into the village during the afternoon, too full of excitement at the proceedings to remember her state of life. However, almost before the sad lovers had said anything to each other, Martha came in in a steaming state.

'Oh, there's such a stoor, Mrs Newberry and Mr Stockdale! The king's excisemen can't get the carts ready nohow at all! They pulled Thomas Ballam's,[31] and William Rogers's, and Stephen Sprake's carts into the road, and off came the wheels, and down fell the carts; and they found there was no linch-pins in the arms; and then they tried Samuel Shane's waggon, and found that the screws were gone from he, and at last they looked at the dairyman's cart, and he's got none neither! They have gone now to the blacksmith's to get some made, but he's nowhere to be found!'

Stockdale looked at Lizzy, who blushed very slightly, and went out of the room, followed by Martha Sarah. But before they had got through the passage there was a rap at the front door, and Stockdale recognized Latimer's voice addressing Mrs Newberry, who had turned back.

'For God's sake, Mrs Newberry, have you seen Hardman the blacksmith up this way? If we could get hold of him, we'd e'en a'most drag him by the hair of his head to his anvil, where he ought to be.'

'He's an idle man, Mr Latimer,' said Lizzy archly. 'What do you want him for?'

'Why, there isn't a horse in the place that has got more than three shoes on, and some have only two. The waggon-wheels be without strakes, and there's no linch-pins to the carts. What with that, and the bother about every set of harness being out of order, we shan't be off before nightfall – upon my soul we shan't. 'Tis a rough lot, Mrs Newberry, that you've got about you here; but they'll play at this game once too often, mark my words they will! There's not a man in the parish that don't deserve to be whipped.'

It happened that Hardman was at that moment a little farther up the lane, smoking his pipe behind a holly-bush. When Latimer had done speaking he went on in this direction, and Hardman, hearing the exciseman's steps, found curiosity too strong for prudence. He peeped out from the bush at the very moment that Latimer's glance was on it. There was nothing left for him to do but to come forward with unconcern.

'I've been looking for you for the last hour!' said Latimer with a glare in his eye.

'Sorry to hear that,' said Hardman. 'I've been out for a stroll, to look for more hid tubs, to deliver 'em up to Gover'ment.'

'Oh yes, Hardman, we know it,' said Latimer, with withering sarcasm. 'We know that you'll deliver 'em up to Gover'ment. We know that all the parish is helping us, and have been all day! Now you please walk along with me down to your shop, and kindly let me hire ye in the king's name.'

They went down the lane together; and presently there resounded from the smithy the ring of a hammer not very briskly swung. However, the carts and horses were got into some sort of travelling condition, but it was not until after the clock had struck six, when the muddy roads were glistening under the horizontal light of the fading day. The smuggled tubs were soon packed into the vehicles, and Latimer, with three of his assistants, drove slowly out of the village in the direction of the port of Budmouth, some considerable number of miles distant, the other excisemen being left to watch for the remainder of the cargo, which they knew to have been sunk somewhere between Ringsworth and Lullstead Cove, and to unearth Owlett, the only person clearly implicated by the discovery of the cave.

Women and children stood at the doors as the carts, each chalked with the Government pitchfork, passed in the increasing twilight; and as they stood they looked at the confiscated property with a melancholy expression that told only too plainly the relation which they bore to the trade.

'Well, Lizzy,' said Stockdale, when the crackle of the wheels had nearly died away. 'This is a fit finish to your adventure. I am truly thankful that you have got off without suspicion, and the loss only of the liquor. Will you sit down and let me talk to you?'

'By-and-by,' she said. 'But I must go out now.'

'Not to that horrid shore again?' he said blankly.

'No, not there. I am only going to see the end of this day's business.'

He did not answer to this, and she moved towards the door slowly, as if waiting for him to say something more.

'You don't offer to come with me,' she added at last. 'I suppose that's because you hate me after all this?'

'Can you say it, Lizzy, when you know I only want to save you from such practices? Come with you! – of course I will, if it is only to take care of you. But why will you go out again?'

'Because I cannot rest indoors. Something is happening, and I must know what. Now, come!' And they went into the dusk together.

When they reached the turnpike-road she turned to the right, and he soon perceived that they were following the direction of the excisemen and their load. He had given her his arm, and every now and then she suddenly pulled it back, to signify that he was to halt a moment and listen. They had walked rather quickly along the first quarter of a mile, and on the second or third time of standing still she said, 'I hear them ahead – don't you?'

'Yes,' he said; 'I hear the wheels. But what of that?'

'I only want to know if they get clear away from the neighbourhood.'

'Ah,' said he, a light breaking upon him. 'Something desperate is to be attempted! – and now I remember there was not a man about the village when we left.'

'Hark!' she murmured. The noise of the cart-wheels had stopped, and given place to another sort of sound.

' 'Tis a scuffle!' said Stockdale. 'There'll be murder! Lizzy, let go my arm; I am going on. On my conscience, I must not stay here and do nothing!'

'There'll be no murder, and not even a broken head,' she said. 'Our men are thirty to four of them: no harm will be done at all.'

'Then there *is* an attack!' exclaimed Stockdale; 'and you knew it was to be. Why should you side with men who break the laws like this?'

'Why should you side with men who take from country traders what they have honestly bought wi' their own money in France?' said she firmly.

'They are not honestly bought,' said he.

'They are,' she contradicted. 'I and Owlett and the others paid thirty shillings for every one of the tubs before they were put on board at Cherbourg, and if a king who is nothing to us sends his people to steal our property, we have a right to steal it back again.'

Stockdale did not stop to argue the matter, but went quickly in the direction of the noise, Lizzy keeping at his side. 'Don't you interfere, will you, dear Richard?' she said anxiously, as they drew near. 'Don't let us go any closer: 'tis at Warm'ell Cross where they are seizing 'em. You can do no good, and you may meet with a hard blow!'

'Let us see first what is going on,' he said. But before they had got much farther the noise of the cart-wheels began again; and Stockdale soon found that they were coming towards him. In another minute the three carts came up, and Stockdale and Lizzy stood in the ditch to let them pass.

Instead of being conducted by four men, as had happened when they went out of the village, the horses and carts were now accompanied by a body of from twenty to thirty, all of whom, as Stockdale perceived to his astonishment, had blackened faces. Among them walked six or eight huge female figures whom, from their wide strides, Stockdale guessed to be men in disguise. As soon as the party discerned Lizzy and her companion four or five fell back, and when the carts had passed, came close to the pair.

'There is no walking up this way for the present,' said one of the gaunt women, who wore curls a foot long, dangling down the sides of her face, in the fashion of the time.[32] Stockdale recognized this lady's voice as Owlett's.

'Why not?' said Stockdale. 'This is the public highway.'

'Now look here, youngster,' said Owlett. 'Oh, 'tis the Methodist parson! – what, and Mrs Newberry! Well, you'd better not go up that way, Lizzy. They've all run off, and folks have got their own again.'

The miller then hastened on and joined his comrades. Stockdale and Lizzy also turned back. 'I wish all this hadn't been forced upon us,' she said regretfully. 'But if those excisemen had got off with the tubs, half the people in the parish would have been in want for the next month or two.'

Stockdale was not paying much attention to her words, and he said, 'I don't think I can go back like this. Those four poor excisemen may be murdered for all I know.'

'Murdered!' said Lizzy impatiently. 'We don't do murder here.'

'Well, I shall go as far as Warm'ell Cross to see,' said Stockdale decisively; and, without wishing her safe home or anything else, the minister turned back. Lizzy stood looking at him till his form was absorbed in the shades; and then, with sadness,[33] she went in the direction of Nether Mynton.

The road was lonely, and after nightfall at this time of the year there was often not a passer for hours. Stockdale pursued his way without hearing a sound beyond that of his own footsteps; and in due time he passed beneath the trees of the plantation which surrounded the Warm'ell Cross-road. Before he had reached the point of intersection he heard voices from the thicket.

'Hoi-hoi-hoi! Help, help!'

The voices were not at all feeble or despairing, but they were unmistakably anxious. Stockdale had no weapon, and before plunging into the pitchy darkness of the plantation he pulled a stake from the hedge, to use in case of need. When he got among the trees he shouted – 'What's the matter – where are you?'

'Here,' answered the voices; and, pushing through the brambles in that direction, he came near the objects of his search.

'Why don't you come forward?' said Stockdale.

'We be tied to the trees.'

'Who are you?'

'Poor Will Latimer the exciseman!' said one plaintively. 'Just come and cut these cords, there's a good man. We were afraid nobody would pass by tonight.'

Stockdale soon loosened them, upon which they stretched their limbs and stood at their ease.

'The rascals!' said Latimer, getting now into a rage, though he had seemed quite meek when Stockdale first came up. ' 'Tis the same set of fellows. I know they were Mynton chaps to a man.'

'But we can't swear to 'em,' said another. 'Not one of 'em spoke.'

'What are you going to do?' said Stockdale.

'I'd fain go back to Mynton, and have at 'em again!' said Latimer.

'So would we!' said his comrades.

'Fight till we die!' said Latimer.

'We will, we will!' said his men.

'But,' said Latimer, more frigidly, as they came out of the plantation, 'we don't *know* that these chaps with black faces were Mynton men? And proof is a hard thing.'

'So it is,' said the rest.

'And therefore we won't do nothing at all,' said Latimer, with complete dispassionateness. 'For my part, I'd sooner be them than we. The clitches of my arms are burning like fire from the cords those

THOMAS HARDY

two strapping women tied round 'em. My opinion is, now I have had
time to think o't, that you may serve your Gover'ment at too high a
price. For these two nights and days I have not had an hour's rest;
and, please God, here's for home-along.'

The other officers agreed heartily to this course; and, thanking
Stockdale for his timely assistance, they parted from him at the Cross,
taking themselves the western road, and Stockdale going back to
Nether Mynton.

During that walk the minister was lost in reverie of the most painful
kind. As soon as he got into the house, and before entering his own
rooms, he advanced to the door of the little back parlour in which
Lizzy usually sat with her mother. He found her there alone. Stockdale
went forward, and, like a man in a dream, looked down upon the
table that stood between him and the young woman, who had her
bonnet and cloak still on. As he did not speak, she looked up from
her chair at him, with misgiving in her eye.

'Where are they gone?' he then said listlessly.

'Who? – I don't know. I have seen nothing of them since. I came
straight in here.'

'If your men can manage to get off with those tubs, it will be a great
profit to you, I suppose?'

'A share will be mine, a share my cousin Owlett's, a share to each
of the two farmers, and a share divided amongst the men who helped
us.'

'And you still think,' he went on slowly, 'that you will not give this
business up?'

Lizzy rose, and put her hand upon his shoulder. 'Don't ask that,'
she whispered. 'You don't know what you are asking. I must tell you,
though I meant not to do it. What I make by that trade is all I have
to keep my mother and myself with.'

He was astonished. 'I did not dream of such a thing,' he said. 'I
would rather have swept the streets,[34] had I been you. What is money
compared with a clear conscience?'

'My conscience is clear. I know my mother, but the king I have
never seen. His dues are nothing to me. But it is a great deal to me
that my mother and I should live.'

84

'Marry me, and promise to give it up. I will keep your mother.'

'It is good of you,' she said, trembling[35] a little. 'Let me think of it by myself. I would rather not answer now.'

She reserved her answer till the next day, and came into his room with a solemn face. 'I cannot do what you wished!' she said passionately. 'It is too much to ask. My whole life ha' been passed in this way.' Her words and manner showed that before entering she had been struggling with herself in private, and that the contention had been strong.

Stockdale turned pale, but he spoke quietly. 'Then, Lizzy, we must part. I cannot go against my principles in this matter, and I cannot make my profession a mockery. You know how I love you, and what I would do for you; but this one thing I cannot do.'

'But why should you belong to that profession?' she burst out. 'I have got this large house; why can't you marry me, and live here with us, and not be a Methodist preacher any more? I assure you, Richard, it is no harm, and I wish you could only see it as I do! We only carry it on in winter: in summer it is never done at all. It stirs up one's dull life at this time o' the year, and gives excitement, which I have got so used to now that I should hardly know how to do 'ithout it. At nights, when the wind blows, instead of being dull and stupid, and not noticing whether it do blow or not, your mind is afield, even if you are not afield yourself; and you are wondering how the chaps are getting on; and you walk up and down the room, and look out o' window, and then you go out yourself, and know your way about as well by night as by day, and have hairbreadth escapes from old Latimer and his fellows, who are too stupid ever to really frighten us, and only make us a bit nimble.'

'He frightened you a little last night, anyhow; and I would advise you to drop it before it is worse.'

She shook her head. 'No, I must go on as I have begun. I was born to it. It is in my blood, and I can't be cured. Oh, Richard, you cannot think what a hard thing you have asked, and how sharp you try me when you put me between this and my love for 'ee!'

Stockdale was leaning with his elbow on the mantelpiece,[36] his hands over his eyes. 'We ought never to have met, Lizzy,' he said. 'It was an ill day for us! I little thought there was anything so hopeless and impossible in our engagement as this. Well, it is too late now to regret consequences in this way. I have had the happiness of seeing you and knowing you at least.'

'You dissent from Church, and I dissent from State,' she said. 'And I don't see why we are not well matched.'

He smiled sadly, while Lizzy remained looking down, her eyes beginning to overflow.

That was an unhappy evening for both of them, and the days that followed were unhappy days. Both she and he went mechanically about their employments, and his depression was marked in the village by more than one of his denomination with whom he came in contact. But Lizzy, who passed her days indoors, was unsuspected of being the cause; for it was generally understood that a quiet engagement to marry existed between her and her cousin Owlett, and had existed for some time.

Thus uncertainly the week passed on; till one morning Stockdale said to her: 'I have had a letter, Lizzy. I must call you that till I am gone.'

'Gone?' said she blankly.

'Yes,' he said. 'I am going from this place. I felt it would be better for us both that I should not stay after what has happened. In fact, I couldn't stay here, and look on you from day to day, without becoming weak and faltering in my course. I have just heard of an arrangement by which the other minister can arrive here in about a week; and let me go elsewhere.'

That he had all this time continued so firmly fixed in his resolution came upon her as a grievous surprise. 'You never loved me!' she said bitterly.

'I might say the same,' he returned; 'but I will not. Grant me one favour. Come and hear my last sermon on the day before I go.'[37]

Lizzy, who was a church-goer on Sunday mornings, frequently attended Stockdale's chapel in the evening with the rest of the double-minded; and she promised.

It became known that Stockdale was going to leave, and a good many people outside his own sect were sorry to hear it. The intervening days flew rapidly away, and on the evening of the Sunday which preceded the morning of his departure Lizzy sat in the chapel to hear him for the last time. The little building was full to overflowing, and he took up the subject which all had expected, that of the contraband trade so extensively practised among them. His hearers, in laying his words to their own hearts, did not perceive that they were most particularly directed against Lizzy, till the sermon waxed warm, and Stockdale nearly broke down with emotion. In truth his own earnestness, and her sad eyes looking up at him, were too much for the young man's equanimity. He hardly knew how he ended. He saw Lizzy, as through a mist, turn and go away with the rest of the congregation; and shortly afterwards followed her home.

She invited him to supper, and they sat down alone, her mother having, as was usual with her on Sunday nights, gone to bed early.

'We will part friends, won't we?' said Lizzy, with forced gaiety, and never alluding to the sermon: a reticence which rather disappointed him.

'We will,' he said, with a forced smile on his part; and they sat down.

It was the first meal that they had ever shared together in their lives, and probably the last that they would so share. When it was over, and the indifferent conversation could no longer be continued, he arose and took her hand. 'Lizzy,' he said, 'do you say we must part – do you?'

'You do,' she said solemnly. 'I can say no more.'

'Nor I,' said he. 'If that is your answer, goodbye!'

Stockdale bent over her and kissed her, and she involuntarily returned his kiss. 'I shall go early,' he said hurriedly. 'I shall not see you again.'

And he did leave early. He fancied, when stepping forth into the grey morning light, to mount the van which was to carry him away, that he saw a face between the parted curtains of Lizzy's window; but the light was faint, and the panes glistened with wet; so he could not be sure. Stockdale mounted the vehicle, and was gone; and on the following Sunday the new minister preached in the chapel of the Mynton Wesleyans.

*

One day, two years after the parting, Stockdale, now settled in a midland town,[38] came into Nether Mynton by carrier in the original way. Jogging alone in the van that afternoon he had put questions to the driver, and the answers that he received interested the minister deeply. The result of them was that he went without the least hesitation to the door of his former lodging. It was about six o'clock in the evening, and the same time of year as when he had left; now, too, the ground was damp and glistening, the west was bright, and Lizzy's snowdrops were raising their heads in the border under the wall.

Lizzy must have caught sight of him from the window, for by the time that he reached the door she was there holding it open; and then, as if she had not sufficiently considered her act of coming out, she drew herself back, saying with some constraint, 'Mr Stockdale!'

'You knew it was,' said Stockdale, taking her hand. 'I wrote to say I should call.'

'Yes, but you did not say when,' she answered.

'I did not. I was not quite sure when my business would lead me to these parts.'

'You only came because business brought you near?'

'Well, that is the fact; but I have often thought I should like to come on purpose to see you . . . But what's all this that has happened? I told you how it would be, Lizzy, and you would not listen to me.'

'I would not,' she said sadly. 'But I had been brought up to that life; and it was second nature to me. However, it is all over now. The officers have blood-money for taking a man dead or alive, and the trade is going to nothing. We were hunted down like rats.'

'Owlett is quite gone, I hear.'

'Yes. He is in America. We had a dreadful struggle that last time, when they tried to take him. It is a perfect miracle that he lived through it; and it is a wonder that I was not killed. I was shot in the hand. It was not by aim; the shot was really meant for my cousin; but I was behind, looking on as usual, and the bullet came to me. It bled terribly, but I got home without fainting; and it healed after a time. You know how he suffered?'

'No,' said Stockdale. 'I only heard that he just escaped with his life.'

'He was shot in the back; but a rib turned the ball. He was badly hurt. We would not let him be took. The men carried him all night across the meads to Bere,[39] and hid him in a barn, dressing his wound as well as they could, till he was so far recovered as to be able to get about.[40] He had gied up his mill for some time; and at last he got to Bristol, and took a passage to America, and he's settled in Wisconsin.'

'What do you think of smuggling now?' said the minister gravely.

'I own that we were wrong,' said she. 'But I have suffered for it. I am very poor now, and my mother has been dead these twelve months . . . But won't you come in, Mr Stockdale?'

Stockdale went in; and it is to be presumed that they came to an understanding; for a fortnight later there was a sale of Lizzy's furniture, and after that a wedding at a chapel in a neighbouring town.

He took her away from her old haunts to the home that he had made for himself in his native county, where she studied her duties as a minister's wife with praiseworthy assiduity. It is said that in after years she wrote an excellent tract called *Render unto Caesar; or, the Repentant Villagers*, in which her own experience was anonymously used as the introductory story. Stockdale got it printed, after making some corrections, and putting in a few powerful sentences of his own; and many hundreds of copies were distributed by the couple in the course of their married life.[41]

I

The shepherd on the east hill could shout out lambing intelligence to the shepherd on the west hill, over the intervening town chimneys, without great inconvenience to his voice, so nearly did the steep pastures encroach upon the burghers' backyards. And at night it was possible to stand in the very midst of the town and hear from their native paddocks on the lower levels of greensward the mild lowing of the farmers' heifers, and the profound, warm blowings of breath in which those creatures indulge. But the community which had jammed itself in the valley thus flanked formed a veritable town, with a real mayor and corporation, and a staple manufacture.[1]

During a certain damp evening five-and-thirty years ago,[2] before the twilight was far advanced, a pedestrian of professional appearance, carrying a small bag in his hand and an elevated umbrella, was descending one of these hills by the turnpike-road when he was overtaken by a phaeton.[3]

'Hullo, Downe – is that you?' said the driver of the vehicle, a young man of pale and refined appearance. 'Jump up here with me, and ride down to your door.'

The other turned a plump, cheery, rather self-indulgent face over his shoulder towards the hailer.

'Oh! good evening, Mr Barnet – thanks,' he said, and mounted beside his acquaintance.

They were fellow-burgesses of the town which lay beneath them, but though old and very good friends, they were differently circumstanced. Barnet was a richer man than the struggling young lawyer Downe, a fact which was to some extent perceptible in Downe's manner towards his companion, though nothing of it ever showed in Barnet's manner towards the solicitor. Barnet's position in the town was none of his own making; his father had been a very successful flax-merchant in the same place, where the trade was still carried on as briskly as the small capacities of its quarters would allow. Having acquired a fair fortune, old Mr Barnet had retired from business, bringing up his son as a gentleman-burgher, and, it must be added, as a well-educated, liberal-minded young man.

'How is Mrs Barnet?' asked Downe.

'Mrs Barnet was very well when I left home,' the other answered constrainedly, exchanging his meditative regard of the horse for one of self-consciousness.

Mr Downe seemed to regret his inquiry, and immediately took up another thread of conversation. He congratulated his friend on his election as a council-man; he thought he had not seen him since that event took place; Mrs Downe had meant to call and congratulate Mrs Barnet, but he feared that she had failed to do so as yet.

Barnet seemed hampered in his replies. 'We should have been glad to see you. I – my wife would welcome Mrs Downe at any time, as you know . . . Yes, I am a member of the corporation – rather an inexperienced member, some of them say. It is quite true; and I should have declined the honour as premature – having other things on my hands just now, too – if it had not been pressed upon me so very heartily.'

'There is one thing you have on your hands which I can never quite see the necessity for,' said Downe, with good-humoured freedom. 'What the deuce do you want to build that new mansion for, when you have already got such an excellent house as the one you live in?'

Barnet's face acquired a warmer shade of colour; but as the question had been idly asked by the solicitor while regarding the surrounding flocks and fields, he answered after a moment with no apparent embarrassment –

'Well, we wanted to get out of the town, you know; the house I am living in is rather old and inconvenient.'

Mr Downe declared that he had chosen a pretty site for the new building. They would be able to see for miles and miles from the windows. Was he going to give it a name? he supposed so.

Barnet thought not. There was no other house near that was likely to be mistaken for it. And he did not care for a name.

'But I think it has a name!' Downe observed: 'I went past – when was it? – this morning; and I saw something, – "Château Ringdale,"[4] I think it was, stuck up on a board!'

'It was an idea she – we had for a short time,' said Barnet hastily. 'But we have decided finally to do without a name – at any rate such a name as that. It must have been a week ago that you saw it. It was taken down last Saturday . . . Upon that matter I am firm!' he added grimly.

Downe murmured in an unconvinced tone that he thought he had seen it yesterday.

Talking thus they drove into the town. The street was unusually still for the hour of seven in the evening; an increasing drizzle had prevailed since the afternoon, and now formed a gauze across the yellow lamps, and trickled with a gentle rattle down the heavy roofs of stone tile, that bent the house-ridges hollow-backed with its weight, and in some instances caused the walls to bulge outwards in the upper story. Their route took them past the little town-hall, the Black-Bull Hotel,[5] and onward to the junction of a small street on the right, consisting of a row of those two-and-two brick residences of no particular age, which are exactly alike wherever found, except in the people they contain.

'Wait – I'll drive you up to your door,' said Barnet, when Downe prepared to alight at the corner. He thereupon turned into the narrow street, when the faces of three little girls could be discerned close to the panes of a lighted window a few yards ahead, surmounted by that of a young matron, the gaze of all four being directed eagerly up the empty street. 'You are a fortunate fellow, Downe,' Barnet continued, as mother and children disappeared from the window to run to the door. 'You must be happy if any man is. I would give a hundred such houses as my new one to have a home like yours.'

'Well – yes, we get along pretty comfortably,' replied Downe complacently.

'That house, Downe, is none of my ordering,' Barnet broke out, revealing a bitterness hitherto suppressed, and checking the horse a moment to finish his speech before delivering up his passenger. 'The house I have already is good enough for me, as you supposed. It is my own freehold; it was built by my grandfather, and is stout enough for a castle. My father was born there, lived there, and died there. I was born there, and have always lived there; yet I must needs build a new one.'

'Why do you?' said Downe.

'Why do I? To preserve peace in the household. I do anything for that; but I don't succeed.[6] I was firm in resisting "Château Ringdale", however; not that I would not have put up with the absurdity of the name, but it was too much to have your house christened after Lord Ringdale, because your wife once had a fancy for him. If you only knew everything,[7] you would think all attempt at reconciliation hopeless. In your happy home you have had no such experiences; and God forbid that you ever should. See, here they are all ready to receive you!'

'Of course! And so will your wife be waiting to receive you,' said Downe. 'Take my word for it she will! And with a dinner prepared for you far better than mine.'

'I hope so,' Barnet replied dubiously.

He moved on to Downe's door, which the solicitor's family had already opened. Downe descended, but being encumbered with his bag and umbrella, his foot slipped, and he fell upon his knees in the gutter.[8]

'Oh, my dear Charles!' said his wife, running down the steps; and, quite ignoring the presence of Barnet, she seized hold of her husband, pulled him to his feet, and kissed him, exclaiming, 'I hope you are not hurt, darling!' The children crowded round, chiming in piteously, 'Poor papa!'

'He's all right,' said Barnet, perceiving that Downe was only a little muddy, and looking more at the wife than at the husband. Almost at any other time – certainly during his fastidious bachelor years – he would have thought her a too demonstrative woman; but those recent circumstances of his own life to which he had just alluded made Mrs Downe's solicitude so affecting that his eye grew damp as he witnessed it. Bidding the lawyer and his family good night he left them, and drove slowly into the main street towards his own house.

The heart of Barnet was sufficiently impressionable to be influenced by Downe's parting prophecy that he might not be so unwelcome home as he imagined: the dreary night might, at least on this one occasion, make Downe's forecast true. Hence it was in a suspense that he could hardly have believed possible that he halted at his door. On entering his wife was nowhere to be seen, and he inquired for her. The servant informed him that her mistress had the dressmaker with her, and would be engaged for some time.

'Dressmaker at this time of day!'

'She dined early, sir, and hopes you will excuse her joining you this evening.'

'But she knew I was coming tonight?'

'Oh yes, sir.'

'Go up and tell her I am come.'

The servant did so; but the mistress of the house merely repeated her former words.

Barnet said nothing more, and presently sat down to his lonely meal,[9] which was eaten abstractedly, the domestic scene he had lately witnessed still impressing him by its contrast with the situation here. His mind fell back into past years upon a certain pleasing and gentle being whose face would loom out of their shades at such times as these. Barnet turned in his chair, and looked with unfocused eyes in a direction southward from where he sat, as if he saw not the room but a long way beyond. 'I wonder if she lives there still!' he said.

II

He rose with a sudden rebelliousness, put on his hat and coat, and went out of the house, pursuing his way along the glistening pavement while eight o'clock was striking from St Mary's tower, and the apprentices and shopmen were slamming up the shutters from end to end of the town. In two minutes only those shops which could boast of no attendant save the master or the mistress remained with open eyes. These were ever somewhat less prompt to exclude customers than the others: for their owners' ears the closing hour had scarcely the cheerfulness that it possessed for the hired servants of the rest. Yet the night being dreary the delay was not for long, and their windows, too, blinked together one by one.

During this time Barnet had proceeded with decided step in a direction at right angles to the broad main thoroughfare of the town, by a long street leading due southward. Here, though his family had no more to do with the flax manufacture, his own name occasionally greeted him on gates and warehouses, being used allusively by small rising tradesmen as a recommendation, in such words as 'Smith, from Barnet and Co.' – 'Robinson, late manager at Barnet's.' The sight led him to reflect upon his father's busy life, and he questioned if it had not been far happier than his own.

The houses along the road became fewer, and presently open ground appeared between them on either side, the tract on the right hand rising to a higher level till it merged in a knoll. On the summit a row of builders' scaffold-poles probed the indistinct sky like spears, and at their bases could be discerned the lower courses of a building lately begun. Barnet slackened his pace and stood for a few moments without leaving the centre of the road, apparently not much interested in the sight, till suddenly his eye was caught by a post in the fore part of the ground, bearing a white board at the top. He went to the rails, vaulted over, and walked in far enough to discern painted upon the board 'Château Ringdale'.

A dismal irony seemed to lie in the words, and its effect was to irritate him. Downe, then, had spoken truly. He stuck his umbrella into the sod and seized the post with both hands, as if intending to loosen and throw it down. Then, like one bewildered by an opposition which would exist none the less though its manifestations were removed, he allowed his arms to sink to his side.

'Let it be,' he said to himself. 'I have declared there shall be peace – if possible.'

Taking up his umbrella he quietly left the enclosure, and went on his way, still keeping his back to the town. He had advanced with more decision since passing the new building, and soon a hoarse murmur rose upon the gloom; it was the sound of the sea. The road led to the harbour, at a distance of a mile from the town, from which the trade of the district was fed. After seeing the obnoxious name-board Barnet had forgotten to open his umbrella, and the rain tapped smartly on his hat, and occasionally stroked his face as he went on.

Though the lamps were still continued at the roadside, they stood at wider intervals than before, and the pavement had given place to common road. Every time he came to a lamp an increasing shine made itself visible upon his shoulders, till at last they quite glistened with wet. The murmur from the shore grew stronger, but it was still some distance off when he paused before one of the smallest of the detached houses by the wayside, standing in its own garden, the latter being divided from the road by a row of wooden palings. Scrutinizing the spot to ensure that he was not mistaken, he opened the gate and gently knocked at the cottage door.

When he had patiently waited minutes enough to lead any man in ordinary cases to knock again, the door was heard to open; though it was impossible to see by whose hand, there being no light in the passage. Barnet said at random, 'Does Miss Savile live here?'

A youthful voice assured him that she did live there, and by a sudden afterthought asked him to come in. It would soon get a light, it said; but, the night being wet, mother had not thought it worth while to trim the passage lamp.

'Don't trouble yourself to get a light for me,' said Barnet hastily; 'it is not necessary at all. Which is Miss Savile's sitting-room?'

The young person, whose white pinafore could just be discerned, signified a door in the side of the passage, and Barnet went forward at the same moment, so that no light should fall upon his face. On entering the room he closed the door behind him, pausing till he heard the retreating footsteps of the child.

He found himself in an apartment which was simply and neatly, though not poorly furnished; everything, from the miniature chiffonnier to the shining little daguerreotype which formed the central ornament of the mantelpiece, being in scrupulous order. The picture was enclosed by a frame of embroidered cardboard – evidently the work of feminine hands – and it represented a thin-faced, elderly lieutenant in the navy. From behind the lamp on the table a female form now rose into view: it was that of a young girl, and a resemblance between her and the portrait was early discoverable. She had been so absorbed in some occupation on the other side of the lamp as to have barely found time to realize her visitor's presence.

They both remained standing for a few seconds without speaking. The face that confronted Barnet had a beautiful outline; the Raffael-esque oval of its contour[10] was remarkable for an English countenance, and that countenance housed in a remote country-road to an unheard-of harbour. But her features did not do justice to this splendid beginning: Nature had recollected that she was not in Italy; and the young lady's lineaments, though not so inconsistent as to make her plain, would have been accepted rather as pleasing than as correct. The preoccupied expression which, like images on the retina, remained with her for a moment after the state that caused it had ceased, now changed into a reserved, half-proud, and slightly indignant look, in which the blood diffused itself quickly across her cheek, and additional brightness broke the shade of her rather heavy eyes.

'I know I have no business here,' he said, answering the look. 'But I had a great wish to see you, and inquire how you were. You can give your hand to me, seeing how often I have held it in past days?'[11]

'I would rather forget than remember all that, Mr Barnet,' she answered, as she coldly complied with the request. 'When I think of the circumstances of our last meeting, I can hardly consider it kind of you to allude to such a thing as our past – or indeed, to come here at all.'

'There was no harm in it surely? I don't trouble you often, Lucy.'

'I have not had the honour of a visit from you for a very long time, certainly, and I did not expect it now,' she said, with the same stiffness in her air. 'I hope Mrs Barnet is very well?'

'Yes, yes!' he impatiently returned. 'At least I suppose so – though I only speak from inference!'

'But she is your wife, sir?' said the young girl tremulously.

The unwonted tones of a man's voice in that feminine chamber had startled a canary that was roosting in its cage by the window; the bird awoke hastily, and fluttered against the bars. She went and stilled it by laying her face against the cage and murmuring a coaxing sound. It might partly have been done to still herself.

'I didn't come to talk of Mrs Barnet,' he pursued; 'I came to talk of you, of yourself alone; to inquire how you are getting on since your great loss.' And he turned towards the portrait of her father.

'I am getting on fairly well, thank you.'

The force of her utterance was scarcely borne out by her look; but Barnet courteously reproached himself for not having guessed a thing so natural; and to dissipate all embarrassment, added, as he bent over the table, 'What were you doing when I came? – painting flowers, and by candlelight?'

'Oh no,' she said, 'not painting them – only sketching the outlines. I do that at night to save time – I have to get three dozen done by the end of the month.'

Barnet looked as if he regretted it deeply. 'You will wear your poor eyes out,' he said, with more sentiment than he had hitherto shown. 'You ought not to do it. There was a time when I should have said you must not. Well – I almost wish I had never seen light with my own eyes when I think of that!'

'Is this a time or place for recalling such matters?' she asked, with dignity. 'You used to have a gentlemanly respect for me, and for yourself. Don't speak any more as you have spoken, and don't come again. I cannot think that this visit is serious, or was closely considered by you.'

'Considered: well, I came to see you as an old and good friend – not to mince matters, to visit a woman I loved. Don't be angry![12] I could not help doing it, so many things brought you into my mind . . . This evening I fell in with an acquaintance, and when I saw how happy he was with his wife and family welcoming him home, though with only one-tenth of my income and chances, and thought what might have been in my case, it fairly broke down my discretion, and off I came here. Now I am here I feel that I am wrong to some extent. But the feeling that I should like to see you, and talk of those we used to know in common, was very strong.'

'Before that can be the case a little more time must pass,' said Miss Savile[13] quietly; 'a time long enough for me to regard with some calmness what at present I remember far too impatiently – though it may be you almost forget it. Indeed you must have forgotten it long before you acted as you did.' Her voice grew stronger and more vivacious as she added: 'But I am doing my best to forget it too, and I know I shall succeed from the progress I have made already!'

She had remained standing till now, when she turned and sat down, facing half away from him.

Barnet watched her moodily. 'Yes, it is only what I deserve,' he said. 'Ambition pricked me on – no, it was not ambition, it was wrongheadedness! Had I but reflected . . .' He broke out vehemently: 'But always remember this, Lucy: if you had written to me only one little line after that misunderstanding, I declare I should have come back to you. That ruined me!' He slowly walked as far as the little room would allow him to go, and remained with his eyes on the skirting.

'But, Mr Barnet, how could I write to you? There was no opening for my doing so.'

'Then there ought to have been,' said Barnet, turning. 'That was my fault!'

'Well, I don't know anything about that; but as there had been nothing said by me which required any explanation by letter, I did not send one. Everything was so indefinite, and feeling your position to be so much wealthier than mine, I fancied I might have mistaken your meaning. And when I heard of the other lady – a woman of whose family even you might be proud – I thought how foolish I had been, and said nothing.'[14]

'Then I suppose it was destiny – accident – I don't know what, that separated us, dear Lucy. Anyhow you were the woman I ought to have made my wife – and I let you slip, like the foolish man that I was!'

'Oh, Mr Barnet,' she said, almost in tears, 'don't revive the subject to me; I am the wrong one to console you – think, sir, – you should not be here — it would be so bad for me if it were known!'

'It would – it would, indeed,' he said hastily. 'I am not right in doing this, and I won't do it again.'

'It is a very common folly of human nature, you know, to think the course you did *not* adopt must have been the best,'[15] she continued, with gentle solicitude, as she followed him to the door of the room. 'And you don't know that I should have accepted you, even if you had asked me to be your wife.' At this his eye met hers, and she dropped her gaze. She knew that her voice belied her. There was a silence till she looked up to add, in a voice of soothing playfulness, 'My family was so much poorer than yours, even before I lost my dear father, that – perhaps your companions would have made it unpleasant for us on account of my deficiencies.'

'Your disposition would soon have won them round,' said Barnet.

She archly expostulated: 'Now, never mind my disposition; try to make it up with your wife! Those are my commands to you. And now you are to leave me at once.'

'I will. I must make the best of it all, I suppose,' he replied, more cheerfully than he had as yet spoken. 'But I shall never again meet with such a dear girl as you!'[16] And he suddenly opened the door, and left her alone. When his glance again fell on the lamps that were sparsely ranged along the dreary level road, his eyes were in a state which showed straw-like motes of light radiating from each flame into the surrounding air.

On the other side of the way Barnet observed a man under an umbrella, walking parallel with himself. Presently this man left the footway, and gradually converged on Barnet's course. The latter then saw that it was Charlson, a surgeon of the town, who owed him money. Charlson was a man not without ability; yet he did not prosper. Sundry circumstances stood in his way as a medical practitioner; he was needy; he was not a coddle; he gossiped with men instead of with women; he had married a stranger instead of one of the town young ladies; and he was given to conversational buffoonery. Moreover, his look was quite erroneous. Those only proper features in the family doctor, the quiet eye, and the thin straight passionless lips which never curl in public either for laughter or for scorn, were not his; he had a full curved mouth, and a bold black eye that made timid people nervous. His companions were what in old times would have been called boon companions – an expression which, though of irreproachable root, suggests fraternization carried to the point of unscrupulousness. All this was against him in the little town of his adoption.

Charlson had been in difficulties, and to oblige him Barnet had put his name to a bill; and, as he had expected, was called upon to meet it when it fell due. It had been only a matter of fifty pounds, which Barnet could well afford to lose, and he bore no ill-will to the thriftless surgeon on account of it. But Charlson had a little too much brazen indifferentism in his composition to be altogether a desirable acquaintance.

'I hope to be able to make that little bill-business right with you in the course of three weeks, Mr Barnet,' said Charlson with hail-fellow friendliness.

Barnet replied good-naturedly that there was no hurry.

This particular three weeks had moved on in advance of Charlson's present with the precision of a shadow for some considerable time.

'I've had a dream,' Charlson continued. Barnet knew from his tone that the surgeon was going to begin his characteristic nonsense, and did not encourage him. 'I've had a dream,' repeated Charlson, who required no encouragement. 'I dreamed that a gentleman, who has been very kind to me, married a haughty lady in haste, before he had quite forgotten a nice little girl he knew before, and that one wet evening, like the present, as I was walking up the harbour-road, I saw him come out of that dear little girl's present abode.'

Barnet glanced towards the speaker. The rays from a neighbouring lamp struck through the drizzle under Charlson's umbrella, so as just to illumine his face against the shade behind, and show that his eye was turned up under the outer corner of its lid, whence it leered with impish jocoseness as he thrust his tongue into his cheek.

'Come,' said Barnet gravely, 'we'll have no more of that.'

'No, no – of course not,' Charlson hastily answered, seeing that his humour had carried him too far, as it had done many times before. He was profuse in his apologies, but Barnet did not reply. Of one thing he was certain – that scandal was a plant of quick root, and that he was bound to obey Lucy's injunction for Lucy's own sake.

THOMAS HARDY

III

He did so, to the letter; and though, as the crocus followed the snowdrop and the daffodil the crocus in Lucy's garden, the harbour-road was a not unpleasant place to walk in, Barnet's feet never trod its stones, much less approached her door. He avoided a saunter that way as he would have avoided a dangerous dram, and took his airings a long distance northward, among severely square and brown ploughed fields, where no other townsman came. Sometimes he went round by the lower lanes of the borough, where the rope-walks stretched in which his family formerly had share, and looked at the rope-makers walking backwards, overhung by apple-trees and bushes, and intruded on by cows and calves, as if trade had established itself there at considerable inconvenience to nature.

One morning, when the sun was so warm as to raise a steam from the south-eastern slopes of those flanking hills that looked so lovely above the old roofs, but made every low-chimneyed house in the town as smoky as Tophet, Barnet glanced from the windows of the town-council room for lack of interest in what was proceeding within. Several members of the corporation were present, but there was not much business doing, and in a few minutes Downe came leisurely across to him, saying that he seldom saw Barnet now.

Barnet owned that he was not often present.

Downe looked at the crimson curtain which hung down beside the panes, reflecting its hot hues into their faces, and then out of the window. At that moment there passed along the street a tall command-ing lady, in whom the solicitor recognized Barnet's wife. Barnet had done the same thing, and turned away.

'It will be all right some day,' said Downe, with cheering sympathy.

'You have heard, then, of her last outbreak?'

Downe depressed his cheerfulness to its very reverse in a moment. 'No, I have not heard of anything serious,' he said, with as long a face as one naturally round could be turned into at short notice. 'I only hear vague reports of such things.'

'You may think it will be all right,' said Barnet drily. 'But I have a different opinion . . . No, Downe, we must look the thing in the face. Not poppy nor mandragora[17] – however, how are your wife and children?'

Downe said that they were all well, thanks; they were out that morning somewhere; he was just looking to see if they were walking that way. Ah, there they were, just coming down the street, and Downe pointed to the figures of two children with a nursemaid, and a lady walking behind them.

'You will come out and speak to her?' he asked.

'Not this morning. The fact is I don't care to speak to anybody just now.'

'You are too sensitive, Mr Barnet. At school I remember you used to get as red as a rose if anybody uttered a word that hurt your feelings.'

Barnet mused. 'Yes,' he admitted, 'there is a grain of truth in that. It is because of that I often try to make peace at home. Life would be tolerable then at any rate, even if not particularly bright.'

'I have thought more than once of proposing a little plan to you,' said Downe with some hesitation. 'I don't know whether it will meet your views, but take it or leave it, as you choose. In fact, it was my wife who suggested it; that she would be very glad to call on Mrs Barnet and get into her confidence. She seems to think that Mrs Barnet is rather alone in the town, and without advisers. Her impression is that your wife will listen to reason. Emily has a wonderful way of winning the hearts of people of her own sex.'

'And of the other sex too, I think. She is a charming woman, and you were a lucky fellow to find her.'

'Well, perhaps I was,' simpered Downe, trying to wear an aspect of being the last man in the world to feel pride. 'However, she will be likely to find out what ruffles Mrs Barnet. Perhaps it is some misunderstanding, you know – something that she is too proud to ask you to explain, or some little thing in your conduct that irritates her because she does not fully comprehend you. The truth is, Emily would have been more ready to make advances if she had been quite sure of her fitness for Mrs Barnet's society, who has of course been accustomed to London people of good position, which made Emily fearful of intruding.'

Barnet expressed his warmest thanks for the well-intentioned prop-osition. There was reason in Mrs Downe's fear – that he owned. 'But do let her call,' he said. 'There is no woman in England I would so soon trust on such an errand. I am afraid there will not be any brilliant result; still I shall take it as the kindest and nicest thing if she will try it, and not be frightened at a repulse.'

When Barnet and Downe had parted, the former went to the Town Savings-Bank, of which he was a trustee, and endeavoured to forget his troubles in the contemplation of low sums of money, and figures in a network of red and blue lines. He sat and watched the working-people making their deposits, to which at intervals he signed his name. Before he left in the afternoon Downe put his head inside the door.

'Emily has seen Mrs Barnet,' he said, in a low voice. 'She has got Mrs Barnet's promise to take her for a drive down to the shore tomorrow, if it is fine. Good afternoon!'

Barnet shook Downe by the hand without speaking, and Downe went away.

IV

The next day was as fine as the arrangement could possibly require. As the sun passed the meridian and declined westward, the tall shadows from the scaffold-poles of Barnet's rising residence streaked the ground as far as to the middle of the highway. Barnet himself was there inspecting the progress of the works for the first time during several weeks. A building in an old-fashioned town five-and-thirty years ago did not, as in the modern fashion, rise from the sod like a booth at a fair. The foundations and lower courses were put in and allowed to settle for many weeks before the superstructure was built up, and a whole summer of drying was hardly sufficient to do justice to the important issues involved. Barnet stood within a window-niche which had as yet received no frame, and thence looked down a slope into the road. The wheels of a chaise were heard, and then his handsome Xantippe,[18] in the company of Mrs Downe, drove past on their way to the shore. They were driving slowly; there was a pleasing light in

Mrs Downe's face, which seemed faintly to reflect itself upon the countenance of her companion – that *politesse du cœur* which was so natural to her having possibly begun already to work results.[19] But whatever the situation, Barnet resolved not to interfere, or do anything to hazard the glory of the day. He might well afford to trust the issue to another when he could never direct it but to ill himself. His wife's clenched rein-hand in its lemon-coloured glove, her stiff erect figure, clad in velvet and lace, and her boldly-outlined face, passed on, exhibiting their owner as one fixed for ever above the level of her companion – socially by her early breeding, and materially by her higher cushion.

Barnet decided to allow them a proper time to themselves, and then stroll down to the shore and drive them home. After lingering on at the house for another hour he started with this intention. A few hundred yards below 'Château Ringdale' stood the cottage in which the late lieutenant's daughter had her lodging. Barnet had not been so far that way for a long time, and as he approached the forbidden ground a curious warmth passed into him, which led him to perceive that, unless he were careful, he might have to fight the battle with himself about Lucy over again. A tenth of his present excuse would, however, have justified him in travelling by that road today.

He came opposite the dwelling, and turned his eyes for a momentary glance into the little garden that stretched from the palings to the door. Lucy was in the enclosure; she was walking and stooping to gather some flowers, possibly for the purpose of painting them, for she moved about quickly, as if anxious to save time. She did not see him; he might have passed unnoticed; but a sensation which was not in strict unison with his previous sentiments that day led him to pause in his walk and watch her. She went nimbly round and round the beds of anemones, tulips, jonquils, polyanthuses, and other old-fashioned flowers, looking a very charming figure in her half-mourning bonnet, and with an incomplete nosegay in her left hand. Raising herself to pull down a lilac blossom she observed him.

'Mr Barnet!' she said, innocently smiling. 'Why, I have been thinking of you many times since your pony-carriage went by, and now here you are!'

'Yes, Lucy,' he said.

Then she seemed to recall particulars of their last meeting, and he believed that she flushed, though it might have been only the fancy of his own super-sensitiveness.

'I am going to the harbour,' he added.

'Are you?' Lucy remarked simply, 'A great many people begin to go there now the summer is drawing on.'

Her face had come more into his view as she spoke, and he noticed how much thinner and paler it was than when he had seen it last. 'Lucy, how weary you look! tell me, can I help you?' he was going to cry out. — 'If I do,' he thought, 'it will be the ruin of us both!' He merely said that the afternoon was fine, and went on his way.

As he went a sudden blast of air came over the hill as if in contradiction to his words, and spoilt the previous quiet of the scene. The wind had already shifted violently, and now smelt of the sea.

The harbour-road soon began to justify its name. A gap appeared in the rampart of hills which shut out the sea, and on the left of the opening rose a vertical cliff, coloured a burning orange by the sunlight, the companion cliff on the right being livid in shade. Between these cliffs, like the Libyan bay which sheltered the ship-wrecked Trojans,[20] was a little haven, seemingly a beginning made by Nature herself of a perfect harbour, which appealed to the passer-by as only requiring a little human industry to finish it and make it famous, the ground on each side as far back as the daisied slopes that bounded the interior valley being a mere layer of blown sand. But the Port-Bredy burgesses a mile inland had, in the course of ten centuries, responded many times to that mute appeal, with the result that the tides had invariably choked up their works with sand and shingle as soon as completed. There were but few houses here: a rough pier, a few boats, some stores, an inn, a residence or two, a ketch unloading in the harbour, were the chief features of the settlement. On the open ground by the shore stood his wife's pony-carriage, empty, the boy in attendance holding the horse.

When Barnet drew nearer, he saw an indigo-coloured spot moving swiftly along beneath the radiant base of the eastern cliff, which proved to be a man in a jersey, running with all his might. He held up his hand to Barnet, as it seemed, and they approached each other. The man was local, but a stranger to him.

'What is it, my man?' said Barnet.

'A terrible calamity!' the boatman hastily explained. Two ladies had been capsized in a boat – they were Mrs Downe and Mrs Barnet of the old town; they had driven down there that afternoon – they had alighted, and it was so fine, that, after walking about a little while, they had been tempted to go out for a short sail round the cliff. Just as they were putting in to the shore, the wind shifted with a sudden gust, the boat listed over, and it was thought they were both drowned. How it could have happened was beyond his mind to fathom, for John Green knew how to sail a boat as well as any man there.

'Which is the way to the place?' said Barnet.

It was just round the cliff.

'Run to the carriage and tell the boy to bring it to the place as soon as you can. Then go to the Harbour Inn and tell them to ride to town for a doctor. Have they been got out of the water?'

'One lady has.'

'Which?'

'Mrs Barnet. Mrs Downe, it is feared, has fleeted out to sea.'

Barnet ran on to that part of the shore which the cliff had hitherto obscured from his view, and there discerned, a long way ahead, a group of fishermen standing. As soon as he came up one or two recognized him, and, not liking to meet his eye, turned aside with misgiving. He went amidst them and saw a small sailing-boat lying draggled at the water's edge; and, on the sloping shingle beside it, a soaked and sandy woman's form in the velvet dress and yellow gloves of his wife.

V

All had been done that could be done. Mrs Barnet was in her own house under medical hands, but the result was still uncertain. Barnet had acted as if devotion to his wife were the dominant passion of his existence. There had been much to decide – whether to attempt

restoration of the apparently lifeless body as it lay on the shore –
whether to carry her to the Harbour Inn – whether to drive with her
at once to his own house. The first course, with no skilled help or
appliances near at hand, had seemed hopeless. The second course
would have occupied nearly as much time as a drive to the town,
owing to the intervening ridges of shingle, and the necessity of crossing
the harbour by boat to get to the house, added to which much time
must have elapsed before a doctor could have arrived down there. By
bringing her home in the carriage some precious moments had slipped
by; but she had been laid in her own bed in seven minutes, a doctor
called to her side, and every possible restorative brought to bear upon
her.

At what a tearing pace he had driven up that road, through the
yellow evening sunlight, the shadows flapping irksomely into his eyes
as each wayside object rushed past between him and the west! Tired
workmen with their baskets at their backs had turned on their homeward journey to wonder at his speed. Half-way between the shore and
Port-Bredy town he had met Charlson, who had been the first surgeon
to hear of the accident. He was accompanied by his assistant in a gig.
Barnet had sent on the latter to the coast in case that Downe's poor
wife should by that time have been reclaimed from the waves, and
had brought Charlson back with him to the house.

Barnet's presence was not needed here, and he felt it to be his next
duty to set off at once and find Downe, that no other than himself
might break the news to him.

He was quite sure that no chance had been lost for Mrs Downe by
his leaving the shore. By the time that Mrs Barnet had been laid in
the carriage, a much larger group had assembled to lend assistance
in finding her friend, rendering his own help superfluous. But the duty
of breaking the news was made doubly painful by the circumstance
that the catastrophe which had befallen Mrs Downe was solely the
result of her own and her husband's loving-kindness towards himself.

He found Downe in his office. When the solicitor comprehended
the intelligence he turned pale, stood up, and remained for a moment
perfectly still, as if bereft of his faculties; then his shoulders heaved,
he pulled out his handkerchief and began to cry like a child. His sobs

might have been heard in the next room. He seemed to have no idea of going to the shore, or of doing anything; but when Barnet took him gently by the hand, and proposed to start at once he quietly acquiesced, neither uttering any further word nor making any effort to repress his tears.

Barnet accompanied him to the shore, where, finding that no trace had as yet been seen of Mrs Downe, and that his stay would be of no avail, he left Downe with his friends and the young doctor, and once more hastened back to his own house.

At the door he met Charlson. 'Well?' Barnet said.

'I have just come down,' said the doctor; 'we have done everything; but without result. I sympathize with you in your bereavement.'

Barnet did not much appreciate Charlson's sympathy, which sounded to his ears as something of a mockery from the lips of a man who knew what Charlson knew about their domestic relations. Indeed there seemed an odd spark in Charlson's full black eye as he said the words; but that might have been imaginary.

'And, Mr Barnet,' Charlson resumed, 'that little matter between us – I hope to settle it finally in three weeks at least.'

'Never mind that now,' said Barnet abruptly. He directed the surgeon to go to the harbour in case his services might even now be necessary there; and himself entered the house.

The servants were coming from his wife's chamber, looking helplessly at each other and at him. He passed them by and entered the room, where he stood mutely regarding the bed for a few minutes, after which he walked into his own dressing-room adjoining, and there paced up and down. In a minute or two he noticed what a strange and total silence had come over the upper part of the house; his own movements, muffled as they were by the carpet, seemed noisy; and his thoughts to disturb the air like articulate utterances. His eye glanced through the window. Far down the road to the harbour a roof detained his gaze: out of it rose a red chimney, and out of the red chimney a curl of smoke, as from a fire newly kindled. He had often seen such a sight before. In that house lived Lucy Savile; and the smoke was from the fire which was regularly lighted at this time to make her tea.

After that he went back to the bedroom, and stood there some time regarding his wife's silent form. She was a woman some years older than himself, but had not by any means overpassed the maturity of good looks and vigour. Her passionate features, well-defined, firm, and statuesque in life, were doubly so now: her mouth and brow, beneath her purplish black hair, showed only too clearly that the turbulency of character which had made a bear-garden of his house had been no temporary phase of her existence. While he reflected, he suddenly said to himself, I wonder if all has been done?

The thought was led up to by his having fancied that his wife's features lacked in its complete form the expression which he had been accustomed to associate with the faces of those whose spirits have fled for ever. The effacement of life was not so marked but that, entering uninformed, he might have supposed her sleeping. Her complexion was that seen in the numerous faded portraits by Sir Joshua Reynolds;[21] it was pallid in comparison with life, but there was visible on a close inspection the remnant of what had once been a flush; the keeping between the cheeks and the hollows of the face being thus preserved, although positive colour was gone. Long orange rays of evening sun stole in through chinks in the blind, striking on the large mirror, and being thence reflected upon the crimson hangings and woodwork of the heavy bedstead, so that the general tone of light was remarkably warm; and it was probable that something might be due to this circumstance. Still the fact impressed him as strange. Charlson had been gone more than a quarter of an hour: could it be possible that he had left too soon, and that his attempts to restore her had operated so sluggishly as only now to have made themselves felt? Barnet laid his hand upon her chest, and fancied that ever and anon a faint flutter of palpitation, gentle as that of a butterfly's wing, disturbed the stillness there – ceasing for a time, then struggling to go on, then breaking down in weakness and ceasing again.

Barnet's mother had been an active practitioner of the healing art among her poorer neighbours, and her inspirations had all been derived from an octavo volume of Domestic Medicine,[22] which at this moment was lying, as it had lain for many years, on a shelf in Barnet's dressing-room. He hastily fetched it, and there read under the head 'Drowning': –

'Exertions for the recovery of any person who has not been immersed for a longer period than half an hour should be continued for at least four hours, as there have been many cases in which returning life has made itself visible even after a longer interval.

'Should, however, a weak action of any of the organs show itself when the case seems almost hopeless, our efforts must be redoubled; the feeble spark in this case requires to be solicited; it will certainly disappear under a relaxation of labour.'

Barnet looked at his watch; it was now barely two hours and a half from the time when he had first heard of the accident. He threw aside the book and turned quickly to reach a stimulant which had previously been used. Pulling up the blind for more light, his eye glanced out of the window. There he saw that red chimney still smoking cheerily, and that roof, and through the roof that somebody. His mechanical movements stopped, his hand remained on the blind-cord, and he seemed to become breathless, as if he had suddenly found himself treading a high rope.

While he stood a sparrow lighted on the window-sill, saw him, and flew away. Next a man and a dog walked over one of the green hills which bulged above the roofs of the town. But Barnet took no notice.

We may wonder what were the exact images that passed through his mind during those minutes of gazing upon Lucy Savile's house, the sparrow, the man and the dog, and Lucy Savile's house again. There are honest men who will not admit to their thoughts, even as idle hypotheses, views of the future that assume as done a deed which they would recoil from doing; and there are other honest men for whom morality ends at the surface of their own heads, who will deliberate what the first will not so much as suppose. Barnet had a wife whose presence distracted his home; she now lay as in death; by merely doing nothing – by letting the intelligence which had gone forth to the world lie undisturbed – he would effect such a deliverance for himself as he had never hoped for,[23] and open up an opportunity of which till now he had never dreamed. Whether the conjuncture had arisen through any unscrupulous, ill-considered impulse of Charlson to help out of a strait the friend who was so kind as never to press him for what was due could not be told; there was nothing to prove it; and it was a question which could never be asked. The triangular situation – himself – his wife – Lucy Savile – was the one clear thing.

From Barnet's actions we may infer that he *supposed* such and such a result, for a moment, but did not deliberate. He withdrew his hazel eyes from the scene without, calmly turned, rang the bell for assistance, and vigorously exerted himself to learn if life still lingered in that motionless frame. In a short time another surgeon was in attendance; and then Barnet's surmise proved to be true. The slow life timidly heaved again; but much care and patience were needed to catch and retain it, and a considerable period elapsed before it could be said with certainty that Mrs Barnet lived. When this was the case, and there was no further room for doubt, Barnet left the chamber. The blue evening smoke from Lucy's chimney had died down to an imperceptible stream, and as he walked about downstairs he murmured to himself, 'My wife was dead, and she is alive again.'

It was not so with Downe. After three hours' immersion his wife's body had been recovered, life, of course, being quite extinct. Barnet, on descending, went straight to his friend's house, and there learned the result. Downe was helpless in his wild grief, occasionally even hysterical. Barnet said little, but finding that some guiding hand was necessary in the sorrow-stricken household, took upon him to supervise and manage till Downe should be in a state of mind to do so for himself.

VI

One September evening, four months later, when Mrs Barnet was in perfect health, and Mrs Downe but a weakening memory, an errand-boy paused to rest himself in front of Mr Barnet's old house, depositing his basket on one of the window-sills. The street was not yet lighted, but there were lights in the house, and at intervals a flitting shadow fell upon the blind at his elbow. Words also were audible from the same apartment, and they seemed to be those of persons in violent altercation. But the boy could not gather their purport, and he went on his way.

Ten minutes afterwards the door of Barnet's house opened, and a tall closely-veiled lady in a travelling-dress came out and descended the free-stone steps. The servant stood in the doorway watching her as she went with a measured tread down the street. When she had been out of sight for some minutes Barnet appeared at the door from within.

'Did your mistress leave word where she was going?' he asked.

'No, sir.'

'Is the carriage ordered to meet her anywhere?'

'No, sir.'

'Did she take a latch-key?'

'No, sir.'

Barnet went in again, sat down in his chair, and leaned back. Then in solitude and silence he brooded over the bitter emotions that filled his heart. It was for this that he had gratuitously restored her to life, and made his union with another impossible! The evening drew on, and nobody came to disturb him. At bedtime he told the servants to retire, that he would sit up for Mrs Barnet himself; and when they were gone he leaned his head upon his hand and mused for hours.

The clock struck one, two; still his wife came not, and, with impatience added to depression, he went from room to room till another weary hour had passed. This was not altogether a new experience for Barnet; but she had never before so prolonged her absence. At last he sat down again and fell asleep.

He awoke at six o'clock to find that she had not returned. In searching about the rooms he discovered that she had taken a case of jewels which had been hers before her marriage. At eight a note was brought him; it was from his wife, in which she stated that she had gone by the coach to the house of a distant relative near London, and expressed a wish that certain boxes, articles of clothing, and so on, might be sent to her forthwith. The note was brought to him by a waiter at the Black-Bull Hotel, and had been written by Mrs Barnet immediately before she took her place in the stage.

By the evening this order was carried out, and Barnet, with a sense of relief, walked out into the town. A fair had been held during the day, and the large clear moon which rose over the most prominent hill flung its light upon the booths and standings that still remained in the street, mixing its rays curiously with those from the flaring naphtha lamps. The town was full of country-people who had come in to enjoy themselves, and on this account Barnet strolled through the streets unobserved. With a certain recklessness he made for the harbour-road, and presently found himself by the shore, where he walked on till he came to the spot near which his friend the kindly Mrs Downe had lost her life, and his own wife's life had been preserved. A tremulous pathway of bright moonshine now stretched over the water which had engulfed them, and not a living soul was near.

Here he ruminated on their characters, and next on the young girl in whom he now took a more sensitive interest than at the time when he had been free to marry her. Nothing, so far as he was aware, had ever appeared in his own conduct to show that such an interest existed. He had made it a point of the utmost strictness to hinder that feeling from influencing in the faintest degree his attitude towards his wife; and this was made all the more easy for him by the small demand Mrs Barnet made upon his attentions, for which she ever evinced the greatest contempt; thus unwittingly giving him the satisfaction of knowing that their severance owed nothing to jealousy, or, indeed, to any personal behaviour of his at all. Her concern was not with him or his feelings, as she frequently told him; but that she had, in a moment of weakness, thrown herself away upon a common burgher when she might have aimed at, and possibly brought down, a peer of the realm. Her frequent depreciation of Barnet in these terms had at times been so intense that he was sorely tempted to retaliate on her egotism by owning that he loved at the same low level on which he lived; but prudence had prevailed, for which he was now thankful.

Something seemed to sound upon the shingle behind him over and above the raking of the wave. He looked round, and a slight girlish shape appeared quite close to him. He could not see her face because it was in the direction of the moon.

'Mr Barnet?' the rambler said, in timid surprise. The voice was the voice of Lucy Savile.

'Yes,' said Barnet. 'How can I repay you for this pleasure?'

FELLOW-TOWNSMEN

'I only came because the night was so clear. I am now on my way home.'

'I am glad we have met. I want to know if you will let me do something for you, to give me an occupation, as an idle man? I am sure I ought to help you, for I know you are almost without friends.'

She hesitated. 'Why should you tell me that?' she said.

'In the hope that you will be frank with me.'

'I am not altogether without friends here. But I am going to make a little change in my life – to go out as a teacher of freehand drawing and practical perspective, of course I mean on a comparatively humble scale, because I have not been specially educated for that profession. But I am sure I shall like it much.'

'You have an opening?'

'I have not exactly got it, but I have advertised for one.'

'Lucy, you must let me help you!'

'Not at all.'

'You need not think it would compromise you, or that I am indifferent to delicacy. I bear in mind how we stand. It is very unlikely that you will succeed as teacher of the class you mention, so let me do something of a different kind for you. Say what you would like, and it shall be done.'

'No; if I can't be a drawing-mistress or governess, or something of that sort, I shall go to India and join my brother.'

'I wish I could go abroad, anywhere, everywhere with you, Lucy, and leave this place and its associations for ever!'

She played with the end of her bonnet-string, and hastily turned aside. 'Don't ever touch upon that kind of topic again,' she said, with a quick severity not free from anger. 'It simply makes it impossible for me to see you, much less receive any guidance from you. No, thank you, Mr Barnet; you can do nothing for me at present; and as I suppose my uncertainty will end in my leaving for India, I fear you never will. If ever I think you *can* do anything, I will take the trouble to ask you. Till then, goodbye.'

The tone of her latter words was equivocal, and while he remained in doubt whether a gentle irony was or was not inwrought with their sound, she swept lightly round and left him alone. He saw her form get smaller and smaller along the damp belt of sea-sand between ebb and flood; and when she had vanished round the cliff into the harbour-road, he himself followed in the same direction.

That her hopes from an advertisement should be the single thread which held Lucy Savile in England was too much for Barnet. On reaching the town he went straight to the residence of Downe, now a widower with four children. The young motherless brood had been sent to bed about a quarter of an hour earlier, and when Barnet entered he found Downe sitting alone. It was the same room as that from which the family had been looking out for Downe at the beginning of the year, when Downe had slipped into the gutter and his wife had been so enviably tender towards him. The old neatness had gone from the house; articles lay in places which could show no reason for their presence, as if momentarily deposited there some months ago, and forgotten ever since; there were no flowers; things were jumbled together on the furniture which should have been in cupboards; and the place in general had that stagnant, unrenovated air which usually pervades the maimed home of the widower.

Downe soon renewed his customary full-worded lament over his wife, and even when he had worked himself up to tears, went on volubly, as if a listener were a luxury to be enjoyed whenever he could be caught.

'She was a treasure beyond compare, Mr Barnet! I shall never see such another. Nobody now to nurse me – nobody to console me in those daily troubles, you know, Barnet, which make consolation so necessary to a nature like mine. It would be unbecoming to repine, for her spirit's home was elsewhere – the tender light in her eyes always showed it; but it is a long dreary time that I have before me, and nobody else can ever fill the void left in my heart by her loss – nobody – nobody!' And Downe wiped his eyes again.

'She was a good woman in the highest sense,' gravely answered Barnet, who, though Downe's words drew genuine compassion from his heart, could not help feeling that a tender reticence would have been a finer tribute to Mrs Downe's really sterling virtues than such a second-class lament as this.

'I have something to show you,' Downe resumed, producing from a drawer a sheet of paper on which was an elaborate design for a canopied tomb. 'This has been sent me by the architect, but it is not exactly what I want.'

'You have got Jones to do it, I see, the man who is carrying out my house,' said Barnet, as he glanced at the signature to the drawing.

'Yes, but it is not quite what I want. I want something more striking – more like a tomb I have seen in St Paul's Cathedral. Nothing less will do justice to my feelings, and how far short of them that will fall!'[24]

Barnet privately thought the design a sufficiently imposing one as it stood, even extravagantly ornate; but, feeling that he had no right to criticize, he said gently, 'Downe, should you not live more in your children's lives at the present time, and soften the sharpness of regret for your own past by thinking of their future?'

'Yes, yes; but what can I do more?' asked Downe, wrinkling his forehead hopelessly.

It was with anxious slowness that Barnet produced his reply – the secret object of his visit tonight. 'Did you not say one day that you ought by rights to get a governess for the children?'

Downe admitted that he had said so, but that he could not see his way to it. 'The kind of woman I should like to have,' he said, 'would be rather beyond my means. No; I think I shall send them to school in the town when they are old enough to go out alone.'

'Now I know of something better than that. The late Lieutenant Savile's daughter Lucy wants to do something for herself in the way of teaching. She would be inexpensive, and would answer your purpose as well as anybody for six or twelve months. She would probably come daily if you were to ask her, and so your housekeeping arrangements would not be much affected.'

'I thought she had gone away,' said the solicitor, musing. 'Where does she live?'

Barnet told him, and added that, if Downe should think of her as suitable, he would do well to call as soon as possible, or she might be on the wing. 'If you do see her,' he said, 'it would be advisable not to mention my name. She is rather stiff in her ideas of me, and it might prejudice her against a course if she knew that I recommended it.'

Downe promised to give the subject his consideration, and nothing more was said about it just then. But when Barnet rose to go, which was not till nearly bedtime, he reminded Downe of the suggestion, and went up the street to his own solitary home with a sense of satisfaction at his promising diplomacy in a charitable cause.

VII

The walls of his new house were carried up nearly to their full height. By a curious though not infrequent reaction, Barnet's feelings about that unnecessary structure had undergone a change; he took considerable interest in its progress as a long-neglected thing, his wife before her departure having grown quite weary of it as a hobby. Moreover, it was an excellent distraction for a man in the unhappy position of having to live in a provincial town with nothing to do. He was probably the first of his line who had ever passed a day without toil, and perhaps something like an inherited instinct[25] disqualifies such men for a life of pleasant inaction, such as lies in the power of those whose leisure is not a personal accident, but a vast historical accretion which has become part of their natures.

Thus Barnet got into a way of spending many of his leisure hours on the site of the new building, and he might have been seen on most days at this time trying the temper of the mortar by punching the joints with his stick, looking at the grain of a floor-board, and meditating where it grew, or picturing under what circumstances the last fire would be kindled in the at present sootless chimney. One day when thus occupied he saw three children pass by in the company of a fair young woman, whose sudden appearance caused him to flush perceptibly.

'Ah, she is there,' he thought. 'That's a blessed thing.'

Casting an interested glance over the rising building and the busy workmen, Lucy Savile and the little Downes passed by; and after that time it became a regular though almost unconscious custom of Barnet to stand in the half-completed house and look from the ungarnished windows at the governess as she tripped towards the sea-shore with her young charges, which she was in the habit of doing on most fine afternoons. It was on one of these occasions, when he had been loitering on the first-floor landing, near the hole left for the staircase, not yet erected, that there appeared above the edge of the floor a little hat, followed by a little head.

Barnet withdrew through a doorway, and the child came to the top of the ladder, stepping on to the floor and crying to her sisters and Miss Savile to follow. Another head rose above the floor, and another, and then Lucy herself came into view. The troop ran hither and thither through the empty, shaving-strewn rooms, and Barnet came forward.

Lucy uttered a small exclamation: she was very sorry that she had intruded; she had not the least idea that Mr Barnet was there: the children had come up, and she had followed.

Barnet replied that he was only too glad to see them there. 'And now, let me show you the rooms,' he said.

She passively assented, and he took her round. There was not much to show in such a bare skeleton of a house, but he made the most of it, and explained the different ornamental fittings that were soon to be fixed here and there. Lucy made but few remarks in reply, though she seemed pleased with her visit, and stole away down the ladder, followed by her companions.

After this the new residence became yet more of a hobby for Barnet. Downe's children did not forget their first visit, and when the windows were glazed, and the handsome staircase spread its broad low steps into the hall, they came again, prancing in unwearied succession through every room from ground-floor to attics, while Lucy stood waiting for them at the door. Barnet, who rarely missed a day in coming to inspect progress, stepped out from the drawing-room.

'I could not keep them out,' she said, with an apologetic blush. 'I tried to do so very much; but they are rather wilful, and we are directed to walk this way for the sea air.'

'Do let them make the house their regular playground, and you yours,' said Barnet. 'There is no better place for children to romp and take their exercise in than an empty house, particularly in muddy or damp weather, such as we shall get a good deal of now; and this place will not be furnished for a long long time – perhaps never. I am not at all decided about it.

'Oh, but it must!' replied Lucy, looking round at the hall. 'The rooms are excellent, twice as high as ours; and the views from the windows are so lovely.'

'I daresay, I daresay,' he said absently.

'Will all the furniture be new?' she asked.

'All the furniture be new – that's a thing I have not thought of. In fact I only come here and look on. My father's house would have been large enough for me, but another person had a voice in the matter, and it was settled that we should build. However, the place grows upon me; its recent associations are cheerful, and I am getting to like it fast.'

A certain uneasiness in Lucy's manner showed that the conversation was taking too personal a turn for her. 'Still, as modern tastes develop, people require more room to gratify them in,' she said, withdrawing to call the children; and serenely bidding him good afternoon she went on her way.

Barnet's life at this period was singularly lonely, and yet he was happier than he could have expected. His wife's estrangement and absence, which promised to be permanent, left him free as a boy in his movements, and the solitary walks that he took gave him ample opportunity for chastened reflection on what might have been his lot if he had only shown wisdom enough to claim Lucy Savile when there was no bar between their lives, and she was to be had for the asking. He would occasionally call at the house of his friend Downe; but there was scarcely enough in common between their two natures to make them more than friends of that excellent sort whose personal knowledge of each other's history and character is always in excess of intimacy, whereby they are not so likely to be severed by a clash of sentiment as in cases where intimacy springs up in excess of knowledge. Lucy was never visible at these times, being either engaged in the school-room, or in taking an airing out of doors; but, knowing that she was now comfortable, and had given up the, to him, depressing idea of going off to the other side of the globe, he was quite content.

The new house had so far progressed that the gardeners were

beginning to grass down the front. During an afternoon which he was passing in marking the curve for the carriage-drive, he beheld her coming in boldly towards him from the road. Hitherto Barnet had only caught her on the premises by stealth; and this advance seemed to show that at last her reserve had broken down.

A smile gained strength upon her face as she approached, and it was quite radiant when she came up, and said, without a trace of embarrassment, 'I find I owe you a hundred thanks – and it comes to me quite as a surprise! It was through your kindness that I was engaged by Mr Downe. Believe me, Mr Barnet, I did not know it until yesterday, or I should have thanked you long and long ago!'

'I had offended you – just a trifle – at the time, I think?' said Barnet, smiling, 'and it was best that you should not know.'

'Yes, yes,' she returned hastily. 'Don't allude to that; it is past and over, and we will let it be. The house is finished almost, is it not? How beautiful it will look when the evergreens are grown! Do you call the style Palladian, Mr Barnet?'

'I – really don't quite know what it is. Yes, it must be Palladian, certainly. But I'll ask Jones, the architect; for, to tell the truth, I had not thought much about the style: I had nothing to do with choosing it, I am sorry to say.'

She would not let him harp on this gloomy refrain, and talked on bright matters till she said, producing a small roll of paper which he had noticed in her hand all the while, 'Mr Downe wished me to bring you this revised drawing of the late Mrs Downe's tomb, which the architect has just sent him. He would like you to look it over.'

The children came up with their hoops, and she went off with them down the harbour-road as usual. Barnet had been glad to get those words of thanks; he had been thinking for many months that he would like her to know of his share in finding her a home, such as it was; and what he could not do for himself, Downe had now kindly done for him. He returned to his desolate house with a lighter tread; though in reason he hardly knew why his tread should be light.

On examining the drawing, Barnet found that, instead of the vast altar-tomb and canopy Downe had determined on at their last meeting, it was to be a more modest memorial even than had been suggested by the architect; a coped tomb of good solid construction, with no useless elaboration at all. Barnet was truly glad to see that Downe had come to reason of his own accord; and he returned the drawing with a note of approval.

He followed up the house-work as before, and as he walked up and down the rooms, occasionally gazing from the windows over the bulging green hills and the quiet harbour that lay between them, he murmured words and fragments of words, which, if listened to, would have revealed all the secrets of his existence. Whatever his reason in going there, Lucy did not call again: the walk to the shore seemed to be abandoned: he must have thought it as well for both that it should be so, for he did not go anywhere out of his accustomed ways to endeavour to discover her.

VIII

The winter and the spring had passed, and the house was complete. It was a fine morning in the early part of June, and Barnet, though not in the habit of rising early, had taken a long walk before breakfast; returning by way of the new building. A sufficiently exciting cause of his restlessness today might have been the intelligence which had reached him the night before, that Lucy Savile was going to India after all, and notwithstanding the representations of her friends that such a journey was unadvisable in many ways for an unpractised girl, unless some more definite advantage lay at the end of it than she could show to be the case. Barnet's walk up the slope to the building betrayed that he was in a dissatisfied mood. He hardly saw that the dewy time of day lent an unusual freshness to the bushes and trees which had so recently put on their summer habit of heavy leafage, and made his newly-laid lawn look as well established as an old manorial meadow. The house had been so adroitly placed between six tall elms which were growing on the site beforehand, that they seemed like real ancestral trees; and the rooks, young and old, cawed melodiously to their visitor.

The door was not locked, and he entered. No workmen appeared to be present, and he walked from sunny window to sunny window of the empty rooms, with a sense of seclusion which might have been very pleasant but for the antecedent knowledge that his almost paternal care of Lucy Savile was to be thrown away by her wilfulness. Footsteps echoed through an adjoining room; and, bending his eyes in that direction, he perceived Mr Jones, the architect. He had come to look over the building before giving the contractor his final certificate. They walked over the house together. Everything was finished except the papering: there were the latest improvements of the period in bell-hanging, ventilating, smoke-jacks, fire-grates, and French windows. The business was soon ended, and Jones, having directed Barnet's attention to a roll of wall-paper patterns which lay on a bench for his choice, was leaving to keep another engagement, when Barnet said, 'Is the tomb finished yet for Mrs Downe?'

'Well – yes: it is at last,' said the architect, coming back and speaking as if he were in a mood to make a confidence. 'I have had no end of trouble in the matter, and, to tell the truth, I am heartily glad it is over.'

Barnet expressed his surprise. 'I thought poor Downe had given up those extravagant notions of his? then he has gone back to the altar and canopy after all? Well, he is to be excused, poor fellow!'

'Oh no – he has not at all gone back to them – quite the reverse,' Jones hastened to say. 'He has so reduced design after design, that the whole thing has been nothing but waste labour for me; till in the end it has become a common headstone, which a mason put up in half a day.'

'A common headstone?' said Barnet.

'Yes. I held out for some time for the addition of a footstone at least. But he said, "Oh no – he couldn't afford it." '

'Ah, well – his family is growing up, poor fellow, and his expenses are getting serious.'

'Yes, exactly,' said Jones, as if the subject were none of his. And again directing Barnet's attention to the wall-papers, the bustling architect left him to keep some other engagement.

'A common headstone,' murmured Barnet, left again to himself. He mused a minute or two, and next began looking over and selecting from the patterns; but had not long been engaged in the work when he heard another footstep on the gravel without, and somebody enter the open porch.

Barnet went to the door – it was his manservant in search of him.

'I have been trying for some time to find you, sir,' he said. 'This letter has come by the post, and it is marked immediate. And there's this one from Mr Downe, who called just now wanting to see you.' He searched his pocket for the second.

Barnet took the first letter – it had a black border, and bore the London postmark. It was not in his wife's handwriting, or in that of any person he knew; but conjecture soon ceased as he read the page, wherein he was briefly informed that Mrs Barnet had died suddenly on the previous day, at the furnished villa she had occupied near London.

Barnet looked vaguely round the empty hall, at the blank walls, out of the doorway. Drawing a long palpitating breath, and with eyes downcast, he turned and climbed the stairs slowly, like a man who doubted their stability. The fact of his wife having, as it were, died once already, and lived on again, had entirely dislodged the possibility of her actual death from his conjecture. He went to the landing, leant over the balusters, and after a reverie, of whose duration he had but the faintest notion, turned to the window and stretched his gaze to the cottage farther down the road, which was visible from his landing, and from which Lucy still walked to the solicitor's house by a cross path. The faint words that came from his moving lips were simply, 'At last!'

Then, almost involuntarily, Barnet fell down on his knees and murmured some incoherent words of thanksgiving. Surely his virtue in restoring his wife to life had been rewarded! But, as if the impulse struck uneasily on his conscience, he quickly rose, brushed the dust from his trousers, and set himself to think of his next movements. He could not start for London for some hours; and as he had no pre-parations to make that could not be made in half an hour, he mechan-ically descended and resumed his occupation of turning over the wall-papers. They had all got brighter for him, those papers. It was all changed – who would sit in the rooms that they were to line? He went on to muse upon Lucy's conduct in so frequently coming to the house with the children; her occasional blush in speaking to him; her evident interest in him. What woman can in the long run avoid being interested in a man whom she knows to be devoted to her? If human solicitation could ever effect anything, there should be no going to India for Lucy now. All the papers previously chosen seemed wrong in their shades, and he began from the beginning to choose again.

While entering on the task he heard a forced 'Ahem!' from without the porch, evidently uttered to attract his attention, and footsteps again advancing to the door. His man, whom he had quite forgotten in his mental turmoil, was still waiting there.

'I beg your pardon, sir,' the man said from round the doorway; 'but here's the note from Mr Downe that you didn't take. He called just after you went out, and as he couldn't wait, he wrote this on your study-table.'

He handed in the letter – no black-bordered one now, but a practical-looking note in the well-known writing of the solicitor.

'DEAR BARNET' – it ran – 'Perhaps you will be prepared for the information I am about to give – that Lucy Savile and myself are going to be married this morning. I have hitherto said nothing as to my intention to any of my friends, for reasons which I am sure you will fully appreciate. The crisis has been brought about by her expressing her intention to join her brother in India. I then discovered that I could not do without her.

'It is to be quite a private wedding; but it is my particular wish that you come down here quietly at ten, and go to church with us; it will add greatly to the pleasure I shall experience in the ceremony, and, I believe, to Lucy's also. I have called on you very early to make the request, in the belief that I should find you at home; but you are beforehand with me in your early rising.
– Yours sincerely,   C. DOWNE.'

'Need I wait, sir?' said the servant after a dead silence.

'That will do, William. No answer,' said Barnet calmly.

When the man had gone Barnet re-read the letter. Turning eventually to the wall-papers, which he had been at such pains to select, he deliberately tore them into halves and quarters, and threw them into the empty fireplace. Then he went out of the house, locked the door, and stood in the front awhile. Instead of returning into the town, he went down the harbour-road and thoughtfully lingered about by the sea, near the spot where the body of Downe's late wife had been found and brought ashore.

Barnet was a man with a rich capacity for misery, and there is no doubt that he exercised it to its fullest extent now. The events that had, as it were, dashed themselves together into one half-hour of this day showed that curious refinement of cruelty in their arrangement which often proceeds from the bosom of the whimsical god at other times known as blind Circumstance. That his few minutes of hope, between the reading of the first and second letters, had carried him to extraordinary heights of rapture was proved by the immensity of his suffering now. The sun blazing into his face would have shown a close watcher that a horizontal line, which he had never noticed before, but which was never to be gone thereafter, was somehow gradually forming itself in the smooth of his forehead. His eyes, of a light hazel, had a curious look which can only be described by the word bruised; the sorrow that looked from them being largely mixed with the surprise of a man taken unawares.

The secondary particulars of his present position, too, were odd enough, though for some time they appeared to engage little of his attention. Not a soul in the town knew, as yet, of his wife's death; and he almost owed Downe the kindness of not publishing it till the day was over: the conjuncture, taken with that which had accompanied the death of Mrs Downe, being so singular as to be quite sufficient to darken the pleasure of the impressible solicitor to a cruel extent, if made known to him. But as Barnet could not set out on his journey to London, where his wife lay, for some hours (there being at this date no railway within a distance of eighty miles),[26] no great reason existed why he should leave the town.

Impulse in all its forms characterized Barnet, and when he heard the distant clock strike the hour of ten his feet began to carry him up the harbour-road with the manner of a man who must do something to bring himself to life. He passed Lucy Savile's old house, his own new one, and came in view of the church. Now he gave a perceptible start, and his mechanical condition went away. Before the church-gate were a couple of carriages, and Barnet then could perceive that the marriage between Downe and Lucy was at that moment being solemnized within. A feeling of sudden, proud self-confidence, an indocile wish to walk unmoved in spite of grim environments, plainly possessed him, and when he reached the wicket-gate he turned in without apparent effort. Pacing up the paved footway, he entered the church and stood for a while in the nave passage. A group of people was standing round the vestry door; Barnet advanced through these and stepped into the vestry.

There they were, busily signing their names. Seeing Downe about to look round, Barnet averted his somewhat disturbed face for a second or two; when he turned again front to front he was calm and quite smiling: it was a creditable triumph over himself, and deserved to be remembered in his native town. He greeted Downe heartily, offering his congratulations.

It seemed as if Barnet expected a half-guilty look upon Lucy's face; but no, save the natural flush and flurry engendered by the service just performed, there was nothing whatever in her bearing which showed a disturbed mind: her grey-brown eyes carried in them now as at other times the well-known expression of common-sensed rectitude which never went so far as to touch on hardness. She shook hands with him, and Downe said warmly, 'I wish you could have come sooner: I called on purpose to ask you. You'll drive back with us now?'

'No, no,' said Barnet; 'I am not at all prepared; but I thought I would look in upon you for a moment, even though I had not time to go home and dress. I'll stand back and see you pass out, and observe the effect of the spectacle upon myself as one of the public.'

Then Lucy and her husband laughed, and Barnet laughed and retired; and the quiet little party went gliding down the nave and towards the porch, Lucy's new silk dress sweeping with a smart rustle round the base-mouldings of the ancient font,[27] and Downe's little daughters following in a state of round-eyed interest in their position, and that of Lucy, their teacher and friend.

So Downe was comforted after his Emily's death, which had taken place twelve months, two weeks, and three days before that time.

When the two flys had driven off and the spectators had vanished, Barnet followed to the door, and went out into the sun. He took no more trouble to preserve a spruce exterior; his step was unequal, hesitating, almost convulsive; and the slight changes of colour which went on in his face seemed refracted from some inward flame. In the churchyard he became pale as a summer cloud, and finding it not easy to proceed he sat down on one of the tombstones and supported his head with his hand.

Hard by was a sexton filling up a grave which he had not found time to finish on the previous evening. Observing Barnet, he went up to him, and recognizing him, said, 'Shall I help you home, sir?'

'Oh no, thank you,' said Barnet, rousing himself and standing up. The sexton returned to his grave, followed by Barnet, who, after watching him awhile, stepped into the grave, now nearly filled, and helped to tread in the earth.

The sexton apparently thought his conduct a little singular, but he made no observation, and when the grave was full, Barnet suddenly stopped, looked far away, and with a decided step proceeded to the gate and vanished. The sexton rested on his shovel and looked after him for a few moments, and then began banking up the mound.

In those short minutes of treading in the dead man Barnet had formed a design, but what it was the inhabitants of that town did not for some long time imagine. He went home, wrote several letters of business, called on his lawyer, an old man of the same place who had been the legal adviser of Barnet's father before him, and during the evening overhauled a large quantity of letters and other documents in his possession. By eleven o'clock the heap of papers in and before Barnet's grate had reached formidable dimensions, and he began to burn them. This, owing to their quantity, it was not so easy to do as he had expected, and he sat long into the night to complete the task.

The next morning Barnet departed for London, leaving a note for Downe to inform him of Mrs Barnet's sudden death, and that he was gone to bury her; but when a thrice-sufficient time for that purpose had elapsed, he was not seen again in his accustomed walks, or in his new house, or in his old one. He was gone for good, nobody knew whither. It was soon discovered that he had empowered his lawyer to dispose of all his property, real and personal, in the borough, and pay in the proceeds to the account of an unknown person at one of the large London banks. The person was by some supposed to be himself under an assumed name; but few, if any, had certain knowledge of that fact.

The elegant new residence was sold with the rest of his possessions; and its purchaser was no other than Downe, now a thriving man in the borough, and one whose growing family and new wife required more roomy accommodation than was afforded by the little house up the narrow side street. Barnet's old habitation was bought by the trustees of the Congregational Baptist body in that town, who pulled down the time-honoured dwelling and built a new chapel on its site.[28] By the time the last hour of that, to Barnet, eventful year had chimed, every vestige of him had disappeared from the precincts of his native place, and the name became extinct in the borough of Port-Bredy, after having been a living force therein for more than two hundred years.

IX

Twenty-one years and six months do not pass without setting a mark even upon durable stone and triple brass: upon humanity such a period works nothing less than transformation. In Barnet's old birthplace vivacious young children with bones like india-rubber had grown up to be stable men and women, men and women had dried in the skin, stiffened, withered, and sunk into decrepitude; while selections from every class had been consigned to the outlying cemetery. Of inorganic differences the greatest was that a railway had invaded the town, tying it on to a main line at a junction a dozen miles off. Barnet's house on the harbour-road, once so insistently new, had acquired a respectable mellowness, with ivy, Virginia creepers, lichens, damp patches, and even constitutional infirmities of its own like its elder fellows. Its architecture, once so very improved and modern, had already become stale in style, without having reached the dignity of being old-fashioned. Trees about the harbour-road had increased in circumference or disappeared under the saw; while the church had had such a tremend-ous practical joke played upon it by some facetious restorer or other as to be scarce recognizable by its dearest old friends.[29]

During this long interval George Barnet had never once been seen or heard of in the town of his fathers.

It was the evening of a market-day, and some half-dozen middle-aged farmers and dairymen were lounging round the bar of the Black-Bull Hotel, occasionally dropping a remark to each other, and less frequently to the two barmaids who stood within the pewter-topped counter in a perfunctory attitude of attention, these latter sighing and making a private observation to one another at odd intervals, on more interesting experiences than the present.

'Days get shorter,' said one of the dairymen, as he looked towards the street, and noticed that the lamplighter was passing by.

The farmers merely acknowledged by their countenances the pro-priety of this remark, and finding that nobody else spoke, one of the barmaids said 'yes' in a tone of painful duty.

'Come fair-day we shall have to light up before we start for home-along.'

'That's true,' his neighbour conceded, with a gaze of blankness.

'And after that we shan't see much further difference all's winter.'

The rest were not unwilling to go even so far as this.

The barmaid sighed again, and raised one of her hands from the counter on which they rested to scratch the smallest surface of her face with the smallest of her fingers. She looked towards the door, and presently remarked, 'I think I hear the 'bus coming in from station.'

The eyes of the dairymen and farmers turned to the glass door dividing the hall from the porch, and in a minute or two the omnibus drew up outside. Then there was a lumbering down of luggage, and then a man came into the hall, followed by a porter with a portmanteau on his poll, which he deposited on a bench.

The stranger was an elderly person, with curly ashen-white hair, a deeply-creviced outer corner to each eyelid, and a countenance baked by innumerable suns to the colour of terra-cotta, its hue and that of his hair contrasting like heat and cold respectively. He walked meditatively and gently, like one who was fearful of disturbing his own mental equilibrium. But whatever lay at the bottom of his breast had evidently made him so accustomed to its situation there that it caused him little practical inconvenience.

He paused in silence while, with his dubious eyes fixed on the barmaids, he seemed to consider himself. In a moment or two he addressed them, and asked to be accommodated for the night. As he waited he looked curiously round the hall, but said nothing. As soon as invited he disappeared up the staircase, preceded by a chambermaid and candle, and followed by a lad with his trunk. Not a soul had recognized him.

A quarter of an hour later, when the farmers and dairymen had driven off to their homesteads in the country, he came downstairs, took a biscuit and one glass of wine, and walked out into the town, where the radiance from the shop-windows had grown so in volume of late years as to flood with cheerfulness every standing cart, barrow, stall, and idler that occupied the wayside, whether shabby or genteel. His chief interest at present seemed to lie in the names painted over the shop-fronts and on doorways, as far as they were visible; these now differed to an ominous extent from what they had been one-and-twenty years before.

The traveller passed on till he came to the bookseller's, where he looked in through the glass door. A fresh-faced young man was standing behind the counter, otherwise the shop was empty. The grey-haired observer entered, asked for some periodical by way of paying for his standing, and with his elbow on the counter began to turn over the pages he had bought, though that he read nothing was obvious.

At length he said, 'Is old Mr Watkins still alive?' in a voice which had a curious youthful cadence in it even now.

'My father is dead, sir,' said the young man.

'Ah, I am sorry to hear it,' said the stranger. 'But it is so many years since I last visited this town that I could hardly expect it should be otherwise.' After a short silence he continued – 'And is the firm of Barnet, Browse, and Company still in existence? – they used to be large flax-merchants and twine-spinners here?'

'The firm is still going on, sir, but they have dropped the name of Barnet. I believe that was a sort of fancy name – at least, I never knew of any living Barnet. 'Tis now Browse and Co.'

'And does Andrew Jones still keep on as architect?'

'He's dead, sir.'

'And the vicar of St Mary's – Mr Melrose?'

'He's been dead a great many years.'

'Dear me!' He paused yet longer, and cleared his voice. 'Is Mr Downe, the solicitor, still in practice?'

'No, sir, he's dead. He died about seven years ago.'

Here it was a longer silence still; and an attentive observer would have noticed that the paper in the stranger's hand increased its imperceptible tremor to a visible shake. The grey-haired gentleman noticed it himself, and rested the paper on the counter. 'Is *Mrs* Downe still alive?' he asked, closing his lips firmly as soon as the words were out of his mouth, and dropping his eyes.

'Yes, sir, she's alive and well. She's living at the old place.'

'In East Street?'

'Oh no; at Château Ringdale. I believe it has been in the family for some generations.'

'She lives with her children, perhaps?'

'No; she has no children of her own. There were some Miss Downes; I think they were Mr Downe's daughters by a former wife; but they are married and living in other parts of the town. Mrs Downe lives alone.'

'Quite alone?'

'Yes, sir; quite alone.'

The newly-arrived gentleman went back to the hotel and dined; after which he made some change in his dress, shaved back his beard to the fashion that had prevailed twenty years earlier, when he was young and interesting, and once more emerging, bent his steps in the direction of the harbour-road. Just before getting to the point where the pavement ceased and the houses isolated themselves, he overtook a shambling, stooping, unshaven man, who at first sight appeared like a professional tramp, his shoulders having a perceptible greasiness[30] as they passed under the gaslight. Each pedestrian momentarily turned and regarded the other, and the tramp-like gentleman started back.

'Good – why – is that Mr Barnet? 'Tis Mr Barnet, surely!'

'Yes; and you are Charlson?'

'Yes – ah – you notice my appearance. The Fates have rather ill-used me. By the bye, that fifty pounds. I never paid it, did I? . . . But I was not ungrateful!' Here the stooping man laid one hand emphatically in the palm of the other. I gave you a chance, Mr George Barnet, which many men would have thought full value received – the chance to marry your Lucy. As far as the world[31] was concerned, your wife was a *drowned woman*, hey?'

'Heaven forbid all that, Charlson!'

'Well, well, 'twas a wrong way of showing gratitude, I suppose. And now a drop of something to drink for old acquaintance sake! And Mr Barnet, she's again free – there's a chance now if you care for it – ha, ha!' And the speaker pushed his tongue into his hollow cheek and slanted his eye in the old fashion.

'I know all,' said Barnet quickly; and slipping a small present into the hands of the needy, saddening man, he stepped ahead and was soon in the outskirts of the town.

He reached the harbour-road, and paused before the entrance to a well-known house. It was so highly bosomed in trees and shrubs planted since the erection of the building that one would scarcely have recognized the spot as that which had been a mere neglected slope till chosen as a site for a dwelling. He opened the swing-gate, closed it noiselessly, and gently moved into the semicircular drive, which remained exactly as it had been marked out by Barnet on the morning when Lucy Savile ran in to thank him for procuring her the post of governess to Downe's children. But the growth of trees and bushes which revealed itself at every step was beyond all expectation; sun-proof and moon-proof bowers vaulted the walks, and the walls of the house were uniformly bearded with creeping plants as high as the first-floor windows.

After lingering for a few minutes in the dusk of the bending boughs, the visitor rang the doorbell, and on the servant appearing, he announced himself as 'an old friend of Mrs Downe's.'

The hall was lighted, but not brightly, the gas being turned low, as if visitors were rare. There was a stagnation in the dwelling: it seemed to be waiting. Could it really be waiting for him? The partitions which had been probed by Barnet's walking-stick when the mortar was green, were now quite brown with the antiquity of their varnish, and the ornamental woodwork of the staircase, which had glistened with a pale yellow newness when first erected, was now of a rich wine-colour. During the servant's absence the following colloquy could be dimly heard through the nearly closed door of the drawing-room.

'He didn't give his name?'

'He only said "an old friend", ma'am.'

'What kind of gentleman is he?'

'A staidish gentleman, with grey hair.'

The voice of the second speaker seemed to affect the listener greatly. After a pause, the lady said, 'Very well, I will see him.'

And the stranger was shown in face to face with the Lucy who had once been Lucy Savile. The round cheek of that formerly young lady had, of course, alarmingly flattened its curve in her modern representative; a pervasive greyness overspread her once dark brown hair, like morning rime on heather. The parting down the middle was wide and jagged; once it had been a thin white line, a narrow crevice between two high banks of shade. But there was still enough left to form a handsome knob behind, and some curls beneath inwrought with a few hairs like silver wires were very becoming. In her eyes the only modification was that their originally mild rectitude of expression had become a little more stringent than heretofore. Yet she was still girlish – a girl who had been gratuitously weighted by destiny with a burden of five-and-forty years instead of her proper twenty.

'Lucy, don't you know me?' he said, when the servant had closed the door.

'I knew you the instant I saw you!' she returned cheerfully. 'I don't know why, but I always thought you would come back to your old town again.'

She gave him her hand, and then they sat down. 'They said you were dead,' continued Lucy, 'but I never thought so. We should have heard of it for certain if you had been.'

'It is a very long time since we met.'

'Yes; what you must have seen, Mr Barnet, in all these roving years, in comparison with what I have seen in this quiet place!' Her face grew more serious. 'You know my husband has been dead a long time? I am a lonely old woman now, considering what I have been; though Mr Downe's daughters – all married – manage to keep me pretty cheerful.'

'And I am a lonely old man, and have been any time these twenty years.'

'But where have you kept yourself? And why did you go off so mysteriously?'

'Well, Lucy, I have kept myself a little in America, and a little in Australia, a little in India, a little at the Cape, and so on; I have not stayed in any place for a long time, as it seems to me, and yet more than twenty years have flown. But when people get to my age two years go like one! – Your second question, why did I go away so mysteriously, is surely not necessary. You guessed why, didn't you?'

'No, I never once guessed,' she said simply; 'nor did Charles, nor did anybody, as far as I know.'

'Well, indeed! Now think it over again, and then look at me, and say if you can't guess?'

She looked him in the face with an inquiring smile. 'Surely not because of me?' she said, pausing at the commencement of surprise.

Barnet nodded, and smiled back again; but his smile was sadder than hers.

'Because I married Charles?' she asked.

'Yes; solely because you married him on the day I was free to ask you to marry me. My wife died four-and-twenty hours before you went to church with Downe. The fixing of my journey at that particular moment was because of her funeral; but once away, I knew I should have no inducement to come back, and took my steps accordingly.'

Her face assumed an aspect of gentle reflection, and she looked up and down his form with great interest in her eyes. 'I never thought of it!' she said. 'I knew, of course, that you had once implied some warmth of feeling towards me, but I concluded that it passed off. And I have always been under the impression that your wife was alive at the time of my marriage. Was it not stupid of me! – But you will have some tea or something? I have never dined late, you know, since my husband's death. I have got into the way of making a regular meal of tea. You will have some tea with me, will you not?'

The travelled man assented quite readily, and tea was brought in. They sat and chatted over the meal, regardless of the flying hour. 'Well, well!' said Barnet presently, as for the first time he leisurely surveyed the room; 'how like it all is, and yet how different! Just where your piano stands was a board on a couple of trestles, bearing the patterns of wall-papers, when I was last here. I was choosing them – standing in this way, as it might be. Then my servant came in at the door, and handed me a note, so. It was from Downe, and announced that you were just going to be married to him. I chose no more wall-papers – tore up all those I had selected, and left the house. I never entered it again till now.'

'Ah, at last I understand it all,' she murmured.

They had both risen and gone to the fireplace. The mantel came almost on a level with her shoulder, which gently rested against it, and Barnet laid his hand upon the shelf close beside her shoulder. 'Lucy,' he said, 'better late than never. Will you marry me now?'

She started back, and the surprise which was so obvious in her wrought even greater surprise in him that it should be so. It was difficult to believe that she had been quite blind to the situation, and yet all reason and common sense went to prove that she was not acting.

'You take me quite unawares by such a question!' she said, with a feverish[32] laugh of uneasiness. It was the first time she had shown any embarrassment at all. 'Why,' she added, 'I couldn't marry you for the world.'

'Not after all this! Why not?'

'It is – I would – I really think I may say it – I would upon the whole rather marry you, Mr Barnet, than any other man I have ever met, if I ever dreamed of marriage again. But I don't dream of it – it is quite out of my thoughts; I have not the least intention of marrying again.'

'But – on my account – couldn't you alter your plans a little? Come!'

'Dear Mr Barnet,' she said with a little flutter, 'I would on your account if on anybody's in existence. But you don't know in the least what it is you are asking – such an impracticable thing – I won't say ridiculous, of course, because I see that you are really in earnest, and earnestness is never ridiculous to my mind.'

'Well, yes,' said Barnet, more slowly, dropping her hand, which he had taken at the moment of pleading, 'I am in earnest. The resolve, two months ago, at the Cape, to come back once more was, it is true, rather sudden, and as I see now, not well considered. But I am in earnest in asking.'

'And I in declining. With all good feeling and all kindness, let me say that I am quite opposed to the idea of marrying a second time.'

'Well, no harm has been done,' he answered, with the same subdued and tender humorousness that he had shown on such occasions in early life. 'If you really won't accept me, I must put up with it, I suppose.' His eye fell on the clock as he spoke. 'Had you any notion that it was so late?' he asked. 'How absorbed I have been!'

She accompanied him to the hall, helped him to put on his overcoat, and let him out of the house herself.

'Good night,' said Barnet, on the doorstep, as the lamp shone in his face. 'You are not offended with me?'

'Certainly not. Nor you with me?'

'I'll consider whether I am or not,' he pleasantly replied. 'Good night.'

She watched him safely through the gate; and when his footsteps had died away upon the road, closed the door softly and returned to the room. Here the modest widow long pondered his speeches, with eyes dropped to an unusually low level. Barnet's urbanity under the blow of her refusal greatly impressed her. After having his long period of probation rendered useless by her decision, he had shown no anger, and philosophically taken her words, as if he deserved no better ones. It was very gentlemanly of him, certainly; it was more than gentlemanly; it was heroic and grand. The more she meditated, the more she questioned the virtue of her conduct in checking him so peremptorily; and went to her bedroom in a mood of dissatisfaction. On looking in the glass she was reminded that there was not so much remaining of her former beauty as to make his frank declaration an impulsive natural homage to her cheeks and eyes; it must undoubtedly have arisen from an old staunch feeling of his, deserving tenderest consideration. She recalled to her mind with much pleasure that he had told her he was staying at the Black-Bull Hotel; so that if, after waiting a day or two, he should not, in his modesty, call again, she might then send him a nice little note. To alter her views for the present was far from her intention; but she would allow herself to be induced to reconsider the case, as any generous woman ought to do.

The morrow came and passed, and Mr Barnet did not drop in. At every knock, light youthful hues flew across her cheek; and she was abstracted in the presence of her other visitors. In the evening she walked about the house, not knowing what to do with herself; the conditions of existence seemed totally different from those which ruled only four-and-twenty short hours ago. What had been at first a tantalizing elusive sentiment was getting acclimatized within her as a definite hope, and her person was so informed by that emotion that she might almost have stood as its emblematical representative by the time the clock struck ten. In short, an interest in Barnet precisely resembling that of her early youth led her present heart to belie her yesterday's words to him, and she longed to see him again.

The next day she walked out early, thinking she might meet him in the street. The growing beauty of her romance absorbed her, and she went from the street to the fields, and from the fields to the shore, without any consciousness of distance, till reminded by her weariness that she could go no farther. He had nowhere appeared. In the evening she took a step which under the circumstances seemed justifiable; she wrote a note to him at the hotel, inviting him to tea with her at seven[33] precisely, and signing her note 'Lucy'.

In a quarter of an hour the messenger came back. Mr Barnet had left the hotel early in the morning of the day before, but he had stated that he would probably return in the course of the week.

The note was sent back, to be given to him immediately on his arrival.

There was no sign from the inn that this desired event had occurred, either on the next day or the day following. On both nights she had been restless, and had scarcely slept half-an-hour.[34]

On the Saturday, putting off all diffidence, Lucy went herself to the Black-Bull, and questioned the staff closely.

Mr Barnet had cursorily remarked when leaving that he might return on the Thursday or Friday, but they were directed not to reserve a room for him unless he should write.

He had left no address.

Lucy sorrowfully took back her note, went home, and resolved to wait.

She did wait – years and years – but Barnet never reappeared.

Among the few features of agricultural England which retain an appearance but little modified by the lapse of centuries, may be reckoned the high, grassy, and furzy downs, coombs, or ewe-leases, as they are indifferently called, that fill a large area of certain counties in the south and south-west. If any mark of human occupation is met with hereon, it usually takes the form of the solitary cottage of some shepherd.

Fifty years ago[1] such a lonely cottage stood on such a down, and may possibly be standing there now. In spite of its loneliness, however, the spot, by actual measurement, was not more than five miles from a county-town. Yet that affected it little. Five miles of irregular upland, during the long inimical seasons, with their sleets, snows, rains, and mists, afford withdrawing space enough to isolate a Timon or a Nebuchadnezzar;[2] much less, in fair weather, to please that less repellent tribe, the poets, philosophers, artists, and others who 'conceive and meditate of pleasant things'.[3]

Some old earthen camp or barrow, some clump of trees, at least some starved fragment of ancient hedge, is usually taken advantage of in the erection of these forlorn dwellings. But, in the present case, such a kind of shelter had been disregarded. Higher Crowstairs,[4] as the house was called, stood quite detached and undefended. The only reason for its precise situation seemed to be the crossing of two footpaths at right angles hard by, which may have crossed there and thus for a good five hundred years. Hence the house was exposed to the elements on all sides. But, though the wind up here blew unmistakably when it did blow, and the rain hit hard whenever it fell, the various weathers of the winter season were not quite so formidable on the coomb as they were imagined to be by dwellers on low ground. The raw rimes were not so pernicious as in the hollows, and the frosts were scarcely so severe. When the shepherd and his family who tenanted the house were pitied for their sufferings from the exposure, they said that upon the whole they were less inconvenienced by 'wuzzes and flames' (hoarses and phlegms) than when they had lived by the stream of a snug neighbouring valley.

The night of March 28, 182–, was precisely one of the nights that were wont to call forth these expressions of commiseration. The level rainstorm smote walls, slopes, and hedges like the clothyard shafts of Senlac and Crecy.[5] Such sheep and outdoor animals as had no shelter stood with their buttocks to the winds; while the tails of little birds trying to roost on some scraggy thorn were blown inside-out like umbrellas. The gable-end of the cottage was stained with wet, and the eavesdroppings flapped against the wall. Yet never was commiseration for the shepherd more misplaced. For that cheerful rustic was entertaining a large party in glorification of the christening of his second girl.

The guests had arrived before the rain began to fall, and they were all now assembled in the chief or living room of the dwelling. A glance into the apartment at eight o'clock on this eventful evening would have resulted in the opinion that it was as cosy and comfortable a nook as could be wished for in boisterous weather. The calling of its inhabitant was proclaimed by a number of highly-polished sheep-crooks without stems that were hung ornamentally over the fireplace, the curl of each shining crook varying from the antiquated type engraved in the patriarchal pictures of old family Bibles to the most approved fashion of the last local sheep-fair. The room was lighted by half a dozen candles, having wicks only a trifle smaller than the grease which enveloped them, in candlesticks that were never used but at high-days, holy-days, and family feasts. The lights were scattered about the room, two of them standing on the chimney-piece. This position of candles was in itself significant. Candles on the chimney-piece always meant a party.

On the hearth, in front of a back-brand to give substance, blazed a fire of thorns, that crackled 'like the laughter of the fool'.[6]

Nineteen persons were gathered here. Of these, five women, wearing gowns of various bright hues, sat in chairs along the wall; girls shy and not shy filled the window-bench; four men, including Charley

Jake the hedge-carpenter, Elijah New the parish-clerk, and John Pitcher, a neighbouring dairyman, the shepherd's father-in-law, lolled in the settle; a young man and maid, who were blushing over tentative *pourparlers* on a life-companionship, sat beneath the corner-cupboard; and an elderly engaged man of fifty or upward moved restlessly about from spots where his betrothed was not to the spot where she was. Enjoyment was pretty general, and so much the more prevailed in being unhampered by conventional restrictions. Absolute confidence in each other's good opinion begat perfect ease, while the finishing stroke of manner, amounting to a truly princely serenity, was lent to the majority by the absence of any expression or trait denoting that they wished to get on in the world, enlarge their minds, or do any eclipsing thing whatever – which nowadays so generally nips the bloom and *bonhomie* of all except the two extremes of the social scale.

Shepherd Fennel had married well, his wife being a dairyman's daughter from the valley below, who brought fifty guineas in her pocket – and kept them there, till they should be required for ministering to the needs of a coming family. This frugal woman had been somewhat exercised as to the character that should be given to the gathering. A sit-still party had its advantages; but an undisturbed position of ease in chairs and settles was apt to lead on the men to such an unconscionable deal of toping that they would sometimes fairly drink the house dry. A dancing-party was the alternative; but this, while avoiding the foregoing objection on the score of good drink, had a counterbalancing disadvantage in the matter of good victuals, the ravenous appetites engendered by the exercise causing immense havoc in the buttery. Shepherdess Fennel fell back upon the intermediate plan of mingling short dances with short periods of talk and singing, so as to hinder any ungovernable rage in either. But this scheme was entirely confined to her own gentle mind: the shepherd himself was in the mood to exhibit the most reckless phases of hospitality.

The fiddler was a boy of those parts,[7] about twelve years of age, who had a wonderful dexterity in jigs and reels, though his fingers were so small and short as to necessitate a constant shifting for the high notes, from which he scrambled back to the first position with sounds not of unmixed purity of tone. At seven the shrill tweedle-dee of this youngster had begun, accompanied by a booming ground-bass from Elijah New, the parish-clerk, who had thoughtfully brought with him his favourite musical instrument, the serpent. Dancing was instantaneous, Mrs Fennel privately enjoining the players on no account to let the dance exceed the length of a quarter of an hour.

But Elijah and the boy, in the excitement of their position, quite forgot the injunction. Moreover, Oliver Giles, a man of seventeen, one of the dancers, who was enamoured of his partner, a fair girl of thirty-three rolling years, had recklessly handed a new crown-piece to the musicians, as a bribe to keep going as long as they had muscle and wind. Mrs Fennel, seeing the steam begin to generate on the countenances of her guests, crossed over and touched the fiddler's elbow and put her hand on the serpent's mouth. But they took no notice, and fearing she might lose her character of genial hostess if she were to interfere too markedly, she retired and sat down helpless. And so the dance whizzed on with cumulative fury, the performers moving in their planet-like courses, direct and retrograde, from apogee to perigee, till the hand of the well-kicked clock at the bottom of the room had travelled over the circumference of an hour.

While these cheerful events were in course of enactment within Fennel's pastoral dwelling, an incident having considerable bearing on the party had occurred in the gloomy night without. Mrs Fennel's concern about the growing fierceness of the dance corresponded in point of time with the ascent of a human figure to the solitary hill of Higher Crowstairs from the direction of the distant town. This personage strode on through the rain without a pause, following the little-worn path which, farther on in its course, skirted the shepherd's cottage.

It was nearly the time of full moon, and on this account, though the sky was lined with a uniform sheet of dripping cloud, ordinary objects out of doors were readily visible. The sad wan light revealed the lonely pedestrian to be a man of supple frame; his gait suggested that he had somewhat passed the period of perfect and instinctive agility, though not so far as to be otherwise than rapid of motion when occasion required. In point of fact, he might have been about forty years of age. He appeared tall, but a recruiting sergeant, or other person accustomed to the judging of men's heights by the eye, would have discerned that this was chiefly owing to his gauntness, and that he was not more than five-feet-eight or nine.

Notwithstanding the regularity of his tread, there was caution in it, as in that of one who mentally feels his way; and despite the fact that it was not a black coat nor a dark garment of any sort that he wore, there was something about him which suggested that he naturally belonged to the black-coated tribes of men. His clothes were of fustian, and his boots hobnailed, yet in his progress he showed not the mud-accustomed bearing of hobnailed and fustianed peasantry.

By the time that he had arrived abreast of the shepherd's premises the rain came down, or rather came along, with yet more determined violence. The outskirts of the little settlement[8] partially broke the force of wind and rain, and this induced him to stand still. The most salient of the shepherd's domestic erections was an empty sty at the forward corner of his hedgeless garden, for in these latitudes the principle of masking the homelier features of your establishment by a conventional frontage was unknown. The traveller's eye was attracted to this small building by the pallid shine of the wet slates that covered it. He turned aside, and, finding it empty, stood under the pent-roof for shelter.

While he stood, the boom of the serpent within the adjacent house, and the lesser strains of the fiddler, reached the spot as an accompaniment to the surging hiss of the flying rain on the sod, its louder beating on the cabbage-leaves of the garden, on the eight or ten beehives just discernible by the path, and its dripping from the eaves into a row of buckets and pans that had been placed under the walls of the cottage. For at Higher Crowstairs, as at all such elevated domiciles, the grand difficulty of housekeeping was an insufficiency of water; and a casual rainfall was utilized by turning out, as catchers, every utensil that the house contained. Some queer stories might be told of the contrivances for economy in suds and dish-waters that are absolutely necessitated in upland habitations during the droughts of summer. But at this season there were no such exigencies: a mere acceptance of what the skies bestowed was sufficient for an abundant store.

At last the notes of the serpent ceased and the house was silent. This cessation of activity aroused the solitary pedestrian from the reverie into which he had lapsed, and, emerging from the shed, with an apparently new intention, he walked up the path to the house-door. Arrived here, his first act was to kneel down on a large stone beside the row of vessels, and to drink a copious draught from one of them. Having quenched his thirst he rose and lifted his hand to knock, but paused with his eye upon the panel. Since the dark surface of the wood revealed absolutely nothing, it was evident that he must be mentally looking through the door, as if he wished to measure thereby all the possibilities that a house of this sort might include, and how they might bear upon the question of his entry.

In his indecision he turned and surveyed the scene around. Not a soul was anywhere visible. The garden-path stretched downward from his feet, gleaming like the track of a snail; the roof of the little well (mostly dry), the well cover, the top rail of the garden-gate, were varnished with the same dull liquid glaze; while, far away in the vale, a faint whiteness of more than usual extent showed that the rivers were high in the meads. Beyond all this winked a few bleared lamplights through the beating drops, lights that denoted the situation of the county-town from which he had appeared to come. The absence of all notes of life in that direction seemed to clinch his intentions, and he knocked at the door.

Within, a desultory chat had taken the place of movement and musical sound. The hedge-carpenter was suggesting a song to the company, which nobody just then was inclined to undertake, so that the knock afforded a not unwelcome diversion.

'Walk in!' said the shepherd promptly.

The latch clicked upward, and out of the night our pedestrian appeared upon the door-mat. The shepherd arose, snuffed two of the nearest candles, and turned to look at him.

Their light disclosed that the stranger was dark in complexion and not unprepossessing as to feature. His hat, which for a moment he did not remove, hung low over his eyes, without concealing that they were large, open, and determined, moving with a flash rather than a glance round the room. He seemed pleased with the survey, and, baring his shaggy head, said, in a rich deep voice, 'The rain is so heavy, friends, that I ask leave to come in and rest awhile.'

'To be sure, stranger,' said the shepherd. 'And faith, you've been lucky in choosing your time, for we are having a bit of a fling for a glad cause – though, to be sure, a man could hardly wish that glad cause to happen more than once a year.'

'Nor less,' spoke up a woman. 'For 'tis best to get your family over and done with, as soon as you can, so as to be all the earlier out of the fag o't.'

'And what may be this glad cause?' asked the stranger.

'A birth and christening,' said the shepherd.

The stranger hoped his host might not be made unhappy either by too many or too few of such episodes, and being invited by a gesture to a pull at the mug, he readily acquiesced. His manner, which, before entering, had been so dubious, was now altogether that of a careless and candid man.

'Late to be traipsing athwart this coomb – hey?' said the engaged man of fifty.

'Late it is, master, as you say. – I'll take a seat in the chimney-corner, if you have nothing to urge against it, ma'am; for I am a little moist on the side that was next the rain.'

Mrs Shepherd Fennel assented, and made room for the self-invited comer, who, having got completely inside the chimney-corner, stretched out his legs and his arms with the expansiveness of a person quite at home.

'Yes, I am rather thin in the vamp,' he said freely, seeing that the eyes of the shepherd's wife fell upon his boots, 'and I am not well fitted either. I have had some rough times lately, and have been forced to pick up what I can get in the way of wearing, but I must find a suit better fit for working-days when I reach home.'

'One of hereabouts?' she inquired.

'Not quite that – farther up the country.'

'I thought so. And so am I; and by your tongue you come from my neighbourhood.'

'But you would hardly have heard of me,' he said quickly. 'My time would be long before yours, ma'am, you see.'

This testimony to the youthfulness of his hostess had the effect of stopping her cross-examination.

'There is only one thing more wanted to make me happy,' continued the new-comer. 'And that is a little baccy, which I am sorry to say I am out of.'

'I'll fill your pipe,' said the shepherd.

'I must ask you to lend me a pipe likewise.'

'A smoker, and no pipe about ye?'

'I have dropped it somewhere on the road.'

The shepherd filled and handed him a new clay pipe, saying, as he did so, 'Hand me your baccy-box – I'll fill that too, now I am about it.'

The man went through the movement of searching his pockets.

'Lost that too?' said his entertainer, with some surprise.

'I am afraid so,' said the man with some confusion. 'Give it to me in a screw of paper.' Lighting his pipe at the candle with a suction that drew the whole flame into the bowl, he resettled himself in the corner, and bent his looks upon the faint steam from his damp legs, as if he wished to say no more.

Meanwhile the general body of guests had been taking little notice of this visitor by reason of an absorbing discussion in which they were engaged with the band about a tune for the next dance. The matter being settled, they were about to stand up, when an interruption came in the shape of another knock at the door.

At sound of the same the man in the chimney-corner took up the poker and began stirring the fire as if doing it thoroughly were the one aim of his existence; and a second time the shepherd said 'Walk in!' In a moment another man stood upon the straw-woven door-mat. He too was a stranger.

This individual was one of a type radically different from the first. There was more of the commonplace in his manner, and a certain jovial cosmopolitanism sat upon his features. He was several years older than the first arrival, his hair being slightly frosted, his eyebrows bristly, and his whiskers cut back from his cheeks. His face was rather full and flabby, and yet it was not altogether a face without power. A few grog-blossoms marked the neighbourhood of his nose. He flung back his long drab greatcoat, revealing that beneath it he wore a suit of cinder-grey shade throughout, large heavy seals, of some metal or other that would take a polish, dangling from his fob as his only personal ornament. Shaking the water-drops from his low-crowned glazed hat, he said, 'I must ask for a few minutes' shelter, comrades, or I shall be wetted to my skin before I get to Casterbridge.'

'Make yourself at home, master,' said the shepherd, perhaps a trifle less heartily than on the first occasion. Not that Fennel had the least tinge of niggardliness in his composition; but the room was far from large, spare chairs were not numerous, and damp companions were not altogether desirable[9] at close quarters for the women and girls in their bright-coloured gowns.

However, the second comer, after taking off his greatcoat, and hanging his hat on a nail in one of the ceiling-beams as if he had been specially invited to put it there, advanced and sat down at the table. This had been pushed so closely into the chimney-corner, to give all available room to the dancers, that its inner edge grazed the elbow of the man who had ensconced himself by the fire; and thus the two strangers were brought into close companionship. They nodded to each other by way of breaking the ice of unacquaintance, and the first stranger handed his neighbour the family[10] mug – a huge vessel of brown ware, having its upper edge worn away like a threshold by the rub of whole generations of thirsty lips that had gone the way of all flesh, and bearing the following inscription burnt upon its rotund side in yellow letters: –

THERE iS NO FUN
UNTiLL i CUM.

The other man, nothing loth, raised the mug to his lips, and drank on, and on, and on – till a curious blueness overspread the countenance of the shepherd's wife, who had regarded with no little surprise the first stranger's free offer to the second of what did not belong to him to dispense.

'I knew it!' said the toper to the shepherd with much satisfaction. 'When I walked up your garden before coming in, and saw the hives all of a row, I said to myself, "Where there's bees there's honey, and where there's honey there's mead." But mead of such a truly comfortable sort as this I really didn't expect to meet in my older days.' He took yet another pull at the mug, till it assumed an ominous elevation.

'Glad you enjoy it!' said the shepherd warmly.

'It is goodish mead,' assented Mrs Fennel with an absence of enthusiasm, which seemed to say that it was possible to buy praise for one's cellar at too heavy a price. 'It is trouble enough to make – and really I hardly think we shall make any more. For honey sells well, and we ourselves can make shift with a drop o' small mead and metheglin for common use from the comb-washings.'

'Oh, but you'll never have the heart!' reproachfully cried the stranger in cinder-grey, after taking up the mug a third time and setting it down empty. 'I love mead, when 'tis old like this, as I love to go to church o' Sundays, or to relieve the needy any day of the week.'

'Ha, ha, ha!' said the man in the chimney-corner, who, in spite of the taciturnity induced by the pipe of tobacco, could not or would not refrain from this slight testimony to his comrade's humour.

Now the old mead of those days, brewed of the purest first-year or maiden honey,[11] four pounds to the gallon – with its due complement of white of eggs, cinnamon, ginger, cloves, mace, rosemary, yeast, and processes of working, bottling, and cellaring – tasted remarkably strong; but it did not taste so strong as it actually was. Hence, presently, the stranger in cinder-grey at the table, moved by its creeping influence, unbuttoned his waistcoat, threw himself back in his chair, spread his legs, and made his presence felt in various ways.

'Well, well, as I say,' he resumed, 'I am going to Casterbridge, and to Casterbridge I must go. I should have been almost there by this time; but the rain drove me into your dwelling, and I'm not sorry for it.'

'You don't live in Casterbridge?' said the shepherd.

'Not as yet; though I shortly mean to move there.'

'Going to set up in trade, perhaps?'

'No, no,' said the shepherd's wife. 'It is easy to see that the gentleman is rich, and don't want to work at anything.'

The cinder-grey stranger paused, as if to consider whether he would accept that definition of himself. He presently rejected it by answering,

'Rich is not quite the word for me, dame. I do work, and I must work. And even if I only get to Casterbridge by midnight I must begin work there at eight tomorrow morning. Yes, het or wet, blow or snow, famine or sword, my day's work tomorrow must be done.'

'Poor man! Then, in spite o' seeming, you be worse off than we?' replied the shepherd's wife.

' 'Tis the nature of my trade, men and maidens. 'Tis the nature of my trade more than my poverty . . . But really and truly I must up and off, or I shan't get a lodging in the town.' However, the speaker did not move, and directly added, 'There's time for one more draught of friendship before I go; and I'd perform it at once if the mug were not dry.'

'Here's a mug o' small,' said Mrs Fennel. 'Small, we call it, though to be sure 'tis only the first wash o' the combs.'

'No,' said the stranger disdainfully. 'I won't spoil your first kindness by partaking o' your second.'

'Certainly not,' broke in Fennel. 'We don't increase and multiply every day, and I'll fill the mug again.' He went away to the dark place under the stairs where the barrel stood. The shepherdess followed him.

'Why should you do this?' she said reproachfully, as soon as they were alone. 'He's emptied it once, though it held enough for ten people; and now he's not contented wi' the small, but must needs call for more o' the strong! And a stranger unbeknown to any of us. For my part, I don't like the look o' the man at all.'

'But he's in the house, my honey; and 'tis a wet night, and a christening. Daze it, what's a cup of mead more or less? there'll be plenty more next bee-burning.'

'Very well – this time, then,' she answered, looking wistfully at the barrel. 'But what is the man's calling, and where is he one of, that he should come in and join us like this?'

'I don't know. I'll ask him again.'

The catastrophe of having the mug drained dry at one pull by the stranger in cinder-grey was effectually guarded against this time by Mrs Fennel. She poured out his allowance in a small cup, keeping the large one at a discreet distance from him. When he had tossed off his portion the shepherd renewed his inquiry about the stranger's occupation.

The latter did not immediately reply, and the man in the chimney-corner, with sudden demonstrativeness, said, 'Anybody may know my trade – I'm a wheelwright.'

'A very good trade for these parts,' said the shepherd.

'And anybody may know mine – if they've the sense to find it out,' said the stranger in cinder-grey.

'You may generally tell what a man is by his claws,' observed the hedge-carpenter, looking at his own hands. 'My fingers be as full of thorns as an old pin-cushion is of pins.'

The hands of the man in the chimney-corner instinctively sought the shade, and he gazed into the fire as he resumed his pipe. The man at the table took up the hedge-carpenter's remark, and added smartly, 'True; but the oddity of my trade is that, instead of setting a mark upon me, it sets a mark upon my customers.'

No observation being offered by anybody in elucidation of this enigma, the shepherd's wife once more called for a song. The same obstacles presented themselves as at the former time – one had no voice, another had forgotten the first verse. The stranger at the table, whose soul had now risen to a good working temperature, relieved the difficulty by exclaiming that, to start the company, he would sing himself. Thrusting one thumb into the arm-hole of his waistcoat, he waved the other hand in the air, and, with an extemporizing gaze at the shining sheep-crooks above the mantelpiece, began: –

> 'Oh my trade it is the rarest one,
>> Simple shepherds all –
> My trade is a sight to see;
> For my customers I tie, and take them up on high,
> And waft 'em to a far countree!'[12]

The room was silent when he had finished the verse – with one exception, that of the man in the chimney-corner, who, at the singer's word, 'Chorus!' joined him in a deep bass voice of musical relish –

> 'And waft 'em to a far countree!'

Oliver Giles, John Pitcher the dairyman, the parish-clerk, the engaged man of fifty, the row of young women against the wall, seemed lost in thought not of the gayest kind. The shepherd looked meditatively on the ground, the shepherdess gazed keenly at the singer, and with some suspicion; she was doubting whether this stranger were merely singing an old song from recollection, or was composing one there and then for the occasion. All were as perplexed at the obscure revelation as the guests at Belshazzar's Feast,[13] except the man in the chimney-corner, who quietly said, 'Second verse, stranger,' and smoked on.

The singer thoroughly moistened himself from his lips inwards, and went on with the next stanza as requested: –

> 'My tools are but common ones,
>> Simple shepherds all,
> My tools are no sight to see:
> A little hempen string, and a post whereon to swing,
> Are implements enough for me!'

Shepherd Fennel glanced round. There was no longer any doubt that the stranger was answering his question rhythmically. The guests one and all started back with suppressed exclamations. The young woman engaged to the man of fifty fainted half-way, and would have proceeded, but finding him wanting in alacrity for catching her she sat down trembling.

'Oh, he's the —!' whispered the people in the background, mentioning the name of an ominous public officer. 'He's come to do it. 'Tis to be at Casterbridge jail tomorrow – the man for sheep-stealing – the poor clock-maker we heard of, who used to live away at Shottsford[14] and had no work to do – Timothy Sommers, whose family were a-starving, and so he went out of Shottsford by the high-road, and took a sheep in open daylight, defying the farmer and the farmer's wife and the farmer's lad, and every man jack among 'em. He' (and they nodded towards the stranger of the deadly trade) 'is come from up the country to do it because there's not enough to do in his own county-town, and he's got the place here now our own county man's dead; he's going to live in the same cottage under the prison wall.'[15]

The stranger in cinder-grey took no notice of this whispered string of observations, but again wetted his lips. Seeing that his friend in the chimney-corner was the only one who reciprocated his joviality in any way, he held out his cup towards that appreciative comrade, who also held out his own. They clinked together, the eyes of the rest of the room hanging upon the singer's actions. He parted his lips for the third verse; but at that moment another knock was audible upon the door. This time the knock was faint and hesitating.

The company seemed scared; the shepherd looked with consternation towards the entrance, and it was with some effort that he resisted his alarmed wife's deprecatory glance, and uttered for the third time the welcoming words, 'Walk in!'

The door was gently opened, and another man stood upon the mat. He, like those who had preceded him, was a stranger. This time it was a short, small personage, of fair complexion, and dressed in a decent suit of dark clothes.

'Can you tell me the way to —?' he began; when, gazing round the room to observe the nature of the company amongst whom he had fallen, his eyes lighted on the stranger in cinder-grey. It was just at the instant when the latter, who had thrown his mind into his song with such a will that he scarcely heeded the interruption, silenced all whispers and inquiries by bursting into his third verse: –

> 'Tomorrow is my working day,
>> Simple shepherds all –
> Tomorrow is a working day for me:
> For the farmer's sheep is slain, and the lad who did it ta'en,
>> And on his soul may God ha' merc-y!'

The stranger in the chimney-corner, waving cups with the singer so heartily that his mead splashed over on the hearth, repeated in his bass voice as before: –

> 'And on his soul may God ha' merc-y!'

All this time the third stranger had been standing in the doorway. Finding now that he did not come forward or go on speaking, the guests particularly regarded him. They noticed to their surprise that he stood before them the picture of abject terror – his knees trembling, his hand shaking so violently that the door-latch by which he supported himself rattled audibly; his white lips were parted, and his eyes fixed on the merry officer of justice in the middle of the room. A moment more and he had turned, closed the door, and fled.

'What a man can it be?' said the shepherd.

The rest, between the awfulness of their late discovery and the odd conduct of this third visitor, looked as if they knew not what to think, and said nothing. Instinctively they withdrew farther and farther from the grim gentleman in their midst, whom some of them seemed to take for the Prince of Darkness himself, till they formed a remote circle, an empty space of floor being left between them and him –

'. . . circulus, cujus centrum diabolus.'[16]

The room was so silent – though there were more than twenty people in it – that nothing could be heard but the patter of the rain against the window-shutters, accompanied by the occasional hiss of a stray drop that fell down the chimney into the fire, and the steady puffing of the man in the corner, who had now resumed his pipe of long clay.

The stillness was unexpectedly broken. The distant sound of a gun reverberated through the air – apparently from the direction of the county-town.

'Be jiggered!' cried the stranger who had sung the song, jumping up.

'What does that mean?' asked several.

'A prisoner escaped from the jail – that's what it means.'

All listened. The sound was repeated, and none of them spoke but the man in the chimney-corner, who said quietly, 'I've often been told that in this county they fire a gun at such times; but I never heard it till now.'

'I wonder if it is *my* man?' murmured the personage in cinder-grey.

'Surely it is!' said the shepherd involuntarily. 'And surely we've seen him! That little man who looked in at the door by now, and quivered like a leaf when he seed ye and heard your song!'

'His teeth chattered, and the breath went out of his body,' said the dairyman.

'And his heart seemed to sink within him like a stone,' said Oliver Giles.

'And he bolted as if he'd been shot at,' said the hedge-carpenter.

'True – his teeth chattered, and his heart seemed to sink; and he bolted as if he'd been shot at,' slowly summed up the man in the chimney-corner.

'I didn't notice it,' remarked the hangman.

'We were all a-wondering what made him run off in such a fright,' faltered one of the women against the wall, 'and now 'tis explained.'

The firing of the alarm-gun went on at intervals, low and sullenly, and their suspicions became a certainty. The sinister gentleman in cinder-grey roused himself. 'Is there a constable here?' he asked in thick tones. 'If so, let him step forward.'

The engaged man of fifty stepped quavering out of the corner, his betrothed beginning to sob on the back of the chair.

'You are a sworn constable?'

'I be, sir.'

'Then pursue the criminal at once, with assistance, and bring him back here. He can't have gone far.'

'I will, sir, I will – when I've got my staff. I'll go home and get it, and come sharp here, and start in a body.'

'Staff! – never mind your staff; the man 'll be gone!'

'But I can't do nothing without my staff – can I, William, and John, and Charles Jake? No; for there's the king's royal crown a painted on en in yaller and gold, and the lion and the unicorn, so as when I raise en up and hit my prisoner, 'tis made a lawful blow thereby. I wouldn't 'tempt to take up a man without my staff – no, not I. If I hadn't the law to gie me courage, why, instead o' my taking up him he might take up me!'

'Now, I'm a king's man myself, and can give you authority enough for this,' said the formidable officer in grey. 'Now then, all of ye, be ready. Have ye any lanterns?'

'Yes – have ye any lanterns? – I demand it!' said the constable.

'And the rest of you able-bodied —'

'Able-bodied men – yes – the rest of ye!' said the constable.

'Have you some good stout staves and pitchforks —'

'Staves and pitchforks – in the name o' the law! And take 'em in yer hands and go in quest, and do as we in authority tell ye!'

Thus aroused, the men prepared to give chase. The evidence was, indeed, though circumstantial, so convincing, that but little argument was needed to show the shepherd's guests that after what they had seen it would look very much like connivance if they did not instantly pursue the unhappy third stranger, who could not as yet have gone more than a few hundred yards over such uneven country.

A shepherd is always well provided with lanterns; and, lighting these hastily, and with hurdle-staves in their hands, they poured out of the door, taking a direction along the crest of the hill, away from the town, the rain having fortunately a little abated.

Disturbed by the noise, or possibly by unpleasant dreams of her baptism, the child who had been christened began to cry heart-brokenly in the room overhead. These notes of grief came down through the chinks of the floor to the ears of the women below, who jumped up one by one, and seemed glad of the excuse to ascend and comfort the baby, for the incidents of the last half-hour greatly oppressed them. Thus in the space of two or three minutes the room on the ground-floor was deserted quite.

But it was not for long. Hardly had the sound of footsteps died away when a man returned round the corner of the house from the direction the pursuers had taken. Peeping in at the door, and seeing nobody there, he entered leisurely. It was the stranger of the chimney-corner, who had gone out with the rest. The motive of his return was shown by his helping himself to a cut piece of skimmer-cake that lay on a ledge beside where he had sat, and which he had apparently forgotten to take with him. He also poured out half a cup more mead from the quantity that remained, ravenously eating and drinking these as he stood. He had not finished when another figure came in just as quietly – his friend[17] in cinder-grey.

'Oh – you here?' said the latter, smiling. 'I thought you had gone to help in the capture.' And this speaker also revealed the object of his return by looking solicitously round for the fascinating mug of old mead.

'And I thought you had gone,' said the other, continuing his skimmer-cake with some effort.

'Well, on second thoughts, I felt there were enough without me,' said the first confidentially, 'and such a night as it is, too. Besides, 'tis the business o' the Government to take care of its criminals – not mine.'

'True; so it is. And I felt as you did, that there were enough without me.'

'I don't want to break my limbs running over the humps and hollows of this wild country.'

'Nor I neither, between you and me.'

'These shepherd-people are used to it – simple-minded souls, you know, stirred up to anything in a moment. They'll have him ready for me before the morning, and no trouble to me at all.'

'They'll have him, and we shall have saved ourselves all labour in the matter.'

'True, true. Well, my way is to Casterbridge; and 'tis as much as my legs will do to take me that far. Going the same way?'

'No, I am sorry to say! I have to get home over there' (he nodded indefinitely to the right), 'and I feel as you do, that it is quite enough for my legs to do before bedtime.'

The other had by this time finished the mead in the mug, after which, shaking hands heartily at the door, and wishing each other well, they went their several ways.

In the meantime the company of pursuers had reached the end of the hog's-back elevation which dominated this part of the coomb. They had decided on no particular plan of action; and, finding that the man of the baleful trade was no longer in their company, they seemed quite unable to form any such plan now. They descended in all directions down the hill, and straightway several of the party fell into the snare set by Nature for all misguided midnight ramblers over this part of the cretaceous formation. The 'lynchets', or flint slopes, which belted the escarpment at intervals of a dozen yards, took the less cautious ones unawares, and losing their footing on the rubbly steep they slid sharply downwards, the lanterns rolling from their hands to the bottom, and there lying on their sides till the horn was scorched through.

When they had again gathered themselves together, the shepherd, as the man who knew the country best, took the lead, and guided them round these treacherous inclines. The lanterns, which seemed rather to dazzle their eyes and warn the fugitive than to assist them in the exploration, were extinguished, due silence was observed; and in this more rational order they plunged into the vale. It was a grassy, briery, moist defile, affording some shelter to any person who had sought it; but the party perambulated it in vain, and ascended on the other side. Here they wandered apart, and after an interval closed together again to report progress. At the second time of closing in they found themselves near a lonely ash, the single tree on this part of the upland, probably sown there by a passing bird some fifty years before. And here, standing a little to one side of the trunk, as motionless as the trunk itself, appeared the man they were in quest of, his outline being well defined against the sky beyond. The band noiselessly drew up and faced him.

'Your money or your life!' said the constable sternly to the still figure.

'No, no,' whispered John Pitcher. ' 'Tisn't our side ought to say that. That's the doctrine of vagabonds like him, and we be on the side of the law.'

'Well, well,' replied the constable impatiently; 'I must say something, mustn't I? and if you had all the weight o' this undertaking upon your mind, perhaps you'd say the wrong thing too! – Prisoner at the bar, surrender, in the name of the Father – the Crown, I mane!'[18]

The man under the tree seemed now to notice them for the first time, and, giving them no opportunity whatever for exhibiting their courage, he strolled slowly towards them. He was, indeed, the little man, the third stranger; but his trepidation had in a great measure gone.

'Well, travellers,' he said, 'did I hear ye speak to me?'

'You did: you've got to come and be our prisoner at once,' said the constable. 'We arrest ye on the charge of not biding in Casterbridge jail in a decent proper manner to be hung tomorrow morning. Neighbours, do your duty, and seize the culpet!'

On hearing the charge, the man seemed enlightened, and, saying not another word, resigned himself with preternatural civility to the search-party, who, with their staves in their hands, surrounded him on all sides, and marched him back towards the shepherd's cottage.

It was eleven o'clock by the time they arrived. The light shining from the open door, a sound of men's voices within, proclaimed to them as they approached the house that some new events had arisen in their absence. On entering they discovered the shepherd's living-room to be invaded by two officers from Casterbridge jail, and a well-known magistrate who lived at the nearest country-seat, intelligence of the escape having become generally circulated.

'Gentlemen,' said the constable, 'I have brought back your man – not without risk and danger; but every one must do his duty! He is inside this circle of able-bodied persons, who have lent me useful aid, considering their ignorance of Crown work. Men, bring forward your prisoner!' And the third stranger was led to the light.

'Who is this?' said one of the officials.

'The man,' said the constable.

'Certainly not,' said the turnkey; and the first corroborated his statement.

'But how can it be otherwise?' asked the constable. 'Or why was he so terrified at sight o' the singing instrument of the law who sat there?' Here he related the strange behaviour of the third stranger on entering the house during the hangman's song.

'Can't understand it,' said the officer coolly. 'All I know is that it is not the condemned man. He's quite a different character from this one; a gauntish fellow, with dark hair and eyes, rather good-looking, and with a musical bass voice that if you heard it once you'd never mistake as long as you lived.'

'Why, souls – 'twas the man in the chimney-corner!'

'Hey – what?' said the magistrate, coming forward after inquiring particulars from the shepherd in the background. 'Haven't you got the man after all?'

'Well, sir,' said the constable, 'he's the man we were in search of, that's true; and yet he's not the man we were in search of. For the man we were in search of was not the man we wanted, sir, if you understand my everyday way; for 'twas the man in the chimney-corner!'

'A pretty kettle of fish altogether!' said the magistrate. 'You had better start for the other man at once.'

The prisoner now spoke for the first time. The mention of the man in the chimney-corner seemed to have moved him as nothing else could do. 'Sir,' he said, stepping forward to the magistrate, 'take no more trouble about me. The time is come when I may as well speak. I have done nothing; my crime is that the condemned man is my brother. Early this afternoon I left home at Shottsford to tramp it all the way to Casterbridge jail to bid him farewell. I was benighted, and called here to rest and ask the way. When I opened the door I saw before me the very man, my brother, that I thought to see in the condemned cell at Casterbridge. He was in this chimney-corner; and jammed close to him, so that he could not have got out if he had tried, was the executioner who'd come to take his life, singing a song about it and not knowing that it was his victim who was close by, joining in to save appearances. My brother looked a glance of agony at me, and I knew he meant, "Don't reveal what you see; my life depends on it." I was so terror-struck that I could hardly stand, and, not knowing what I did, I turned and hurried away.'

The narrator's manner and tone had the stamp of truth, and his story made a great impression on all around. 'And do you know where your brother is at the present time?' asked the magistrate.

'I do not. I have never seen him since I closed this door.'

'I can testify to that, for we've been between ye ever since,' said the constable.

'Where does he think to fly to? – what is his occupation?'

'He's a watch-and-clock-maker, sir.'

' 'A said 'a was a wheelwright – a wicked rogue,' said the constable.

'The wheels of clocks and watches he meant, no doubt,' said Shepherd Fennel. 'I thought his hands were palish for's trade.'

'Well, it appears to me that nothing can be gained by retaining this poor man in custody,' said the magistrate; 'your business lies with the other, unquestionably.'

And so the little man was released off-hand; but he looked nothing the less sad on that account, it being beyond the power of magistrate or constable to raze out the written troubles in his brain, for they concerned another whom he regarded with more solicitude than himself. When this was done, and the man had gone his way, the night was found to be so far advanced that it was deemed useless to renew the search before the next morning.

Next day, accordingly, the quest for the clever sheep-stealer became general and keen, to all appearance at least. But the intended punishment was cruelly disproportioned to the transgression, and the sympathy of a great many country-folk in that district was strongly on the side of the fugitive. Moreover, his marvellous coolness and daring in hob-and-nobbing with the hangman, under the unprecedented circumstances of the shepherd's party, won their admiration. So that it may be questioned if all those who ostensibly made themselves so busy in exploring woods and fields and lanes were quite so thorough when it came to the private examination of their own lofts and outhouses. Stories were afloat of a mysterious figure being occasionally seen in some old overgrown trackway or other, remote from turnpike-roads; but when a search was instituted in any of these suspected quarters nobody was found. Thus the days and weeks passed without tidings.

In brief, the bass-voiced man of the chimney-corner was never recaptured. Some said that he went across the sea, others that he did not, but buried himself in the depths of a populous city. At any rate, the gentleman in cinder-grey never did his morning's work at Casterbridge, nor met anywhere at all, for business purposes, the genial comrade with whom he had passed an hour of relaxation in the lonely house on the coomb.

The grass has long been green on the graves of Shepherd Fennel and his frugal wife; the guests who made up the christening party have mainly followed their entertainers to the tomb; the baby in whose honour they all had met is a matron in the sere and yellow leaf.[19] But the arrival of the three strangers at the shepherd's that night, and the details connected therewith, is a story as well known as ever in the country about Higher Crowstairs.

THE ROMANTIC ADVENTURES
OF A MILKMAID

'Where are you going, my pretty maid?'
'I'm going a milking, Sir,' she said.[1]

I

It was half-past five o'clock, on the morning of the 5th of May. A dense white fog hung over the valley of the Swenn,[2] and spread up the hills on either side.

But though nothing in the vale could be seen from higher ground, notes of differing kinds gave pretty clear indications that bustling phases of life had existence there. This audible presence and visual absence of an active scene was very peculiar. Nature had laid a white hand over the creatures ensconced within the vale, as a hand might be laid over a nest of chirping birds.

The noises that ascended through the pallid coverlid were perturbed lowings, mingled with human voices in sharps and flats, and the bark of a dog. These, followed by the slamming of a gate, explained as well as eyesight could have done, to any inhabitant of the district, that Dairyman Tucker's under-milker was driving the cows from the meads into the stalls. When a rougher accent joined in the vociferations of man and beast, that same inhabitant would have distinguished that Dairyman Tucker himself had come out to meet the cows, pail in hand, and white pinafore on; and when, moreover, some women's voices joined in the chorus, that the cows were stalled and proceedings about to commence.

A comparative hush followed, the atmosphere being so stagnant that the milk could be heard buzzing into the pails, together with the words of the milkmaids and men whenever they spoke above gossiping tones.

'Don't ye bide about long upon the road, Margery. You can be back again by skimming-time.'

The rough voice described as Dairyman Tucker's was the vehicle of this remark. Then the barton-gate slammed again, and in two or three minutes a something became visible, rising out of the fog in that quarter.

First, the shape revealed itself as that of a woman; next, the gait, which was the gait of one young and agile. Next, the colours and other details of her dress – a bright pink cotton frock (because winter was over); a small woollen shawl of shepherd's plaid (because summer was not come); a white handkerchief tied over her head-gear, because it was so foggy, so damp, and so early; and a straw bonnet and ribbons peeping from under the handkerchief, because it was likely to be a sunny May day.

Her face was of the hereditary type among families down in these parts: sweet in expression, perfect in hue, and somewhat irregular in feature. Her eyes were of a liquid brown. On her arm she carried a withy basket,[3] in which lay several butter-rolls in a nest of wet cabbage-leaves. She was, no doubt, the 'Margery' of the voice, who had been told not to 'bide about long upon the road'.

She went on her way across the fields, not much perplexed by the fog, except when the track was so indefinite that it ceased to be a guide to the next stile. She carefully avoided treading on the innumerable earthworms that lay in couples across the path[4] till, startled even by her light tread, they withdrew suddenly into their holes. She kept clear of all trees. Why was that? There was no danger of lightning on such a morning as this. But though the roads were dry the fog had gathered in the boughs, causing them to set up such a dripping as would go clean through the protecting handkerchief like bullets, and spoil the ribbons beneath. The beech and ash were particularly shunned, for they dripped more maliciously than any. It was an instance of woman's keen appreciativeness of nature's moods and peculiarities: a man crossing those fields might hardly have perceived that the trees dripped at all.

In less than an hour she had traversed a distance of four miles, and arrived at a latticed cottage in a secluded spot. An elderly woman, scarce awake, answered her knocking. Margery delivered up the butter, and said, 'How is granny this morning? I can't stay to go up to her, but tell her I have returned what we owed her.'

Her grandmother was no worse than usual: and receiving back the empty basket the girl proceeded to carry out some intention which had not been included in her orders. Instead of returning to the light labours of skimming-time, she hastened on, her direction being towards a little neighbouring town. Before, however, Margery had proceeded far, she met the postman, laden to the neck with letter-bags, of which he had not yet deposited one.

'Are the shops open yet, Samuel?' she said.

'O no,' replied that stooping pedestrian, not waiting to stand upright. 'They won't be open yet this hour, except the saddler and ironmonger and little tacker-haired machine-man for the farm folk. They downs their shutters at half-past six, then the baker's at half-past seven, then the draper's at eight.'

'O, the draper's at eight.' It was plain that Margery had wanted the draper's.

The postman turned up a side-path, and the young girl, as though deciding within herself that if she could not go shopping at once she might as well get back for the skimming, retraced her steps. The public road home from the point to which she had arrived was easy of access, but devious. By far the nearest way was by getting over a fence adjoining, and crossing the private grounds of a picturesque old country-house, whose chimneys were just visible through the trees. As the house had been shut up for many months, the girl decided to take the straight cut. She pushed her way through the laurel bushes, sheltering her bonnet with the shawl as an additional safeguard, scrambled over the wire boundary, went along through more shrubberies, and stood ready to emerge upon the open lawn. Before doing so she looked around in the wary manner of a poacher. It was not the first time that she had broken fence in her life; but somehow, and all of a sudden, she had felt herself too near womanhood to indulge in such practices with freedom. However, she moved forth, and the house-front stared her in the face, unobscured by the fog because close at hand.

It was a building of the medium size, and unpretending, the façade being of stone; and of the Italian elevation made familiar by the works of Inigo Jones.[5] There was a doorway to the lawn, standing at the head of a flight of steps. The shutters of the house were closed, and the blinds of the bedrooms drawn down. Her perception of the fact that no crusty caretaker could see her from the windows led her at once to slacken her pace, and stroll through the flower-beds coolly. A house unblinded is a possible spy, and must be treated accordingly; a house with the shutters closed is an insensate heap of stone and mortar, to be faced with indifference.

On the other side of the house the greensward rose to an eminence, whereon stood one of those curious summer shelters that are sometimes erected on exposed points of view, called an all-the-year-round. In the present case it consisted of four walls radiating from a centre like the arms of a turnstile, with seats in each angle, so that whencesoever the wind came, it was always possible to find a screened corner from which to observe the landscape.

The milkmaid's trackless course led her up the hill and past this erection. At ease as to being watched and scolded as an intruder, her mind flew to other matters; till, at the moment when she was not a yard from the shelter, she heard a foot or feet scraping on the gravel behind it. Some one was in the all-the-year-round, apparently occupying the seat on the other side; as was proved when, on turning, she saw an elbow, a man's elbow, projecting over the edge.

Now the young woman did not much like the idea of going down the hill under the eyes of this person, which she would have to do if she went on, for as an intruder she was liable to be called back and questioned upon her business there. Accordingly she crept softly up and sat in the seat behind, intending to remain there until her companion should leave.

This he by no means seemed in a hurry to do. What could possibly have brought him there, what could detain him there, at six o'clock on a morning of dense mist when there was nothing to be seen or enjoyed, puzzled her not a little. But he remained quite still, and Margery grew impatient. She discerned the track of his feet in the dewy grass, forming a line from the house steps, which announced that he was an inhabitant and not a chance passer-by. At last she peeped round.

II

A fine-framed dark-mustachioed gentleman, in dressing-gown and slippers, was sitting there in the fog without a hat on. With one hand he was tightly grasping his forehead, with the other his knee. The attitude bespoke with sufficient clearness a certain mental condition – anguish. He was quite a different being from any of the men to whom her eyes were accustomed.[6] His hands and his face were white – to her view deadly white – and he heeded nothing outside his own existence. There he remained as motionless as the unwafted bushes around him; indeed, he scarcely seemed to breathe.

Having imprudently advanced thus far, Margery's wish was to get back again in the same unseen manner; but in moving her foot for the purpose it grated slightly on the gravel. He started up with an air of bewilderment, and slipped something into the pocket of his dressing-gown.[7] The pair then stood looking blankly at each other.

'Who are you?' he at length asked sternly, and with not altogether an English articulation. 'What do you do here?'

Margery had already begun to be frightened at her own boldness in invading the lawn and pleasure-seat. The house had a master, and she had not known of it. 'My name is Margaret Tucker, sir,' she said meekly. 'My father is Dairyman Tucker. We live at Stickleford Dairy-house.'[8]

'What were you doing here at this hour of the morning?'

She told him, even to the fact that she had climbed over the fence.

'And what made you peep round at me?'

'I saw your elbow, sir; and I wondered what you were doing?'

'And what was I doing?'

'Nothing. You had one hand on your forehead and the other on your knee. I do hope you be not ill, sir,[9] or in deep trouble?'

'What difference would it make to you if I were ill or in trouble? You don't know me, and cannot care for me.'

She returned no answer, feeling that she might have taken a liberty in expressing sympathy. But, looking furtively up at him, she discerned to her surprise that he seemed affected by her humane wish, simply as it had been expressed. She had scarcely conceived that such a tall dark man could know what gentle feelings were.

'Well, I am much obliged to you for caring how I am,' said he with a faint smile and an affected lightness of manner which, even to her, only rendered more apparent the real gloom beneath. 'I have not slept this past night. I suffer from sleeplessness. Probably you don't.'[10]

Margery laughed a little, and he glanced with interest at the comely picture she presented; her fresh face, brown hair, candid eyes, unpractised manner, country dress, pink hands, empty wicker-basket, and the handkerchief over her bonnet.

'Well,' he said, after his scrutiny, 'I need hardly have asked such a question of one who is Nature's own image . . . Ah, but my good little friend,' he added, recurring to his bitter tone and sitting wearily down, 'you don't know what great clouds can hang over some people's lives, and what cowards some men are in face of them. To escape themselves they travel, take picturesque houses, and engage in country sports. But here it is so dreary, and the fog was horrible this morning.'

'Why, this is only the pride of the morning!' said Margery brightly. 'By-and-by it will be a beautiful day.'

She was going on her way forthwith; but he detained her – detained her with words, talking on every innocent little subject he could think of. The feint of this was so transparent that one thing was beyond question: he had an object in keeping her there more serious than his words would imply. It was as if he feared to be left alone.

While they still stood the misty figure of the postman, whom Margery had left a quarter of an hour earlier to follow his sinuous course, crossed the grounds below them on his way to the house. First signifying to Margery by a wave of his hand that she was to step back out of sight, in the hinder angle of the shelter, the gentleman beckoned to the postman to bring the bag to where he stood. The man, who recognized him, did so, and again resumed his journey.

The stranger unlocked the bag and threw it on the seat, having taken one letter from within. This he read attentively, and his countenance changed.

The effect was as if the sun had burst through the fog upon that face: it became clear, bright, almost radiant. The change was almost phantasmagorial; yet it was but a change that may take place in the commonest human being, provided his countenance be not too wooden, or his artifice have not grown to second nature. He turned to Margery, who was again edging off, and, seizing her hand, appeared as though he were about to embrace her. Checking his impulse, he said, 'My guardian angel[11] – my good friend – you have saved me!'

'What from?' she ventured to ask.

'That you may never know!' he replied solemnly.

She guessed that the letter he had just received had been the means of effecting this change for the better in his mood; but made no observation till he went on to say, 'What did you tell me was your name, dear girl?'

She repeated her name.

'Margaret Tucker.' He stopped, and pressed her hand. 'Sit down for a moment – one moment,' he said, pointing to the end of the seat, and taking the extremest further end for himself, not to discompose her. She sat down.

'It is to ask a question,' he went on, 'and there must be confidence between us. You have saved me from indescribable folly! What can I do for you?'

'Nothing, sir.'

'Nothing?'

'Father is very well off, and we don't want anything.'

'But there must be some service I can render, some kindness I can bestow – some votive offering which I could make, and so imprint on your memory as long as you live that I am not an ungrateful man?'

'Why should you be grateful to me, sir?'

He shook his head. 'Some things are best left unspoken. Now think. What would you like to have best in the world?'

Margery made a pretence of reflecting – then fell to reflecting seriously; but the negative was ultimately as undisturbed as ever: she could not decide on anything she would like best in the world; it was too difficult, too sudden.

'Very well – don't hurry yourself. Think it over all day. I ride this afternoon. You live – where?'

'Stickleford Dairy-house.'

'I will ride that way homeward this evening. Do you consider by eight o'clock what little article, what little treat, you would most like of any.'

'I will, sir,' said Margery, now warming up a little to the idea. 'And where shall I meet you? Or will you call at the house, sir?'

'Ah – no. I should not wish the circumstances to be known out of which our acquaintance arose. It would be more proper – but no.'

Margery, too, seemed rather anxious that he should not call. 'I could come out, sir,' she said. 'My father is odd-tempered, and perhaps —'

It was ultimately agreed that she should look over a stile at the top of her father's garden, and that he should ride along a bridle-path without, to receive her answer. 'Margery,' said the gentleman in conclusion, 'now that you have discovered me under peculiar conditions, are you going to reveal them, and make me an object for the gossip of the curious?'

'No, no, sir!' she replied earnestly. 'Why should I do that?'

'You will never tell?'

'Never, never will I tell what has happened here this morning.'

'Neither to your father, nor to your friends, nor to any one?'

'To no one at all,' she said, a little puzzled.

'It is sufficient,' he answered. 'You mean what you say, my dear maiden. Now you want to leave me. Goodbye!'

She descended the hill, walking with some awkwardness; for she felt the stranger's eyes were upon her till the fog had enveloped her from his gaze. She took no notice now of the dripping from the trees; she was lost in thought on other things. How had she saved this handsome, melancholy, sleepless, foreign gentleman who had had a trouble on his mind till the letter came? What had he been going to do? Margery did not know. Strange as the incident had been in itself, to her it had seemed stranger even than it was. Contrasting colours heighten each other by being juxtaposed; it is the same with contrasting lives.

Reaching the opposite side of the park there appeared before her for the third time that little old man, the foot-post. As the turnpike-road ran, the postman's beat was twelve miles a day; six miles out from Anglebury, and six miles back at night. But what with zigzags, devious ways, offsets to country seats, horse-shoe curves to farms, looped courses and isosceles triangles to outlying hamlets, the ground actually covered by him was nearer one-and-twenty miles. Hence it was that Margery, who had come straight, was still abreast of him, despite her long pause.

The weighty sense that she was mixed up in a tremendous and tragical secret with an unknown, mysterious, and handsome stranger, prevented her joining very readily in chat with the postman for some time. But a keen interest in her adventure caused her to respond at once when the bowed man of mails said, 'You hit athwart the grounds of Mount Lodge,[12] Miss Margery, or you wouldn't ha' met me here. Well, somebody hev took the old place at last.'

In acknowledging her route Margery brought herself to ask who the new gentleman might be.

'Guide the girl's heart, what don't she know! And yet how should ye – he's only just a-come. – Well, primary, he's a fishing gentleman, come for the summer only. Then, more to the subject, 'a's a foreign noble that's lived in England so long as to be a kind of mule as to country: some of his letters call him Baron, some Squire, so that 'a must be born to something that didn't come by reason. But to return to the real compass of this matter, whether 'a's a rich man in my eye and a poor man in's own, or a rich man in his own and mine too, I can't interpret no more than Pharaoh.[13] – 'A was out this morning a-watching the fog. "Postman," 'a said, "give me the bag," quite easy-like. O, yes, 'a's a civil genteel noble enough, that's true.'

'Took the house for fishing, did he?'

'Well, that's what they say, and as it can't be for nothing else I suppose it's true. But, in final, his health's not good, 'a b'lieve; and he's been living too rithe. The London smoke got into his keakhorn, till 'a couldn't eat. However, I shouldn't mind having the run of his kitchen.'

'And what is his name?'

'Ah – there you have me! 'Tis a name no man's tongue can tell, or even woman's, except by pen-and-ink and good scholarship. It begins with X, and who, without the machinery of a clock in's inside, can speak that? But here 'tis – from his letters.' The postman with his walking-stick wrote upon the ground,

'BARON VON XANTEN.'

III

The day, as she had prognosticated, turned out fine; for weather-wisdom was imbibed along with their milk-sops by the children of Swenn Vale. The impending meeting moved Margery deeply,[14] and she performed her daily duties in her father's house with mechanical unconsciousness.

Milking, skimming, cheesemaking were done. Her father was asleep in the settle, the milkmen and maids were gone home to their cottages, and the clock showed a quarter to eight. She dressed herself with care, went to the top of the garden, and looked over the stile. The view was eastward, and a great moon hung before her in a sky which had not a cloud. Nothing was moving except on the minutest scale, and she remained leaning over, the night-jar sounding his rattle from the bough of an isolated tree on the open hill side.

Here Margery waited till the appointed time had passed by three-quarters of an hour; but no foreign baron came. She was full of an idea, and her heart sank with disappointment. And then at last the pacing of a horse became audible on the soft path without, leading up from the water-meads, simultaneously with which she beheld the form of the stranger drawing near. He was riding home.

The moonlight so flooded her face as to make her very conspicuous in the garden-gap. 'Ah – Margery!' he said, starting. 'How came you here? But of course I remember – we were to meet. And it was to be at eight – *proh pudor*![15] – I have kept you waiting!'

'It doesn't matter, sir. – I've thought of something.'

'Thought of something?'

'Yes, sir. You said this morning that I was to think what I would like best in the world, and I have made up my mind.'

'I did say so – to be sure I did,' he replied, collecting his thoughts. 'I remember to have had good reason for gratitude to you.' He placed his hand to his brow, and in a minute alighted, and came up to her with the bridle in his hand. 'I was to give you a treat or present, and you could not think of one. Now you have done so. Let me hear what it is, and I'll be as good as my word.'

'To go to the Yeomanry Ball that's to be given this month.'

'The Yeomanry Ball – Yeomanry Ball?' he murmured, as if, of all requests in the world, this was what he had least expected. 'Where is what you call the Yeomanry Ball?'

'At Casterbridge.'

'Have you ever been to it before?'

'No, sir.'

'Or to any ball?'

'No.'

'But did I not say a present?'

'Or a treat?'

'Ah, yes, or a treat,' he echoed, with the air of one who finds himself in a slight fix. 'But with whom would you propose to go?'

'I don't know. I have not thought of that yet.'

'You have no friend who could take you, even if I got you an invitation?'

Margery looked at the moon. 'No one who can dance,' she said; adding, with hesitation, 'I was thinking that perhaps —'

'But, my dear Margery,' he said, stopping her, as if he half-divined what her simple dream of a cavalier had been; 'it is very odd that you can think of nothing else than going to a Yeomanry Ball. Think again. You are sure there's nothing else?'

'Quite sure, sir,' she decisively answered. At first nobody would have noticed in that pretty young face any sign of such decision; yet it was discoverable. The mouth, though soft, was firm in line; the eyebrows were distinct, and extended near to each other. 'I have thought of it all day,' she continued, sadly. 'Still, sir, if you are sorry you offered me anything, I can let you off.'

'Sorry? – Certainly not, dear Margery,' he said, rather nettled. 'I'll show you that whatever hopes I have raised in your breast I am honourable enough to gratify. If it lies in my power,' he added with sudden firmness, 'you *shall* go to the Yeomanry Ball. In what building is it to be held?'

'In the Assembly Rooms.'

'And would you be likely to be recognized there? Do you know many people?'

'Not many, sir. None, I may say. I know nobody who goes to balls.'

'Ah, well; you must go, since you wish it; and if there is no other way of getting over the difficulty of having nobody to take you, I'll take you myself. Would you like me to do so? I can dance.'

'Oh, yes, sir; I know that, and I thought you might offer to do it. But would you bring me back again?'

'Of course I'll bring you back. But, by-the-by, can *you* dance?'

'Yes – reels, and jigs, and country-dances like the New-Rigged-Ship, and Follow-my-Lover, and Haste-to-the-Wedding, and the College Hornpipe, and the Favourite Quickstep, and Captain White's Dance.'

'Not a bad list; but unluckily I fear they don't dance any of those now. But if you have the instinct we may soon cure your ignorance. Let me see you dance a moment.'

She glanced around, and saw nobody. 'You will promise not to tell, sir?'[16]

'Can you ask it! Have you not some secret of mine?'

She stood out into the garden-path, the stile being still between them, and seizing a side of her skirt with each hand, performed the movements which are even yet far from uncommon in the dances of the villagers of merry England. But her motions, though graceful, were not precisely those which appear in the figures of a modern ball-room.

'Well, my good friend, it is a very pretty sight,' he said, warming up to the proceedings. 'But you dance too well – you dance all over your person – and that's too thorough a way for the present day. I should say it was exactly how they danced in the time of the poet Chaucer; but as people don't dance like it now, we must consider. First I must inquire more about this ball, and then I must see you again.'

'If it is a great trouble to you, sir, in —'

'O no, no. I will think it over. So far so good.'

The baron mentioned an evening and an hour when he would be passing that way again; then mounted his horse and rode away.

On the next occasion, which was just when the sun was changing places with the moon as an illuminator of Stickleford Dairy, she found him at the spot before her, and unencumbered by a horse. The melancholy that had so weighed him down at their first interview, and had been perceptible at their second, had quite disappeared. He pressed her right hand between both his own across the stile.

'My dear girl, God bless you!' said he warmly. 'I cannot help thinking of that morning! I was too much over-shadowed at first to take in the whole force of it. You don't know all; but your presence was a miraculous intervention. Now to more cheerful matters. I have a great deal to tell – that is, if your wish about the ball be still the same?'

'Oh yes, sir – if you don't object,' said the persistent maiden.

'Never think of my objecting. What I have found out is something which simplifies matters amazingly. In addition to your Yeomanry Ball at Casterbridge, there is also to be one in the next county about the same time. This ball is not to be held at the Town Hall of the county-town as usual, but at Lord Blakemore's,[17] who is colonel of the regiment, and who, I suppose, wishes to please the yeomen because his brother is going to stand for the county. Now I find I could take you there very well, and the great advantage of that ball over the Yeomanry Ball in this county is, that there you would be absolutely unknown, and I also. But do you prefer your own county?'

'Oh no, sir. It is a ball I long to see – I don't know what it is like; it does not matter where.'

'Then I shall be able to make much more of you there, where there is no possibility of recognition. That being settled, the next thing is the dancing. Now reels and such things won't do. For think of this –

there is a new dance at Almack's and everywhere else, over which the world has gone crazy.'[18]

'How dreadful!'

'Ah – but that is a mere expression – gone mad. It is really an ancient Scythian dance; but, such is the power of fashion, that, having once been adopted by Society, this dance has made the tour of the Continent in one season.'

'What is its name, sir?'

'The polka. Young people, who always dance, are ecstatic about it, and old people, who have not danced for years, have begun to dance again on its account. All share the excitement. It arrived in London only some few months ago – it is now all over the country. Now this is your opportunity, my good Margery. To learn this one dance will be enough. They will dance scarce anything else at that ball. While, to crown all, it is the easiest dance in the world, and as I know it quite well I can practise you in the step. Suppose we try?'

Margery showed some hesitation before crossing the stile: it was a Rubicon in more ways than one.[19] But the curious reverence which was stealing over her for all that this stranger said and did was too much for prudence. She crossed the stile.

Withdrawing with her to a nook where two high hedges met, and where the grass was elastic and dry, he lightly rested his arm on her waist, and practised with her the new step of fascination. Instead of music he whispered numbers, and she, as may be supposed, showed no slight aptness in following his instructions. Thus they moved round together, the moon-shadows from the twigs racing over their forms as they turned.

The interview lasted about half-an-hour. Then he somewhat abruptly handed her over the stile and stood looking at her from the other side.

'Well,' he murmured, 'what has come to pass is strange! My whole business after this will be to recover my right mind!'

Margery (to whose recollections the writer is indebted for the details of this interview)[20] always declared that there seemed to be some power in the stranger that was more than human, something magical and compulsory, when he seized her and gently trotted her round. But the lapse of many many years[21] may have led her memory to play pranks with the scene, and her vivid imagination at that youthful age must be taken into account in believing her. However, there is no doubt that the stranger, whoever he might be, and whatever his powers, taught her the elements of modern dancing at a certain interview by moonlight at the top of her father's garden, as was proved by her possession of knowledge on the subject that could have been acquired in no other way.

His was of the first rank of commanding figures, she was one of the most graceful of milkmaids, and to casual view it would have seemed all of a piece with Nature's doings that things should go on thus. But there was another side to the case; and whether the strange gentleman were a wild olive tree, or not,[22] it was questionable if the acquaintance would lead to happiness. 'A fleeting romance and a possible calamity';[23] thus it might have been summed up by the practical.

Margery was in Paradise; and yet she was not distinctly in love with the stranger. What she felt was something more mysterious, more of the nature of veneration. As he looked at her across the stile she spoke timidly, on a subject which had apparently occupied her long.

'I ought to have a ball-dress, ought I not, sir?'

'Certainly. And you shall have a ball-dress.'

'Really?'

'No doubt of it. I won't do things by halves for my best friend. I have thought of the ball-dress, and of other things also.'

'And is my dancing good enough?'

'Quite – quite.' He paused, lapsed into thought, and looked at her. 'Margery,' he said, 'do you trust yourself unreservedly to me?'

'Oh yes, sir,' she replied brightly; 'if I am not too much trouble: if I am good enough to be seen in your society.'

The Baron laughed in a peculiar way. 'Really, I think you may assume as much as that. – However, to business. The ball is on the twenty-fifth, that is next Thursday week; and the only difficulty about the dress is the size. Suppose you lend me this?' And he touched her on the shoulder to signify a tight little jacket she wore.

Margery was all obedience. She took it off and handed it to him.

The Baron rolled and compressed it with all his force till it was about as large as a cricket-ball,[24] and put it into his pocket.

'The next thing,' he said, 'is about getting the consent of your friends to your going. Have you thought of this?'

'There is only my father. I can tell him I am invited to a party, and I don't think he'll mind. Though I would rather not tell him.'

'But it strikes me that you must inform him something of what you intend? I would strongly advise you to do so.' He spoke as if rather perplexed as to the probable custom of the English peasantry in such matters, and added, 'However, it is for you to decide. I know nothing of the circumstances. As to getting to the ball, the plan I have arranged is this. The direction to Lord Blakemore's being the other way from my house, you must meet me at Three-Walks-End in Chillington Wood,[25] two miles or more from here. You know the place? Good. By meeting there we shall save five or six miles of journey, a consideration, as it is a long way. – Now for the last time: are you still firm in your wish for this particular treat and no other? It is not too late to give it up. Cannot you think of something else – something better – some useful household articles you require?'

Margery's countenance, which before had been beaming with expectation, lost its brightness: her eyes became moist,[26] and her voice broken. 'You have offered to take me, and now —'

'No, no, no,' he said, patting her cheek. 'We will not think of anything else. You shall go.'

IV

But whether the Baron, in naming such a distant spot for the rendezvous, was in hope she might fail him, and so relieve him after all of his undertaking, cannot be said; though it might have been strongly suspected from his manner that he had no great zest for the responsibility of escorting her.

But he little knew the firmness of the young woman he had to deal with. She was one of those soft natures whose power of adhesiveness to an acquired idea seems to be one of the special attributes of that softness. To go to a ball with this glorious and mysterious personage of romance was her most ardent desire and aim; and none the less in that she trembled with fear and excitement at her position in so aiming. She felt the deepest awe, tenderness, and humility towards the Baron of the strange name; and yet she was prepared to stick to her point.

Thus it was that the afternoon of the eventful day found Margery trudging her way up the slopes from the vale to the place of appointment. She walked to the music of innumerable birds,[27] which increased as she drew away from the open meads towards the groves. She had overcome all difficulties. After thinking out the question of telling or not telling her father, she had decided that to tell him was to be forbidden to go. Her contrivance therefore was this: to leave home this evening on a visit to her invalid grandmother, who lived not far from the Baron's house; to arrive at her grandmother's by breakfast time next morning. Who would suspect the existence of a *lacuna* of twelve hours, during which she would be off to the ball? That this piece of deception was extremely wrong she afterwards owned readily enough; but she did not stop to think of it then.

It was sunset within Chillington Wood by the time she reached Three-Walks-End – the converging point of radiating trackways, now floored with a carpet of matted grass, which had never known other scythes than the teeth of rabbits and hares. The twitter overhead had ceased, except from a few braver and larger birds, including the cuckoo, who did not fear night at this pleasant time of year. Nobody seemed to be on the spot when she first drew near, but no sooner did Margery stand at the intersection of the roads than a slight crashing became audible, and her patron appeared. He was so transfigured in dress that she scarcely knew him. Under a light great-coat, which was flung open, instead of his ordinary clothes he wore a suit of thin black cloth, a waistcoat open all down the front, a white tie, shining boots, no thicker than a glove, a coat that made him look like a bird, and a hat that seemed as if it would open and shut like an accordion.

'I am dressed for the ball – nothing worse,' he said, drily smiling. 'So will you be soon.'

'Why did you choose this place for our meeting, Sir?' she asked, looking around and acquiring confidence.

'Why did I choose it? Well, because in riding past one day I observed a large hollow tree close by here, and it occurred to me when I was last with you that this would be useful for our purpose. Have you told your father?'

'I have not yet told him, Sir?'

'That's very bad of you, Margery. How have you arranged it, then?'

She briefly related her plan, on which he made no comment, but, taking her by the hand as if she were a little child, he led her through the undergrowth to a spot where the trees were older, and standing at wider distances. Among them was the tree he had spoken of – an elm; huge, hollow, distorted, and headless, with a rift in its side.

'Now go inside,' he said, 'before it gets any darker. You will find there everything you want. At any rate, if you do not you must do without it. I'll keep watch; and don't be longer than you can help to be.'

'What am I to do, sir?' asked the puzzled maiden.

'Go inside, and you will see. When you are ready wave your handkerchief at that hole.'

She stooped into the opening. The cavity within the tree formed a lofty circular apartment, four or five feet in diameter, to which daylight entered at the top, and also through a round hole about six feet from the ground, marking the spot at which a limb had been amputated in the tree's prime. The decayed wood of cinnamon-brown, forming the inner surface of the tree, and the warm evening glow reflected in at the top, suffused the cavity with a faint mellow radiance.

But Margery had hardly given herself time to heed these things. Her eye had been caught by objects of quite another quality. A large white oblong paper box lay against the inside of the tree; over it, on a splinter, hung a small oval looking-glass.

Margery seized the idea in a moment. She pressed through the rift into the tree, lifted the cover of the box, and behold, there was disclosed within a lovely white apparition in a somewhat flattened state. It was the ball-dress.

This marvel of art was, briefly, a sort of heavenly cobweb. It was a gossamer texture of precious manufacture, artistically festooned in a dozen flounces or more.

Margery lifted it, and could hardly refrain from kissing it. Had any one told her before this moment that such a dress could exist, she would have said, 'No; it's impossible!' She drew back, went forward, flushed, laughed, raised her hands. To say that the maker of that dress had been an individual of talent was simply understatement: he was a genius; and she sunned herself in the rays of his creation.

She then remembered that her friend without had told her to make haste, and she spasmodically proceeded to array herself. In removing the dress she found satin slippers, gloves, a handkerchief nearly all lace, a fan, and even flowers for the hair. 'Oh, how could he think of it!' she said, clasping her hands and almost crying with agitation. 'And the glass – how good of him!'

Everything was so well prepared, that to clothe herself in these garments was a matter of ease. In a quarter of an hour she was ready, even to shoes and gloves. But what led her more than anything else into admiration of the Baron's foresight was the discovery that there were half-a-dozen pairs each of shoes and gloves, of varying sizes, out of which she selected a fit.

Margery glanced at herself in the mirror, or at as much as she could see of herself: the image presented was superb. Then she hastily rolled up her old dress, put it in the box, and thrust the latter on a ledge as high as she could reach. Standing on tiptoe, she waved the handkerchief through the upper aperture, and bent to the rift to go out.

But what a trouble stared her in the face. The dress was so airy, so fantastical, and so extensive, that to get out in her new clothes by the rift which had admitted her in her old ones was an impossibility. She heard the Baron's steps crackling over the dead sticks and leaves.

'Oh, sir!' she began in despair.

'What – can't you dress yourself?' he inquired from the back of the trunk.

'Yes; but I can't get out of this dreadful tree!'

He came round to the opening, stooped, and looked in. 'It is obvious that you cannot,' he said, taking in her compass at a glance; and adding to himself, 'Charming! who would have thought that clothes could do so much! – Wait a minute, my little maid: I have it!' he said more loudly.

With all his might he kicked at the sides of the rift, and by that means broke away several pieces of the rotten touchwood. But being thinly armed about the feet he abandoned that process, and went for a fallen branch which lay near. By using the large end as a lever, he tore away pieces of the wooden shell which enshrouded Margery and all her loveliness,[28] till the aperture was large enough for her to pass without tearing her dress. She breathed her relief: the silly girl had begun to fear that she would not get to the ball after all.

He now carefully wrapped round her a cloak he had brought with him: it was hooded, and of a length which covered her to the heels.

'The carriage is waiting down the other path,' he said, and gave her his arm. A short trudge over the soft dry leaves brought them to the place indicated. There stood the brougham, the horses, the coachman, all as still as if they were growing on the spot, like the trees. Margery's eyes rose with some timidity to the coachman's figure.

'You need not mind him,' said the Baron. 'He is a foreigner, and heeds nothing.'

In the space of a short minute she was handed inside; the Baron buttoned up his overcoat, and surprised her by mounting with the coachman. The carriage moved off silently over the long grass of the vista, the shadows deepening to black as they proceeded. Darker and darker grew the night as they rolled on; the neighbourhood familiar to Margery was soon left behind, and she had not the remotest idea of the direction they were taking. The stars blinked out, the coachman lit his lamps, and they bowled on again.

In the course of an hour and a-half they arrived at a small town, where they pulled up at the chief inn, and changed horses; all being done so readily that their advent had plainly been expected. The journey was resumed immediately. Her companion never descended to speak to her; whenever she looked out there he sat upright on his perch, with the mien of a person who had a difficult duty to perform, and who meant to perform it properly at all costs. But Margery could not help feeling a certain dread at her situation – almost, indeed, a wish that she had not come. Once or twice she thought, 'Suppose he is a wicked man, who is taking me off to a foreign country, and will never bring me home again.'

But her characteristic persistence in an original idea sustained her against these misgivings except at odd moments. One incident in particular had given her confidence in her escort: she had seen a tear in his eye when she expressed her sorrow for his troubles. He may have divined that her thoughts would take an uneasy turn, for when they stopped for a moment in ascending a hill he came to the window. 'Are you tired, Margery?' he asked kindly.

'No, sir.'

'Are you afraid?'

'N – no, sir. But it is a long way.'

'We are almost there,' he answered. 'And now, Margery,' he said in a lower tone, 'I must tell you a secret. I have obtained this invitation in a peculiar way. I thought it best for your sake not to come in my own name, and this is how I have managed. A man in this county, for whom I have lately done a service, one whom I can trust, and who is personally as unknown here as you and I, has (privately) transferred his card of invitation to me. So that we go under his name. I explain this that you may not say anything imprudent by accident. Keep your ears open and be cautious.' Having said this the Baron retreated again to his place.

'Then he is a wicked man after all!' she said to herself; 'for he is going under a false name.' But she soon had the temerity not to mind it: wickedness of that sort was the one ingredient required just now to finish him off as a hero in her eyes.

They descended a hill, passed a lodge, then up an avenue; and presently there beamed upon them the light from other carriages, drawn up in a row, which moved on by degrees; and at last they halted before a large arched doorway, round which a group of people stood.

'We are among the latest arrivals, on account of the distance,' said the Baron, reappearing. 'But never mind; there are three hours at least for your enjoyment.'

The steps were promptly flung down, and they alighted. The steam from the flanks of their swarthy steeds[29] ascended in clouds to the parapet of the porch, and from their nostrils the hot breath jetted forth like smoke out of volcanoes, attracting the attention of all.

V

The bewildered Margery was led by the Baron up the steps to the interior of the house, whence the sounds of music and dancing were already proceeding. The tones were strange. At every fourth beat a deep and mighty note throbbed through the air, reaching Margery's soul with all the force of a blow.

'What is that powerful tune, sir – I have never heard anything like it?' she said.

'The Drum Polka,' answered the Baron.

Her surprise was not lessened when, at the entrance to the ball-room, she heard the names of her conductor and herself announced as 'Mr and Miss Brown.'

However, nobody seemed to take any notice of the announcement, the room beyond being in a perfect turmoil of gaiety, and Margery's consternation at sailing under false colours subsided. At the same moment she observed awaiting them a handsome, dark-haired, rather *petite* lady in cream-coloured satin. 'Who is she?' asked Margery of the Baron.

'She is the lady of the mansion,' he whispered. 'She is the wife of a peer of the realm, the daughter of a marquis, has five Christian names; and hardly ever speaks to commoners, except for political purposes.'

'How heavenly – what joy to be here!' murmured Margery, as she contemplated the diamonds that flashed from the head of her ladyship; who was just inside the ball-room door, in front of a little gilded chair, upon which she sat in the intervals between one arrival and another. She had come down from London at great inconvenience to herself, openly to promote this entertainment.

As Mr and Miss Brown expressed absolutely no meaning to Lady Blakemore (for there were three Browns already present in this rather mixed assembly), and as there was possibly a slight awkwardness in poor Margery's manner, Lady Blakemore touched their hands lightly with the tips of her long gloves, said, 'How d'ye do,' and turned round for more comers.

'Ah, if she only knew we were a rich Baron and his friend, and not Mr and Miss Brown at all, she wouldn't receive us like that, would she?' whispered Margery confidentially.

'Indeed, she wouldn't!' drily said the Baron. 'Now let us drop into the dance at once; some of the people here, you see, dance much worse than you.'

Almost before she was aware she had obeyed his mysterious influence, by giving him one hand, placing the other upon his shoulder, and swinging with him round the room.

At the first gaze the apartment had seemed to her to be floored with black ice; the figures of the dancers appearing upon it upside down. At last she realized that it was highly-polished oak, but she was none the less afraid to move.

'I am afraid of falling down,' said she.

'Lean on me; you will soon get used to it,' he replied.

His words, like all his words to her, were quite true. She found it amazingly easy in a brief space of time. The floor, far from hindering her, was a positive assistance to one of her natural agility and litheness. Moreover, her marvellous dress of twelve flounces inspired her as nothing else could have done. Externally a new creature, she was prompted to new deeds. To feel as well-dressed as the other women around her is to set any woman at her ease, whencesoever she may have come: to feel much better dressed is to add radiance to that ease.

Her prophet's statement on the popularity of the polka at this juncture was amply borne out. It was among the first seasons of its general adoption in country houses; the enthusiasm it excited tonight was beyond description, and scarcely credible to the youth of the present day. A new motive power had been introduced into the world of poesy – the polka, as a counterpoise to the new motive power that had been introduced into the world of prose – steam.

Twenty finished musicians sat in the music gallery at the end, with romantic mop-heads of raven hair,[30] under which their faces and eyes shone like fire under coals.

The nature and object of the ball had led to its being very inclusive. Every rank was there, from the peer to the smallest yeoman, and

Margery got on exceedingly well, particularly when the recuperative powers of supper had banished the fatigue of her long drive.

Sometimes she heard people saying, 'Who are they? – brother and sister – father and daughter? And never dancing except with each other – how odd?' But of this she took no notice.

When not dancing the watchful Baron took her through the drawing-rooms and picture-galleries adjoining, which tonight were thrown open like the rest of the house; and there, ensconcing her in some curtained nook, he drew her attention to scrap-books, prints, and albums, and left her to amuse herself with turning them over till the dance in which she was practised should again be called. Margery would much have preferred to roam about during these intervals; but the words of the Baron were law, and as he commanded so she acted. In such alternations the evening winged away; till at last came the gloomy words, 'Margery, our time is up.'

'One more – only one!' she coaxed, for the longer they stayed the more freely and gaily moved the dance. This entreaty he granted; but on her asking for yet another, he was inexorable. 'No,' he said. 'We have a long way to go.'

Then she bade adieu to the wondrous scene, looking over her shoulder as they withdrew from the hall; and in a few minutes she was cloaked and in the carriage. The Baron mounted to his seat on the box, where she saw him light a cigar; they plunged under the trees, and she leant back, and gave herself up to contemplate the images that filled her brain. The natural result followed: she fell asleep.

She did not awake till they stopped to change horses; when she saw against the stars the Baron sitting as erect as ever. 'He watches like the Angel Gabriel, when all the world is asleep!'[31] she thought.

With the resumption of motion she slept again, and knew no more till he touched her hand and said, 'Our journey is done – we are in Chillington Wood.'

It was almost daylight. Margery scarcely knew herself to be awake till she was out of the carriage and standing beside the Baron, who, having told the coachman to drive on to a certain point indicated, turned to her.

'Now,' he said smiling, 'run across to the hollow tree; you know where it is. I'll wait as before, while you perform the reverse operation that you did last night.' She took no heed of the path now, nor regarded whether her pretty slippers became scratched by the brambles or no. A walk of a few steps brought her to the particular tree which she had left about nine hours earlier. It was still gloomy at this spot, the morning not being clear.

She entered the trunk, dislodged the box containing her old clothing, pulled off the satin shoes, and gloves, and dress, and in ten minutes emerged in the cotton gown and shawl of shepherd's plaid.

The Baron was not far off. 'Now you look the milkmaid again,' he said, coming towards her. 'Where is the finery?'

'Packed in the box, sir, as I found it.' She spoke with more humility now. The difference between them was greater than it had been at the ball.

'Good,' he said. 'I must just dispose of it; and then away we go.'

He went back to the tree, Margery following at a little distance. Bringing forth the box, he pulled out the dress as carelessly as if it had been rags. But this was not all. He gathered a few dry sticks, crushed the lovely garment into a loose billowy heap, threw the gloves, fan, and shoes on the top, then struck a light and ruthlessly set fire to the whole.

Margery was agonized. She ran forward; she implored and entreated. 'Please, sir – do spare it – do! My lovely dress – my dear, dear slippers – my fan – it is cruel! Don't burn them, please!'

'Nonsense. We shall have no further use for them if we live a hundred years.'

'But spare a bit of it – one little piece, sir – a scrap of the lace – one bow of the ribbon – the lovely fan – just something!'

But he was as immoveable as Rhadamanthus.[32] 'No,' he said, with a stern gaze of his aristocratic eye. 'It is of no use for you to speak like that. The things are my property. I undertook to gratify you in what you might desire because you had saved my life. To go to a ball, you said. You might much more wisely have said anything else, but no; you said, to go to a ball. I have taken you to a ball. I have brought you back. The clothes were only the means, and I dispose of them my own way. Have I not a right to?'

'Yes, sir,' she said meekly.

He gave the fire a stir, and lace and ribbons, and the twelve flounces, and the embroidery, and all the rest crackled and disappeared. He then put in her hands the butter basket she had brought to take on to her grandmother's, and accompanied her to the edge of the wood, where it merged in the undulating open country in which her grand-dame dwelt.

'Now, Margery,' he said, 'here we part. I have performed my contract – at some awkwardness, if I was recognized. But never mind that. How do you feel – sleepy?'

'Not at all, sir,' she said.

'That long nap refreshed you, eh? Now you must make me a promise. That if I require your presence at any time, you will come to me . . . I am a man of more than one mood,' he went on with sudden solemnity; 'and I may have desperate need of you again, to deliver me from that darkness as of Death which sometimes encompasses me. Promise it, Margery – promise it; that, no matter what stands in the way, you will come to me if I require you.'

'I would have if you had not burnt my things!' she pouted.

'Ah – ungrateful!'

'Indeed, then, I will promise, sir,' she said from her heart. 'Wherever I am, if I have bodily strength I will come to you.'

He pressed her hand. 'It is a solemn promise,' he replied. 'Now I must go, for you know your way.'

'I shall hardly believe that it has not been all a dream!' she said, with a childish instinct to cry at his withdrawal. 'There will be nothing left of last night – nothing of my dress, nothing of my pleasure, nothing of the place!'

'You shall remember it in this way,' said he. 'We'll cut our initials on this tree as a memorial, so that whenever you walk this path you will see them.'

Then with a knife he inscribed on the smooth bark of a beech tree the letters M. T., and underneath a large X.

'What, have you no Christian name, sir?' she said.

'Yes, but I don't use it. Now, goodbye, my little friend. – What will you do with yourself today, when you are gone from me?' he lingered to ask.

'Oh – I shall go to my granny's,' she replied with some gloom; 'and have breakfast, and dinner, and tea with her, I suppose; and in the evening I shall go home to Stickleford Dairy, and perhaps Jim will come to meet me, and all will be the same as usual.'

'Who is Jim?'

'O, he's nobody – only the young man I've got to marry some day.'

'What! – you engaged to be married? – Why didn't you tell me this before?'

'I – I don't know, sir.'

'What is the young man's name?'

'James Hayward,[33] sir.'

'What is he?'

'A master lime-burner.'

'Engaged to a master lime-burner, and not a word of this to me! Margery, Margery! when shall a straightforward one of your sex be found! Subtle even in your simplicity! What mischief have you caused me to do, through not telling me this? I wouldn't have so endangered anybody's happiness for a thousand pounds. Wicked girl that you were; why didn't you tell me?'

'I thought I'd better not, sir!' said Margery, beginning to be frightened.

'But don't you see and understand that if you are already the property of a young man, and he were to find out this night's excursion, he may be angry with you and part from you for ever? With him already in the field I had no right to take you at all; he undoubtedly ought to have taken you; which really might have been arranged, if you had not deceived me by saying you had nobody.'

Margery's face wore that aspect of woe which comes from the repentant consciousness of having been guilty of an enormity. 'But he wasn't good enough to take me, sir!' she said, almost crying; 'and he isn't absolutely my master until I have married him, is he?'

'That's a subject I cannot go into. However, we must alter our tactics. Instead of advising you, as I did at first, to tell of this experience to your friends, I must now impress on you that it will be best to keep a silent tongue on the matter – perhaps for ever and ever. It may come right some day, and you may be able to say "All's well that ends well."[34] Now, good morning, my friend. Think of Jim, and forget me.'

'Ah, perhaps I can't do that,' she said, with a tear in her eye, and a full throat.

'Well – do your best. I can say no more.'

He turned and retreated into the wood, and Margery, sighing, went on her way.

VI

Between six and seven o'clock in the evening of the same day a young man might have been seen descending the hills into the valley of the Swenn, at a point about midway between Stickleford and the residence of Margery's grandmother, four miles to the west.

He was a thoroughbred son of the country, as far removed from what is known as the provincial, as the latter is from the out-and-out gentleman of culture. His trousers and waistcoat were of fustian, almost white; but he wore a jacket of old-fashioned blue West-of-England cloth, so well preserved that evidently the article was relegated to a nail whenever its owner engaged in such active occupations as he usually pursued. His complexion was fair, almost florid, and he had scarcely any beard.

A novel attraction about this young man, which a glancing stranger would know nothing of, was a rare and curious freshness of atmosphere that appertained to him, to his clothes, to all his belongings, even to the room in which he had been sitting. It might almost have been said that by adding him and his implements to an overcrowded apartment you made it healthful. This resulted from his trade. He was a lime-burner; he handled lime daily; and in return the lime rendered him an incarnation of salubrity. His hair was dry, fair, and frizzled, the latter possibly by the operation of the same caustic agent. He carried as a walking-stick a green sapling, whose growth had been contorted to a corkscrew pattern by a twining honeysuckle.[35]

As he descended to the level ground of the water-meadows he cast his glance westward, with a frequency that revealed him to be in search of some object in the distance. It was rather difficult to do this, the low sunlight dazzling his eyes by glancing from the river away there, and from the 'carriers' (as they were called) in his path – narrow artificial brooks for conducting the water over the grass. His course was something of a zigzag from the necessity of finding points in these carriers convenient for jumping. Thus peering and leaping and winding, he drew near the Swenn, the central river of the miles-long mead.

A moving spot became visible to him in the direction of his scrutiny, mixed up with the rays of the same river. The spot got nearer, and revealed itself to be a slight thing of pink cotton and shepherd's plaid, which pursued a path on the brink of the stream. The young man so shaped his trackless course as to impinge on the path a little ahead of this coloured form, and when he drew near her he smiled and reddened. The girl smiled back to him; but her smile had not the life in it that the young man's had shown.

'My dear Margery – here I am!' he said gladly in an undertone, as with a last leap he crossed the last intervening carrier, and stood at her side.

'You've come all the way from the kiln, on purpose to meet me, and you shouldn't have done it,' she reproachfully returned.

'We finished there at four, so it was no trouble; and if it had been – why, I should ha' come.'

A small sigh was the response.

'What, you are not even so glad to see me as you would be to see your dog or cat?' he continued. 'Come, Mis'ess Margery, this is rather hard. But, by George, how tired you do look! Why, if you'd been up all night your eyes couldn't be more like tea-saucers. You've walked too far, that's what it is. The weather is getting warm now, and the air of these low-lying meads is not strengthening in summer. I wish you lived up on higher ground with me, beside the kiln. You'd get as strong as a hoss! Well, there; all that will come in time.'

Instead of saying yes, the fair maid repressed another sigh.

'What, won't it, then?' he said.

'I suppose so,' she answered. 'If it is to be, it is.'

'Well said – very well said, my dear.'

'And if it isn't to be it isn't.'

'What? Who's been putting that into your head? Your grumpy granny, I suppose. However, how is she? Margery, I have been thinking today – in fact, I was thinking it yesterday and all the week – that really we might settle our little business this summer.'

'This summer?' she repeated, with some dismay. 'But the partnership? Remember it was not to be till after that was completed.'

'There I have you!' said he, taking the liberty to pat her shoulder, and the further liberty of advancing his hand behind it to the other. 'The partnership is settled. 'Tis "Vine and Hayward, lime-burners", now, and "Richard Vine" no longer. Yes, Cousin Richard has settled it so, for a time at least, and 'tis to be painted on the carts this week – blue letters – yaller ground. I'll hoss one of 'em, and drive en round to your door as soon as the paint is dry, to show ye how it looks?'

'Oh, I am sure you needn't take that trouble, Jim; I can see it quite well enough in my mind,' replied the young girl – not without a flitting accent of superiority.

'Hullo,' said Jim, taking her by the shoulders, and looking at her hard. 'What do that bit of incivility mean? Now, Margery, let's sit down here, and have this cleared.' He rapped with his stick upon the rail of a little bridge they were crossing, and seated himself firmly, leaving a place for her.

'But I want to get home-along, dear Jim,' she coaxed.

'Fidgets. Sit down, there's a dear. I want a straightforward answer, if you please. In what month, and on what day of the month, will you marry me?'

'Oh, Jim,' she said, sitting gingerly on the edge, 'That's too plain-spoken for you yet. Before I look at it in that business light I should have to – to –'

'But your father has settled it long ago, and you said it should be as soon as I became a partner. So, dear, you must not mind a plain man wanting a plain answer. Come, name your time.'

She did not reply at once. What thoughts were passing through her brain during the interval? Not images raised by his words, but whirling figures of men and women in red and white and blue, reflected from a glassy floor, in movements timed by the thrilling beats of the Drum

Polka. At last she said slowly, 'Jim, you don't know the world, and what a woman's wants can be.'

'But I can make you comfortable. I am in lodgings as yet, but I can have a house for the asking; and as to furniture, you shall choose of the best for yourself – the very best.'

'The best! Far are you from knowing what that is!' said the little woman. 'There be ornaments such as you never dream of; work-tables that would set you in amaze; silver candlesticks, tea and coffee pots that would dazzle your eyes; tea-cups, and saucers, gilded all over with guinea-gold; heavy velvet curtains, gold clocks, pictures, and looking-glasses beyond your very dreams. So don't say I shall have the best.'

'H'm!' said Jim gloomily; and fell into reflection. 'Where did you get those high notions from, Margery?' he presently inquired. 'I'll swear you hadn't got 'em a week ago.' She did not answer, and he added, '*You* don't expect to have such things, I hope; deserve them as you may?'

'I was not exactly speaking of what I wanted,' she said severely. 'I said, things a woman *could* want.'

'You are a pink-and-white conundrum, Margery,' he said; 'and I give you up for tonight. Anybody would think the d— had showed you the kingdoms of the world since I saw you last!'[36]

She reddened; then arose, he following her; and they soon reached Margery's home, approaching it from the lower or meadow side – the opposite to that of the garden top, where she had met the Baron.

'You'll come in, won't you, Jim?' she said, with more ceremony than heartiness.

'No – I think not tonight,' he answered. 'I'll consider what you've said.'

'You are very good, Jim,' she returned lightly. 'Goodbye.'

VII

Jim thoughtfully retraced his steps. He was a village character, and he had a villager's simplicity: that is, the simplicity which comes from the lack of a complicated experience. But simple by nature he certainly was not. Among the rank and file of rustics he was quite a Talleyrand,[37] or rather had been one, till he lost a good deal of his self-command by falling in love.

Now, however, that the charming object of his distraction was out of sight he could deliberate, and measure, and weigh things with some approach to keenness. The substance of his queries was, What change had come over Margery – whence these new notions?

Ponder as he would he could evolve no answer save one, which, eminently unsatisfactory as it was, he felt it would be unreasonable not to accept: that she was simply skittish and ambitious by nature, and would not be hunted into matrimony till he had provided a well-adorned home.

Jim returned to the kiln, and looked to the fires. The kiln stood in a peculiar, interesting, even impressive spot. It was at the end of a short ravine in the lower chalk formation, and all around was an open hilly down or coomb. The nearest house was that of Jim's cousin and partner, which stood on the outskirts of the down beside the turnpike-road. From this house a little lane wound between the steep escarpments of the ravine till it reached the kiln, which faced down the miniature valley, commanding it as a fort might command a defile.

The idea of a fort in this association owed little to imagination. For on the nibbled green steep above the kiln stood a bye-gone, worn-out specimen of such an erection, huge, impressive, and difficult to scale even now in its decay. It was a British castle or entrenchment,[38] with triple rings of defence, rising roll behind roll, their outlines cutting sharply against the sky, and Jim's kiln nearly undermining their base. When the lime-kiln flared up in the night, which it often did, its fires lit up the front of these ramparts to a great majesty. They were old friends of his, and while keeping up the heat through the long darkness, as it was sometimes his duty to do, he would imagine the dancing lights and shades about the stupendous earthwork to be the forms of those giants who (he supposed) had heaped it up. Often he clambered upon it, and walked about the summit, thinking out the problems connected with his business, his partner, his future, his Margery.

It was what he did this evening, continuing the meditation on the young girl's manner that he had begun upon the road, and still, as then, finding no clue to the change.

While thus engaged he observed a man coming up the ravine to the kiln. Business messages were almost invariably left at the house below, and Jim watched the man with the interest excited by a belief that he had come on a personal matter. On nearer approach Jim recognized him as the gardener at Mount Lodge. If this meant business, the Baron (of whose arrival Jim had vaguely heard) was a new and unexpected customer.

It meant nothing else, apparently. The man's errand was simply to inform Jim that the Baron required a load of lime for the garden.

'You might have saved yourself trouble by leaving word at Mr Vine's,' said Jim.

'I was to see you personally,' said the gardener, 'and to say that the Baron would like to inquire of you about the different qualities of lime proper for such purposes.'

'Couldn't you tell him yourself?' said Jim.

'He said I was to tell you that,' replied the gardener; 'and it wasn't for me to interfere.'

No motive other than the ostensible one could possibly be conjectured by Jim Hayward at this time; and the next morning he started with great pleasure, in his best business suit of clothes. By eleven o'clock he and his horse and cart had arrived on the Baron's premises, and the lime was deposited where directed; an exceptional spot, just within view of the windows of the south front.

Baron Von Xanten, pale and melancholy, was sauntering in the sun on the slope between the house and the all-the-year-round. He looked across to where Jim and the gardener were standing, and the identity of Hayward being established by what he brought, the Baron came down, and the gardener withdrew.

The Baron's first inquiries were, as Jim had been led to suppose they would be, on the exterminating effects of lime upon slugs and snails in its different conditions of slaked and unslaked, ground and in the lump. He appeared to be much interested by Jim's explanations, and eyed the young man closely whenever he had an opportunity.

'And I hope trade is prosperous with you this year,' said the Baron.

'Very, my noble lord,' replied Jim, who, in his uncertainty on the proper method of address, wisely concluded that it was better to err by giving too much honour than by giving too little. 'In short, trade is looking so well that I've become a partner in the firm.'

'Indeed; I am glad to hear it. So now you are settled in life.'

'Well, my lord; I am hardly settled, even now. For I've got to finish it – I mean, to get married.'

'That's an easy matter, compared with the partnership.'

'Now a man might think so, my lord,' said Jim, getting more confidential. 'But the real truth is, 'tis the hardest part of all for me.'

'Your suit prospers, I hope?'

'It don't,' said Jim. 'It don't at all just at present. In short, I can't for the life o' me think what's come over the young woman lately.' And he fell into deep reflection.

Though Jim did not observe it, the Baron's brow became shadowed with self-reproach as he heard those simple words, and his eyes had a look of pity. 'Indeed – since when?' he asked.

'Since yesterday, my noble lord.' Jim spoke meditatively. He was resolving upon a bold stroke. Why not make a confidant of this kind gentleman, instead of the parson, as he had intended? The thought was no sooner conceived than acted on. 'My lord,' he resumed, 'I have heard that you are a nobleman of great scope and talent, who has seen more strange countries and characters than I have ever heard of, and know the insides of men well. Therefore I would fain put a question to your noble lordship, if I may so trouble you, and having nobody else in the world who could inform me so truly.'

'Any advice I can give is at your service, Hayward. What do you wish to know?'

'It is this, my lord. What can I do to bring down a young woman's ambition that's got to such a towering height there's no reaching it or compassing it: how get her to be pleased with me and my station as she used to be when I first knew her?'

'Truly, that's a hard question, my man. What does she aspire to?'

'She's got a craze for fine furniture.'

'How long has she had it?'

'Only just now.'

The Baron seemed still more to experience regret. 'What furniture does she specially covet?' he asked.

'Silver candlesticks, work-tables, looking-glasses, gold tea-things, silver tea-pots, gold clocks, curtains, pictures, and I don't know what all – things I shall never get if I live to be a hundred – not so much that I couldn't raise the money to buy 'em, as that I ought to put it to other uses, or save it for a rainy day.'

'You think the possession of those articles would make her happy?'

'I really think they might, my lord.'

'Good. Open your pocket-book and write as I tell you.'

Jim in some astonishment did as commanded, and elevating his pocket-book against the garden-wall, thoroughly moistened his pencil, and wrote at the Baron's dictation:

'Pair of silver candlesticks: inlaid work-table and work-box: one large mirror: two small ditto: one gilt china tea and coffee service: one silver tea-pot, coffee-pot, sugar-basin, jug, and dozen spoons: French clock: pair of curtains: six large pictures.'

'Now,' said the Baron, 'tear out that leaf and give it to me. Keep a close tongue about this; go home, and don't be surprised at anything that may come to your door.'

'But, my noble lord, you don't mean that your lordship is going to give —'

'Never mind what I am going to do. Only keep your own counsel. I perceive that, though a plain countryman, you are by no means deficient in tact and understanding. If sending these things to you gives me pleasure, why should you object? The fact is, Hayward, I occasionally take an interest in people, and like to do a little for them. I take an interest in you. Now go home, and a week hence invite Marg—the young woman and her father, to tea with you. The rest is in your own hands.'

A question often put to Jim in after times was why it had not occurred to him at once that the Baron's liberal conduct must have been dictated by something more personal than sudden spontaneous generosity to him, a stranger. To which Jim always answered that, admitting the existence of such generosity, there had appeared nothing remarkable in the Baron selecting himself as its object. The Baron had told him that he took an interest in him; and self-esteem, even with the most modest, is usually sufficient to over-ride any little difficulty that might occur to an outsider in accounting for a preference. He moreover considered that foreign noblemen, rich and eccentric, might have habits of acting which were quite at variance with those of their English compeers.

So he drove off homeward with a lighter heart than he had known for several days. To have a foreign gentleman take a fancy to him – what a triumph to a plain sort of fellow, who had scarcely expected the Baron to look in his face. It would be a fine story to tell Margery when the Baron gave him liberty to speak out.

Jim lodged at the house of his cousin and partner, Richard Vine, a widower of fifty odd years. Having failed in the development of a household of direct descendants this tradesman had been glad to let his chambers to his much younger relative, when the latter entered on the business of lime manufacture; and their intimacy had led to a partnership. Jim lived upstairs; his partner lived down; and the furniture of all the rooms was so plain and old fashioned as to excite the special dislike of Miss Margery Tucker, and even to prejudice her against Jim for tolerating it. Not only were the chairs and tables queer, but, with due regard to the principle that a man's surroundings should bear the impress of that man's life and occupation, the chief ornaments of the dwelling were a curious collection of calcinations, that had been discovered from time to time in the lime-kiln – misshapen ingots of strange substance, some of them like Pompeian remains.[39]

The head of the firm was a quiet-living, narrow-minded, though friendly, man of fifty; and he took a serious interest in Jim's love-suit, frequently inquiring how it progressed, and assuring Jim that if he chose to marry he might have all the upper floor at a low rent, he, Mr Vine, contenting himself entirely with the ground level. It had been so convenient for discussing business matters to have Jim in the same house, that he did not wish any change to be made in consequence of a change in Jim's state. Margery knew of this wish, and of Jim's concurrent feeling; and did not like the idea at all.

About four days after the young man's interview with the Baron, there drew up in front of Jim's house at noon a waggon laden with cases and packages, large and small. They were all addressed to 'Mr

Hayward', and they had come from the largest furnishing warehouses in that part of England.

Three-quarters of an hour were occupied in getting the cases to Jim's rooms. The wary Jim did not show the amazement he felt at his patron's munificence; and presently the senior partner came into the passage, and wondered what was lumbering upstairs.

'Oh – it's only some things of mine,' said Jim.

'Bearing upon the coming event – eh?' said his partner.

'Exactly,' replied Jim.

Mr Vine, with some astonishment at the number of cases, shortly after went away to the kiln; whereupon Jim shut himself into his rooms, and there he might have been heard ripping up and opening boxes with a cautious hand, afterwards appearing outside the door with them empty, and carrying them off to the outhouse.

A triumphant look lit up his face when, a little later in the afternoon, he ran across the meads to the dairy, and invited Margery and her father to his house to supper.

She was not unsociable that day, and, her father expressing a hard and fast acceptance of the invitation, she perforce agreed to go with him. Again at home, Jim made himself as mysteriously busy as before in those rooms of his, and when his partner returned he too was asked to join in the supper.

At dusk Hayward went to the door, where he stood till he heard the voices of his guests from the direction of the low grounds, now covered with their frequent fleece of fog. The voices grew more distinct, and then on the white surface of the fog there appeared two trunkless heads, from which bodies gradually extended as the approaching pair rose towards the house.

When they had entered Jim pressed Margery's hand and conducted her up to his rooms, her father waiting below to say a few words to the senior lime-burner.

'Bless me,' said Jim to her, on entering the sitting-room; 'I quite forgot to get a light beforehand; but I'll have one in a jiffy.'

Margery stood in the middle of the dark room, while Jim struck a match; and then the young girl's eyes were conscious of a burst of light, and the rise into being of a pair of handsome silver candlesticks containing two candles that Jim was in the act of lighting.

'Why – where – you have candlesticks like that?' said Margery. Her eyes flew round the room as the growing candle-flames showed other articles. 'Pictures too – and lovely china – why I knew nothing of this, I declare.'

'Yes – a few things that came to me by accident,' said Jim quietly.

'And a great gold clock under a glass, and a cupid swinging for a pendulum; and oh what a lovely work-table – woods of every colour – and a work-box to match. May I look inside that work-box, Jim? – whose is it?'

'Oh yes; look at it of course. It is a poor enough thing, but 'tis mine; and it will belong to the woman I marry, whoever she may be, as well as all the other things here.'

'And the curtains and the looking-glasses: why I declare I can see myself in a hundred places.'

'That tea-set,' said Jim, placidly pointing to a gorgeous china service and a large silver tea-pot on the side table, 'I don't use at present, being a bachelor-man; but, says I to myself, "whoever I marry will want some such things for giving her parties; or I can sell em" – but I haven't took steps for't yet —'

'Sell 'em – no, I should think not,' said Margery with earnest reproach. 'Why, I hope you wouldn't be so foolish! Why, this is exactly the kind of thing I was thinking of when I told you of the things women could want – of course not meaning myself particularly. I had no idea that you had such valuable —' Margery was unable to speak coherently, so much was she amazed at the wealth of Jim's possessions.

At this moment her father and the lime-burner came upstairs; and to appear womanly and proper to Mr Vine, Margery repressed the remainder of her surprise. As for the two elderly worthies, it was not till they entered the room and sat down that their slower eyes discerned anything brilliant in the appointments. Then one of them stole a glance at some article, and the other at another; but each being unwilling to express his wonder in the presence of his neighbours, they received the objects before them with quite an accustomed air; the lime-burner inwardly trying to conjecture what all this meant, and the dairyman musing that if Jim's business allowed him to accumulate at this rate, the sooner Margery became his wife the better. Margery retreated to the work-table, work-box, and tea-service, which she examined with hushed exclamations.

An entertainment thus surprisingly begun could not fail to progress well. Whenever Margery's crusty old father felt the need of a civil sentence, the flash of Jim's fancy articles inspired him to one; while the lime-burner, having reasoned away his first ominous thought that all this had come out of the firm, also felt proud and blithe.

Jim accompanied his dairy friends part of the way home. Her father, finding that Jim wanted to speak to her privately, and that she exhibited some elusiveness, turned to Margery and said, 'Come, come, my lady; no more of this nonsense. You just step behind with that young man.'

Margery, a little scared at her father's peremptoriness, obeyed. It was plain that Jim had won the old man by that night's stroke, if he had not won her.

'I know what you are going to say, Jim,' she began, less ardently now, for she was no longer under the novel influence of the shining silver and glass. 'Well, as you desire it, and as my father desires it, and as I suppose it will be the best course for me, I will fix the day – not this evening, but as soon as I can think it over.'

VIII

Notwithstanding a press of business, Jim went and did his duty in thanking the Baron. The latter saw him in his fishing-tackle room, an apartment littered with every appliance that a votary of the rod could require.

'And when is the wedding-day to be, Hayward?' the Baron asked, after Jim had told him that matters were settled.

'It is not quite certain yet, my noble lord,' said Jim cheerfully. 'But I hope 'twill not be long after the time when God A'mighty christens the little apples.'[40]

'And when is that?'

'St Swithin's – the middle of July. 'Tis to be some time in that month, she tells me.'

When Jim was gone the Baron seemed meditative. He went out, ascended the mount, and entered the weather-screen, where he looked at the seats, as though re-enacting in his fancy the scene of that memorable morning of fog. He turned his eyes to the angle of the shelter, round which Margery had suddenly appeared like a vision, and it was plain that he would not have minded her appearing there then. The juncture had indeed been such an impressive and critical one that she must have seemed rather a heavenly messenger than a passing milkmaid, more especially to a man like the Baron, who, despite the mystery of his origin and life, revealed himself to be a melancholy, emotional character – the Jacques of this forest and stream.[41]

Behind the mount the ground rose yet higher, ascending to a plantation which sheltered the house. The Baron strolled up here, and bent his gaze over the distance. The valley of the Swenn lay before him, with its shining river, the brooks that fed it, and the brimming carriers that fed the brooks. The situation of Margery's house was visible, though not the house itself; and the Baron gazed that way for an infinitely long time, till, remembering himself, he moved on.

Instead of returning to the house he went along the ridge till he arrived at the verge of Chillington Wood, and in the same desultory manner roamed under the trees, not pausing till he had come to Three-Walks-End, and the hollow elm hard by. He peeped in at the rift. In the soft dry layer of wood-dust that floored the hollow Margery's tracks were still visible, as she had made them there when dressing for the ball.

'Little Margery!' murmured the Baron.

In a moment he thought better of this mood, and turned to go home. But behold, a form stood behind him – that of the girl whose name had been on his lips.

She was in utter confusion. 'I – I – did not know you were here, sir!' she began. 'I was out for a little walk.' She could get no further; her eyes filled with tears. That spice of wilfulness, even hardness, which characterized her in Jim's company, magically disappeared in the presence of the Baron.

'Never mind, never mind,' said he, masking under a severe manner whatever he felt. 'The meeting is awkward, and ought not to have occurred, especially if, as I suppose, you are shortly to be married to James Hayward. But it cannot be helped now. You had no idea I was here, of course. Neither had I of seeing you. Remember you cannot be too careful,' continued the Baron, in the same grave tone; 'and I strongly request you as a friend to do your utmost to avoid meetings like this. When you saw me before I turned, why did you not go away?'

'I did not see you, sir. I did not think of seeing you. I was walking this way, and I only looked in to see the tree.'

'That shows you have been thinking of things you should not think of,' returned the Baron. 'Good morning.'

Margery could answer nothing. A brow-beaten glance, almost of misery, was all she gave him. He took a slow step away from her; then turned suddenly back and, stooping, impulsively kissed her cheek, taking her as much by surprise as ever a woman was taken in her life.

Immediately after he went off with a flushed face and rapid strides, which he did not check till he was within his own boundaries.

The haymaking season now set in vigorously, and the weir-hatches were all down[42] in the meads to drain off the water. The carriers ran themselves dry, and there was no longer any difficulty in walking about among them. The Baron could very well witness from the elevations about his house the activity which followed these preliminaries. The white shirt-sleeves of the mowers glistened in the sun, the scythes flashed, voices echoed, snatches of song floated about, and there were glimpses of red waggon-wheels, purple gowns, and many-coloured handkerchiefs.

The Baron had been told that the haymaking was to be followed by the wedding, and had he gone down to the dairy he would have had plenty of evidence to that effect. Dairyman Tucker's house was in a whirlpool of bustle, and among other difficulties was that of turning the cheese-room into a genteel apartment for the time being, and hiding the awkwardness of having to pass through the milk-house to get to the parlour door. These household contrivances appeared to interest Margery much more than the great question of dressing for the ceremony and the ceremony itself. In all relating to that she showed an indescribable backwardness, which later on was well remembered.

'If it were only somebody else, and I was one of the bridesmaids, I really think I should like it better!' she murmured one afternoon.

'Away with thee – that's only your shyness!' said one of the milkmaids.

It is said that about this time the Baron seemed to feel the effects of solitude strongly. Solitude revives the simple instincts of primitive man, and lonely country nooks afford rich soil for wayward emotions. Moreover, idleness waters those unconsidered impulses which a short season of turmoil would stamp out. It is difficult to speak with any exactness of the bearing of such conditions on the mind of the Baron – a man of whom so little was ever truly known – but there is no doubt that his mind ran much on Margery as an individual, without reference to her rank or quality, or to the question whether she would marry Jim Hayward that summer. She was the single lovely human thing within his present horizon, for he lived in absolute seclusion; and her image unduly affected him.

But, leaving conjecture, let us state what happened. One Saturday evening, two or three weeks after his accidental meeting with her in the wood, he wrote the note following: –

'DEAR MARGERY, –

'You must not suppose that, because I spoke somewhat severely to you at our chance encounter by the hollow tree, I have any feeling against you. Far from it. Now, as ever, I have the most grateful sense of your considerate kindness to me on a momentous occasion which shall be nameless.

'You solemnly promised to come and see me whenever I should send for you. Can you call for five minutes as soon as possible? and disperse those plaguy glooms from which I am so unfortunate as to suffer? If you refuse I will not answer for the consequences. I shall be in the summer-shelter on the mount tomorrow morning at half-past ten. If you come I shall be grateful. I have also something for you.

'Yours,
'X.'

In keeping with the tenor of this epistle the desponding, self-oppressed Baron ascended the mount on Sunday morning and sat down. There was nothing here to exactly signify the hour, but before the church bells had begun he heard somebody approaching at the back. The light footstep moved timidly, first to one recess, and then to another; then to the third, where he sat in the shade. Poor Margery stood before him.

She looked worn and weary, and her little shoes and the skirts of her dress were covered with dust. The weather was sultry, the sun being already high and powerful, and rain had not fallen for weeks. The Baron, who walked little, had thought nothing of the effects of this heat and drought in inducing fatigue. A distance which had been but a reasonable exercise on a foggy morning was a drag for Margery now. She was out of breath; and anxiety, even unhappiness was written on her everywhere.

He rose to his feet, and took her hand. He was vexed with himself at sight of her. 'My dear little girl!' he said. 'You are tired – you should not have come.'

'You sent for me, sir; and I was afraid you were ill; and my promise to you was sacred.'

He bent over her, looking upon her downcast face, and still holding her hand; then he dropped it, and took a pace or two backwards.

'It was a whim, nothing more,' he said, sadly. 'I wanted to see my little friend, to express good wishes – and to present her with this.' He held forward a small morocco case, and showed her how to open it, disclosing a pretty locket, set with pearls. 'It is intended as a wedding present,' he continued. 'To be returned to me again if you do not marry Jim this summer – it is to be this summer I think?'

'It was, sir,' she said with agitation. 'But it is so no longer. And, therefore, I cannot take this.'

'What do you say?'

'It was to have been today; but now it cannot be.'

'The wedding today – Sunday?' he cried.

'We fixed Sunday not to hinder much time at this busy season of the year,' replied she.

'And have you, then, put it off – surely not?'

'You sent for me, and I have come,' she answered humbly, like an obedient familiar in the employ of some great enchanter. Indeed, the Baron's power over this innocent girl was curiously like enchantment, or mesmeric influence. It was so masterful that the sexual element was almost eliminated. It was that of Prospero over the gentle Ariel.[43] And yet it was probably only that of the cosmopolite over the recluse, of the experienced man over the simple maid.

'You have come — on your wedding-day! — Oh, Margery, this is a mistake. Of course, you should not have obeyed me, since, though I thought your wedding would be soon, I did not know it was today.'

'I promised you, sir; and I would rather keep my promise to you than be married to Jim.'

'Margery, that must not be — the feeling is wrong!' he murmured, looking at the distant hills. 'There seems to be a fate in all this; I get out of the frying-pan into the fire. What a recompense to you for your goodness! The fact is, I was out of health and out of spirits, so I — but no more of that. Now instantly to repair this tremendous blunder that we have made — that's the question.'

After a pause, he went on hurriedly, 'Walk down the hill; get into the road. By that time I shall be there with a phaeton. We may get back in time. What time is it now? If not, no doubt the wedding can be tomorrow; so all will come right again. Don't cry, my dear girl. Keep the locket, of course — you'll marry Jim.'

IX

He hastened down towards the stables, and she went on as directed. It seemed as if he must have put in the horse himself, so quickly did he reappear with the phaeton on the open road. Margery silently took her seat, and the Baron seemed cut to the quick with self-reproach as he noticed the listless indifference with which she acted. There was no doubt that in her heart she had preferred obeying the apparently important mandate that morning to becoming Jim's wife; but there was no less doubt that had the Baron left her alone she would quietly have gone to the altar.

He drove along furiously, in a cloud of dust. There was much to contemplate in that peaceful Sunday morning – the windless trees and fields, the shaking sunlight, the pause in human stir. Yet neither of them heeded, and thus they drew near to the dairy. His first expressed intention had been to go indoors with her, but this he abandoned as impolitic in the highest degree.

'You may be soon enough,' he said, springing down, and helping her to follow. 'Tell the truth: say you were sent for to receive a wedding present – that it was a mistake on my part – a mistake on yours; and I think they'll forgive . . . And, Margery, my last request to you is this: that if I send for you again, you do not come. Promise solemnly, my dear girl, that any such request shall be unheeded.'

Her lips moved, but the promise was not articulated. 'Oh, sir, I cannot promise it!' she said at last.

'But you must; your salvation may depend on it!' he insisted almost fiercely.[44] 'You don't know what I am.'

'Then, sir, I promise,' she replied. 'Now leave me to myself, please, and I'll go indoors and manage matters.'

He turned the horse and drove away, but only for a little distance. Out of sight he pulled rein suddenly. 'Only to go back and propose it to her, and she'd come,' he murmured.

He stood up in the phaeton, and by this means he could see over the hedge. Margery still sat listlessly in the same place; there was not a lovelier flower in the field. 'No,' he said; 'no, no – never!' He reseated himself, and the wheels sped lightly back over the soft dust to Mount Lodge.

Meanwhile Margery had not moved. If the Baron could dissimulate on the side of severity she could dissimulate on the side of calm. He did not know what had been veiled by the quiet promise to manage matters indoors. Rising at length she first turned away from the house; and, by-and-bye, having apparently forgotten till then that she carried it in her hand, she opened the case, and looked at the locket. This seemed to give her courage. She turned, set her face towards the dairy in good earnest, and though her heart faltered when the gates came in sight, she kept on and drew near the door.

On the threshold she stood listening. The house was silent. Decorations were visible in the passage, and also the carefully swept and sanded path to the gate, which she was to have trodden as a bride; but the sparrows hopped over it as if it were abandoned; and all appeared to have been checked at its climacteric, like a clock stopped on the strike. Till this moment of confronting the suspended animation of the scene she had not realized the full shock of the convulsion which her disappearance must have caused. It is quite certain – apart from her own repeated assurances to that effect in later years – that in hastening off that morning to her sudden engagement, Margery had not counted the cost of such an enterprise; while a dim notion that she might get back again in time for the ceremony, if the message meant nothing serious, should also be mentioned in her favour. But, upon the whole, she had obeyed the call with an unreasoning obedience, worthy of a disciple in primitive times. A conviction that the Baron's life might depend upon her presence – for she had by this time divined the tragical event she had interrupted on the foggy morning – took from her all will to judge and consider calmly. The simple affairs of her and hers seemed nothing beside the possibility of harm to him.

A well-known step moved on the sanded floor within, and she went forward. That she saw her father's face before her, just within the door, can hardly be said: it was rather Reproach and Rage in a human mask.

'What! ye have dared to come back alive, hussy, to look upon the dupery you have practised on honest people! You've mortified us all; I don't want to see ye; I don't want to hear ye; I don't want to know anything!' He walked up and down the room, unable to command himself. 'Nothing but being dead could have excused ye for not meeting and marrying that man this morning; and yet you have the brazen impudence to stand there as well as ever! What be you here for?'

'I've come back to marry Jim, if he wants me to,' she said faintly. 'And if not – perhaps so much the better. I was sent for this morning early. I thought —' She halted. To say that she had thought a man's death might happen by his own hand if she did not go to him, would never do. 'I was obliged to go,' she said. 'I had given my word.'

'Why didn't you tell us then, so that the wedding could be put off, without making fools o' us?'

'Because I was afraid you wouldn't let me go, and I had made up my mind to go.'

'To go where?'

She was silent; till she said, 'I will tell Jim all, and why it was; and if he's any friend of mine he'll excuse me.'

'Not Jim – he's no such fool. Jim had put all ready for you, Jim had called at your house, a dressed up in his new wedding clothes, and a smiling like the sun; Jim had told the parson, had got the ringers in tow, and the clerk a waiting; and then – you was *gone*! Then Jim turned as pale as rendlewood, and busted out, "If she don't marry me today," 'a said, "she don't marry me at all! No; let her look elsewhere for a husband. For two years I've put up with her hontish tricks and her takings," 'a said. "I've droudged and I've traipsed, I've bought and I've sold, all wi' an eye to her; I've suffered horseflesh," he says – yes, them was his noble words – "but I'll suffer it no longer. She shall go!" "Jim," says I, "you be a man. If she's alive, I commend ye; if she's dead, I pity my old age." "She isn't dead," says he; "for I've just heard she was seen walking off across the fields this morning, looking all of a scornful triumph." He turned round and went, and the rest o' the neighbours went; and here be I left to the reproach o't.'

'He was too hasty,' murmured Margery. 'For now he's said this I can't marry him tomorrow, as I might ha' done; and perhaps so much the better.'

'You can be so calm about it, can ye? Be my arrangements nothing, then, that you should break 'em up, and say off hand what wasn't done today might ha' been done tomorrow, and such flick-flack? Out o' my sight! I won't hear any more. I won't speak to ye any more.'

'I'll go away, and then you'll be sorry!'

'Very well, go. Sorry – not I.'

He turned and stamped his way into the cheese-room. Margery went upstairs. She too was excited now, and instead of fortifying herself in her bedroom till her father's rage had blown over, as she had often done on lesser occasions, she packed up a bundle of articles, crept down again, and went out of the house. She had a place of refuge in these cases of necessity, and her father knew it, and was less alarmed at seeing her depart than he might otherwise have been. This place was Rook's Gate,[45] the house of her grandmother, who always took Margery's part when that young woman was particularly in the wrong.

The devious way she pursued, to avoid the vicinity of Mount Lodge, was tedious, and she was already weary. But the cottage was a restful place to arrive at, for she was her own mistress there – her grandmother never coming down stairs – and Edy, the woman who lived with and attended her, being a cipher except in muscle and voice. The approach was by a straight open road, bordered by thin lank trees, all sloping away from the south-west wind-quarter, and the scene bore a strange resemblance to certain bits of Dutch landscape which have been imprinted on the world's eye by Hobbema and his school.[46]

Having explained to her granny that the wedding was put off, and that she had come to stay, one of Margery's first acts was carefully to pack up the locket and case, her wedding present from the Baron. The conditions of the gift were unfulfilled, and she wished it to go back instantly. Perhaps, in the intricacies of her bosom, there lurked a greater satisfaction with the reason for returning the present than she would have felt just then with a reason for keeping it.

To send the article was difficult. In the evening she wrapped herself up, searched and found a gauze veil that had been used by her grandmother in past years for hiving swarms of bees, buried her face in it, and sallied forth with a palpitating heart till she drew near the tabernacle of her demi-god the Baron. She ventured only to the back-door, where she handed in the parcel addressed to him, and quickly came away.

Now it seems that during the day the Baron had been unable to learn the result of his attempt to return Margery in time for the event he had interrupted. Wishing, for obvious reasons, to avoid direct inquiry by messenger, and being too unwell to go far himself, he could learn no particulars. He was sitting in thought after a lonely dinner when the parcel intimating failure was brought in. The footman, whose curiosity had been excited by the mode of its arrival, peeped through the keyhole after closing the door, to learn what the packet meant. Directly the Baron had opened it he thrust out his feet vehemently from his chair, and began cursing his ruinous conduct in bringing about such a disaster, for the return of the locket denoted not only no wedding that day, but none tomorrow, or at any time.

'I have done that innocent woman a great wrong!' he murmured. 'Deprived her of, perhaps, her only opportunity of becoming mistress of a happy home!'

X

A considerable period of inaction followed among all concerned.

Nothing tended to dissipate the obscurity which veiled the life of the Baron. The position he occupied in the minds of the country-folk around was one which combined the mysteriousness of a legendary character with the unobtrusive deeds of a modern gentleman. To this day whoever takes the trouble to go down to Stickleford and make inquiries will find existing there almost a superstitious feeling for the moody melancholy stranger who resided in the Lodge some forty years ago.

Whence he came, whither he was going, were alike unknown. It was said that his mother had been an English lady of noble family who had married a foreigner not unheard of in circles where men pile up 'the cankered heaps of strange-achieved gold'[47] – that he had been born and educated in England, taken abroad, and so on. But the facts of a life in such cases are of little account beside the aspect of a life; and hence, though doubtless the years of his existence contained their share of trite and homely circumstance, the curtain which masked all this was never lifted to gratify such a theatre of spectators as those at Stickleford. Therein lay his charm. His life was a vignette, of which the central strokes only were drawn with any distinctness, the environment shading away to a blank.

He might have been said to resemble that solitary bird the heron. The still, lonely stream was his frequent haunt: on its banks he would stand for hours with his rod, looking into the water, beholding the tawny inhabitants with the eye of a philosopher, and seeming to say,

'Bite or don't bite – it's all the same to me.' He was often mistaken for a ghost by children; and for a pollard willow by men, when, on their way home in the dusk, they saw him motionless by some rushy bank, unobservant of the decline of day.

Why did he come to fish at Stickleford? That was never explained. As far as was known he had no relatives near; the fishing there was not exceptionally good; the society thereabout was decidedly meagre. That he had committed some folly or hasty act, that he had been wrongfully accused of some crime, thus rendering his seclusion from the world desirable for a while, squared very well with his frequent melancholy. But such as he was there he lived, well supplied with fishing-tackle, and tenant of a furnished house, just suited to the requirements of such an eccentric being as he.

Margery's father, having privately ascertained that she was living with her grandmother, and getting into no harm, refrained from communicating with her, in the hope of seeing her contrite at his door. It had, of course, become known about Stickleford that at the last moment Margery refused to wed Hayward, by absenting herself from the house. Jim was pitied, yet not pitied much, for it was said that he ought not to have been so eager for a woman who had shown no anxiety for him.

And where was Jim himself? It must not be supposed that that tactician had all this while withdrawn from mortal eye to tear his hair in silent indignation and despair. He had, in truth, merely retired up the lonesome defile between the downs to his smouldering kiln, and the ancient ramparts above it; and there, after his first hours of natural discomposure, he quietly waited for overtures from the possibly repentant Margery. But no overtures arrived, and then he meditated anew on the absorbing problem of her skittishness, and how to set about another campaign for her conquest, notwithstanding his late disastrous failure. Why had he failed? To what was her strange conduct owing? That was the thing which puzzled him.

He had made no advance in solving the riddle when, one morning, a stranger appeared on the down above him, looking as if he had lost his way. The man had a good deal of black hair below his felt hat, and carried under his arm a case containing a musical instrument.

Descending to where Jim stood, he asked if there were not a short cut across that way to Budmouth.

'Well, yes, there is,' said Jim. 'But 'tis an enormous distance for ye.'

'Oh, yes,' replied the musician. 'I wish to intercept the carrier on the highway.'

The nearest way was precisely in the direction of Rook's Gate, where Margery, as Jim knew, was staying. Having some time to spare, Jim was strongly impelled to make a kind act to the lost musician a pretext for taking observations in that neighbourhood, and telling his acquaintance that he was going the same way, he started without further ado.

They skirted the long length of meads, and in due time arrived at the back of Rook's Gate, where the path joined the high road. A hedge divided the public way from the cottage garden. Jim drew up at this point and said, 'Your road is straight on: I turn back here.'

But the musician was standing fixed, as if in great perplexity. Thrusting his hand into his forest of black hair, he murmured, 'Surely it is the same – surely!'

Jim, following the direction of his neighbour's eyes, found them to be fixed on a figure till that moment hidden from himself – Margery Tucker – who was crossing the garden to an opposite gate with a little cheese in her arms, her head thrown back, and her face quite exposed.

'What of her?' said Jim.

'Two months ago I formed one of the band at the Yeomanry Ball given by Lord Blakemore. I saw that young lady dancing the polka there in robes of gauze and lace. Now I see her carry a cheese!'

'Never!' said Jim incredulously.

'But I do not mistake. I say it is so!'

Jim ridiculed the idea; the bandsman protested, and was about to lose his temper, when Jim gave in with the good-nature of a person who can afford to despise opinions; and the musician went his way.

As he dwindled out of sight Jim began to think more carefully over what he had said. The young man's thoughts grew quite to an excitement, for there came into his mind the Baron's extraordinary kindness in regard to furniture, hitherto accounted for by the assumption that the nobleman had taken a fancy to him. Could it be, among all the amazing things of life, that the Baron was at the bottom of this mischief, and that he had amused himself by taking Margery to a ball?

Doubts and suspicions which distract some lovers to imbecility only served to bring out Jim's great qualities. Where he trusted he was the most trusting fellow in the world; where he doubted he could be guilty of the slyest strategy. Once suspicious, he became one of those subtle, watchful characters who, without integrity, make good thieves; with a little, good jobbers; with a great deal, master politicians. Jim was honest, and he considered what to do.

Retracing his steps, he peeped again. She had gone in; but she would soon reappear, for it could be seen that she was carrying little new cheeses one by one to a spring-cart and horse tethered outside the gate – her grandmother, though not a regular dairywoman, still managing a few cows by means of a man and maid. With the lightness of a cat Jim crept round to the gate, took a piece of chalk from his pocket, and wrote upon the boarding '*The Baron*'. Then he retreated to the other side of the garden where he had just watched Margery.

In due time she emerged with another little cheese, came on to the garden-door, and glanced upon the chalked words which confronted her. She started; the cheese rolled from her arms to the ground, and broke into pieces like a pudding.

She looked fearfully round, her face burning like sunset, and, seeing nobody, stooped to pick up the flaccid lumps. Jim, with a pale face, departed as invisibly as he had come. He had proved the bandsman's tale to be true. On his way back he formed a resolution. It was to beard the lion in his den[48] – to call on the Baron.

Meanwhile Margery had recovered her equanimity, and gathered up the broken cheese. But she could by no means account for the handwriting. Jim was just the sort of fellow to play her such a trick at ordinary times, but she imagined him to be far too incensed against her to do it now; and she suddenly wondered if it were any sort of signal from the Baron himself.

Of him she had lately heard nothing. If ever monotony pervaded a life it pervaded hers at Rook's Gate; and she had begun to despair of any happy change. But it is precisely when the social atmosphere seems stagnant that great events are brewing. Margery's quiet was broken first, as we have seen, by a slight start, only sufficient to make her drop a cheese; and then by a more serious matter.

She was inside the same garden one day when she heard two watermen talking without. The conversation was to the effect that the strange gentleman who had taken Mount Lodge for the season was seriously ill.

'How ill?' cried Margery through the hedge, which screened her from recognition.

'Bad abed,' said one of the watermen.

'Inflammation of the lungs,' said the other.

'Got wet, fishing,' the first chimed in.

Margery could gather no more. An ideal admiration rather than any positive passion existed in her breast for the Baron: she had of late seen too little of him to allow any incipient views of him as a lover to grow to formidable dimensions. It was an extremely pure and romantic feeling,[49] delicate as an aroma, capable of quickening to an active principle, or dying to 'a painless sympathy',[50] as the case might be.

This news of his illness, coupled with the mysterious chalking on the gate, troubled her, and revived his image much. She took to walking up and down the garden-paths, looking into the hearts of flowers, and not thinking what they were. His last request had been that she was not to go to him if he should send for her; and now she asked herself, was the name on the gate a hint to enable her to go without infringing the letter of her promise? Thus unexpectedly had Jim's manoeuvre operated.

Ten days passed. All she could hear of the Baron were the same words, 'Bad abed', till one afternoon, after a gallop of the physician to the Lodge, the tidings spread like lightning that the Baron was dying.

Margery distressed herself with the question whether she might be permitted to visit him and say her prayers at his bedside; but she feared to venture; and thus eight-and-forty hours slipped away, and the Baron still lived. Despite her shyness and awe of him she had almost made up her mind to call when, just at dusk on that October evening, somebody came to the door and asked for her.

She could see the messenger's head against the low new moon. He was a man-servant. He said he had been all the way to her father's, and had been sent thence to her here. He simply brought a note, and, delivering it into her hands, went away.

'MARGERY TUCKER (ran the note): –

'They say I am not likely to live, so I want to see you. Be here at eight o'clock this evening. Come quite alone to the side-door, and tap four times softly. My trusty man will admit you. The occasion is an important one. Prepare yourself for a solemn ceremony, which I wish to have performed while it lies in my power.

'VON XANTEN.'

XI

Margery's face flushed up, and her neck and arms glowed in sympathy. The quickness of youthful imagination, and the assumptiveness of woman's reason, sent her straight as an arrow this thought: 'He wants to marry me!'

She had heard of similar strange proceedings, in which the orange-flower and the sad cypress were inter-twined. People sometimes wished on their death-beds, from motives of esteem, to form a legal tie which they had not cared to establish as a domestic one during their active life.

For a few minutes Margery could hardly be called excited; she was excitement itself. Between surprise and modesty she blushed and trembled by turns. She became grave, sat down in the solitary room, and looked into the fire. At seven o'clock she rose resolved, and went quite tranquilly upstairs, where she speedily began to dress.

In making this hasty toilet nine-tenths of her care were given to her hands. The summer had left them slightly brown, and she held them up and looked at them with some misgiving, the fourth finger of her left hand more especially. Hot washings and cold washings, certain products from bee and flower known only to country girls, everything she could think of, were used upon those little sunburnt hands, till she persuaded herself that they were really as white as could be wished by a husband with a hundred titles. Her dressing completed, she left word with Edy that she was going for a long walk, and set out in the direction of Mount Lodge.

She no longer tripped like a girl, but walked like a woman. While crossing the park she murmured 'Baroness Xanten' in a pronunciation of her own. The sound of that title caused her such agitation that she was obliged to pause, with her hand upon her heart.

The house was so closely neighboured by shrubberies on three of its sides, that it was not till she had gone nearly round it that she found the little door. The resolution she had been an hour in forming failed her when she stood at the portal. While pausing for courage to tap, a carriage drove up to the front entrance a little way off, and peeping round the corner she saw alight a clergyman, and a gentleman in whom Margery fancied that she recognized a well-known solicitor from the neighbouring town. She had no longer any doubt of the nature of the ceremony proposed. 'It is sudden – but I must obey him!' she murmured: and tapped four times.

The door was opened so quickly that the servant must have been standing immediately inside. She thought him the man who had driven them to the ball – the silent man who could be trusted. Without a word he conducted her up the back staircase, and through a door at the top, into a wide corridor. She was asked to wait in a little dressing-room, where there was a fire, and an old metal-framed looking-glass over the mantelpiece, in which she caught sight of herself. A red spot burnt in each of her cheeks; the rest of her face was pale; and her eyes were like diamonds of the first water.

Before she had been seated many minutes the man came back noiselessly, and she followed him to a door covered by a red and black curtain, which he lifted, and ushered her into a large chamber. A screened light stood on a table before her, and on her left the hangings of a tall dark four-post bedstead obstructed her view of the centre of the room. Everything here seemed of such a magnificent type to her eyes that she felt confused, diminished to half her height, half her strength, half her prettiness. The man who had conducted her retired at once, and some one came softly round the angle of the bed-curtains. He held out his hand kindly – rather patronizingly: it was the solicitor whom she knew by sight. This gentleman led her forward, as if she had been a lamb rather than a woman, till the occupant of the bed was revealed.

The Baron's eyes were closed, and her entry had been so noiseless that he did not open them. The pallor of his face nearly matched the white bed-linen, and his dark hair and heavy black moustache were like dashes of ink on a clean page. Near him sat the parson and another gentleman, whom she afterwards learnt to be a London physician; and on the parson whispering a few words the Baron opened his eyes. As soon as he saw her he smiled faintly, and held out his hand.

Margery would have wept for him, if she had not been too overawed and palpitating to do anything. She quite forgot what she had come for, shook hands with him mechanically, and could hardly return an answer to his weak 'Dear Margery, you see how I am – how are you?'

In preparing for marriage she had not calculated on such a scene as this. Her affection for the Baron had too much of the vague in it to afford her trustfulness now. She wished she had not come. On a sign from the Baron the lawyer brought her a chair, and the oppresive silence was broken by the Baron's words.

'I am pulled down to death's door, Margery,' he said; 'and I suppose I soon shall pass through . . . My peace has been much disturbed in this illness, for just before it attacked me I received – that present you returned, from which, and in other ways, I learnt that you had lost your chance of marriage . . . Now it was I who did the harm, and you can imagine how the news has affected me. It has worried me all the illness through, and I cannot dismiss my error from my mind . . . I want to right the wrong I have done you before I die. Margery, you have always obeyed me, and, strange as the request may be, will you obey me now?'

She whispered, or seemed to whisper,[51] 'Yes.'

'Well, then,' said the Baron, 'these three gentlemen are here for a special purpose: one helps the body – he's called a physician; another helps the soul – he's a parson; the other helps the understanding –

he's a lawyer. They are here partly on my account, and partly on yours.'

The speaker then made a sign to the lawyer, who went out of the door. He came back almost instantly, but not alone. Behind him, dressed up in his best clothes, with a flower in his buttonhole and a bridegroom's air, walked – Jim.

XII

Margery could hardly repress a scream. As for flushing and blushing, she had turned hot and turned pale so many times already during the evening, that there was really now nothing of that sort left for her to do; and she remained in complexion much as before. Oh, the mockery of it! That secret dream – that sweet word 'Baroness'! – which had sustained her all the way along. Instead of a Baron there stood Jim, white-waistcoated, demure, every hair in place, and, if she mistook not, even a deedy spark in his eye.

Jim's surprising presence on the scene may be briefly accounted for. His resolve to seek an explanation with the Baron at all risks had proved unexpectedly easy: the interview had at once been granted, and then, seeing the crisis at which matters stood, the Baron had generously revealed to Jim the whole of his indebtedness to and knowledge of Margery. The truth of the Baron's statement, the inno- cent nature of the acquaintanceship, his sorrow for the rupture he had produced, was so evident that, far from having any further doubts of his patron, Jim frankly asked his advice on the next step to be pursued. At this stage the Baron fell ill, and, desiring much to see the two young people united before his death, he had sent anew to Hayward, and proposed the plan which they were now about to attempt – a marriage at the bedside of the sick man by special licence. The influence at Lambeth of some relatives of the Baron's, and the charitable bequests of his late mother to several deserving Church funds, were generally supposed to be among the reasons why the application for the licence was not refused.

This, however, is of small consequence. The Baron probably knew, in proposing this method of celebrating the marriage, that his enormous power over her would outweigh any sentimental obstacles which she might set up – inward objections that, without his presence and firmness, might prove too much for her acquiescence. Doubtless he foresaw, too, the advantage of getting her into the house before making the individuality of her husband clear to her mind.

Now, the Baron's conjectures were right as to the event, but wrong as to the motives. Margery was a perfect little dissembler on some occasions, and one of them was when she wished to hide any sudden mortification that might bring her into ridicule. She had no sooner recovered from her first fit of discomfiture than pride bade her suffer anything rather than reveal her absurd disappointment. Hence the scene progressed as follows:

'Come here, Hayward,' said the invalid. Hayward came near. The Baron, holding her hand in one of his own, and her lover's in the other, continued, 'Will you, in spite of your recent vexation with her, marry her now if she does not refuse?'

'I will, sir,' said Jim, promptly.

'And Margery, what do you say? It is merely a setting of things right. You have already promised this young man to be his wife, and should, of course, perform your promise. You don't dislike Jim?'

'O, no, sir,' she said, in a low, dry voice.

'I like him better than I can tell you,' said the Baron. 'He is an honourable man, and will make you a good husband. You must remember that marriage is a life contract, in which general compatibility of temper and worldly position is of more importance than fleeting passion, which never long survives. Now, will you, at my earnest request, and before I go to the South of Europe to die, agree to make this good man happy? I have expressed your views on the subject, haven't I, Hayward?'

'To a T, sir,' said Jim emphatically; with a motion of raising his hat to his influential ally, till he remembered he had no hat on. 'And, though I could hardly expect Margery to gie in for my asking, I feels she ought to gie in for yours.'

'And you accept him, my little friend?'

'Yes, sir,' she murmured, 'if he'll agree to a thing or two.'

'Doubtless he will – what are they?'

'That I shall not be made to live with him till I am in the mind for it; and that my having him shall be kept unknown for the present.'

'Well, what do you think of it, Hayward?'

'Anything that you or she may wish I'll do, my noble lord,' said Jim.

'Well, her request is not unreasonable, seeing that the proceedings are, on my account, a little hurried. So we'll proceed. You rather expected this, from my allusion to a ceremony in my note, did you not, Margery?'

'Yes, sir,' said she, with an effort.

'Good; I thought so; you looked so little surprised.'

We now leave the scene in the bedroom for a moment to describe a very peculiar proceeding that might have been watched at that time in a spot not many yards off.

When the carriage seen by Margery at the door was driving up to Mount Lodge it arrested the attention, not only of the young girl, but of a man who had for some time been moving slowly about the opposite lawn, engaged in some operation while he smoked a short pipe. A short observation of his doings would have shown that he was sheltering some delicate plants from an expected frost, and that he was the gardener. When the light at the door fell upon the entering forms of parson and lawyer – the former a stranger, the latter known to him – the gardener walked thoughtfully round the house. Reaching the small side-entrance he was further surprised to see it noiselessly open to a young woman, in whose momentarily illumined features he recognized those of Margery Tucker.

Altogether there was something curious in this. The man returned to the lawn front, and perfunctorily went on putting shelters over certain plants, though his thoughts were plainly otherwise engaged. On the grass his footsteps were noiseless, and the night moreover being still, he could presently hear a murmuring from the bedroom window over his head.

The gardener took from a tree a ladder that he had used in nailing that day, set it under the window, and ascended half-way, hoodwinking his conscience by seizing a nail or two with his hand and testing their twig-supporting powers. He soon heard enough to satisfy him. The words of the marriage service in the strange parson's voice were audible in snatches through the blind: they were the words he knew to be part of the service, such as 'wedded wife', 'richer for poorer', and so on; the less familiar parts being a mere confused sound.

Satisfied that a wedding service was being solemnized there, the gardener did not for a moment dream that one of the contracting parties could be other than the sick Baron. He descended the ladder and again walked round the house, waiting only till he saw Margery emerge from the same little door; when, fearing that he might be discovered, he withdrew in the direction of his own cottage.

This building stood at the lower corner of the garden, and as soon as the gardener entered he was accosted by a handsome woman in a widow's cap, who called him father, and said that supper had been ready for a long time. They sat down, but during the meal the gardener was so abstracted and silent that his daughter put her head winningly to one side and said, 'What is it, father dear?'

'Ah – what is it!' cried the gardener. 'Something that makes very little difference to me, but may be of great account to you, if you play your cards well. *There's been a wedding at the Lodge tonight!*' He related to her, with a caution to secrecy, all that he had heard and seen.

'We are folk that have got to get their living,' he said, 'and such ones mustn't tell tales about their betters, – Lord forgive the mockery o' the word! – but there's something to be made of it. She's a nice maid; so, Harriet, do you take the first chance you get for honouring her, before others know what has happened. Since this is done so privately it will be kept private for some time – till after his death, no question; when I expect she'll take this house for herself, and blaze out as a widow-lady ten thousand pound strong. You being a widow, she may make you her company-keeper; and so you'll have a home by a little contriving.'

While this conversation progressed at the gardener's Margery was on her way out of the Baron's house. She was, indeed, married. But, as we know, she was not married to the Baron. The ceremony over she seemed but little discomposed, and expressed a wish to return alone as she had come. To this, of course, no objection could be offered under the terms of the agreement, and wishing Jim a frigid goodbye, and the Baron a very quiet farewell, she went out by the door which had admitted her. Once safe and alone in the darkness of the park she burst into tears, which dropped upon the grass as she passed along. In the Baron's room she had seemed scared and helpless; now her reason and emotions returned. The further she got away from the glamour of that room, and the influence of its occupant, the more she became of opinion that she had acted absurdly. She had disobediently left her father's house, to obey him here. She had pleased everybody but herself.

However, thinking was now too late. How she got into her grand-mother's house she hardly knew; but without a supper, and without confronting either her relative or Edy, she went to bed.

XIII

On going out into the garden next morning, with a strange sense of being another person than herself, she beheld Jim leaning mutely over the gate.

He nodded. 'Good morning, Margery,' he said civilly.

'Good morning,' said Margery in the same tone.

'I beg your pardon,' he continued. 'But which way was you going this morning?'

'I am not going anywhere just now, thank you. But I shall go to my father's by-and-bye with Edy.' She went on with a sigh, 'I have done what he has all along wished, that is, married you; and there's no longer reason for enmity atween him and me.'

'True – true. Well, as I am going the same way, I can give you a lift in the trap, for the distance is long.'

'No thank you – I am used to walking,' she said.

They remained in silence, the gate between them, till Jim's convictions would apparently allow him to hold his peace no longer. 'This is a bad job!' he murmured.

'It is,' she said, as one whose thoughts have only too readily been identified. 'How I came to agree to it is more than I can tell!' And tears began rolling down her cheeks.

'The blame is more mine than yours, I suppose,' he returned. 'I ought to have said No, and not backed up the gentleman in carrying out this scheme. 'Twas his own notion entirely, as perhaps you know. I should never have thought of such a plan; but he said you'd be willing, and that it would be all right; and I was too ready to believe him.'

'The thing is, how to remedy it,' said she bitterly. 'I believe, of course, in your promise to keep this private, and not to trouble me by calling.'

'Certainly,' said Jim. 'I don't want to trouble you. As for that, why, my dear Mrs Hayward —'

'Don't Mrs Hayward me!' said Margery sharply. 'I won't be Mrs Hayward.'

Jim paused. 'Well, you be she by law, and that was all I meant,' he said mildly.

'I said I would acknowledge no such thing, and I won't. A thing can't be legal when it's against the wishes of the persons the laws are made to protect. So I beg you not to call me that any more.'

'Very well, Miss Tucker,' said Jim deferentially. 'We can live on exactly as before. We can't marry anybody else, that's true; but beyond that there's no difference, and no harm done. Your father ought to be told, I suppose, even if nobody else is? It will partly reconcile him to you, and make your life smoother.'

Instead of directly replying, Margery exclaimed in a low voice,

'Oh, it is a mistake – I didn't see it all, owing to not having time to reflect! I agreed, thinking that at least I should get reconciled to father by the step. But perhaps he would as soon have me not married at all as married and parted. I must ha' been enchanted – bewitched – when I gave my consent to this! I only did it to please that dear good dying nobleman – though why he should have wished it so much I can't tell!'

'Nor I neither,' said Jim. 'Yes, we've been fooled into it, Margery,' he said, with extraordinary gravity. 'He's had his way wi' us, and now we've got to suffer for it. Being a gentleman of patronage, and having bought several loads of lime o' me, and having given me all that splendid furniture, I could hardly refuse —'

'What, did he give you that?'

'Ay sure – to help me win ye.'

Margery covered her face with her hands; whereupon Jim stood up from the gate and looked critically at her. ' 'Tis a cruel conspiracy between you two men to – ensnare me!' she exclaimed. 'Why should you have done it – why should he have done it – when I've not deserved to be treated so! He bought the furniture – did he! Oh, I've been taken in – I've been wronged!' The grief and vexation of finding that long ago, when fondly believing the Baron to have lover-like feelings himself for her, he was still conspiring to favour Jim's suit, was more than she could endure.

Jim with distant courtesy waited, nibbling a straw, till her paroxysm was over. 'One word, Miss Tuck – Mrs – Margery,' he then recommenced gravely. 'You'll find me man enough to respect your wish, and to leave you to yourself – for ever and ever, if that's all. But I've just one word of advice to render ye. That is, that before you go to Stickleford Dairy yourself you let me drive ahead and call on your father. He's friends with me, and he's not friends with you. I can break the news, a little at a time, and I think I can gain his good will for you now, even though the wedding be no natural wedding at all. At any count, I can hear what he's got to say about ye, and come back here and tell ye.'

She nodded a cool assent to this, and he left her strolling about the garden in the sunlight while he went on to reconnoitre as agreed. It must not be supposed that Jim's dutiful echoes of Margery's regret at her precipitate marriage were all gospel; and there is no doubt that his private intention, after telling the old dairyman what had happened, was to ask his temporary assent to her caprice, till, in the course of time, she should be reasoned out of her whims and induced to settle down with Jim in a natural manner. He had, it is true, been somewhat nettled by her firm objection to him, and her keen sorrow for what she had done to please another; but he hoped for the best.

But, alas for the astute Jim's calculations! He drove on to the dairy, whose white walls now gleamed in the morning sun; made fast the horse to a ring in the wall, and entered the barton. Before knocking, he perceived the dairyman walking across from a gate in the other direction, as if he had just come in. Jim went over to him. Since the unfortunate incident on the morning of the intended wedding they had merely been on nodding terms, from a sense of awkwardness in their relations.

'What – is that thee?' said Dairyman Tucker, in a voice which unmistakably startled Jim by its abrupt fierceness. 'A pretty fellow thou be'st!'

It was a bad beginning for the young man's life as a son-in-law, and augured ill for the delicate consultation he desired.

'What's the matter?' said Jim.

'Matter! I wish some folks would burn their lime without burning other folks' property along wi' it. You ought to be ashamed of yourself. You call yourself a man, Jim Hayward, and a honest lime-burner, and a respectable, market-keeping Christen, and yet at six o'clock this morning, instead o' being where you ought to ha' been – at your work, there was neither vell or mark o' thee to be seed!'

'Faith, I don't know what you be raving at,' said Jim.

'Why – the vlankers from thy couch-heap blowed over upon my hayrick, and the rick's burnt to ashes; and all to come out o' my well-squeezed pocket. I'll tell thee what it is, young man. There's no business in ye. I've known Stickleford folk, quick and dead, for the last couple-o'-score year, and I've never knowed one so three-cunning for harm as thee, my gentleman lime-burner; and I reckon it one o' the luckiest days o' my life when I 'scaped having thee in my family. That maid of mine was right; I was wrong. She seed thee to be a drawlacheting rogue, and 'twas her wisdom to go off that morning and get rid o' thee. I commend her for't, and I'm going to fetch her home tomorrow.'

'You needn't take the trouble. She's coming home-along tonight of her own accord. I have seen her this morning, and she told me so.'

'So much the better. I'll welcome her warm. Nation! I'd sooner see her married to the parish fool than thee. Not you – you didn't care for my hay. Tarrying about where you shouldn't be, in bed, no doubt; that's what you was a doing. Now, don't you darken my doors again, and the sooner you be off my bit o' ground the better I shall be pleased.'

Jim looked, as he felt, stultified. If the rick had been really destroyed a little blame certainly attached to him, but he could not understand how it had happened. However, blame or none, it was clear he could not, with any self-respect, declare himself to be this peppery old gaffer's son-in-law in the face of such an attack as this.

For months – almost years – the one transaction that had seemed necessary to compose these two families satisfactorily was Jim's union with Margery. No sooner had it been completed than it appeared on all sides as the gravest mishap for both. Stating coldly that he would discover how much of the accident was to be attributed to his negligence, and pay the damage, he went out of the barton, and returned the way he had come.

Margery had been keeping a look-out for him, particularly wishing him not to enter the house, lest others should see the seriousness of their interview; and as soon as she heard wheels she went to the gate, which was out of view.

'Surely father has been speaking roughly to you!' she said, on seeing his face.

'Not the least doubt that he hev',' said Jim.

'But is he still angry with me?'

'Not in the least. He's waiting to welcome ye.'

'Ah! because I've married you.'

'Because he thinks you have *not* married me! He's jawed me up hill and down. He hates me; and for your sake I have not explained a word.'

Margery looked towards home with a sad, severe gaze. 'Mr Hayward,' she said, 'we have made a great mistake, and we are in a strange position.'

'True, but I'll tell ye what, mistress – I won't stand —' He stopped suddenly. 'Well, well; I've promised!' he quietly added.

'We must suffer for our mistake,' she went on. 'The way to suffer least is to keep our own counsel on what happened last evening, and not to meet. I must now return to my father.'

He inclined his head in indifferent assent, and she went indoors, leaving him there.

XIV

Margery returned home, as she had decided, and resumed her old life at Stickleford. And, seeing her father's animosity towards Jim, she told him not a word of the marriage.

Her inner life, however, was not what it once had been. She had suffered a mental and emotional displacement – a shock, which had set a shade of astonishment on her face as a permanent thing.

Her indignation with the Baron for collusion with Jim, at first bitter, lessened with the lapse of a few weeks, and at length vanished in the interest of some tidings she received one day.

The Baron was not dead, but he was no longer at the Lodge. To the surprise of the physicians, a sufficient improvement had taken place in his condition to permit of his removal before the cold weather came. His desire for removal had been such, indeed, that it was advisable to carry it out at almost any risk. The plan adopted had been to have him borne on men's shoulders in a sort of palanquin to the shore, a distance of only a few miles, where a steam yacht lay awaiting him in a little cove. By this means the noise and jolting of a carriage, and several miles of turnpike-road, were avoided. The singular procession over the fields took place at night, and was witnessed by but few people, one being a labouring man, who described the scene to Margery. When the seaside was reached a long, narrow gangway was laid from the deck of the yacht to the shore, which was so steep in the cove as to allow the yacht to lie quite near. The men, with their burden, ascended by the light of lanterns, the sick man was laid in the cabin, and, as soon as his bearers had returned to the shore, the gangway was removed, a rope was heard skirring over wood in the darkness, the yacht quivered, started her wheels, spread her woven wings to the air, and moved away through the miniature Pillars of Hercules which formed the mouth of the cove.[52] Soon she was but a small, shapeless phantom upon the wide breast of the sea.

It was said that the yacht was bound for Algiers.[53]

When the inimical autumn and winter weather came on, Margery wondered if he were still alive. The house being shut up, and the servants gone, she had no means of knowing, till, on a particular Saturday, her father drove her to market. Here, in attending to his business, he left her to herself for awhile. Walking in a quiet street in the professional quarter of the town, she saw coming towards her the solicitor who had been present at the wedding, and who had acted for the Baron in various small local matters during his brief residence at the Lodge.

She reddened to peony hues, averted her eyes, and would have passed him. But he crossed over and barred the pavement, and when she met his glance he was looking with friendly severity at her. The street was quiet, and he said in a low voice, 'How's the husband?'

'I don't know, sir,' said she.

'What – and are your stipulations about secrecy and separate living still in force?'

'They will always be,' she replied decisively. 'Mr Hayward and I agreed on the point, and we have not the slightest wish to change the arrangement.'

'H'm. Then 'tis Miss Tucker to the world, Mrs Hayward to me and one or two others only.'

Margery nodded. Then she nerved herself by an effort, and though blushing painfully asked, 'May I put one question, sir? Is the Baron dead?'

'He is dead to you and to all of us. Why should you ask?'

'Because, if he's alive, I am sorry I married James Hayward. If he is dead I do not much mind my marriage.'

'I repeat, he is dead to you,' said the lawyer emphatically. 'I'll tell you all I know. My professional services for him ended with his departure from this place; but I think I should have heard from him if he had been alive still. I have not heard at all: and this, taken in connection with the nature of his illness, leaves no doubt in my mind that he is dead.'

Margery sighed, and thanking the lawyer she left him with a tear for the Baron in her eye. After this incident she became more restful; and the time drew on for her periodical visit to her grand-mother.

A few days subsequent to her arrival her aged relative asked her to go with a message to the gardener at Mount Lodge (who still lived on there, keeping the grounds in order for the landlord). Margery hated that direction now, but she went. The lodge, which she saw over the trees, was to her like a skull from which the warm and living flesh had vanished. It was twilight by the time she reached the cottage at the bottom of the Lodge garden, and, the room being illuminated within, she saw through the window a woman she had never seen before. She was dark, and rather handsome, and when Margery knocked she opened the door. It was the gardener's widowed daughter, who had been advised to make friends with Margery. ·

She now found her opportunity. Margery's errand was soon completed, the young widow, to her surprise, treating her with preternatural respect, and afterwards offering to accompany her home. Margery was not sorry to have a companion in the gloom, as they walked on together. The widow, Mrs Peach, was demonstrative and confidential; and told Margery all about herself. She had come quite recently to live with her father – during the Baron's illness, in fact – and her husband had been captain of a ketch.

'I saw you one morning, ma'am,' she said. 'But you didn't see me. It was when you were crossing the hill in sight of the Lodge. You looked at it, and sighed. 'Tis the lot of widows to sigh, ma'am, is it not?'

'Widows – yes, I suppose; but what do you mean?'

Mrs Peach lowered her voice. 'I can't say more, ma'am, with proper respect. But there seems to be no question of the poor Baron's death; and though these foreign princes can take (as my husband used to tell me) what they call left-handed wives, and leave them behind when they go abroad, widowhood is widowhood, left-handed or right. And really, to be the left-handed wife of a foreign baron is nobler than to be married all round to a common man. You'll excuse my freedom, ma'am; but being a widow myself, I have pitied you from my heart; so young as you are, and having to keep it a secret, and (excusing me) having no money out of his vast riches because 'tis swallowed up by Baroness Number One.'

Now Margery did not understand a word more of this than the bare fact that Mrs Peach suspected her to be the Baron's unendowed widow, and, such was the milkmaid's nature, that she did not distinctly deny the widow's impeachment.[54] The latter continued –

'But ah, ma'am, all your troubles are straight backward in your memory – while I have troubles before as well as grief behind.'

'What may they be, Mrs Peach?' inquired Margery, with a slight air of the Baroness.

The other dropped her voice to revelation tones: 'I have been forgetful enough of my first man to lose my heart to a second!'

'You shouldn't do that – it is wrong. You should control your feelings.'

'But how am I to control my feelings?'

'By going to your dead husband's grave, and things of that sort.'

'Do you go to your dead husband's grave?'

'How can I go to Algiers?'

'Ah – too true! Well, I've tried everything to cure myself – read the words against it, and all sorts. But, avast my shipmate! – as my poor man used to say – there, 'tis just the same. In short, I've made up my mind to encourage the new one. 'Tis flattering that I, a new-comer, should have been found out by a young man so soon.'

'Who is he?' said Margery, listlessly.

'A master lime-burner.'

'A master lime-burner?'

'That's his profession. He's a partner-in-co., doing very well indeed.'

'But what's his name?'

'I don't like to tell you his name, for, though 'tis night, that covers all shame-facedness, my face is as hot as a 'Talian iron, I declare! Do you just feel it.'

Margery put her hand on Mrs Peach's face, and, sure enough, hot it was. 'Does he come courting?' she asked quickly.

'Well – only in the way of business. He never comes unless lime is wanted in the neighbourhood. He's in the Yeomanry, too, and will look very fine when he comes out in his regimentals for drill in May.'

'Oh – in the Yeomanry,' she said, with a slight relief. 'Then it can't — is he a young man?'

'Yes, junior partner-in-co.'

The description had an odd resemblance to Jim, of whom Margery had not heard a word for months. He had promised silence and absence, and had fulfilled his promise literally, with a gratuitous addition that was rather amazing, if indeed, it were Jim whom the widow loved. One point in the description puzzled Margery: Jim was not in the Yeomanry, unless, by a surprising development of enterprise, he had entered it recently.

At parting, Margery said, with an interest quite tender, 'I should like to see you again, Mrs Peach, and hear of your attachment. When can you call?'

'Oh – any time, ma'am, I'm sure – if you think I am good enough.'

'Indeed, I do, Mrs Peach. Come as soon as you've seen the lime-burner again.'

XV

Seeing that Jim lived five miles from the widow, Margery was rather surprised, and even felt a slight sinking of the heart, when her new acquaintance appeared at her door so soon as the evening of the following Monday. She asked Margery to walk out with her, which the young woman readily did.

'I am come at once,' said the widow, breathlessly, as soon as they were in the lane, 'for it is so exciting that I can't keep it. I must tell it to somebody, if only a bird or a cat, or a garden snail.'

'What is it?' asked her companion eagerly.[55]

'I've pulled grass from my husband's grave to cure it – wove the blades into true lover's knots; took off my shoes upon the sod; but, avast, my shipmate, —'

'Upon the sod – why?'

'To feel the damp earth he's in, and make the sense of it enter my soul. But no. It has swelled to a head; he is going to meet me at the Yeomanry Review.'

'The master lime-burner?'

The widow nodded.'

'When is it to be?'

'Tomorrow. He looks so lovely in his accoutrements! He's such a splendid soldier; that was the last straw that kindled my soul to say yes. He's home from Casterbridge for a night between the drills,' continued Mrs Peach. 'He goes back tomorrow morning for the review, and when it's over he's going to meet me . . . But, guide my heart, there he is!'

Her exclamation had rise in the sudden appearance of a brilliant red uniform through the trees, and the tramp of a horse carrying the wearer thereof. In another half-minute the military gentleman, whoever he might be, would have turned the corner, and faced them.

'He'd better not see me; he'll think I know too much,' said Margery precipitately. 'I'll go up here.'

The widow, whose thoughts had evidently been of the same cast, seemed much relieved to see Margery disappear in the plantation, in the midst of a spring chorus of birds. Once among the trees, Margery turned her head, and, before she could see the rider's person she recognized the horse as Tony, the lightest of three that Jim and his partner owned, for the purpose of carting out lime to their customers.

Jim, then, had joined the Yeomanry since his estrangement from Margery. A man who had worn the Queen's uniform for seven days only could not be expected to look as if it were a part of his person, in the manner of long-trained soldiers; but he was a well-formed young fellow, and of an age when few positions came amiss to one who has the capacity to adapt himself to circumstances.

Meeting the blushing Mrs Peach (to whom Margery in her mind sternly denied the right to blush at all), Jim alighted and moved on with her, probably at Mrs Peach's own suggestion; so that what they said, how long they remained together, and how they parted, Margery knew not. She might have known some of these things by waiting; but the presence of Jim had bred in her heart a sudden disgust for the widow, and a general sense of discomfiture. She went away in an opposite direction, turning her head and saying to the unconscious Jim, 'There's a fine rod in pickle for you, my gentleman, if you carry out that pretty scheme!'

Jim's military *coup* had decidedly astonished her. What he might do next she could not conjecture. The idea of his doing anything sufficiently brilliant to arrest her attention would have seemed ludicrous, had not Jim, by entering the Yeomanry, revealed a capacity for dazzling exploits which made it unsafe to predicate any limitation to his powers.

Margery was now absolutely excited. The sly daring of the wretched Jim in bursting into scarlet amazed her as much as his doubtful acquaintanceship with the demonstrative Mrs Peach. To go to that Review, to watch the pair, to eclipse Mrs Peach in brilliancy, to meet and pass them in withering contempt – if she only could do it! But, alas! she was a forsaken woman. 'If the Baron were alive, or in England,' she said to herself (for sometimes she thought he might possibly be alive), 'and he were to take me to this Review, wouldn't I show that forward Mrs Peach what a lady is like, and keep among the select company, and not mix with the common people at all!'

It might at first sight be thought that the best course for Margery at this juncture would have been to go to Jim, and nip the intrigue in the bud without further scruple. But her own declaration in after days was that whoever could say that was far from realizing her situation. It was hard to break such ice as divided their two lives now, and to attempt it at that moment was a too humiliating proclamation of defeat. The only plan she could think of – perhaps not a wise one in the circumstances – was to go to the Review herself, and be the gayest there.

A method of doing this with some propriety soon occurred to her. She dared not ask her father, who scorned to waste time in sight-seeing, and whose animosity towards Jim knew no abatement; but she might call on her old acquaintance, Mr Vine, Jim's partner, who would probably be going with the rest of the holiday-folk, and ask if she might accompany him in his spring-trap. She had no sooner perceived the feasibility of this than she decided to call upon the old man early the next morning.

In the mean time Jim and Mrs Peach had walked slowly along the road together, Jim leading the horse, and Mrs Peach informing him that her father the gardener was at Stickleford, and that she had come this way to meet him. Jim, for reasons of his own, was going to sleep at his partner's that night, and thus their route was the same. The shades of eve closed in upon them as they walked, and by the time they reached the lime-kiln, which it was necessary to pass to get to the village, it was quite dark. Jim stopped at the kiln, to see if matters had progressed rightly in his seven days' absence, and Mrs Peach, who stuck to him like a teasle, stopped also, saying she would wait for her father there.

She held the horse, while he ascended to the top of the kiln. Then rejoining her, and not quite knowing what to do, he stood beside her looking at the flames, which tonight burnt up brightly, shining a long way into the dark air, even up to the ramparts of the earthwork above them, and overhead into the bosoms of the clouds.

It was during this proceeding that a carriage, drawn by a pair of coal-black horses, came along the turnpike-road. The light of the kiln caused the horses to swerve a little, and the occupant of the carriage looked out. He saw the bluish, lightning-like flames from the limestone, rising from the top of the furnace, and hard by the figures of Jim Hayward, the widow, and the horse, standing out with spectral distinctness against the mass of night behind. The scene wore the aspect of some unholy assignation in Pandaemonium, and it was all the more impressive from the fact that both Jim and the woman were quite unconscious of the striking spectacle they presented. The gentleman in the carriage watched them till he was borne out of sight.

Having seen to the kiln, Jim and the widow walked on again, and soon Mrs Peach's father met them, and relieved Jim of the lady. When they had parted, Jim, with an expiration not unlike a breath of relief, went on to Mr Vine's, and having put the horse into the stable entered the house. His partner was seated at the table, solacing himself after the labours of the day by luxurious alternations between a long clay pipe and a mug of ale.

'Well,' said Jim eagerly, 'what's the news – how do she take it?'

'Sit down – sit down,' said Vine. ' 'Tis working well; not but that I deserve something o' thee for the trouble I've had in watching her. The soldiering was a fine move; but the woman is a better! – who invented it?'

'I myself,' said Jim modestly.

'Well; jealousy is making her rise like a thunderstorm, and in a day or two you'll have her for the asking, my sonny. What's the next step?'

'The widow is getting rather a weight upon a feller, worse luck,' said Jim. 'But I must keep it up until tomorrow, at any rate. I have promised to see her at the Review, and now the great thing is that Margery should see we a smiling together – I in my full-dress uniform and clinking arms o' war. 'Twill be a good strong sting, and will end the business, I hope. Couldn't you manage to put the hoss in and drive her there? She'd go if you were to ask her.'

'With all my heart,' said Mr Vine, moistening the end of a new pipe in his ale. 'I can call at her grammer's for her – 'twill be all in my way.'

XVI

Margery duly followed up her intention by arraying herself the next morning in her loveliest guise, and keeping watch for Mr Vine's appearance upon the high road, feeling certain that his would form one in the procession of carts and carriages which set in towards Casterbridge that day. Jim had gone by at a very early hour, and she did not see him pass. Her anticipation was verified by the advent of Mr Vine about eleven o'clock, dressed to his highest effort; but Margery was surprised to find that, instead of her having to stop him, he pulled in towards the gate of his own accord. The invitation planned between Jim and the old man on the previous night was now promptly given, and, as may be supposed, as promptly accepted. Such a strange coincidence she had never before known. She was quite ready, and they drove onward at once.

The Review was held on some high ground a little way out of the town, and her conductor suggested that they should put up the horse at the inn, and walk to the field – a plan which pleased her well, for it was more easy to take preliminary observations on foot without being seen herself than when sitting elevated in a vehicle.

They were just in time to secure a good place near the front, and in a few minutes after their arrival the reviewing officer came on the ground. Margery's eye had rapidly run over the troop in which Jim was enrolled, and she discerned him in one of the ranks, looking remarkably new and bright, both as to uniform and countenance. Indeed, if she had not worked herself into such a desperate state of mind she would have felt proud of him then and there. His shapely upright figure was quite noteworthy in the rotund selection of farmers on his right and left; while his charger Tony expressed by his bearing, even more than Jim, that he knew nothing about lime-carts whatever, and everything about trumpets and glory. How Jim could have scrubbed Tony to such shining blackness she could not tell, for the horse in his natural state was ingrained with lime-dust, that burnt the colour out of his coat as it did out of Jim's hair. Now he pranced martially, and was a war-horse every inch of him.

Having discovered Jim her next search was for Mrs Peach, and, by dint of some oblique glancing Margery indignantly discovered the widow in the most forward place of all, her head and bright face conspicuously advanced; and, what was more shocking, she had abandoned her mourning for a violet drawn-bonnet and a gay spencer, together with a parasol luxuriously fringed in a way Margery had never before seen. 'Where did she get the money?' said Margery, under her breath. 'And to forget that poor sailor so soon!'

These general reflections were precipitately postponed by her discovering that Jim and the widow were perfectly alive to each other's whereabouts, and in the active interchange of telegraphic signs of affection, which on the latter's part took the form of a playful fluttering of her handkerchief or waving of her parasol. Richard Vine had placed Margery in front of him, to protect her from the crowd, as he said, he himself surveying the scene over her bonnet. Margery would have been even more surprised than she was if she had known that Jim was not only aware of Mrs Peach's presence, but also of her own, the treacherous Mr Vine having drawn out his flame-coloured handkerchief and waved it to Jim over the young woman's head as soon as they had taken up their position.

'My partner makes a tidy soldier, eh – Miss Tucker?' said the senior lime-burner. 'It is my belief as a Christian that he's got a party here that he's making signs to – that handsome figure o' fun straight over-right him.'

'Perhaps so,' she said with the utmost indifference on the surface of her face.

'And it's growing warm between 'em if I don't mistake,' continued the merciless Vine.

Margery was silent, biting her lip; and the troops being now set in motion, all signalling ceased for the present between soldier Hayward and his pretended sweetheart.

'Have you a piece of paper that I could make a memorandum on, Mr Vine?' asked Margery.

Vine took out his pocket-book and tore a leaf from it, which he handed her with a pencil.

'Don't move from here – I'll return in a minute,' she continued, with the innocence of a woman who means mischief. And, withdrawing herself to the back, where the grass was clear, she pencilled down the words

'JIM'S MARRIED.'

Armed with this document she crept into the throng behind the unsuspecting Mrs Peach, slipped the paper into her pocket on the top of her handkerchief, and withdrew unobserved, rejoining Mr Vine with a bearing of *nonchalance*.

By-and-by the troops were in different order, Jim taking a left-hand position almost close to Mrs Peach. He bent down and said a few words to her. From her manner of nodding assent it was surely some arrangement about a meeting by-and-by when Jim's drill was over, and Margery was the more certain of the fact when, the Review having ended, and the people having strolled off to another part of the field where sports were to take place, Mrs Peach tripped away in the direction of the town.

'I'll just say a word to my partner afore he goes off the ground, if you'll spare me a minute,' said the old lime-burner. 'Please stay here till I'm back again.' He edged along the front till he reached Jim.

'How is she?' said the latter.

'In a trimming sweat,' said Mr Vine. 'And my counsel to ye is to carry this larry no further. 'Twill do no good. She's as ready to make friends wi' ye as any wife can be; and more showing off can only do harm.'

'But I must finish off with a spurt,' said Jim. 'And this is how I am going to do it. I have arranged with Mrs Peach that, as soon as we soldiers have entered the town and been dismissed, I'll meet her there. It is really to say Goodbye, but she don't know that; and I wanted it to look like a lopement to Margery's eyes. When I'm clear of Mrs Peach I'll come back here and make it up with Margery on the spot. But don't say I'm coming, or she may be inclined to throw off again. Just hint to her that I may be meaning to be off to London with the widow.'

The old man still insisted that this was carrying the *ruse* too far.

'No, no, it isn't,' said Jim. 'I know how to manage her. 'Twill just mellow her heart nicely by the time I come back. I must bring her down real tender, or 'twill all fail.'

His senior reluctantly gave in and returned to Margery. A short time afterwards the Yeomanry band struck up and Jim with the regiment followed towards the town.

'Yes, yes; they are going to meet,' said Margery to herself, perceiving that Mrs Peach had so timed her departure as to be in the town at Jim's dismounting.

'Now we will go and see the games,' said Mr Vine; 'they be really worth seeing. There's greasy poles, and jumping in sacks, and other trials of the intellect, that nobody ought to miss who wants to be abreast of his generation.'

Margery felt so miserable at the apparent assignation, which seemed about to take place despite her anonymous writing, that she helplessly assented to go anywhere, dropping behind Vine, that he might not see she was crying.

Jim followed out his programme with literal exactness. No sooner was the troop dismissed in the town that he sent Tony to stable and joined Mrs Peach, who stood on the edge of the pavement expecting him. But this acquaintance was to end: he meant to part from her for ever and in the quickest time, though civilly; for it was important to be with Margery as soon as possible. He had nearly completed the manoeuvre to his satisfaction when, in drawing her handkerchief from her pocket to wipe the tears from her eyes, Mrs Peach's hand grasped the paper, which she read at once.

'What! is that true?' she said, holding it out to Jim.

Jim started and admitted that it was, beginning an elaborate explanation and apologies. But Mrs Peach was thoroughly roused, and then overcome. 'He's married, he's married!' she said, and swooned, or feigned to swoon, so that Jim was obliged to support her.

'He's married, he's married!' said a boy hard by who watched the scene with interest.

'He's married, he's married!' said a hilarious group of other boys near, with smiles several inches broad, and shining teeth; and so the exclamation echoed down the street.

Jim cursed his ill-luck; the loss of time that this dilemma entailed grew serious; for Mrs Peach was now in such a hysterical state that he could not leave her with any good grace or feeling. It was necessary to take her to a refreshment room, lavish restoratives upon her, and altogether to waste nearly half an hour. When she had kept him as long as she chose, she forgave him; and thus at last he got away, his heart swelling with tenderness towards Margery. He at once hurried up the street to effect the reconciliation with her.

'How shall I do it?' he said to himself. 'Why, I'll step round to her side, fish for her hand, draw it through my arm as if I wasn't aware of it. Then she'll look in my face, I shall look in hers, and we shall march off the field triumphant, and the thing will be done without takings or tears.'

He entered the field and went straight as an arrow to the place appointed for the meeting. It was at the back of a refreshment tent outside the mass of spectators, and divided from their view by the tent itself. He turned the corner of the canvas, and there beheld Vine at the indicated spot. But Margery was not with him.

Vine's hat was thrust back into his poll. His face was pale, and his manner bewildered. 'Hullo? what's the matter?' said Jim. 'Where's my Margery?'

'You've carried this game too far, my man!' exclaimed Vine, with the air of a friend who has 'always told you so.' 'You ought to have dropped it several days ago, when she would have come to ye like a cooing dove. Now this is the end o't!'

'Hey! what, my Margery? Has anything happened, for God's sake?'

'She's gone.'

'Where to?'

'That's more than earthly man can tell! I never see such a thing! 'Twas a stroke o' the black art – as if she were sperrited away. When we got to the games I said – mind, you told me to! – I said, "Jim Hayward thinks o' going off to London with that widow woman" – mind, you told me to! She showed no wonderment, though a' seemed very low. Then she said to me, "I don't like standing here in this mean crowd. I shall feel more at home among the gentle-people." And then she went to where the carriages were drawn up, and near her there was a grand coach, a-blazing with lions and unicorns, and hauled by two coal-black horses. I hardly thought much of it then, and by degrees lost sight of her behind it. Presently the other carriages moved off, and I thought still to see her standing there. But no, she had vanished; and then I saw the grand coach rolling away, and glimpsed Margery in it, beside a fine dark gentleman with black moustachios, and a very pale prince-like face. As soon as the horses got into the hard road they rattled on like h—-and-skimmer, and went out of sight in the dust, and – that' all. If you'd come back a little sooner you'd ha' caught her.'

Jim had turned whiter than his pipeclay. 'Oh, this is too bad – too bad!' he cried in anguish, striking his brow. 'That paper and that fainting woman kept me so long. Who could have done it? But 'tis my fault. I've stung her too much. I shouldn't have carried it so far.'

'You shouldn't – just what I said,' replied his senior.

'She thinks I've gone off with that cust widow; and to spite me she's gone off with the man! Do you know who that stranger wi' the lions and unicorns is? Why, 'tis that foreigner who calls himself a Baron, and took Mount Lodge for six months last year to make mischief – a villain! O, my Margery – that it should come to this! She's lost, she's ruined! – Which way did they go?'

Jim turned to follow in the direction indicated, when, behold, there stood at his back her father, Dairyman Tucker.

'Now look here, young man,' said Dairyman Tucker. 'I've just heard all that wailing – and straightway will ask ye to stop it sharp. 'Tis like your brazen impudence to teave and wail when you be another woman's husband; yes, faith, I see'd her a-fainting in yer arms when you wanted to get away from her, and honest folk a-standing round who knew you'd married her, and said so. I heard it, though you didn't see me. "He's married!" says they. Some sly registrar's-office business, no doubt; but sly doings will out. As for Margery – who's to be called higher titles in these parts hencefor'ard – I'm her father, and I say it's all right what she's done. Don't I know private news, hey? Haven't I just learnt that secret weddings of high people can happen at expected deathbeds by special licence, as well as low people at registrars' offices? And can't husbands come back and claim their own when they choose? Be gone, young man, and leave noblemen's wives alone; and I thank God I shall be rid of a numskull!'

Swift words of explanation rose to Jim's lips, but they paused there and died. At that last moment he could not, as Margery's husband, announce Margery's shame and his own, and transform her father's triumph to wretchedness at a blow.

'I – I – must leave here,' he stammered. Going from the place in an opposite course to that of the fugitives, he doubled when out of sight, and in an incredibly short space had entered the town. Here he made inquiries for the emblazoned carriage, and gained from one or two persons a general idea of its route. It had taken the highway to London. Saddling poor Tony before he had half eaten his corn, Jim galloped along the same road.

XVII

Now Jim was quite mistaken in supposing that by leaving the field in a roundabout manner he had deceived Dairyman Tucker as to his object. That astute old man immediately divined that Jim was meaning to track the fugitives, in ignorance (as the dairyman supposed) of their lawful relation. He was soon assured of the fact, for, creeping to a remote angle of the field, he saw Jim hastening into the town. Vowing vengeance on the young lime-burner for his mischievous interference between a nobleman and his secretly-wedded wife, the dairyman determined to balk him.

Tucker had ridden on to the Review ground, so that there was no necessity for him, as there had been for poor Jim, to re-enter the town before starting. The dairyman hastily untied his mare from the row of other horses, mounted, and descended to a bridle-path which would take him obliquely into the London road at Winford Hill. The old man's route being along one side of an equilateral triangle, while Jim's was along two sides of the same, the former was at the point of intersection long before Hayward.

Arrived here, the dairyman pulled up and looked around. Winford Hill was a spot at which the highway forked; the left arm, the more important, led on through Melchester to London; the right to Stickleford, Anglebury, and the coast. Nothing was visible on the white track to London; but on the other there appeared the back of a carriage, which rapidly ascended a distant hill and vanished under the trees. It was the Baron's who, according to the sworn information of the gardener at Mount Lodge, had made Margery his wife.

The carriage having vanished, the dairyman gazed in the opposite direction, towards Casterbridge. Here he beheld Jim in his regimentals, laboriously ascending the hill on Tony's back.

Soon he reached the summit, and saw the dairyman by the wayside. But Jim did not halt. Then the dairyman committed the greatest error of his life.[56]

'Right along the London road, if you want to catch 'em!' he said.

'Thank ye, dairyman, thank ye!' cried Jim, his pale face lighting up with gratitude, for he believed that Tucker had learnt his mistake from Vine, and had come to his assistance. Without drawing rein he diminished down the hill, along the road not taken by the flying pair. The dairyman rubbed his hands with delight, and returned to the town.

Jim pursued his way through the dust, up hill and down hill; but never saw ahead of him the vehicle of his search. That vehicle was passing along a diverging lane at a distance of many miles from where he rode. Still he sped onwards, till Tony showed signs of breaking down; and then Jim gathered from inquiries he made that he had come the wrong way. Suddenly it burst upon his mind that the dairyman, still ignorant of the truth, had misinformed him. Heavier in his heart than words can describe he turned Tony's drooping head, and resolved to drag his way home.

But the horse was now so jaded that it was impossible to proceed far. Having gone about half-a-mile back he came again to a small roadside hamlet and inn, where he put up Tony for a rest and feed. As for himself, there was no quiet in him. He tried to sit and eat in the inn kitchen; but he could not stay there. He went out, and paced up and down the road.

This hamlet had once been a populous village.[57] It bore the name of Letscombe Cross. In the middle, where most of the houses had formerly stood, a road from the hills traversed the highway at right angles down to the water-meads, and at the intersection rose the remains of the old mediaeval cross which shared its name with the hamlet. The interesting relic of ante-Renaissance times was sadly nibbled by years and weather, but it still retained some of its old ornament, and was often copied into the pocket-book of the vagrant artist. Jim Hayward was standing in sight of this object when he beheld, advancing towards it from the opposite direction, the black horses and carriage he sought, now gilded and glorious with the dying fires[58] of the western sun.

The why and wherefore of this sudden appearance he did not pause to consider. His resolve to intercept the carriage was instantaneous. He ran forwards to the cross-roads, and there, doggedly waiting, barred the way to the advancing equipage.

The Baron's coachman shouted, but Jim stood firm as a rock, and, on the former attempting to push past him, Jim drew his sword, resolving to cut the horses down rather than be displaced. The animals were thrown nearly back upon their haunches, and at this juncture a gentleman looked out of the window. It was the Baron himself.

'Who's there?' he inquired.

'James Hayward,' replied the young man fiercely. 'And he demands his wife.'

The Baron leapt out, and told the coachman to drive back out of sight and wait for him.

'I was hastening to find you,' he said to Jim, in a stern tone. 'Your wife is where she ought to be, and where you ought to be also – by your own fireside. Where's the other woman?'

Jim, without replying, looked incredulously into the carriage as it turned. Margery was certainly not there. 'The other woman is nothing to me,' he said, bitterly. 'I used her to warm up Margery: I have now done with her. The question I ask, my lord, is, What business had you with Margery today?'

'My business was to help her to regain the husband she had seemingly lost. I saw her; she told me you had eloped by the Anglebury road with another. I, who have – mostly – had her happiness at heart, told her I would help her to follow you if she wished. She gladly agreed; we drove after, but could hear no tidings of you in front of us. Then I took her – to your house – and there she awaits you. I promised to send you to her if human effort could do it, and was tracking you for that purpose.'

'Then you've been a pursuing after me?'

'You and the widow.'

'And I've been pursuing after you and Margery! . . . My noble lord, your actions seem to show that I ought to believe you in this; and, when you say you've her happiness at heart, I don't forget that you've formerly proved it to be so. Well, Heaven forbid that I should think wrongfully of you if you don't deserve it. A mystery to me you have always been, my noble lord; and in this business more than in any.'

'I am glad to hear you say no worse. In one hour you'll have proof of my conduct – good and bad. Can I do anything more? Say the word, and I'll try.'

Jim reflected. 'Baron,' he said, 'I am a plain man, and wish only to lead a quiet life with my wife, as a man should. You have great power over her – power to any extent, for good or otherwise. If you command her anything on earth, righteous or questionable, that she'll do. So that, since you ask me if you can do more for me, I'll answer this, you can promise never to see her again. I mean no harm, my lord; but your presence can do no good; you will trouble us. If I return to her, will you for ever stay away?'

They had met, as has been observed, by the cross. Nobody was within sight; and, taking Jim by the arm, the Baron mounted the four octagonal steps, and laid his hand upon the body of the structure.

'Hayward,' said the Baron, 'I swear to you by this holy stone that I will disturb you and your wife by my presence no more.'

In relating this curious incident to the present chronicler, Jim used to declare that, to his fancy, the ruddy light of the setting sun burnt with more than earthly fire on the Baron's face and on the cross, as the solemn words were spoken; and that the ruby flash of his eye in the same light was what he never witnessed before nor since in the eye of mortal man. After this there was nothing more to do or say in that place. Jim accompanied his never-to-be forgotten acquaintance to the carriage, closed the door after him, waved his hat to him, and from that hour he and the Baron met not again on earth.

A few words will suffice to explain the fortunes of Margery while the foregoing events were in action elsewhere. On leaving her companion Vine, she had gone distractedly among the carriages, the rather to escape his observation than of any set purpose. Standing here she thought she heard her name pronounced, and turning she saw her foreign friend, whom she had supposed to be, if not dead, a thousand miles off. He beckoned, and she went close. 'You are ill – you are wretched,' he said, looking keenly into her face. 'Where's your husband?'

She briefly told him her sad suspicion that Jim had run away from her. The Baron reflected, and inquired a few other particulars of her late life. Then he said, 'You and I must find him – come with me.' At this word of command from the Baron she had entered the carriage as docilely as a child, and there she sat beside him till he chose to speak, which was not till they were some way out of the town, and the Baron had discovered that Jim was certainly not, as they had supposed, making off from Margery along the London Road.

'To pursue him in this way is useless, I perceive,' he said. 'And the proper course now is that I should take you to his house. That done I will return, and bring him to you, if mortal persuasion can do it.'

'I didn't want to go to his house without him, sir,' said she, tremblingly.

'Didn't want to!' he answered peremptorily.[59] 'Let me remind you,

Margery Hayward, that your place is in your husband's house. Till you are there you have no right to criticize his conduct, however wild it may be. Why have you not been there before?'

'I don't know, sir,' she murmured, her tears falling silently upon her hand.

'Don't you think you ought to be there?'

'Yes, sir.'

'Of course you ought.'

The Baron sank into silence, and allowed his eye to rest on her. What thoughts were all at once engaging his mind after those moments of reproof? Margery had given herself into his hands without a remonstrance. Her husband had apparently deserted her. She was absolutely in his power, and they were on the high road.

That his first impulse in inviting her to accompany him had been the legitimate one denoted by his words, cannot reasonably be doubted. That his second was quite otherwise soon became revealed, though not at first to her, for she was too bewildered to notice where they were going. Instead of pulling up at Jim's house, the Baron, as if influenced suddenly by her reluctance to return thither if Jim was playing truant, kept straight along the road, till, at a signal from him, the coachman turned sharply to the right.

They soon approached the coast. The carriage stopped. Margery awoke from her reverie.

'Where are we?' she said, looking out of the window with a start. Before her was a semi-circular cove between rocks, and in the middle of the cove rode a yacht, its masts repeating as if from memory the rocking they had practised in their native forest.

'At a little seaside nook, where my yacht lies at anchor,' he said tentatively. 'Now Margery; in five minutes we can be aboard, and in half an hour we can be steaming away all the world over. Will you come?'

'I cannot,' she said simply.

'Why not?'

'Because Jim is not with me, and perhaps it would offend him very much if he were to hear of it.'

Then, on a sudden, Margery seemed to see all: she became white as a fleece, and an agonized look came into her eyes. With clasped hands she bent to the Baron. 'Oh, sir!' she gasped, 'I once saved your life – save me now, for pity's sake!'

Baron Xanten averted his face, opened the carriage door, quickly mounted outside; and in a second or two the carriage left the cove behind, and ascended the road by which it had come.

In half an hour they reached Stickleford, and Jim Hayward's home. The Baron alighted, and spoke to her through the window, 'Margery, can you forgive a bad impulse, which I swear was unpremeditated?' he asked. 'If you can, shake my hand.'

She did not do it, but eventually allowed him to help her out of the carriage. He seemed to feel his error keenly; and seeing it she said, 'I forgive you, sir, on one condition. That you send my husband to me.'

'I will, if any man can,' said he. 'Such penance is milder than I deserve! God bless you and give you happiness. I shall never see you again!' He turned, entered the carriage, and was gone; and having found out Jim's course, came up with him upon the road.

In due time the latter reached his lodging at his partner's. The woman who took care of the house in Vine's absence at once told Jim that a lady who had come in a carriage was waiting for him in his sitting-room. Jim proceeded thither with agitation, and beheld shrinkingly ensconced in the large slippery chair, and surrounded by the brilliant articles that had so long awaited her, his long-estranged wife.

Margery's eyes were round and fear-stricken. She essayed to speak, but Jim, strangely enough, found the readier tongue then. 'Why did I do it, you would ask,' he said. 'I cannot tell. Do you forgive my deception? Oh, Margery – you are my Margery still! But how could you trust yourself in the Baron's hands this afternoon, without knowing him better?'

'He said I was to come, and I went,' she said as well as she could for tearfulness.

'You obeyed him blindly.'

'I did. But perhaps I was not justified in doing it.'

'I don't know,' said Jim, musingly. 'I think he's a good man.' Margery did not explain. And then a sunnier mood succeeded her tremblings and tears; till old Mr Vine came into the house below, and Jim went down to declare that all was well, and sent off his partner to break the news to Margery's father, who as yet remained unenlightened.

The Dairyman bore the intelligence of his daughter's untitled state as best he could, and punished her by not coming near her for several weeks, though at last he grumbled his forgiveness, and made up matters with Jim. The handsome Mrs Peach vanished to Budmouth, and found another sailor, not without a reasonable complaint against Jim and Margery both that she had been unfairly used.

As for the mysterious gentleman who had exercised such an influence over their lives, he kept his word, and was a stranger to Stickleford thenceforward. Baron or no Baron, Englishman or foreigner, he had shown a genuine interest in Jim, and real sorrow for a certain doubtful[60] phase of his acquaintance with Margery. That he had a more tender feeling towards the young girl than he wished her or any one else to perceive there could be no doubt; that he was strongly tempted at times to adopt other than straightforward courses with regard to her is also clear, particularly at that critical hour when she rolled along the high road with him in the carriage, in obedience to his suggestion that they should pursue Jim. But at other times he schooled doubtful sentiments into fair conduct, which even erred on the side of harshness. In after years there was a report that another attempt on his life, during one of those fits of sick moodiness to which he seemed constitutionally liable, had been effectual; but nobody in Stickleford was in a position to ascertain the truth.

There he is still regarded as one who had something about him magical and unearthly. In his mystery let him remain; for a man, no less than a landscape, who awakens an interest under uncertain lights, and touches of unfathomable shade, may cut but a poor figure in a garish noontide shine.

When she heard of his possible[61] death Margery sat in her nursing-chair, gravely thinking for nearly ten minutes, to the total neglect of her infant in the cradle. Jim, from the other side of the fire-place said, 'You are sorry enough for him, Margery. I am sure of that.'

'Yes, yes,' she murmured, 'I am sorry.'

'Suppose he were to suddenly appear and say in a voice of command, "Margery, come with me"'!'

'I believe I should have no power to disobey,' she returned, with a mischievous look. 'He was like a magician to me. I think he was one. He could move me as a loadstone moves a speck of steel . . . Yet no,' she added, hearing the baby cry, 'he would not move me now.'

'Well,' said Jim, with no great concern (for his 'la jalousie rétrospective,' as George Sand terms it,[62] had nearly died out of him); 'however he might move ye, my love, he'll never come. He swore it to me: and he was a man of his word.'

I

The north road from Casterbridge is tedious and lonely, especially in winter-time. Along a part of its course it connects with Holloway Lane,[1] a monotonous track without a village or hamlet for many miles, and with very seldom a turning. Unapprised wayfarers who are too old, or too young, or in other respects too weak for the distance to be traversed, but who, nevertheless, have to walk it, say, as they look wistfully ahead, 'Once at the top of that hill, and I must surely see the end of Holloway Lane!' But they reach the hilltop, and Holloway Lane stretches in front as mercilessly as before.

Some few years ago a certain farmer was riding through this lane in the gloom of a winter evening. The farmer's friend, a dairyman, was riding beside him. A few paces in the rear rode the farmer's man. All three were well horsed on strong, round-barrelled cobs; and to be well horsed was to be in better spirits about Holloway Lane than poor pedestrians could attain to during its passage.

But the farmer did not talk much to his friend as he rode along. The enterprise which had brought him there filled his mind; for in truth it was important. Not altogether so important was it, perhaps, when estimated by its value to society at large; but if the true measure of a deed be proportionate to the space it occupies in the heart of him who undertakes it, Farmer Charles Darton's business tonight could hold its own with the business of kings.

He was a large farmer. His turnover, as it is called, was probably thirty thousand pounds a year. He had a great many draught horses, a great many milch cows, and of sheep a multitude. This comfortable position was, however, none of his own making.[2] It had been created by his father, a man of a very different stamp from the present representative of the line.

Darton, the father, had been a one-idea'd character, with a buttoned-up pocket and a chink-like eye brimming with commercial subtlety. In Darton the son, this trade subtlety had become transmuted into emotional, and the harshness had disappeared; he would have been called a sad man but for his constant care not to divide himself from lively friends by piping notes out of harmony with theirs. Contemplative, he allowed his mind to be a quiet meeting-place for memories and hopes. So that, naturally enough, since succeeding to the agricultural calling, and up to his present age of thirty-two, he had neither advanced nor receded as a capitalist – a stationary result which did not agitate one of his unambitious, unstrategic nature, since he had all that he desired. The motive of his expedition tonight showed the same absence of anxious regard for Number one.

The party rode on in the slow, safe trot proper to night-time and bad roads, Farmer Darton's head jigging rather unromantically up and down against the sky, and his motions being repeated with bolder emphasis by his friend Japheth Johns;[3] while those of the latter were travestied in jerks still less softened by art in the person of the lad who attended them. A pair of whitish objects hung one on each side of the latter, bumping against him at each step, and still further spoiling the grace of his seat. On close inspection they might have been perceived to be open rush baskets – one containing a turkey, and the other some bottles of wine.

'D'ye feel ye can meet your fate like a man, neighbour Darton?' asked Johns, breaking a silence which had lasted while five-and-twenty hedgerow trees had glided by.

Mr Darton with a half-laugh murmured, 'Ay – call it my fate! Hanging and wiving go by destiny.'[4] And then they were silent again.

The darkness thickened rapidly, at intervals shutting down on the land in a perceptible flap like the wave of a wing. The customary close of day was accelerated by a simultaneous blurring of the air. With the fall of night had come a mist just damp enough to incommode, but not sufficient to saturate them. Countrymen as they were – born, as may be said, with only an open door between them and the four seasons – they regarded the mist but as an added obscuration, and ignored its humid quality.

They were travelling in a direction that was enlivened by no modern current of traffic, the place of Darton's pilgrimage being an old-fashioned village – one of the Hintocks (several of which lay there-about)[5] – where the people make the best cider and cider-wine in all Wessex, and where the dunghills smell of pomace instead of stable refuse as elsewhere. The lane was sometimes so narrow that the brambles of the hedge, which hung forward like anglers' rods over a stream, scratched their hats and curry-combed their whiskers as they passed. Yet this neglected lane had been a highway to Queen Eliza-beth's court, and other cavalcades of the past. Its day was over now, and its history as a national artery done for ever.

'Why I have decided to marry her,' resumed Darton (in a measured musical voice of confidence which revealed a good deal of his compo-sition) as he glanced round to see that the lad was not too near, 'is not only that I like her, but that I can do no better, even from a fairly practical point of view. That I might ha' looked higher is possibly true, though it is really all nonsense. I have had experience enough in looking above me. "No more superior women for me," said I – you know when. Sally is a comely, independent, simple character, with no make-up about her, who'll think me as much a superior to her as I used to think – you know who I mean – was to me.'

'Ay,' said Johns. 'However, I shouldn't call Sally Hall simple. Primary, because no Sally is; secondary, because if some could be, this one wouldn't. 'Tis a wrong denomination to apply to a woman, Charles, and affects me, as your best man, like cold water. 'Tis like recommending a stage play by saying there's neither murder, villany, nor harm of any sort in it, when that's what you've paid your half-crown to see.'

'Well; may your opinion do you good. Mine's a different one.' And turning the conversation from the philosophical to the practical, Darton expressed a hope that the said Sally had received what he'd sent on by the carrier that day.

Johns wanted to know what that was.

'It is a dress,' said Darton. 'Not exactly a wedding-dress, though she may use it as one if she likes. It is rather serviceable than showy – suitable for the winter weather.'

'Good,' said Johns. 'Serviceable is a wise word in a bridegroom. I commend ye, Charles.'

'For,' said Darton, 'why should a woman dress up like a rope-dancer because she's going to do the most solemn deed of her life except dying?'

'Faith, why? But she will, because she will, I suppose,' said Dairyman Johns.

'H'm,' said Darton.

The lane they followed had been nearly straight for several miles, but it now took a turn, and winding uncertainly for some distance forked into two. By night country roads are apt to reveal ungainly qualities which pass without observation during day; and though Darton had travelled this way before, he had not done so frequently, Sally having been wooed at the house of a relative near his own. He never remembered seeing at this spot a pair of alternative ways looking so equally probable as these two did now. Johns rode on a few steps.

'Don't be out of heart, sonny,' he cried. 'Here's a handpost. Enoch – come and climb this post, and tell us the way.'

The lad dismounted, and jumped into the hedge where the post stood under a tree.

'Unstrap the baskets, or you'll smash up that wine!' cried Darton, as the young man began spasmodically to climb the post, baskets and all.

'Was there ever less head in a brainless world?' said Johns. 'Here, simple Nocky, I'll do it.' He leapt off, and with much puffing climbed the post, striking a match when he reached the top, and moving the light along the arm, the lad standing and gazing at the spectacle.

'I have faced tantalization these twenty years with a temper as mild as milk!' said Japheth; 'but such things as this don't come short of devilry!' And flinging the match away, he slipped down to the ground.

'What's the matter?' asked Darton.

'Not a letter, sacred or heathen – not so much as would tell us the way to the great fireplace[6] – ever I should sin to say it! Either the moss and mildew have eaten away the words, or we have arrived in a land where the natives have lost the art of writing, and should have brought our compass like Christopher Columbus.'

'Let us take the straightest road,' said Darton placidly; 'I shan't be sorry to get there – 'tis a tiresome ride. I would have driven if I had known.'

'Nor I neither, sir,' said Enoch. 'These straps plough my shoulder like a zull. If 'tis much farther to your lady's home, Maister Darton, I shall ask to be let carry half of these good things in my innerds – hee, hee!'

'Don't you be such a reforming radical,[7] Enoch,' said Johns sternly. 'Here, I'll take the turkey.'

This being done, they went forward by the right-hand lane, which ascended a hill, the left winding away under a plantation. The pit-a-pat of their horses' hoofs lessened up the slope; and the ironical directing-post stood in solitude as before, holding out its blank arms to the raw breeze, which brought a snore from the wood as if Skrymir the Giant were sleeping there.[8]

II

Three miles to the left of the travellers, along the road they had not followed, rose an old house with mullioned windows of Ham-hill stone, and chimneys of lavish solidity. It stood at the top of a slope beside Hintock village-street;[9] and immediately in front of it grew a large sycamore-tree, whose bared roots formed a convenient staircase from the road below to the front door of the dwelling. Its situation gave the house what little distinctive name it possessed, namely, 'The Knap'. Some forty yards off a brook dribbled past, which, for its size, made a great deal of noise. At the back was a dairy barton, accessible for vehicles and live-stock by a side 'drong'. Thus much only of the character of the homestead could be divined out of doors at this shady evening-time.

But within there was plenty of light to see by, as plenty was construed at Hintock. Beside a Tudor fireplace, whose moulded four-centred arch was nearly hidden by a figured blue-cloth blower, were seated two women – mother and daughter – Mrs Hall, and Sarah, or Sally; for this was a part of the world where the latter modification had not as yet been effaced as a vulgarity by the march of intellect. The owner of the name was the young woman by whose means Mr Darton purposed to put an end to his bachelor condition on the approaching day.

The mother's bereavement had been so long ago as not to leave much mark of its occurrence upon her now, either in face or clothes. She had resumed the mob-cap of her early married life, enlivening its whiteness by a few rose-du-Barry ribbons. Sally required no such aids to pinkness. Roseate good-nature lit up her gaze; her features showed curves of decision and judgement; and she might have been regarded without much mistake as a warm-hearted, quick-spirited, handsome girl.

She did most of the talking, her mother listening with a half-absent air, as she picked up fragments of redhot wood ember with the tongs, and piled them upon the brands. But the number of speeches that passed was very small in proportion to the meanings exchanged. Long experience together often enabled them to see the course of thought in each other's minds without a word being spoken. Behind them, in the centre of the room, the table was spread for supper, certain whiffs of air laden with fat vapours, which ever and anon entered from the kitchen, denoting its preparation there.

'The new gown he was going to send you stays about on the way like himself,' Sally's mother was saying.

'Yes, not finished, I daresay,' cried Sally independently. 'Lord, I shouldn't be amazed if it didn't come at all! Young men make such kind promises when they are near you, and forget 'em when they go away. But he doesn't intend it as a wedding-gown – he gives it to me merely as a gown to wear when I like – a travelling dress is what it would be called by some. Come rathe or come late it don't much matter, as I have a dress of my own to fall back upon. But what time is it?'

She went to the family clock and opened the glass, for the hour was not otherwise discernible by night, and indeed at all times was rather a thing to be investigated than beheld, so much more wall than window was there in the apartment. 'It is nearly eight,' said she.

'Eight o'clock, and neither dress nor man,' said Mrs Hall.

'Mother, if you think to tantalize me by talking like that, you are much mistaken! Let him be as late as he will – or stay away altogether – I don't care,' said Sally. But a tender, minute quaver in the negation showed that there was something forced in that statement.

Mrs Hall perceived it, and drily observed that she was not so sure about Sally not caring. 'But perhaps you don't care so much as I do, after all,' she said. 'For I see what you don't, that it is a good and flourishing match for you; a very honourable offer in Mr Darton. And I think I see a kind husband in him. So pray God 'twill go smooth, and wind up well.'

Sally would not listen to misgivings. Of course it would go smoothly, she asserted. 'How you are up and down, mother!' she went on. 'At this moment, whatever hinders him, we are not so anxious to see him as he is to be here, and his thought runs on before him, and settles down upon us like the star in the east. Hark!' she exclaimed, with a breath of relief, her eyes sparkling. 'I heard something. Yes – here they are!'

The next moment her mother's slower ear also distinguished the familiar reverberation occasioned by footsteps clambering up the roots of the sycamore.

'Yes, it sounds like them at last,' she said. 'Well, it is not so very late after all, considering the distance.'

The footfall ceased, and they arose, expecting a knock. They began to think it might have been, after all, some neighbouring villager under Bacchic influence,[10] giving the centre of the road a wide berth, when their doubts were dispelled by the newcomer's entry into the passage. The door of the room was gently opened, and there appeared, not the pair of travellers with whom we have already made acquaintance, but a pale-faced man in the garb of extreme poverty – almost in rags.

'Oh, it's a tramp – gracious me!' said Sally, starting back.

His cheeks and eye-orbits were deep concaves – rather, it might be, from natural weakness of constitution than irregular living, though there were indications that he had led no careful life. He gazed at the two women fixedly for a moment; then with an abashed, humiliated demeanour, dropped his glance to the floor, and sank into a chair without uttering a word.

Sally was in advance of her mother, who had remained standing by the fire. She now tried to discern the visitor across the candles.

'Why – mother,' said Sally faintly, turning back to Mrs Hall. 'It is Phil, from Australia!'

Mrs Hall started, and grew pale, and a fit of coughing seized the man with the ragged clothes. 'To come home like this!' she said. 'Oh, Philip – are you ill?'

'No, no, mother,' replied he impatiently, as soon as he could speak.

'But for God's sake how do you come here – and just now too?'

'Well, I am here,' said the man. 'How it is I hardly know. I've come home, mother, because I was driven to it. Things were against me out there, and went from bad to worse.'

'Then why didn't you let us know? – you've not writ a line for the last two or three years.'

The son admitted sadly that he had not. He said that he had hoped and thought he might fetch up again, and be able to send good news. Then he had been obliged to abandon that hope, and had finally come home from sheer necessity – previous to making a new start. 'Yes, things are very bad with me,' he repeated, perceiving their commiserating glances at his clothes.

They brought him nearer the fire, took his hat from his thin hand, which was so small and smooth as to show that his attempts to fetch up again had not been in a manual direction. His mother resumed her inquiries, and dubiously asked if he had chosen to come that particular night for any special reason.

For no reason, he told her. His arrival had been quite at random. Then Philip Hall looked round the room, and saw for the first time that the table was laid somewhat luxuriously, and for a larger number than themselves; and that an air of festivity pervaded their dress. He asked quickly what was going on.

'Sally is going to be married in a day or two,' replied the mother; and she explained how Mr Darton, Sally's intended husband, was coming there that night with the bridesman, Mr Johns, and other details. 'We thought it must be their step when we heard you,' said Mrs Hall.

The needy wanderer looked again on the floor. 'I see – I see,' he murmured. 'Why, indeed, should I have come tonight? Such folk as I are not wanted here at these times, naturally. And I have no business here – spoiling other people's happiness.'

'Phil,' said his mother, with a tear in her eye, but with a thinness of lip and severity of manner which were presumably not more than past events justified; 'since you speak like that to me, I'll speak honestly to you. For these three years you have taken no thought for us. You left home with a good supply of money, and strength and education, and you ought to have made good use of it all. But you come back like a beggar; and that you come in a very awkward time for us cannot be denied. Your return tonight may do us much harm. But mind – you are welcome to this home as long as it is mine. I don't wish to turn you adrift. We will make the best of a bad job; and I hope you are not seriously ill?'

'Oh no. I have only this infernal cough.'

She looked at him anxiously. 'I think you had better go to bed at once,' she said.

'Well – I shall be out of the way there,' said the son wearily. 'Having ruined myself, don't let me ruin you by being seen in these togs, for Heaven's sake. Who do you say Sally is going to be married to – a Farmer Darton?'

'Yes – a gentleman-farmer – quite a wealthy man. Far better in station than she could have expected. It is a good thing, altogether.'

'Well done, little Sal!' said her brother, brightening and looking up at her with a smile. 'I ought to have written; but perhaps I have thought of you all the more. But let me get out of sight. I would rather go and jump into the river than be seen here. But have you anything I can drink? I am confoundedly thirsty with my long tramp.'

'Yes, yes; we will bring something upstairs to you,' said Sally, with grief in her face.

'Ay, that will do nicely. But, Sally and mother —' He stopped, and they waited. 'Mother, I have not told you all,' he resumed slowly, still looking on the floor between his knees. 'Sad as what you see of me is, there's worse behind.'

His mother gazed upon him in grieved suspense, and Sally went and leant upon the bureau, listening for every sound, and sighing.

Suddenly she turned round, saying, 'Let them come, I don't care! Philip, tell the worst, and take your time.'

'Well, then,' said the unhappy Phil, 'I am not the only one in this mess. Would to Heaven I were ! But —'

'Oh, Phil!'

'I have a wife as destitute as I.'

'A wife?' said his mother.

'Unhappily.'

'A wife! Yes, that is the way with sons!'

'And besides —' said he.

'Besides! Oh, Philip, surely —'

'I have two little children.'

'Wife and children!' whispered Mrs Hall, sinking down confounded.[11]

'Poor little things!' said Sally involuntarily.

His mother turned again to him. 'I suppose these helpless beings are left in Australia?'

'No. They are in England.'

'Well, I can only hope you've left them in a respectable place.'

'I have not left them at all. They are here – within a few yards of us. In short, they are in the stable.'

'Where?'

'In the stable. I did not like to bring them indoors till I had seen you, mother, and broken the bad news a bit to you. They were very tired, and are resting out there on some straw.'

Mrs Hall's fortitude visibly broke down. She had been brought up not without refinement, and was even more moved by such a collapse of genteel aims as this than a substantial dairyman's widow would in ordinary have been moved. 'Well, it must be borne,' she said, in a low voice, with her hands tightly joined. 'A starving son, a starving wife, starving children! Let it be. But why is this come to us now, today, tonight? Could no other misfortune happen to helpless women than this, which will quite upset my poor girl's chance of a happy life? Why have you done us this wrong, Philip? What respectable man will come here, and marry open-eyed into a family of vagabonds?'

'Nonsense, mother!' said Sally vehemently, while her face flushed.

'Charley isn't the man to desert me. But if he should be, and won't marry me because Phil's come, let him go and marry elsewhere. I won't be ashamed of my own flesh and blood for any man in England – not I!' And then Sally turned away and burst into tears.

'Wait till you are twenty years older and you will tell a different tale,' replied her mother.

The son stood up. 'Mother,' he said bitterly, 'as I have come, so I will go. All I ask of you is that you will allow me and mine to lie in your stable tonight. I give you my word that we'll be gone by break of day, and trouble you no further!'

Mrs Hall, the mother, changed at that. 'Oh no,' she answered hastily; 'never shall it be said that I sent any of my own family from my door. Bring 'em in, Philip, or take me out to them.'

'We will put 'em all into the large bedroom,' said Sally, brightening, 'and make up a large fire. Let's go and help them in, and call Susannah.' (Susannah was the woman who assisted at the dairy and housework; she lived in a cottage hard by, with her husband who attended to the cows.)

Sally went to fetch a lantern from the back-kitchen, but her brother said, 'You won't want a light. I lit the lantern that was hanging there.'

'What must we call your wife?' asked Mrs Hall.

'Helena,' said Philip.

With shawls over their heads they proceeded towards the back door.

'One minute before you go,' interrupted Philip. 'I – I haven't confessed all.'

'Then Heaven help us!' said Mrs Hall, pushing to the door and clasping her hands in calm despair.

'We passed through Verton[12] as we came,' he continued, 'and I just looked in at the "Dog" to see if old Mike still kept on there as usual. The carrier had come in from Sherton Abbas at that moment, and guessing that I was bound for this place – for I think he knew me – he asked me to bring on a dressmaker's parcel for Sally that was marked "immediate". My wife had walked on with the children. 'Twas a flimsy parcel, and the paper was torn, and I found on looking at it that it was a thick warm gown. I didn't wish you to see poor Helena in a shabby state. I was ashamed that you should – 'twas not what she was born to. I untied the parcel in the road, took it on to her where she was waiting in the Lower Barn, and told her I had managed to get it for her, and that she was to ask no question. She, poor thing, must have supposed I obtained it on trust, through having reached a place where I was known, for she put it on gladly enough. She has it on now. Sally has other gowns, I daresay.'

Sally looked at her mother, speechless.

'You have others, I daresay!' repeated Phil, with a sick man's impatience. 'I thought to myself, "Better Sally cry than Helena freeze." Well, is the dress of great consequence? 'Twas nothing very ornamental, as far as I could see.'

'No – no; not of consequence,' returned Sally sadly, adding in a gentle voice, 'You will not mind if I lend her another instead of that one, will you?'

Philip's agitation at the confession had brought on another attack of the cough, which seemed to shake him to pieces. He was so obviously unfit to sit in a chair that they helped him upstairs at once; and having hastily given him a cordial and kindled the bedroom fire, they descended to fetch their unhappy new relations.

III

It was with strange feelings that the girl and her mother, lately so cheerful, passed out of the back door into the open air of the barton, laden with hay scents and the herby breath of cows. A fine sleet had begun to fall, and they trotted across the yard quickly. The stable-door was open; a light shone from it – from the lantern which always hung there, and which Philip had lit, as he said. Softly nearing the door, Mrs Hall pronounced the name 'Helena!'

There was no answer for the moment. Looking in she was taken by surprise. Two people appeared before her. For one, instead of the drabbish woman she had expected, Mrs Hall saw a pale, dark-eyed, lady-like creature, whose personality ruled her attire rather than was ruled by it. She was in a new and handsome dress, of course, and an old bonnet. She was standing up, agitated; her hand was held by her companion – none else than Sally's affianced, Farmer Charles Darton, upon whose fine figure the pale stranger's eyes were fixed, as his were fixed upon her. His other hand held the rein of his horse, which was standing saddled as if just led in.

At sight of Mrs Hall they both turned, looking at her in a way neither quite conscious nor unconscious, and without seeming to recollect that words were necessary as a solution to the scene. In another moment Sally entered also, when Mr Darton dropped his companion's hand, led the horses aside, and came to greet his betrothed and Mrs Hall.

'Ah!' he said, smiling – with something like forced composure – 'this is a roundabout way of arriving you will say, my dear Mrs Hall. But we lost our way, which made us late. I saw a light here, and led in my horse at once – my friend Johns and my man have gone on to the "Sheaf of Arrows" with theirs, not to crowd you too much. No sooner had I entered than I saw that this lady had taken temporary shelter here – and found I was intruding.'

'She is my daughter-in-law,' said Mrs Hall calmly. 'My son, too, is in the house, but he has gone to bed unwell.'

Sally had stood staring wonderingly at the scene until this moment, hardly recognizing Darton's shake of the hand. The spell that bound her was broken by her perceiving the two little children seated on a heap of hay. She suddenly went forward, spoke to them, and took one on her arm and the other in her hand.

'And two children?' said Mr Darton, showing thus that he had not been there long enough as yet to understand the situation.

'My grandchildren,' said Mrs Hall, with as much affected ease as before.

Philip Hall's wife, in spite of this interruption to her first rencounter, seemed scarcely so much affected by it as to feel any one's presence in addition to Mr Darton's. However, arousing herself by a quick reflection, she threw a sudden critical glance of her sad eyes upon Mrs Hall; and, apparently finding her satisfactory, advanced to her in a meek initiative. Then Sally and the stranger spoke some friendly words to each other, and Sally went on with the children into the house. Mrs Hall and Helena followed, and Mr Darton followed these, looking at Helena's dress and outline, and listening to her voice like a man in a dream.

By the time the others reached the house Sally had already gone upstairs with the tired children. She rapped against the wall for Susannah to come in and help to attend to them, Susannah's house being a little 'spit-and-dab' cabin leaning against the substantial stonework of Mrs Hall's taller erection. When she came a bed was made up for the little ones, and some supper given to them. On descending the stairs after seeing this done Sally went to the sitting-room. Young Mrs Hall entered it just in advance of her, having in the interim retired with her mother-in-law to take off her bonnet, and otherwise make herself presentable. Hence it was evident that no further communication could have passed between her and Mr Darton since their brief interview in the stable.

Mr Japheth Johns now opportunely arrived, and broke up the restraint of the company, after a few orthodox meteorological commentaries had passed between him and Mrs Hall by way of introduction. They at once sat down to supper, the present of wine and turkey not being produced for consumption tonight, lest the premature display of those gifts should seem to throw doubt on Mrs Hall's capacities as a provider.

'Drink bold, Mr Johns – drink bold,' said that matron magnanimously. 'Such as it is there's plenty of. But perhaps cider-wine is not to your taste? – though there's body in it.'

'Quite the contrary, ma'am – quite the contrary,' said the dairyman. 'For though I inherit the malt-liquor principle from my father, I am a cider-drinker on my mother's side. She came from these parts, you know. And there's this to be said for't – 'tis a more peaceful liquor, and don't lie about a man like your hotter drinks. With care, one may live on it a twelvemonth without knocking down a neighbour, or getting a black eye from an old acquaintance.'

The general conversation thus begun was continued briskly, though it was in the main restricted to Mrs Hall and Japheth, who in truth required but little help from anybody. There being slight call upon Sally's tongue, she had ample leisure to do what her heart most desired, namely, watch her intended husband and her sister-in-law with a view of elucidating the strange momentary scene in which her mother and herself had surprised them in the stable. If that scene meant anything, it meant, at least, that they had met before. That there had been no time for explanation Sally could see, for their manner was still one of suppressed amazement at each other's presence there. Darton's eyes, too, fell continually on the dress worn by Helena, as if this were an added riddle to his perplexity; though to Sally it was the one feature in the case which was no mystery. He seemed to feel that fate had impishly changed his *vis-à-vis* in the lover's jig he was about to tread; that while the gown had been expected to enclose a Sally, a Helena's face looked out from the bodice; that some long-lost hand met his own from the sleeves.

Sally could see that whatever Helena might know of Darton, she knew nothing of how the dress entered into his embarrassment. And at moments the young girl would have persuaded herself that Darton's looks at her sister-in-law were entirely the fruit of the clothes query. But surely at other times a more extensive range of speculation and sentiment was expressed by her lover's eye than that which the changed dress would account for.

Sally's independence made her one of the least jealous of women. But there was something in the relations of these two visitors which ought to be explained.

Japheth Johns continued to converse in his well-known style, interspersing his talk with some private reflections on the position of Darton and Sally, which, though the sparkle in his eye showed them to be highly entertaining to himself, were apparently not quite communicable to the company. At last he withdrew for the night, going off to the 'Sheaf of Arrows', whither Darton promised to follow him in a few minutes.

Half-an-hour passed, and then Mr Darton also rose to leave, Sally and her sister-in-law simultaneously wishing him good night as they retired upstairs to their rooms. But on his arriving at the front door with Mrs Hall a sharp shower of rain began to come down, when the widow suggested that he should return to the fireside till the storm ceased.

Darton accepted her proposal, but insisted that, as it was getting late, and she was obviously tired, she should not sit up on his account, since he could let himself out of the house, and would quite enjoy smoking a pipe by the hearth alone. Mrs Hall assented; and Darton was left by himself. He spread his knees to the brands, lit up his tobacco as he had said, and sat gazing into the fire, and at the notches of the chimney-crook which hung above.

An occasional drop of rain rolled down the chimney with a hiss, and still he smoked on; but not like a man whose mind was at rest. In the long run, however, despite his meditations, early hours afield and a long ride in the open air produced their natural result. He began to doze.

How long he remained in this half-unconscious state he did not know. He suddenly opened his eyes. The back-brand had burnt itself in two, and ceased to flame; the light which he had placed on the mantelpiece had nearly gone out. But in spite of these deficiencies there was a light in the apartment, and it came from elsewhere. Turning his head, he saw Philip Hall's wife standing at the entrance of the room with a bed-candle in one hand, a small brass tea-kettle in the other, and *his* gown, as it certainly seemed, still upon her.

'Helena!' said Darton, starting up.

Her countenance expressed dismay, and her first words were an apology. 'I – did not know you were here, Mr Darton,' she said, while a blush flashed to her cheek. 'I thought every one had retired – I was coming to make a little water boil; my husband seems to be worse. But perhaps the kitchen fire can be lighted up again.'

'Don't go on my account. By all means put it on here as you intended,' said Darton. 'Allow me to help you.' He went forward to take the kettle from her hand, but she did not allow him, and placed it on the fire herself.

They stood some way apart, one on each side of the fireplace, waiting till the water should boil, the candle on the mantel between them, and Helena with her eyes on the kettle. Darton was the first to break the silence. 'Shall I call Sally?' he said.

'Oh no,' she quickly returned. 'We have given trouble enough already. We have no right here. But we are the sport of fate, and were obliged to come.'

'No right here!' said he in surprise.

THOMAS HARDY

'None. I can't explain it now,' answered Helena. 'This kettle is very slow.'

There was another pause; the proverbial dilatoriness of watched pots was never more clearly exemplified.

Helena's face was of that sort which seems to ask for assistance without the owner's knowledge – the very antipodes of Sally's, which was self-reliance expressed. Darton's eyes travelled from the kettle to Helena's face, then back to the kettle, then to the face for rather a longer time. 'So I am not to know anything of the mystery that has distracted me all the evening?' he said. 'How is it that a woman, who refused me because (as I supposed) my position was not good enough for her taste, is found to be the wife of a man who certainly seems to be worse off than I?'

'He had the prior claim,' said she.

'What! you knew him at that time?'

'Yes, yes. Please say no more,' she implored. 'Whatever my errors, I have paid for them during the last five years!'

The heart of Darton was subject to sudden overflowings. He was kind to a fault. 'I am sorry from my soul,' he said, involuntarily approaching her. Helena withdrew a step or two, at which he became conscious of his movement, and quickly took his former place. Here he stood without speaking, and the little kettle began to sing.

'Well, you might have been my wife if you had chosen,' he said at last. 'But that's all past and gone. However, if you are in any trouble or poverty I shall be glad to be of service, and as your relative by marriage I shall have a right to be. Does your uncle know of your distress?'

'My uncle is dead. He left me without a farthing. And now we have two children to maintain.'

'What, left you nothing? How could he be so cruel as that?'

'I disgraced myself in his eyes.'

'Now,' said Darton earnestly, 'let me take care of the children, at least while you are so unsettled. *You* belong to another, so I cannot take care of you.'

'Yes you can,' said a voice; and suddenly a third figure stood beside them. It was Sally. 'You can, since you seem to wish to!' she repeated.

266

'She no longer belongs to another . . . My poor brother is dead!'

Her face was red, her eyes sparkled, and all the woman came to the front. 'I have heard it!' she went on to him passionately. 'You can protect her now as well as the children!' She turned then to her agitated sister-in-law. 'I heard something,' said Sally (in a gentle murmur, differing much from her previous passionate words), 'and I went into his room. It must have been the moment you left. He went off so quickly, and weakly, and it was so unexpected, that I couldn't leave even to call you.'

Darton was just able to gather from the confused discourse which followed that, during his sleep by the fire, this brother whom he had never seen had become worse; and that during Helena's absence for water the end had unexpectedly come. The two young women hastened upstairs, and he was again left alone.

After standing there a short time he went to the front door and looked out; till, softly closing it behind him, he advanced and stood under the large sycamore-tree. The stars were flickering coldly, and the dampness which had just descended upon the earth in rain now sent up a chill from it. Darton was in a strange position, and he felt it. The unexpected appearance, in deep poverty, of Helena – a young lady, daughter of a deceased naval officer, who had been brought up by her uncle, a solicitor, and had refused Darton in marriage years ago – the passionate, almost angry demeanour of Sally at discovering them, the abrupt announcement that Helena was a widow; all this coming together was a conjuncture difficult to cope with in a moment, and made him question whether he ought to leave the house or offer assistance. But for Sally's manner he would unhesitatingly have done the latter.

He was still standing under the tree when the door in front of him opened, and Mrs Hall came out. She went round to the garden-gate at the side without seeing him. Darton followed her, intending to speak. Pausing outside, as if in thought, she proceeded to a spot where the sun came earliest in spring-time, and where the north wind never blew; it was where the row of beehives stood under the wall. Discerning her object, he waited till she had accomplished it.

It was the universal custom thereabout to wake the bees by tapping at their hives whenever a death occurred in the household,[13] under the belief that if this were not done the bees themselves would pine away and perish during the ensuing year. As soon as an interior buzzing responded to her tap at the first hive Mrs Hall went on to the second, and thus passed down the row. As soon as she came back he met her.

'What can I do in this trouble, Mrs Hall?' he said.

'Oh – nothing, thank you, nothing,' she said in a tearful voice, now just perceiving him. 'We have called Susannah and her husband, and they will do everything necessary.' She told him in a few words the particulars of her son's arrival, broken in health – indeed, at death's very door, though they did not suspect it – and suggested, as the result of a conversation between her and her daughter, that the wedding should be postponed.

'Yes, of course,' said Darton. 'I think now to go straight to the inn and tell Johns what has happened.' It was not till after he had shaken hands with her that he turned hesitatingly and added, 'Will you tell the mother of his children that, as they are now left fatherless, I shall be glad to take the eldest of them, if it would be any convenience to her and to you?'

Mrs Hall promised that her son's widow should be told of the offer, and they parted. He retired down the rooty slope and disappeared in the direction of the 'Sheaf of Arrows', where he informed Johns of the circumstances. Meanwhile Mrs Hall had entered the house. Sally was downstairs in the sitting-room alone, and her mother explained to her that Darton had readily assented to the postponement.

'No doubt he has,' said Sally, with sad emphasis. 'It is not put off for a week, or a month, or a year. I shall never marry him, and she will.'

IV

Time passed, and the household on the Knap became again serene under the composing influences of daily routine. A desultory, very desultory, correspondence, dragged on between Sally Hall and Darton, who, not quite knowing how to take her petulant words on the night of her brother's death, had continued passive thus long. Helena and her children remained at the dairy-house, almost of necessity, and Darton therefore deemed it advisable to stay away.

One day, seven months later on, when Mr Darton was as usual at his farm, twenty miles from Hintock, a note reached him from Helena. She thanked him for his kind offer about her children, which her mother-in-law had duly communicated, and stated that she would be glad to accept it as regarded the eldest, the boy. Helena had, in truth, good need to do so, for her uncle had left her penniless, and all application to some relatives in the north had failed. There was, besides, as she said, no good school near Hintock to which she could send the child.

On a fine summer day the boy came. He was accompanied half-way by Sally and his mother – to the 'Pack-Horse', a roadside inn[14] – where he was handed over to Darton's bailiff in a shining spring-cart, who met them there.

He was entered as a day-scholar at a popular school at Casterbridge, three or four miles from Darton's, having first been taught by Darton to ride a forest-pony, on which he cantered to and from the aforesaid fount of knowledge, and (as Darton hoped) brought away a promising headful of the same at each diurnal expedition. The thoughtful taciturnity into which Darton had latterly fallen was quite dissipated by the presence of this boy.

When the Christmas holidays came it was arranged that he should spend them with his mother. The journey was, for some reason or other, performed in two stages, as at his coming, except that Darton in person took the place of the bailiff, and that the boy and himself rode on horseback.

Reaching the renowned 'Pack-Horse', Darton inquired if Miss and young Mrs Hall were there to meet little Philip (as they had agreed to be). He was answered by the appearance of Helena alone at the door.

'At the last moment Sally would not come,' she faltered.

That meeting practically settled the point towards which these long-severed persons were converging. But nothing was broached about it for some time yet. Sally Hall had, in fact, imparted the first decisive motion to events by refusing to accompany Helena. She soon gave them a second move by writing the following note: –

'[*Private.*]

'DEAR CHARLES – Living here so long and intimately with Helena, I have naturally learnt her history, especially that of it which refers to you. I am sure she would accept you as a husband at the proper time, and I think you ought to give her the opportunity. You inquire in an old note if I am sorry that I showed temper (which it *wasn't*) that night when I heard you talking to her. No, Charles, I am not sorry at all for what I said then. – Yours sincerely,

'SALLY HALL.'

Thus set in train, the transfer of Darton's heart back to its original quarters proceeded by mere lapse of time. In the following July Darton went to his friend Japheth to ask him at last to fulfil the bridal office which had been in abeyance since the previous January twelvemonths.

'With all my heart, man o' constancy!' said Dairyman Johns warmly. 'I've lost most of my genteel fair complexion haymaking this hot weather, 'tis true, but I'll do your business as well as them that look better. There be scents and good hair-oil in the world yet, thank God, and they'll take off the roughest o' my edge. I'll compliment her. "Better late than never, Sally Hall", I'll say.'

'It is not Sally,' said Darton hurriedly. 'It is young Mrs Hall.'

Japheth's face, as soon as he really comprehended, became a picture of reproachful dismay. 'Not Sally?' he said. 'Why not Sally? I can't believe it! Young Mrs Hall! Well, well – where's your wisdom?'

Darton shortly explained particulars; but Johns would not be reconciled. 'She was a woman worth having if ever woman was,' he cried. 'And now to let her go!'

'But I suppose I can marry where I like,' said Darton.

'H'm,' replied the dairyman, lifting his eyebrows expressively. 'This don't become you, Charles – it really do not. If I had done such a thing you would have sworn I was a d— no'thern fool to be drawn off the scent by such a red-herring doll-oll-oll.'

Farmer Darton responded in such sharp terms to this laconic opinion that the two friends finally parted in a way they had never parted before. Johns was to be no groomsman to Darton after all. He had flatly declined. Darton went off sorry, and even unhappy, particularly as Japheth was about to leave that side of the county, so that the words which had divided them were not likely to be explained away or softened down.

A short time after the interview Darton was united to Helena at a simple matter-of-fact wedding; and she and her little girl joined the boy who had already grown to look on Darton's house as home.

For some months the farmer experienced an unprecedented happiness and satisfaction. There had been a flaw in his life, and it was as neatly mended as was humanly possible. But after a season the stream of events followed less clearly, and there were shades in his reveries. Helena was a fragile woman, of little staying power, physically or morally, and since the time that he had originally known her – eight or ten years before – she had been severely tried. She had loved herself out, in short, and was now occasionally given to moping. Sometimes she spoke regretfully of the gentilities of her early life, and instead of comparing her present state with her condition as the wife of the unlucky Hall, she mused rather on what it had been before she took the first fatal step of clandestinely marrying him. She did not care to please such people as those with whom she was thrown as a thriving farmer's wife. She allowed the pretty trifles of agricultural domesticity to glide by her as sorry details, and had it not been for the children Darton's house would have seemed but little brighter than it had been before.

This led to occasional unpleasantness, until Darton sometimes declared to himself that such endeavours as his to rectify early deviations of the heart by harking back to the old point mostly failed of success. 'Perhaps Johns was right,' he would say. 'I should have gone on with Sally. Better go with the tide and make the best of its course than stem it at the risk of a capsize.' But he kept these unmelodious thoughts to himself, and was outwardly considerate and kind.

This somewhat barren tract of his life had extended to less than a year and a half when his ponderings were cut short by the loss of the woman they concerned. When she was in her grave he thought better of her than when she had been alive; the farm was a worse place without her than with her, after all. No woman short of divine could have gone through such an experience as hers with her first husband without becoming a little soured. Her stagnant sympathies, her sometimes unreasonable manner, had covered a heart frank and well meaning, and originally hopeful and warm. She left him a tiny red infant in white wrappings. To make life as easy as possible to this touching object became at once his care.

As this child learnt to walk and talk Darton learnt to see feasibility in a scheme which pleased him. Revolving the experiment which he had hitherto made upon life, he fancied he had gained wisdom from his mistakes and caution from his miscarriages.

What the scheme was needs no penetration to discover. Once more he had opportunity to recast and rectify his ill-wrought situations by returning to Sally Hall, who still lived quietly on under her mother's roof at Hintock. Helena had been a woman to lend pathos and refinement to a home; Sally was the woman to brighten it. She would not, as Helena did, despise the rural simplicities of a farmer's fireside. Moreover, she had a pre-eminent qualification for Darton's household; no other woman could make so desirable a mother to her brother's two children and Darton's one as Sally – while Darton, now that Helena had gone, was a more promising husband for Sally than he had ever been when liable to reminders from an uncured sentimental wound.

Darton was not a man to act rapidly, and the working out of his reparative designs might have been delayed for some time. But there came a winter evening precisely like the one which had darkened over that former ride to Hintock, and he asked himself why he should postpone longer, when the very landscape called for a repetition of that attempt.

He told his man to saddle the mare, booted and spurred himself with a younger horseman's nicety, kissed the two youngest children, and rode off. To make the journey a complete parallel to the first, he would fain have had his old acquaintance Japheth Johns with him. But Johns, alas! was missing. His removal to the other side of the county had left unrepaired the breach which had arisen between him and Darton; and though Darton had forgiven him a hundred times, as Johns had probably forgiven Darton, the effort of reunion in present circumstances was one not likely to be made.

He screwed himself up to as cheerful a pitch as he could without his former crony, and became content with his own thoughts as he rode, instead of the words of a companion. The sun went down; the boughs appeared scratched in like an etching against the sky; old crooked men with faggots at their backs said 'Good night, sir,' and Darton replied 'Good night' right heartily.

By the time he reached the forking roads it was getting as dark as it had been on the occasion when Johns climbed the directing-post. Darton made no mistake this time. 'Nor shall I be able to mistake, thank Heaven, when I arrive,' he murmured. It gave him peculiar satisfaction to think that the proposed marriage, like his first, was of the nature of setting in order things long awry, and not a momentary freak of fancy.

Nothing hindered the smoothness of his journey, which seemed not half its former length. Though dark, it was only between five and six o'clock when the bulky chimneys of Mrs Hall's residence appeared in view behind the sycamore-tree. He put up at the 'Sheaf of Arrows' as in former time; and when he had plumed himself before the inn mirror, called for a glass of negus, and smoothed out the incipient wrinkles of care, he walked on to the Knap with a quick step.

V

That evening Sally was making 'pinners' for the milkers, who were now increased by two, for her mother and herself no longer joined in milking the cows themselves. But upon the whole there was little change in the household economy, and not much in its appearance, beyond such minor particulars as that the crack over the window, which had been a hundred years coming, was a trifle wider; that the beams were a shade blacker; that the influence of modernism had supplanted the open chimney corner by a grate; that Susannah, who had worn a cap when she had plenty of hair, had left it off now she had scarce any, because it was reported that caps were not fashionable; and that Sally's face had naturally assumed a more womanly and experienced cast.

Mrs Hall was actually lifting coals with the tongs, as she had used to do.

'Five years ago this very night, if I am not mistaken —' she said, laying on an ember.

'Not this very night – though 'twas one night this week,' said the correct Sally.

'Well, 'tis near enough. Five years ago Mr Darton came to marry you, and my poor boy Phil came home to die.' She sighed. 'Ah, Sally,' she presently said, 'if you had managed well Mr Darton would have had you, Helena or none.'

'Don't be sentimental about that, mother,' begged Sally. 'I didn't care to manage well in such a case. Though I liked him, I wasn't so anxious. I would never have married the man in the midst of such a hitch as that was,' she added with decision; 'and I don't think I would if he were to ask me now.'

'I am not sure about that, unless you have another in your eye.'

'I wouldn't; and I'll tell you why. I could hardly marry him for love at this time o' day. And as we've quite enough to live on if we give up the dairy tomorrow, I should have no need to marry for any meaner reason . . . I am quite happy enough as I am, and there's an end o't.'

Now it was not long after this dialogue that there came a mild rap at the door, and in a moment there entered Susannah, looking as though a ghost had arrived. The fact was that that accomplished skimmer and churner (now a resident in the house) had overheard the desultory observations between mother and daughter, and on opening the door to Mr Darton thought the coincidence must have a grisly meaning in it. Mrs Hall welcomed the farmer with warm surprise, as did Sally, and for a moment they rather wanted words.

'Can you push up the chimney-crook for me, Mr Darton? the notches hitch,' said the matron. He did it, and the homely little act bridged over the awkward consciousness that he had been a stranger for four years.

Mrs Hall soon saw what he had come for, and left the principals together while she went to prepare him a late tea, smiling at Sally's late hasty assertions of indifference, when she saw how civil Sally was. When tea was ready she joined them. She fancied that Darton did not look so confident as when he had arrived; but Sally was quite light-hearted, and the meal passed pleasantly.

About seven he took his leave of them. Mrs Hall went as far as the door to light him down the slope. On the doorstep he said frankly –

'I came to ask your daughter to marry me; chose the night and everything, with an eye to a favourable answer. But she won't.'

'Then she's a very ungrateful girl!' emphatically said Mrs Hall.

Darton paused to shape his sentence, and asked, 'I – I suppose there's nobody else more favoured?'

'I can't say that there is, or that there isn't,' answered Mrs Hall. 'She's private in some things. I'm on your side, however, Mr Darton, and I'll talk to her.'

'Thank ye, thank ye!' said the farmer in a gayer accent; and with this assurance the not very satisfactory visit came to an end. Darton descended the roots of the sycamore, the light was withdrawn, and the door closed. At the bottom of the slope he nearly ran against a man about to ascend.

'Can a jack-o'-lent believe his few senses on such a dark night, or can't he?' exclaimed one whose utterance Darton recognized in a moment, despite its unexpectedness. 'I dare not swear he can, though I fain would!' The speaker was Johns.

Darton said he was glad of this opportunity, bad as it was, of putting an end to the silence of years, and asked the dairyman what he was travelling that way for.

Japheth showed the old jovial confidence in a moment. 'I'm going to see your – relations – as they always seem to me,' he said – 'Mrs Hall and Sally. Well, Charles, the fact is I find the natural barbarousness of man is much increased by a bachelor life, and, as your leavings were always good enough for me, I'm trying civilization here.' He nodded towards the house.

'Not with Sally – to marry her?' said Darton, feeling something like a rill of ice water between his shoulders.

'Yes, by the help of Providence and my personal charms. And I think I shall get her. I am this road every week – my present dairy is only four miles off, you know, and I see her through the window. 'Tis rather odd that I was going to speak practical tonight to her for the first time. You've just called?'

'Yes, for a short while. But she didn't say a word about you.'

'A good sign, a good sign. Now that decides me. I'll swing the mallet[15] and get her answer this very night as I planned.'

A few more remarks, and Darton, wishing his friend joy of Sally in a slightly hollow tone of jocularity, bade him goodbye. Johns promised to write particulars, and ascended, and was lost in the shade of the house and tree. A rectangle of light appeared when Johns was admitted, and all was dark again.

'Happy Japheth!' said Darton. 'This, then, is the explanation!'

He determined to return home that night. In a quarter of an hour he passed out of the village, and the next day went about his swede-lifting and storing as if nothing had occurred.

He waited and waited to hear from Johns whether the wedding-day was fixed: but no letter came. He learnt not a single particular till, meeting Johns one day at a horse-auction, Darton exclaimed genially – rather more genially than he felt – 'When is the joyful day to be?'

To his great surprise a reciprocity of gladness was not conspicuous in Johns. 'Not at all,' he said, in a very subdued tone. ' 'Tis a bad job; she won't have me.'

Darton held his breath till he said with treacherous solicitude, 'Try again – 'tis coyness.'

'Oh no,' said Johns decisively. 'There's been none of that. We talked it over dozens of times in the most fair and square way. She tells me plainly, I don't suit her. 'Twould be simply annoying her to ask her again. Ah, Charles, you threw a prize away when you let her slip five years ago.'

'I did – I did,' said Darton.

He returned from that auction with a new set of feelings in play. He had certainly made a surprising mistake in thinking Johns his successful rival. It really seemed as if he might hope for Sally after all.

This time, being rather pressed by business, Darton had recourse to pen-and-ink, and wrote her as manly and straightforward a proposal as any woman could wish to receive. The reply came promptly: –

'DEAR MR DARTON – I am as sensible as any woman can be of the goodness that leads you to make me this offer a second time. Better women than I would be proud of the honour, for when I read your nice long speeches on mangold-wurzel,[16] and such like topics, at the Casterbridge Farmers' Club, I do feel it an honour, I assure you. But my answer is just the same as before. I will not try to explain what, in truth, I cannot explain – my reasons; I will simply say that I must decline to be married to you. With good wishes as in former times, I am, your faithful friend,

'SALLY HALL.'

Darton dropped the letter hopelessly. Beyond the negative, there was just a possibility of sarcasm in it – 'nice long speeches on mangold-wurzel' had a suspicious sound. However, sarcasm or none, there was the answer, and he had to be content.

He proceeded to seek relief in a business which at this time engrossed much of his attention – that of clearing up a curious mistake just current in the county, that he had been nearly ruined by the recent failure of a local bank. A farmer named Darton had lost heavily, and the similarity of name had probably led to the error. Belief in it was so persistent that it demanded several days of letter-writing to set matters straight, and persuade the world that he was as solvent as ever he had been in his life. He had hardly concluded this worrying task when, to his delight, another letter arrived in the handwriting of Sally.

Darton tore it open; it was very short.

'DEAR MR DARTON – We have been so alarmed these last few days by the report that you were ruined by the stoppage of —'s Bank, that, now it is contradicted, I hasten, by my mother's wish, to say how truly glad we are to find there is no foundation for the report. After your kindness to my poor brother's children, I can do no less than write at such a moment. We had a letter from each of them a few days ago. – Your faithful friend,

'SALLY HALL.'

'Mercenary little woman!' said Darton to himself with a smile. 'Then that was the secret of her refusal this time – she thought I was ruined.'

Now, such was Darton, that as hours went on he could not help feeling too generously towards Sally to condemn her in this. What did he want in a wife? he asked himself. Love and integrity. What next? Worldly wisdom. And was there really more than worldly wisdom in her refusal to go aboard a sinking ship? She now knew it was otherwise. 'Begad,' he said, 'I'll try her again.'

The fact was he had so set his heart upon Sally, and Sally alone, that nothing was to be allowed to baulk him; and his reasoning was purely formal.

Anniversaries having been unpropitious, he waited on till a bright day late in May – a day when all animate nature was fancying, in its trusting, foolish way, that it was going to bask out of doors for evermore. As he rode through Holloway Lane it was scarce recognizable as the track of his two winter journeys. No mistake could be made now, even with his eyes shut. The cuckoo's note was at its best, between April tentativeness and mid-summer decrepitude, and the reptiles in the sun behaved as winningly as kittens on a hearth. Though afternoon, and about the same time as on the last occasion, it was broad day and sunshine when he entered Hintock, and the details of the Knap dairy-house were visible far up the road. He saw Sally in the garden, and was set vibrating. He had first intended to go on to the inn; but 'No,' he said; 'I'll tie my horse to the garden-gate. If all goes well, it can soon be taken round: if not, I mount and ride away.'

The tall shade of the horseman darkened the room in which Mrs Hall sat, and made her start, for he had ridden by a side path to the top of the slope, where riders seldom came. In a few seconds he was in the garden with Sally.

Five – ay, three minutes – did the business at the back of that row of bees. Though spring had come, and heavenly blue consecrated the scene, Darton succeeded not. '*No*,' said Sally firmly. 'I will never, never marry you, Mr Darton. I would have done it once; but now I never can.'

'But' – implored Mr Darton. And with a burst of real eloquence he went on to declare all sorts of things that he would do for her. He would drive her to see her mother every week – take her to London – settle so much money upon her – Heaven knows what he did not promise, suggest, and tempt her with. But it availed nothing. She interposed with a stout negative, which closed the course of his argument like an iron gate across a highway. Darton paused.

'Then,' said he simply, 'you hadn't heard of my supposed failure when you declined last time?'

'I had not,' she said. 'But if I had 'twould have been all the same.'[17]

'And 'tis not because of any soreness from my slighting you years ago?'

'No. That soreness is long past.'

'Ah – then you despise me, Sally!'

'No,' she slowly answered. 'I don't altogether despise you. I don't think you quite such a hero as I once did – that's all. The truth is, I am happy enough as I am; and I don't mean to marry at all. Now, may I ask a favour, sir?' She spoke with an ineffable charm, which, whenever he thought of it, made him curse his loss of her as long as he lived.

'To any extent.'

'Please do not put this question to me any more. Friends as long as you like, but lovers and married never.'

'I never will,' said Darton. 'Not if I live a hundred years.'

And he never did. That he had worn out his welcome in her heart was only too plain.

When his step-children had grown up, and were placed out in life, all communication between Darton and the Hall family ceased. It was only by chance that, years after, he learnt that Sally, notwithstanding the solicitations her attractions drew down upon her, had refused several offers of marriage, and steadily adhered to her purpose of leading a single life.

I

Whoever had perceived the yeoman's tall figure standing on Squire Everard's lawn in the dusk of that October evening fifty years ago,[1] might have said at first sight that he was loitering there from idle curiosity. For a large five-light window of the manor-house in front of him was unshuttered and uncurtained, so that the illuminated room within could be scanned almost to its four corners. Obviously nobody was ever expected to be in this part of the grounds after nightfall.

The apartment thus commanded by an eye from without was occupied by two persons only; they were sitting over dessert, the tablecloth having been removed in the old-fashioned way. The fruits were local, consisting of apples, pears, nuts, and such other products of the summer as might be presumed to grow on the estate. There was strong ale and rum on the table, and but little wine. Moreover, the appointments of the dining-room were simple and homely even for the date, betokening a countrified household of the smaller gentry, without much wealth or ambition – formerly a numerous class, but now in great part ousted by the territorial landlords.

One of the two sitters was a young lady in white muslin, who listened somewhat impatiently to the remarks of her companion, an elderly, rubicund personage, whom the merest stranger could have pronounced to be her father. The watcher evinced no signs of moving, and it became evident that affairs were not so simple as they first had seemed. The tall farmer was in fact no accidental spectator, and he stood by premeditation close to the trunk of a tree, so that had any traveller passed along the road without the park gate, or even along the drive to the door, that person would scarce have noticed the other, notwithstanding that the gate was quite near at hand, and the park little larger than a paddock. There was still light enough in the western heaven to faintly brighten one side of the man's face, and to show against the dark mass of foliage behind the admirable cut of his profile; also to reveal that the front of the manor-house, small though it seemed, was solidly built of stone in that never-to-be-surpassed style for the English country residence – the mullioned and transomed Elizabethan.

The lawn, although neglected, was still as level as a bowling-green – which indeed it might once have served for; and the blades of grass before the window were raked by the candle-shine, which stretched over them so far as to touch faintly the yeoman's face on that side.

Within the dining-room there were also, with one of the twain, the same signs of a hidden purpose that marked the farmer. The young lady's mind was straying as clearly into the shadows as that of the loiterer was fixed upon the room – nay, it could be said that she was even cognisant of the presence of him outside. Impatience caused her little foot to beat silently on the carpet, and she more than once rose to leave the table. This proceeding was checked by her father, who would put his hand upon her shoulder, and unceremoniously press her down into her chair, till he should have concluded his observations. Her replies were brief enough, and there was factitiousness in her smiles of assent to his views. A small iron casement between two of the mullions was open, so that some occasional words of the dialogue were audible without.

'As for drains – how can I put in drains? The pipes don't cost much, that's true; but the labour in sinking the trenches is ruination. And then the gates – they should be hung to stone posts, otherwise there's no keeping them up through harvest.' The Squire's voice was strongly toned with the local accent, so that he said 'draïns' and 'geäts' like the rustics on his estate.

The landscape without grew darker, and the young man's figure seemed to be absorbed into the trunk of the tree. The small stars filled in between the larger, the nebulae between the small stars, the trees quite lost their voice; and if there was still a sound, it was the purl of a stream which stretched along under the trees that bounded the lawn on its northern side.

At last the young girl did get to her feet, and so secured her retreat. 'I have something to do, papa,' she said. 'I shall not be in the drawing-room just yet.'

'Very well,' replied he. 'Then I won't hurry.' And closing the door behind her, he drew his decanters together, and settled down in his chair.

Three minutes after that, a female shape emerged from a little garden-door which admitted from the lawn to the entrance front, and came across the grass. She kept well clear of the dining-room window, but enough of its light fell on her to show, escaping from the long dark-hooded cloak that she wore, stray verges of the same light dress which had figured but recently at the dinner-table. The hood was contracted tight about her face with a drawing-string, making her countenance small and baby-like, and lovelier even than before.

Without hesitation she brushed across the grass to the tree under which the young man stood concealed. The moment she had reached him he enclosed her form with his arm. The meeting and embrace, though by no means formal, were yet not passionate; the whole proceeding was that of persons who had repeated the act so often as to be unconscious of its performance. She turned within his arm, and faced in the same direction with himself, which was towards the window; and thus they stood without speaking, the back of her head leaning against his shoulder. For a while each seemed to be thinking his and her diverse thoughts.

'You have kept me waiting a long time, dear Christine,' he said at last. 'I wanted to speak to you particularly, or I should not have stayed. How came you to be dining at this time o' night?'

'My father has been out all day, and dinner was put back till five o'clock. I know I have kept you; but Nicholas, how can I help it sometimes, if I am not to run any risk? My poor father insists upon my listening to all he has to say; since my brother left he has had nobody else to listen to him; and tonight he was particularly tedious on his usual topics – draining, and tenant-farmers, and the village people. I must take daddy to London; he gets so narrow always staying here.'

'And what did you say to it all?'

'Oh, I took the part of the tenant-farmers,[2] of course, as the beloved of one should in duty do.' There followed a little break or gasp, implying a strangled sigh.

'You are sorry you have encouraged that beloving one?'

'O no, Nicholas . . . What is it you want to see me for particularly?'

'I know you *are* sorry, as time goes on, and everything is at a dead lock, with no prospect of change, and your rural swain loses his freshness! Only think, this secret understanding between us has lasted near three year, ever since you was a little over sixteen.'

'Yes; it has been a long time.'

'And I an untamed uncultivated man, who has never seen London, and who knows nothing about society at all.'

'Not uncultivated, dear Nicholas. Untravelled, socially unpractised, if you will,' she said smiling. 'Well, I did sigh; but not because I regret being your plighted one. What I do sometimes regret is that the scheme, which my meetings with you are but a part of, has not been carried out in its entirety. You said, Nicholas, that if I consented to swear to keep faith with you, you would go away and travel, and see nations, and peoples, and cities, and take a professor with you, and study books and art, simultaneously with your study of men and manners; and then come back at the end of two years, when I should find that my father would by no means be indisposed to accept you as a son-in-law. You said your reason for wishing to get my promise before starting was that your mind would then be more at rest when you were far away, and so could give itself more completely to know-ledge, than if you went as my unaccepted lover only, fuming with anxiety as to my favour when you came back. I saw how reasonable that was; and solemnly plighted myself to you in consequence. But instead of going to see the world, you stay on and on here to see me.'

'And you don't want me to see you?'

'Yes – no – it is not that. It is that I have latterly felt frightened at what I am doing when not in your actual presence. It seems so wicked not to tell my father that I have a lover close at hand, within touch and view of both of us; whereas, if you were absent my conduct would not seem quite so treacherous. The realities would not stare at one so. You would be a pleasant dream to me, which I should be free to indulge in without reproach of my conscience; I should live in hopeful expectation of your returning fully qualified to boldly claim me of my father. There, I have been terribly frank, I know.'

He in his turn had lapsed into gloomy breathings now. 'I did plan it as you state,' he answered. 'I did mean to go away the moment I had your promise. But, dear Christine, I did not foresee two or three things. I did not know what a lot of pain it would cost to tear myself from you. And I did not know that my miserly uncle – heaven forgive me calling him so! – would so positively refuse to advance me money for my purpose – the scheme of travelling with an accomplished tutor costing a formidable sum o' money. You have no idea what it would cost!'

'But I have said that I'll find the money.'

'Ah, there,' he returned, 'you have hit a sore place. To speak truly, dear, I would rather stay unpolished a hundred years than take your money.'

'But why? Men continually use the money of the women they marry.'

'Yes; but not till afterwards. No man would like to touch your money at present, and I should feel very mean if I were to do so in present circumstances. That brings me to what I was going to propose. But no – upon the whole I will not propose it now.'

'Ah! I would guarantee expenses, and you won't let me! The money is my personal possession: it comes to me from my late grandfather, and not from my father at all.'

He laughed forcedly and pressed her hand. 'There are more reasons why I cannot tear myself away,' he added. 'What would become of my uncle's farming? Six hundred acres in this parish, and five hundred in the next – a constant traipsing from one farm to the other; he can't be in two places at once. Still, that might be got over if it were not for the other matters. Besides, dear, I still should be a little uneasy, even though I have your promise, lest somebody should snap you up away from me.'

'Ah, you should have thought of that before. Otherwise I have committed myself for nothing.'

'I should have thought of it,' he answered, gravely. 'But I did not. There lies my fault, I admit it freely. Ah, if you would only commit yourself a little more, I might at least get over that difficulty! But I won't ask you. You have no idea how much you are to me still; you could not argue so coolly if you had. What property belongs to you I hate the very sound of; it is you I care for. I wish you hadn't a farthing in the world but what I could earn for you!'

'I don't altogether wish that,' she murmured.

'I wish it, because it would have made what I was going to propose much easier to do than it is now. Indeed I will not propose it, although I came on purpose, after what you have said in your frankness.'

'Nonsense, Nic. Come, tell me. How can you be so touchy!'

'Look at this then, Christine dear.' He drew from his breast-pocket a sheet of paper and unfolded it, when it was observable that a seal dangled from the bottom.

'What is it?' She held the paper sideways, so that what there was of window-light fell on its surface. 'I can only read the old-English letters – why – our names! Surely it is not a marriage-licence?'

'It is.'

She trembled. 'Oh, Nic; how could you do this – and without telling me!'

'Why should I have thought I must tell you? You had not spoken "frankly" then as you have now. We have been all to each other more than these two years, and I thought I would propose that we marry privately, and that I then leave you on the instant. I would have taken my travelling-bag to church, and you would have gone home alone. I should not have started on my adventures in the brilliant manner of our original plan, but should have roughed it a little at first; my great gain would have been that the absolute possession of you would have enabled me to work with spirit and purpose, such as nothing else could do. But I dare not ask you now – so frank as you have been.'

She did not answer. The document he had produced gave such unexpected substantiality to the venture with which she had so long toyed as a vague dream merely, that she was, in truth, frightened a little. 'I – don't know about it!' she said.

'Perhaps not. Ah, my little lady, you are wearying of me!'

'No, Nic,' responded she, creeping closer. 'I am not. Upon my word, and truth, and honour, I am not, Nic.'

'A mere tiller of the soil, as I should be called,' he continued, without heeding her. 'And you – well, a daughter of one of the – I won't say oldest families, because that's absurd, all families are the same age – one of the longest chronicled families about here, whose name is actually the name of the place.'

'That's not much, I am sorry to say! My poor brother – but I won't speak of that . . . Well,' she murmured mischievously, after a pause, 'you certainly would not need to be uneasy if I were to do this that you want me to do. You would have me safe enough in your trap then; I couldn't get away!'

'That's just it!' he said vehemently. 'It *is* a trap – you feel it so, and that though you wouldn't be able to get away from me you might particularly wish to! Ah, if I had asked you two years ago you would have agreed instantly. But I thought I was bound to wait for the proposal to come from you as the superior!'

'Now you are angry, and take seriously what I meant purely in fun. You don't know me even yet! To show you that you have not been mistaken in me, I *do* propose to carry out this licence. I'll marry you, dear Nicholas, tomorrow morning.'

'Ah, Christine! I am afraid I have stung you on to this, so that I cannot —'

'No, no, no!' she hastily rejoined; and there was something in her tone which suggested that she had been put upon her mettle and would not flinch. 'Take me whilst I am in the humour.³ What church is the licence for?'

'That I've not looked to see – why our parish church here, of course. Ah, then we cannot use it! We dare not be married here.'

'We do dare,' said she. 'And we will too, if you'll be there.'

'*If* I'll be there!'

They speedily came to an agreement that he should be in the church-porch at ten minutes to eight on the following morning, awaiting her; and that, immediately after the conclusion of the service which would make them one, Nicholas should set out on his long-deferred educational tour, towards the cost of which she was resolving to bring a substantial subscription with her to church. Then, slipping from him, she went indoors by the way she had come, and Nicholas bent his steps homewards.

II

Instead of leaving the lawn by the gate, he flung himself over the fence, and pursued a direction towards the river under the trees. And it was now, in his lonely progress, that he showed for the first time outwardly that he was not altogether unworthy of her. He wore long water-boots reaching above his knees, and, instead of making a circuit to find a bridge by which he might cross the Swenn – as the river aforesaid was called – he made straight for the point whence proceeded the low roar that was at this hour the only evidence of the stream's existence. He speedily stood on the verge of the waterfall which caused the noise, and stepping into the water at the top of the same, waded through with the sure tread of one who knew every inch of his footing, even though the canopy of trees rendered the darkness almost absolute, and a false step would have precipitated him into the pool beneath. Soon reaching the boundary of the grounds, he continued in the same direct line to traverse the alluvial valley, full of brooks and tributaries to the main stream – in former times quite impassable, and impassable in winter now. Sometimes he would cross a deep gulley on a plank not wider than the hand; at another time he ploughed his way through beds of spear-grass, where at a few feet to the right or left he might have been sucked down into a morass. At last he reached firm land on the other side of this watery tract, and came to his house on the rise behind – an ordinary farmstead, from the back of which rose indistinct breathings, belchings, and snortings, the rattle of halters, and other familiar features of an agriculturist's home.

While Nicholas Long was packing his bag in an upper room of this dwelling, Miss Christine Everard sat at a desk in her own chamber at Swenn-Everard manor-house, looking with pale fixed countenance at the candles.

'I ought – I must now!' she whispered to herself. 'I should not have begun it if I had not meant to carry it through! It runs in the blood of us, I suppose.' She alluded to a fact unknown to her lover, the clandestine marriage of an aunt under circumstances somewhat similar to the present.[4] In a few minutes she had penned the following note: –

'October 13, 1838.

'DEAR MR EASTMAN, – Can you make it convenient to yourself to meet me at the Church tomorrow morning at eight? I name the early hour because it would suit me better than later on in the day. You will find me in the chancel, if you can come. An answer yes or no by the bearer of this will be sufficient.

'CHRISTINE EVERARD.'

She sent the note to the rector immediately, waiting at a small side-door of the house till she heard the servant's footsteps returning along the lane, when she went round and met him in the passage. The rector had taken the trouble to write a line, and answered that he would meet her with pleasure.

A dripping fog which ushered in the next morning was highly favourable to the scheme of the pair. At that time of the century Swenn-Everard House had not been altered into a farm-homestead; the public lane passed close under its walls; and there was a door opening directly from one of the old parlours – the south parlour, as it was called – into the lane which led to the village. Christine came out this way, and after following the lane for a short distance entered upon a path within a belt of plantation, by which the church could be reached privately. She even avoided the churchyard gate, walking along to a place where the turf without the low wall rose into a mound, enabling her to mount upon the coping and spring down inside. She crossed the wet graves, and so glided round to the door. He was there, with his bag in his hand. He kissed her with a sort of surprise, as if he had expected that at the last moment her heart would fail her.

Though it had not failed her, there was, nevertheless, no great ardour in Christine's bearing – merely the momentum of an antecedent impulse. They went up the aisle together, the bottle-green glass of the old lead quarries[5] admitting but little light at that hour, and under such an atmosphere. They stood by the altar-rail in silence, Christine's skirt visibly quivering at each beat of her heart.

Presently a quick step ground upon the gravel, and Mr Eastman came round by the front. He was a quiet bachelor, courteous towards

Christine, and not at first recognizing in Nicholas a neighbouring yeoman (for he lived in a remote part of the parish),[6] advanced to her without revealing any surprise at her unusual request. But in truth he was surprised, the keen interest taken by many country young women at the present day in church decoration and festivals being then unknown.

'Good morning,' he said; and repeated the same words to Nicholas more mechanically.

'Good morning,' she replied gravely. 'Mr Eastman, I have a serious reason for asking you to meet me – us, I may say. We wish you to marry us.'

The rector's gaze hardened to fixity, rather between than upon either of them, and he neither moved nor replied for some time.

'Ah!' he said at last.

'And we are quite ready.'

'I had no idea —'

'It has been kept rather private,' she said calmly.

'Where are your witnesses?'

'They are outside in the meadow, sir. I can call them in a moment,' said Nicholas.

'Oh – I see it is – Mr Nicholas Long,' said Mr Eastman, and turning again to Christine, 'Does your father know of this?'

'Is it necessary that I should answer that question, Mr Eastman?'

'I am afraid it is – highly necessary.'

Christine began to look concerned.

'Where is the licence?' the rector asked; 'since there have been no banns.'

Nicholas produced it, Mr Eastman read it, an operation which occupied him several minutes – or at least he made it appear so; till Christine said impatiently, 'We are quite ready, Mr Eastman. Will you proceed? Mr Long has to take a journey of a great many miles today.'

'And you?'

'No. I remain.'

Mr Eastman assumed firmness. 'There is something wrong in this,' he said. 'I cannot marry you without your father's presence.'

'But have you a right to refuse us?' interposed Nicholas. 'I believe we are in a position to demand your fulfilment of our request.'

'No you are not! Is Miss Everard of age? I think not. I think she is far⁷ from being so. Eh, Miss Everard?'

'Am I bound to tell that?'

'Certainly. At any rate you are bound to write it. Meanwhile I refuse to solemnize the service. And let me entreat you two young people to do nothing so rash as this, even if by going to some strange church, you may do so without discovery. The tragedy of marriage —'

'Tragedy?'

'Certainly. It is full of crises and catastrophes, and ends with the death of one of the actors. The tragedy of marriage, as I was saying, is one I shall not be a party to your beginning with such light hearts, and I shall feel bound to put your father on his guard, Miss Everard. Think better of it, I entreat you! Remember the proverb, "Marry in haste and repent at leisure." '

Christine grew passionate, almost stormed at him. Nicholas implored; but nothing would turn that obstinate rector. She sat down and painfully reflected. By-and-bye she confronted Mr Eastman.

'Our marriage is not to be this morning, I see,' she said. 'Now grant me one favour, and in return I'll promise you to do nothing rashly. Do not tell my father a word of what has happened here.'

'I agree – if you undertake not to elope.'

She looked at Nicholas, and he looked at her. 'Do you wish me to elope, Nic?' she asked.

'No,' he said.

So the compact was made and they left the church singly, Nicholas remaining till the last, and closing the door. On his way home, carrying the well-packed bag which was just now to go no further, the two men who were mending water-carriers in the meadows approached the hedge, as if they had been on the alert all the time.

'You said you mid want us for zummat, sir?'

'All right – never mind,' he answered through the hedge. 'I did not require you after all.'

III

At a neighbouring manor there lived a queer and primitive couple who had lately been blessed with a son and heir. The christening took place during the week under notice, and this had been followed by a feast to the parishioners. Christine's father, one of the same generation and kind, had been asked to drive over and assist in the entertainment, and Christine, as a matter of course, accompanied him.

When they reached Eldhampton Hall,[8] as the house was called, they found the usually quiet nook a lively spectacle. Tables had been spread in the apartment which lent its name to the whole building – the hall proper – covered with a fine open-timbered roof, whose braces, purlins and rafters made a brown thicket of oak overhead. Here tenantry of all ages sat with their wives and families, and the servants were assisted in their ministrations by the sons and daughters of the owner's friends and neighbours. Christine lent a hand among the rest.

She was holding a plate in each hand towards a huge brown platter of baked rice-pudding, from which a footman was scooping a large spoonful, when a voice reached her ear over her shoulder: 'Allow me to hold them for you.'

Christine turned, and recognized in the speaker the nephew of the entertainer, a young man from London, whom she had already met on two or three occasions. She accepted the proffered help, and from that moment, whenever he passed her in their marchings to and fro during the remainder of the serving, he smiled acquaintance. When their work was done, he improved the few words into a conversation. He plainly had been attracted by her fairness.

Bellston was a self-assured young man, not particularly good-looking, with more colour in his skin than even Nicholas had. He had flushed a little in attracting her notice, though the flush had nothing of nervousness in it – the air with which it was accompanied making it curiously suggestive of a flush of anger; and even when he laughed it was difficult to banish that fancy.

The rich autumn sunlight streamed in through the window-panes upon the heads and shoulders of the venerable patriarchs of the hamlet, and upon the middle-aged, and upon the young; upon men and women who had played out, or were to play, tragedies or tragi-comedies in that nook of civilization not less great, humanly, than those which, enacted on more central arenas, fix the attention of the world. One of the party was a cousin of Nicholas Long's, who sat with her husband and children.[9]

To make himself as locally harmonious as possible, Mr Bellston remarked to his companion on the scene –

'It does one's heart good,' he said, 'to see these simple peasants enjoying themselves.'

'Oh, Mr Bellston!' exclaimed Christine; 'don't be too sure about that word "simple"! You little think what they see and meditate! Their reasonings and emotions are as complicated as ours.'

She spoke with a vehemence which would have been hardly present in her words but for her own relation to Nicholas. The sense of that produced in her a nameless depression thenceforward. The young man, however, still followed her up.

'I am glad to hear you say it,' he returned warmly. 'I was merely attuning myself to your mood, as I thought. The real truth is that I know more of the Parthians, and Medes, and dwellers in Mesopotamia[10] – almost of any people, indeed – than of the English rustics. Travel and exploration are my profession, not the study of the British peasantry.'

Travel. There was sufficient coincidence between his declaration and the course she had urged upon her lover, to lend Bellston's account of himself a certain interest in Christine's ears. He might perhaps be able to tell her something that would be useful to Nicholas, if their dream were carried out. A door opened from the hall into the garden, and she somehow found herself outside, chatting with Mr Bellston on this topic, till she thought that, upon the whole, she liked the young man. The garden being his uncle's, he took her round it with an air of proprietorship; and they went on amongst the Michaelmas-daisies and chrysanthemums,[11] and through a door to the fruit-garden. A green-house was open, and he went in and cut her a bunch of grapes.

'How daring of you! They are your uncle's.'

'Oh, he don't mind – I do anything here. A rough old buffer, isn't he?'

She was thinking of her Nic, and felt that by comparison with her present acquaintance, the farmer more than held his own as a fine and intelligent fellow; but the harmony with her own existence in little things, which she found here, imparted an alien tinge to Nicholas just now. The latter, idealized by moonlight, or a thousand miles of distance, was altogether a more romantic object for a woman's dream than this smart new-lacquered man; but in the sun of afternoon, and amid a surrounding company, Mr Bellston was a very tolerable companion.

When they re-entered the hall, Bellston entreated her to come with him up a spiral stair in the thickness of the wall, leading to a passage and gallery, whence they could look down upon the scene below. The people had finished their feast, the newly-christened baby had been exhibited, and a few words having been spoken to them they began, amid a racketing of forms, to make for the greensward without, Nicholas's cousin and cousin's wife and cousin's children among the rest. While they were filing out, a voice was heard calling –

'Hullo! – here, Jim; where are you?' said Bellston's uncle. The young man descended, Christine following at leisure.

'Now will ye be a good fellow,' the Squire continued, 'and set them going outside in some dance or other that they know? I'm dead tired, and I want to have a vew words with Mr Everard before we join 'em – hey, Everard? They are shy till somebody starts 'em; afterwards they'll keep gwine brisk enough.'

'Ay, that they wool,' said Squire Everard.

They followed to the lawn; and here it proved that James Bellston was as shy, or rather as averse, as any of the tenantry themselves, to acting the part of fugleman. Only the parish people had been at the feast, but outlying neighbours had now strolled in for a dance.

'They want "Speed the Plough",' said Bellston, coming up breathless. 'It must be a country dance, I suppose? Now, Miss Everard, do have pity upon me. I am supposed to lead off; but really I know no more about speeding the plough than a child just born! Would you take one of the villagers? – just to start them, my uncle says. Suppose you take that handsome young farmer over there – I don't know his name, but I dare say you do – and I'll come on with one of the dairyman's daughters as second couple.'

Christine turned in the direction signified, and changed colour – though in the shade nobody noticed it. 'Oh, yes – I know him,' she said coolly. 'He is from our own place – Mr Nicholas Long.'

'That's capital – then you can easily make him stand as first couple with you. Now I must pick up mine.'

'I – I think I'll dance with you, Mr Bellston,' she said with some trepidation. 'Because, you see,' she explained eagerly, 'I know the figure, and you don't – so that I can help you; while Nicholas Long, I know, is familiar with the figure, and that will make two couples who know it – which is necessary, at least.'

Bellston showed his gratification by one of his angry-pleasant flushes – he had hardly dared to ask for what she proffered freely; and having requested Nicholas to take the dairyman's daughter, led Christine to her place, Long promptly stepping up second with his charge. There were grim silent depths in Nic's character; a small deedy spark in his eye, as it caught Christine's, was all that showed his consciousness of her. Then the fiddlers began – the celebrated Mellstock fiddlers[12] who, given free stripping, could play from sunset to dawn without turning a hair. The couples wheeled and swung, Nicholas taking Christine's hand in the course of business with the figure, when she waited for him to give it a little squeeze; but he did not.

Christine had the greatest difficulty in steering her partner through the maze, on account of his self-will, and when at last they reached the bottom of the long line, she was breathless with her hard labour. Resting here, she watched Nic and his lady; and, though she had decidedly cooled off in these later months, began to admire him anew. Nobody knew these dances like him, after all, or could do anything of this sort so well. His performance with the dairyman's daughter so won upon her, that when 'Speed the Plough' was over she contrived to speak to him.

'Nic, you are to dance with me next time.'

He said he would, and presently asked her in a formal public manner, lifting his hat gallantly. She showed a little backwardness, which he quite understood, and allowed him to lead her to the top, a row of enormous length appearing below them as if by magic as soon as they had taken their places. Truly the Squire was right when he said that they only wanted starting.

'What is it to be?' whispered Nicholas.

She turned to the band. ' "The Honeymoon",' she said.

And then they trod the delightful last-century measure of that name, which if it had been ever danced better, was never danced with more zest. The perfect responsiveness which their tender acquaintance threw into the motions of Nicholas and his partner lent to their gyrations the fine adjustment of two interacting parts of a single machine. The excitement of the movement carried Christine back to the time – the unreflecting passionate time, about two years before – when she and Nic had been incipient lovers only; and it made her forget the carking anxieties, the vision of social breakers ahead, that had begun to take the gilding off her position now. Nicholas, on his part, had never ceased to be a lover; no personal worries had as yet made him conscious of any staleness, flatness, or unprofitableness[13] in his admiration of Christine.

'Not quite so wildly, Nic,' she whispered. 'I don't object personally; but they'll notice us. How came you here?'

'I heard that you had driven over; and I set out – on purpose for this.'

'What – you have walked?'

'Yes. If I had waited for one of uncle's horses I should have been too late.'

'Eleven miles here and eleven back – two-and-twenty miles on foot – merely to dance!'

'With you. What made you think of this old "Honeymoon" thing?'

'Oh! it came into my head when I saw you, as what would have been a reality with us if you had not been stupid about that licence, and had got it for a distant church.'

'Shall we try again?'

'No – I don't know. I'll think it over.'

The villagers admired their grace and skill, as the dancers themselves perceived; but they did not know what accompanied that admiration in one spot, at least.

'People who wonder they can foot it so featly together should know what some others think,' a waterman was saying to his neighbour. 'Then their wonder would be less.'

His comrade asked for information.

'Well – really I hardly believe it – but 'tis said they be man and wife. Yes, sure – went to church and did the job a'most afore 'twas light one morning. But mind, not a word of this; for 'twould be the loss of a winter's work to me if I had spread such a report and it were not true.'

When the dance had ended she rejoined her own section of the company. Her father and Mr Bellston the elder had now come out from the house, and were smoking in the background. Presently she found that her father was at her elbow.

'Christine, don't dance too often with young Long – as a mere matter of prudence, I mean, as volk might think it odd, he being oone of our own parish people. I should not mention this to 'ee if he were an ordinary young fellow; but being superior to the rest it behoves you to be careful.'

'Exactly, papa,' said Christine.

But the revived sense that she was deceiving him threw a damp over her spirits. 'But, after all,' she said to herself, 'he is a young man of Swenn-Everard,[14] handsome, able, and the soul of honour; and I am a young woman of that place, who have been constantly thrown into communication with him. Is it not, by nature's rule, the most proper thing in the world that I should marry him, and is it not an absurd conventional regulation which says that such a union would be wrong?'

It may be concluded that the strength of Christine's large-minded argument was rather an evidence of weakness than of strength in the passion it concerned, which had required neither argument nor reasoning of any kind for its maintenance when full and flush in its early days.

When driving home in the dark with her father, she sank into pensive silence. She was thinking of Nicholas having to trudge on foot all those eleven miles after his exertions on the sward. Mr Everard, arousing himself from a nap, said suddenly, 'I have something to mention to ye, by George – so I have, Chris! You probably know what it is?'

She wondered if her father had discovered anything of her secret.

'Well, according to *him* you know. But I will tell 'ee. Perhaps you noticed young Jim Bellston walking me off down the lawn with him? – whether or no, we walked together a good while; and he informed me that he wanted to pay his addresses to 'ee. I naturally said that it depended upon yourself; and he replied that you was willing enough; you had given him particular encouragement – showing your preference for him by specially choosing him for your partner – hey? "In that case," says I, "go on and conquer – settle it with her – I have no objection." The poor fellow was very grateful, and in short, there we left the matter. He'll propose tomorrow.'

She saw now to her dismay what James Bellston had read as encouragement. 'He has mistaken me altogether,' she said. 'I had no idea of such a thing.'

'What, you won't have him?'

'Indeed, I cannot!'

'Chrissy,' said Mr Everard with emphasis, 'there's *noo*body whom I should so like you to marry as that young man. He's a thoroughly clever fellow, and fairly well provided for. He's travelled all over the temperate zone; but he says that directly he marries he's going to give up all that, and be a regular stay-at-home. You would be nowhere safer than in his hands.'

'It is true,' she answered. 'He *is* a highly desirable match, and I *should* be well provided for, and probably very safe in his hands.'

'Then don't be skittish, and stand-to.'

She had spoken from her conscience and understanding, and not to please her father. As a reflecting woman she believed that such a marriage would be a wise one. In great things Nicholas was closest to her nature; in little things Bellston seemed immeasurably nearer than Nic; and life was made up of little things.

Altogether the firmament looked black for Nicholas Long, notwithstanding her half-hour's ardour for him when she saw him dancing with the dairyman's daughter. Most great passions, movements, and beliefs – individual and national – burst during their decline into a temporary irradiation, which rivals their original splendour; and then they speedily become extinct. Perhaps the dance had given the last flare-up to Christine's love. It seemed to have improvidently consumed for its immediate purpose all her ardour forwards, so that for the future there was nothing left but frigidity.

Nicholas had certainly been very foolish about that licence!

IV

This laxity of emotional tone was further increased by an incident, when, two days later, she kept an appointment with Nicholas in the Sallows. The Sallows was an extension of shrubberies and plantations along the banks of the Swenn, accessible from the lawn of Swenn-Everard House only, except by wading through the river at the waterfall or elsewhere. Near the fall was a thicket of box in which a trunk lay prostrate; this had been once or twice their trysting-place, though it was by no means a safe one; and it was here she sat awaiting him now.

The noise of the stream muffled any sound of footsteps, and it was before she was aware of his approach that she looked up and saw him wading across at the top of the waterfall.

Noontide lights and dwarfed shadows always banished the romantic aspect of her love for Nicholas. Moreover, something new had occurred to disturb her; and if ever she had regretted giving way to a tenderness for him – which perhaps she had not done with any distinctness – she regretted it now. Yet in the bottom of their hearts those two were excellently paired, the very twin halves of a perfect whole;[15] and their love was pure. But at this hour surfaces showed garishly, and obscured the depths. Probably her regret appeared in her face.

He walked up to her without speaking, the water running from his boots; and, taking one of her hands in each of his own, looked narrowly into her eyes.

'Have you thought it over?'

'What?'

'Whether we shall try again; you remember saying you would at the dance?'

'Oh, I had forgotten that!'

'You are sorry we tried at all!' he said accusingly.

'I am not so sorry for the fact as for the rumours,' she said.

'Ah! rumours?'

'They say we are already married.'

'Who?'

'I cannot tell exactly. I heard some whispering to that effect. Some-body in the village told one of the servants, I believe. This man said that he was crossing the churchyard early on that unfortunate foggy morning, and heard voices in the chancel, and peeped through the window as well as the dim panes would let him; and there he saw you and me and Mr Eastman, and so on; but thinking his surmises would be dangerous knowledge, he hastened on. And so the story got afloat. Then your aunt, too —'

'Good Lord! – what has she done?'

'The story was told her, and she said proudly. "Oh yes, it is true enough. I have seen the licence. But it is not to be known yet." '

'Seen the licence? How the —'

'Accidentally, I believe, when your coat was hanging somewhere.'

The information, coupled with the infelicitous word 'proudly', caused Nicholas to flush with mortification. He knew that it was in his aunt's nature to make a brag of that sort; but worse than the brag was the fact that this was the first occasion on which Christine had deigned to show her consciousness that such a marriage would be a source of pride to his relatives – the only two he had in the world.

'You are sorry, then, even to be thought my wife, much less to be it.' He dropped her hand, which fell lifelessly.

'It is not sorry exactly, dear Nic. But I feel uncomfortable and vexed, that after screwing up my courage, my fidelity, to the point of going to church, you should have so muddled – managed the matter that it has ended in neither one thing nor the other. How can I meet acquaintances, when I don't know what they are thinking of me?'

'Then, dear Christine, let us mend the muddle. I'll go away for a few days and get another licence, and you can come to me.'

She shrank from this perceptibly. 'I cannot screw myself up to it a second time,' she said. 'I am sure I cannot! Besides, I promised Mr Eastman. And yet how can I continue to see you after such a rumour? We shall be watched now, for certain.'

'Then don't see me.'

'I fear I must not for the present. Altogether —'

'What?'

'I am very depressed.'

These views were not very inspiriting to Nicholas, as he construed them. It may indeed have been possible that he construed them wrongly, and should have insisted upon her making the rumour true. Unfortunately, too, he had come to her in a hurry through brambles and briars, water and weed, and the shaggy wildness which hung about his appearance at this fine and correct time of day lent an impracticability to the look of him.

'You blame me – you repent your courses – you repent that you ever, ever owned anything to me!'

'No, Nicholas, I do not repent that,' she returned gently, though with firmness. 'But I think that you ought not to have got that licence without asking me first; and I also think that you ought to have known how it would be if you lived on here in your present position, and made no effort to better it. I can bear whatever comes, for social ruin is not personal ruin, or even personal disgrace. But as a sensible, new-risen poet says,[16] whom I have been reading this morning –

> "The world and its ways have a certain worth:
> And to press a point while these oppose
> Were simple policy."

As soon as you had got my promise, Nic, you should have gone away – yes – and made a name, and come back to claim me. That was my silly girlish dream about my hero.'

'Perhaps I can do as much yet! And would you have indeed liked better to live away from me for family reasons, than to run a risk in seeing me for affection's sake? O what a cold heart it has grown! If I had been a prince, and you a dairymaid, I'd have stood by you in the face of the world!'

She shook her head. 'Ah – you don't know what society is – you don't know.'

'Perhaps not. Who was that strange gentleman of about seven-and-twenty I saw at Mr Bellston's christening feast?'

'Oh – that was his nephew James. Now he is a man who has seen an unusual extent of the world for his age. He is a great traveller, you know.'

'Indeed.'

'In fact an explorer. He is very entertaining.'

'No doubt.'

Nicholas received no shock of jealousy from her announcement. He knew her so well that he could see she was not in the least in love with Bellston. But he asked if Bellston were going to continue his explorations.

'Not if he settles in life. Otherwise he will, I suppose.'

'Perhaps I could be a great explorer, too, if I tried.'

'You could, I am sure.'

They sat apart, and not together; each looking afar off at vague objects, and not in each other's eyes. Thus the sad autumn afternoon waned, while the waterfall hissed sarcastically of the inevitableness of the unpleasant. Very different this from the time when they had first met there.

The nook was most picturesque; but it looked horridly common and stupid now. Their sentiment had set a colour hardly less visible than a material one on surrounding objects, as sentiment must where life is but thought. Nicholas was as devoted as ever to the fair Christine: but unhappily he too had moods and humours; and the division between them was not closed.

She had no sooner got indoors and sat down to her work-table than her father entered the drawing-room. She handed him his newspaper; he took it without a word; went and stood on the hearthrug, and flung the paper on the floor.

'Christine, what's the meaning of this terrible story? I was just on my way to look at the register.'

She looked at him without speech.

'You have married – Nicholas Long?'

'No, father.'

'No? Can you say no in the face of such facts as I have been put in possession of?'

'Yes.'

'But – the note you wrote to the rector – and the going to church?'

She briefly explained that their attempt had failed.

'Ah! Then this is what that dancing meant, was it? By —, it makes me —. How long has this been going on, may I ask?'

'This what?'

'What, indeed? Why, making him your beau. Now listen to me. All's well that ends well;[17] from this day, madam, this moment, he is to be nothing more to you. You are not to see him. Cut him adrift instantly! I only wish his volk were on my farm – out they should go, or I would know the reason why. However, you are to write him a letter to this effect at once.'

'How can I cut him adrift?'

'Why not? You must, my good maid!'

'Well, though I have not actually married him, I have solemnly sworn to be his wife when he comes home from abroad to claim me. It would be gross perjury not to fulfil my promise. Besides, no woman can go to church with a man to deliberately solemnize matrimony, and refuse him afterwards, if he does nothing wrong meanwhile.'

The uttered sound of her strong conviction seemed to kindle in Christine a livelier perception of all its bearings than she had known while it had lain unformulated in her mind. For when she had done speaking she fell down on her knees before her father, covered her face, and said, 'Please, please forgive me, papa! How *could* I do it without letting you know! I don't know, I don't know!'

When she looked up she found that, in the turmoil of his mind, her father was moving about the room. 'You are within an ace of ruining yourself, ruining me, ruining us all!' he said. 'You are nearly as bad as your brother, begad!'

'Perhaps I am – yes – perhaps I am!'

'That I should father such a harum-scarum brood!'

'It is very bad; but Nicholas —'

'He's a scoundrel!'

'He is *not* a scoundrel!' cried she, turning quickly. 'He's as good and worthy as you or I, or anybody bearing our name or any nobleman in the kingdom, if you come to that! Only – only' – she could not continue the argument on those lines. 'Now, father, listen!' she sobbed; 'if you taunt me I'll go off and join him at his farm this very day, and marry him tomorrow, that's what I'll do!'

'I don't taant ye!'

'I wish to avoid unseemliness as much as you.'

She went away. When she came back a quarter of an hour later, thinking to find the room empty, he was standing there as before, never having apparently moved. His manner had quite changed. He seemed to take a resigned and entirely different view of circumstances.

'Christine, I have suffered more in this last haaf hour than I hope you may suffer all your life.[18] But since this was to happen, I'll bear it, and not complain. All volk have crosses, and this is one of mine. Well, this is what I've got to say – I almost feel that you must carry out this attempt at marrying Nicholas Long. Faith, you must! The rumour will become a scandal if you don't – that's my view. I have tried to look at the brightest side of the case. Nicholas Long is a young man superior to most of his class, and fairly presentable. And he's not poor – at least his uncle is not. I believe the old muddler could buy me up any day. However, a farmer's wife you must be, as far as I can see. As you've made your bed, so ye must lie. Parents propose, and ungrateful children dispose.[19] You shall marry him, and immediately.'

Christine hardly knew what to make of this. 'He is quite willing to wait, and so am I. We can wait for two or three years, and then he will be as worthy as —'

'You must marry him. And the sooner the better, if 'tis to be done at all . . . And yet I did wish you could have been Jim Bellston's wife. I did wish it! But no.'

'I did wish it, and do still, in one sense,' she returned gently. His moderation had won her out of her defiant mood, and she was willing to reason with him.

'You do?' he said, surprised.

'I see that in a worldly sense my conduct may be considered a mistake.'

'H'm – I am glad to hear that – after my death you may see it more clearly still; and you won't have long to wait, to my reckoning.'

She fell into bitter repentance, and kissed him in her anguish. 'Don't say that!' she cried. 'Tell me what to do?'

'If you'll leave me for an hour or two I'll think. Drive to the market and back – the carriage is at the door – and I'll try to collect my senses. Dinner can be put back till you return.'

In a few minutes she was dressed, and the carriage bore her up the hill which divided the village and manor from the market-town.

V

A quarter of an hour brought her into the High Street, and for want of a more important errand she called at the harness-maker's for a dog-collar that she required.

It happened to be market-day, and Nicholas, having postponed the engagements which called him thither to keep the appointment with her in the Sallows, rushed off at the end of the afternoon to attend to them as well as he could. Arriving thus in a great hurry on account of the lateness of the hour, he still retained the wild, amphibious appearance which had marked him when he came up from the meadows to her side – an exceptional condition of things which had scarcely ever before occurred. When she crossed the pavement from the shop door, the shopman bowing and escorting her to the carriage, Nicholas chanced to be standing at the road-waggon office, talking to the master of the waggons. There were a good many people about, and those near paused and looked at her transit, in the full stroke of the level October sun, which went under the brims of their hats, and pierced through their button-holes. From the group she heard murmured the words: 'Mrs Nicholas Long'.

The unexpected remark, not without distinct satire in its tone, took her so greatly by surprise that she was confounded. Nicholas was by this time nearer, though coming against the sun he had not yet perceived her. Influenced by her father's lecture, she felt angry with him for being there and causing this awkwardness. Her notice of him was therefore slight, supercilious perhaps, slurred over; and her vexation at his presence showed distinctly in her face as she sat down in her seat. Instead of catching his waiting eye, she positively turned her head away.

A moment after she was sorry she had treated him so; but he was gone.

Reaching home she found on her dressing-table a note from her father. The statement was brief:

'I have considered and am of the same opinion. You must marry him. He can leave home at once and travel as proposed. I have written to him to this effect. I don't want any victuals, so don't wait dinner for me.'

Nicholas was the wrong sort of man to be blind to his Christine's mortification, though he did not know its entire cause. He had lately foreseen something of this sort as possible.

'It serves me right,' he thought, as he trotted homeward. 'It was absurd – wicked of me to lead her on so. The sacrifice would have been too great – too cruel!' And yet, though he thus took her part, he flushed with indignation every time he said to himself, 'She is ashamed of me!'

On the ridge which overlooked Swenn-Everard he met a neighbour of his – a stock-dealer – in his gig, and they drew rein and exchanged a few words. A part of the dealer's conversation had much meaning for Nicholas.

'I've had occasion to call on Squire Everard,' the former said; 'but he couldn't see me on account of being quite knocked up at some bad news he has heard.'

Nicholas rode on past Swenn-Everard to Homeston Farm, pondering. He had new and startling matter for thought as soon as he got there. The Squire's note had arrived. At first he could not credit its import; then he saw further, took in the tone of the letter, saw the writer's contempt behind the words, and understood that the letter was written as by a man hemmed into a corner. Christine was defiantly

– insultingly – hurled at his head. He was accepted because he was so despised.

And yet with what respect he had treated her and hers! Now he was reminded of what an agricultural friend had said years ago, when the eyes of Nicholas were once fixed on Christine as on an angel as she passed: 'Better a little fire to warm ye than a great one to burn ye. No good can come of throwing your heart there.' He went into the mead, sat down, and asked himself four questions: –

1. How could she live near her acquaintance as his wife, even in his absence, without suffering martyrdom from the stings of their contempt?

2. Would not this entail total estrangement between Christine and her family also, and her own consequent misery?

3. Must not such isolation extinguish her affection for him?

4. Supposing that her father rigged them out as colonists and sent them off to America, was not the effect of such exile upon one of her gentle nurture likely to be as the last?

In short, whatever they should embark in together would be cruelty to her, and his death would be a relief. It would, indeed, in one aspect be a relief to her now, if she were so ashamed of him as she had appeared to be that day. Were he dead, this little episode with him would fade away like a dream.

Mr Everard was a good-hearted man at bottom, but to take his enraged offer seriously was impossible. The least thing that he could do would be to go away and never trouble her more. To travel and learn and come back in two years, as mapped out in their first sanguine scheme, required a staunch heart on her side, if the necessary expenditure of time and money were to be afterwards justified; and it were folly to calculate on that when he had seen today that her heart was failing her already. To travel and disappear and not be heard of for many years would be a far more independent stroke, and it would leave her entirely unfettered. Perhaps he might rival in this kind the accomplished Mr Bellston, of whose journeyings he had heard so much.

He sat and sat, and the fog rose out of the river, enveloping him like a fleece; first his feet and knees, then his arms and body, and finally submerging his head. When he had come to a decision he went up again into the homestead. He would be independent, if he died for it, and he would free Christine. Exile was the only course. The first step was to inform his uncle of his determination.

Two days later Nicholas was on the same spot in the mead, at almost the same hour of eve. But there was no fog now; a blusterous autumn wind had ousted the still, golden days and misty nights; and he was going, full of purpose, in the opposite direction. When he had last entered the mead he was an inhabitant of the Swenn valley; in forty-eight hours he had severed himself from that spot as completely as if he had never belonged to it. All that appertained to him in the Swenn valley now was circumscribed by the portmanteau in his hand.

In making his preparations for departure he had unconsciously held a faint, foolish hope that she would communicate with him and make up their estrangement in some soft womanly way. But she had given no signal, and it was too evident to him that her latest mood had grown to be her fixed one, proving how well-founded had been his impulse to set her free.

He entered the Sallows, found his way in the dark to the garden-door of the house, slipped under it a note to tell her of his departure, and explaining its true reason to be a consciousness of her growing feeling that he was an encumbrance and a humiliation. Of the direction of his journey and of the date of his return he said nothing.

His course now took him into the high road, which he pursued for some miles in a north-easterly direction, still spinning the thread of sad inferences, and asking himself why he should ever return. At daybreak he stood on the hill above Shottsford-Forum, and awaited a coach which passed about this time along that highway towards Salisbury and London.

VI

Some fifteen years after the date of the foregoing incidents, a man who had dwelt in far countries, and viewed many cities, arrived at Troyton Inn, an isolated tavern on the old western turnpike-road, not five miles from Swenn-Everard. He was still barely of middle-age, but it could be seen that a haze of grey was settling upon the locks of his hair, and that his face had lost colour and curve, as if by exposure to bleaching climates and strange atmospheres, or from ailments contracted therein. He seemed to observe little around him, by reason of the intrusion of his musings upon the scene. In truth Nicholas Long was just now the creature of old hopes and fears consequent upon his arrival – this man who once had not cared if his name were blotted out from that district. The evening light showed wistful lines which he could not smooth out by the worldling's gloss of nonchalance that he had learnt to fling over his face.

Troyton Inn was a somewhat unusual place for a man of this sort to choose as a house of sojourn. Before he left home it had been a lively old tavern at which High-flyers, and Heralds, and Tally-hoes had changed horses on their stages up and down the country; but now the house was rather cavernous and chilly, the stable-roofs were hollow-backed, the landlord was asthmatic, and the traffic gone.

He arrived in the afternoon, and when he had sent back the fly and was having a nondescript meal, he put a question to the waiting-maid, with a mien of indifference.

'Squire Everard, of Swenn-Everard Manor, has been dead some years, I believe?'

She replied in the affirmative.

'And are any of the family left there still?'

'Oh no, bless you, sir! They sold the place years ago – Squire Everard's son did – and went away. I've never heard where they went to. They came quite to nothing.'

'Never heard anything of the young lady – the Squire's daughter?'

'No. You see 'twas before I came to these parts.'

When the waitress had left the room, Nicholas pushed aside his plate and gazed out of the window. He was not going over into the Swenn Valley altogether on Christine's account, but she had greatly animated his motive in coming that way. Anyhow he would push on there now that he was so near, and not ask questions here where he was liable to be wrongly informed. The fundamental inquiry he had not ventured to make – whether Christine had married before the family went away. He had abstained because of an absurd dread of extinguishing hopeful surmise. That the Everards had left their old home was bad enough intelligence for one day.

Rising from the table he put on his hat and went out, ascending towards the upland which divided this district from his native vale. The first familiar feature that met his eye was a little spot on the distant sky – a clump of trees standing on a barrow which surmounted a yet more remote upland – a point where, in his childhood, he had believed people could stand and see America. He reached the further verge of the plateau on which he had entered. Ah, there was the valley – a greenish-grey stretch of colour – still looking placid and serene, as though it had not much missed him. If Christine was no longer there, why should he pause over it this evening? His uncle and aunt were dead, and tomorrow would be soon enough to inquire for remoter relatives. Thus, disinclined to go further, he turned to retrace his way to the inn.

In the backward path he now perceived the figure of a woman, who had been walking at a distance behind him; and as she drew nearer he began to be startled. Surely, despite the variations introduced into that figure by changing years, its ground-lines were those of Christine?

Nicholas had been sentimental enough to write to Christine immediately on landing at Southampton a day or two before this, addressing his letter at a venture to the old house, and merely telling her that he planned to reach Troyton Inn on the present afternoon. The news of the scattering of the Everards had dissipated his hope of hearing of her; but here she was.

So they met – there, alone, on the open down by a pond, just as if the meeting had been carefully arranged.

She threw up her veil. She was still beautiful, though the years had touched her; a little more matronly – much more homely. Or was it only that he was much less homely now – a man of the world – the sense of homeliness being relative? Her face had grown to be pre-eminently of the sort that would be called interesting. Her habiliments were of a demure and sober cast, though she was one who had used to dress so airily and so gaily. Years had laid on a few shadows too in this.

'I received your letter,' she said, when the momentary embarrassment of their first approach had passed. 'And I thought I would walk across the hills today, as it was fine. I have just called at the inn, and they told me you were out. I was now on my way homeward.'

He hardly listened to this, though he intently gazed at her. 'Christine,' he said; 'one word. Are you free?'

'I – I am in a certain sense,' she replied, colouring.

The announcement had a magical effect. The intervening time between past and present closed up for him, and moved by an impulse which he had combated for fifteen years, he seized her two hands and drew her towards him.

She started back, and became almost a mere acquaintance. 'I have to tell you,' she gasped, 'that I have – been married.'

Nicholas's rose-coloured dream was immediately toned down to a greyish tinge.

'I did not marry till many years after you left,' she continued in the humble tones of one confessing to a crime. 'Oh Nic,' she cried reproachfully, 'how could you stay away so long!'

'Whom did you marry?'

'Mr Bellston.'

'I – ought to have expected it.' He was going to add, 'And is he dead?' but he checked himself. Her dress unmistakably suggested widowhood; and she had said she was free.

'I must now hasten home,' said she. 'I felt that, considering my shortcomings at our parting so many years ago, I owed you the initiative now.'

'There is some of your old generosity in that. I'll walk with you, if I may. Where are you living, Christine?'

'In the same house, but not on the old conditions. I have part of it on lease; the farmer now tenanting the premises found the whole more than he wanted, and the owner allowed me to keep what rooms I chose. I am poor now, you know, Nicholas, and almost friendless. My brother sold the Swenn-Everard estate when it came to him, and the person who bought it turned our home into a farm-house. Till my father's death my husband and I lived in the manor-house with him, so that I have never lived away from the spot.'

She was poor. That, and the change of name, sufficiently accounted for the inn-servant's ignorance of her continued existence within the walls of her old home.

It was growing dusk, and he still walked with her. A woman's head arose from the declivity before them, and as she drew nearer, Christine asked him to go back. 'This is the wife of the farmer who shares the house,' she said. 'She is accustomed to come out and meet me whenever I walk far and am benighted. I am obliged to walk everywhere now.'

The farmer's wife, seeing that Christine was not alone, paused in her advance, and Nicholas said, 'Dear Christine, if you are obliged to do these things, I am not, and what wealth I can command you may command likewise. They say rolling stones gather no moss; but they gather dross sometimes. I was one of the pioneers to the gold-fields,[20] you know, and made a sufficient fortune there for my wants. What is more, I kept it. When I had done this I was coming home, but hearing of my uncle's death I changed my plan, travelled, speculated, and increased my fortune. Now, before we part: you remember you stood with me at the altar once, and therefore I speak with less preparation than I should otherwise use. Before we part then I ask, shall another again intrude between us? Or shall we complete the union we began?'

She trembled – just as she had done at that very minute of standing with him in the church, to which he had recalled her mind. 'I will not enter into that now, dear Nicholas,' she replied. 'There will be more to talk of and consider first – more to explain, which it would have spoiled this meeting to have entered into now.'

'Yes, yes; but —'

'Further than the brief answer I first gave, Nic, don't press me tonight. I still have the old affection for you, or I should not have sought you. Let that suffice for the moment.'

'Very well, dear one. And when shall I call to see you?'

'I will write and fix an hour. I will tell you everything of my history then.'

And thus they parted, Nicholas feeling that he had not come here fruitlessly. When she and her companion were out of sight he retraced his steps to Troyton, where he made himself as comfortable as he could in the deserted old inn of his boyhood's days. He missed her companionship this evening more than he had done at any time during the whole fifteen years; and it was as though instead of separation there had been constant communion with her throughout that period. The tones of her voice had stirred his heart in places which had lain stagnant ever since he last heard them. They recalled the woman to whom he had once lifted his eyes as to a goddess. Her announcement that she had been another's came as a little shock to him, and he did not now lift his eyes to her in precisely the same way as he had lifted them at first. But he forgave her for marrying Bellston; what could he expect after fifteen years?

He slept at Troyton Inn that night, and in the morning there was a short note from her, repeating more emphatically her statement of the previous evening – that she wished to inform him clearly of her circumstances, and to calmly consider with him the position in which she was placed. Would he call upon her on Sunday afternoon, when she was sure to be alone?

'Nic,' she wrote on, 'what a cosmopolite you are! I expected to find my old yeoman still; but I was quite awed in the presence of such a citizen of the world. Did I seem rusty and unpractised? Ah – you seemed so once to me!'

Tender, playful words; the old Christine was in them. She said Sunday afternoon, and it was now only Saturday morning. He wished she had said today; that short revival of her image had vitalized to sudden heat feelings that had almost been stilled. Whatever she might have to explain as to her position – and it was awkwardly narrowed, no doubt – he could not give her up. Miss Everard or Mrs Bellston, what mattered it? – she was the same Christine.

He did not go outside the inn all Saturday. He had no wish to see or do anything but to await the coming interview. So he smoked, and read the local newspaper of the previous week, and stowed himself in the chimney-corner. In the evening he felt that he could remain indoors no longer, and the moon being near the full, he started from the inn on foot in the same direction as that of yesterday, with the view of contemplating the old village and its precincts, and hovering round her house under the cloak of night.

With a stout stick in his hand he climbed over the five miles of upland in a comparatively short space of time. Nicholas had seen many strange lands and trodden many strange ways since he last walked that path, but as he trudged he seemed wonderfully like his old self, and had not the slightest difficulty in finding the way. In descending to the meads the streams perplexed him a little, some of the old foot-bridges having been removed; but he ultimately got across the larger water-courses, and pushed on to the village, avoiding her residence for the moment, lest she should encounter him, and think he had not respected the time of her appointment.

He found his way to the churchyard, and first ascertained where lay the two relations he had left alive at his departure; then he observed the gravestones of other inhabitants with whom he had been well acquainted, till by degrees he seemed to be in the society of all the elder Swenn-Everard population, as he had known the place. Side by side as they had lived in his day here were they now. They had moved house in mass.

But no tomb of Mr Bellston was visible, though, as he had lived at the manor-house, it would have been natural to find it here. In truth Nicholas was more anxious to discover that than anything, being curious to know how long he had been dead. Seeing from the glimmer of a light in the church that somebody was there cleaning for Sunday he entered, and looked round upon the walls as well as he could. But there was no monument to her husband, though one had been erected to the Squire.

Nicholas addressed the young man who was sweeping. 'I don't see any monument or tomb to the late Mr Bellston?'

'Oh no, sir; you won't see that,' said the young man drily.

'Why, pray?'

'Because he's not buried here. He's not Christian-buried anywhere, as far as we know. In short, perhaps he's not buried at all; and between ourselves, perhaps he's alive.'

Nicholas sank an inch shorter. 'Ah,' he answered.

'Then you don't know the peculiar circumstances, sir?'

'I am a stranger here – as to late years.'

'Mr Bellston was a traveller – an explorer – it was his calling; you may have heard his name as such?'

'I remember.' Nicholas recalled the fact that this very bent of Mr Bellston's was the incentive to his own roaming.

'Well, when he married he came and lived here with his wife and his wife's father, and said he would travel no more. But after a time he got weary of biding quiet here, and weary of her – he was not a good husband to the young lady by any means – and he betook himself again to his old trick of roving – with her money. Away he went, quite out of the realm of human foot, into the bowels of Asia, and never was heard of more. He was murdered, it is said, but nobody knows; though as that was nine years ago he's dead enough in principle, if not in corporation. His widow lives quite humble, for between her husband and her brother she's left in very lean pasturage.'

Nicholas went back to Troyton Inn without hovering round her dwelling. This then was the explanation which she had wanted to make. Not dead, but missing. How could he have expected that the first fair promise of happiness held out to him would remain untarnished? She had said that she was free; and legally she was free, no doubt. Moreover, from her tone and manner he felt himself justified in concluding that she would be willing to run the risk of a union with him, in the improbability of her husband's existence. Even if that husband lived, his return was not a likely event, to judge from his character. A man who could spend her money on his own personal adventures would not be anxious to disturb her poverty after such a lapse of time.

Well, the prospect was not so unclouded as it had seemed. But could he, even now, give up Christine?

VII

Two months more brought the year nearly to a close, and found Nicholas Long tenant of a spacious house in the market-town nearest to Swenn-Everard. A man of means, genial character, and a bachelor, he was an object of great interest to his neighbours, and to his neighbours' wives and daughters. But he took little note of this, and had made it his business to go twice a-week, no matter what the weather, to the now farm-house at Swenn-Everard, a wing of which had been retained as the refuge of Christine. He always walked, to give no trouble in putting up a horse to a housekeeper whose staff was limited.

The two had put their heads together on the situation, had gone to a solicitor, had balanced possibilities, and had resolved to make the plunge of matrimony. 'Nothing venture nothing have,' Christine had said, with some of her old audacity.

With almost gratuitous honesty they had let their intentions be widely known. Christine, it is true, had rather shrunk from publicity at first; but Nicholas argued that their boldness in this respect would have good results. With his friends he held that there was not the slightest probability of her being other than a widow, and a challenge to the missing man now, followed by no response, would stultify any unpleasant remarks which might be thrown at her after their union. To this end a paragraph was inserted in the Wessex papers, announcing that their marriage was proposed to be celebrated on such and such a day in December.

His periodic walks along the south side of the valley to visit her were among the happiest experiences of his life. The yellow leaves falling around him in the foreground, the well-watered meads on the right hand, and the woman he loved awaiting him at the back of the scene, promised a future of much serenity, as far as human judgment could foresee. On arriving, he would sit with her in the 'parlour' of the wing she retained, her general sitting-room, where the only relics of her early surroundings were an old clock from the other end of the house, and her own piano. Before it was quite dark they would stand, hand in hand, looking out of the window across the flat turf to the dark clump of trees which hid further view from their eyes.

'Do you wish you were still mistress here, dear?' he once said.

'Not at all,' said she cheerfully. 'I have a good enough room, and a good enough fire, and a good enough friend. Besides, my latter days as mistress of the house were not happy ones, and they spoilt the place for me. It was a punishment for my faithfulness. Nic, you do forgive me? Really you do?'

The twenty-third of December, the eve of the wedding-day, had arrived at last in the train of such uneventful ones as these. Nicholas had arranged to visit her that day a little later than usual, and see that everything was ready with her for the morrow's event and her removal to his house; for he had begun to look after her domestic affairs, and to lighten as much as possible the duties of her housekeeping.

He was to come to an early supper, which she had arranged to take the place of a wedding-breakfast next day – the latter not being feasible in her present situation. An hour or so after dark the wife of the farmer who lived in the other part of the house entered Christine's parlour to lay the cloth.

'What with getting the ham skinned, and the black-puddings hotted up,' she said; 'it will take me all my time before he's here, if I begin this minute.'

'I'll lay the table myself,' said Christine, jumping up. 'Do you attend to the cooking.'

'Thank you, ma'am. And perhaps 'tis no matter, seeing that it is the last night you'll have to do such work. I knew this sort of life wouldn't last long for ye, being born to better things.'

'It has lasted rather long, Mrs Wake. And if he had not found me out it would have lasted all my days.'

'But he did find you out.'

'He did. And I'll lay the cloth immediately.'

Mrs Wake went back to the kitchen, and Christine began to bustle about. She greatly enjoyed preparing this table for Nicholas and herself with her own hands. She took artistic pleasure in adjusting each article to its position, as if half an inch error were a point of high importance. Finally she placed the two candles where they were to stand, and sat down by the fire.

Mrs Wake re-entered and regarded the effect. 'Why not have another candle or two, ma'am?' she said. ' 'Twould make it livelier. Say four.'

'Very well,' said Christine; and four candles were lighted. 'Really,' she added, surveying them, 'I have been now so long accustomed to little economies that they look quite extravagant.'

'Ah, you'll soon think nothing of forty in his grand new house! Shall I bring in supper directly he comes, ma'am?'

'No, not for half an hour; and, Mrs Wake, you and Betsy are busy in the kitchen, I know; so when he knocks don't disturb yourselves; I can let him in.'

She was again left alone, and, as it still wanted some time to Nicholas's appointment, she stood by the fire, looking at herself in the glass over the mantel. Reflectively raising a lock of her hair just above her temple she uncovered a small scar. That scar had a history. The terrible temper of her late husband – those sudden moods of irascibility which had made even his friendly excitements look like anger – had once caused him to set that mark upon her with the bezel of a ring he wore. He declared that the whole thing was an accident. She was a woman, and kept her own opinion.

Christine then turned her back to the glass and scanned the table and the candles, shining one at each corner like types of the four Evangelists,[21] and thought they looked too assuming – too confident. She glanced up at the clock, which stood also in this room, there not being space enough for it in the passage. It was nearly seven, and she expected Nicholas at half-past. She liked the company of this venerable article in her lonely life: its tickings and whizzings were a sort of conversation. It now began to strike the hour. At the end something grated slightly. Then without any warning, the clock slowly inclined forward and fell at full length upon the floor.[22]

The crash brought the farmer's wife rushing into the room. Christine had well-nigh sprung out of her shoes. Mrs Wake's inquiry what had happened was answered by the evidence of her own eyes.

'How did it occur?' she said.

'I cannot say; it was not firmly fixed, I suppose. Dear me, how sorry I am! My dear father's hall-clock! And now I suppose it is ruined.'

Assisted by Mrs Wake, she lifted the clock. Every inch of glass was, of course, shattered, but very little harm besides appeared to be done. They propped it up temporarily, though it would not go again.

Christine had soon recovered her composure, but she saw that Mrs

Wake was gloomy. 'What does it mean, Mrs Wake?' she said. 'Is it ominous?'

'It is a sign of a violent death in the family.'

'Don't talk of it. I don't believe such things; and don't mention it to Mr Long when he comes. *He's* not in the family yet, you know.'

'Oh, no, it cannot refer to him,' said Mrs Wake musingly.

'Some remote cousin, perhaps,' observed Christine, no less willing to humour her than to get rid of a shapeless dread which the incident had caused in her own mind. 'And – supper is almost ready, Mrs Wake?'

'In three-quarters of an hour.'

Mrs Wake left the room, and Christine sat on. Though it still wanted fifteen minutes to the hour at which Nicholas had promised to be there, she began to grow impatient. After the accustomed ticking the dead silence was oppressive. But she had not to wait so long as she had expected; steps were heard approaching the door, and there was a knock.

Christine was already there to open to it. The entrance had no lamp, but it was not particularly dark out of doors. She could see the outline of a man, and cried cheerfully, 'You are early; it is very good of you.'[23]

'Early am I? I thought I was late.'

The voice was not the voice of Nicholas.

'I beg pardon,' said she. 'I did not – I expected some one else. Will you come in? You wish to see Mrs Wake?'

The new-comer did not answer, but followed her up the passage and into her own room. She turned to look at him, and by degrees recognized that her husband, James Bellston, stood before her.

She sank into a chair. He was now a much-bearded man, his beard growing almost straight from his face like spines. Corpulent he was too, and short in his breathing, but unmistakable. He placed a small leather portmanteau of a common kind on the floor and said, 'You did not expect me?'

'I did not,' she gasped. 'I thought you were —'

'Dead. Good. So did others. It was natural, Christine, and I have a good deal to blame myself for in that respect; but I could bring you

home neither money nor fame, and what was the use of my coming?
However, I heard, or rather read, the account of your approaching
marriage, and that forced my hand. It was to have been tomorrow?'

'Yes.'

'I knew by seeing the date mentioned in the papers. That was why
I came tonight, though I had the greatest difficulty in getting here,
owing to my having taken passage in a sailing vessel, which was delayed
by contrary winds. I meant to have arrived much sooner. And so the
old house and manor are gone from your family at last?' he said,
seating himself.

'Yes,' said she; and then she spasmodically began to tell him of
things that were more pertinent to the moment – how Nicholas Long
had come back a comparatively rich man; that he was going to call
that evening, and that the very supper-table before their eyes was laid
for him.

'Then he may enter at any minute?' said her husband.

'Certainly.'

'That will be awkward. In common civility he ought to be fore-
warned. All this comes of my being so delayed . . . My dear, I think
the proper plan will be for me to go out for half-an-hour, during which
time he will arrive, I presume. You can break to him what has
happened, and please convey my apologies to him for this abrupt
return, which I really could not help. I will come back to the house
when he is gone, and so an unpleasant encounter will be avoided. If
I allow him an hour from this time to be out of the house it will be
long enough probably?'

'Yes. And the supper —'

'Can wait till I come. Thank you, dear. Now I'll go and stroll round,
and see how the familiar old places look after such a long interval.'

He placed his portmanteau in a corner, imprinted a business-like
kiss upon her cheek, and withdrew.

She was alone; but what a solitude!

She stood in the middle of the room just as he had left her, in the
gloomy silence of the stopped clock, till at length she heard another
tread without, coming from an opposite direction to that of her
husband's retreat, and there was a second knocking at the door.

She did not respond to it; and Nicholas – for it was he – thinking that he was not heard by reason of concentration on tomorrow's proceedings, opened the door softly, and came on to the door of her room, which stood unclosed, just as it had been left by her husband.

Nicholas uttered a blithe greeting, cast his eye round the parlour, which with its tall candles, blazing fire, snow-white cloth, and prettily-spread table, formed a cheerful spectacle enough for a man who had been walking in the dark for an hour.

'My bride – almost, at last!' he cried, encircling her with his arms.

Instead of responding, her figure became limp, frigid, heavy; her head fell back, and he found that she had fainted.

It was natural, he thought. She had had many little worrying matters to attend to, and but slight assistance. He ought to have seen more effectually to her affairs; the closeness of the event had over-excited her. Nicholas kissed her unconscious face – more than once, little thinking whose lips had lately made a lodging there. Loth to call Mrs Wake, he carried Christine to a couch and laid her down. This had the effect of reviving her. Nicholas bent and whispered in her ear, 'Lie quiet, dearest, no hurry; and dream, dream, dream of happy days. It is only I. You will soon be better.' He held her by the hand.

'No, no, no!' she moaned. 'Oh, how can this be?'

Nicholas was alarmed and perplexed, but the disclosure was not long delayed. When she had sat up, and by degrees made the stunning event known to him, he stood as if transfixed.

'Ah – is it so!' said he. Then, becoming quite meek, 'And why was he so cruel as to – delay his return till now?'

She dutifully recited the explanation her husband had given her; but her mechanical manner of telling it showed how much she doubted its truth. It was too unlikely that his arrival at such a dramatic moment should not be a contrived surprise, quite of a piece with his previous dealings towards her.

'He – seems very kind now – not as he used to be,' she faltered. 'And perhaps, Nicholas, he is a changed man – we'll hope he is. I suppose I ought not to have listened to my legal advisers, and assumed his death so surely! Anyhow, I am roughly received back into – the right way!'

Nicholas burst out bitterly: 'Oh what too, too honest fools we were! – to so court daylight upon our intention! Why could we not have married privately, and gone away, so that he would never have known what had become of you, even if he had returned? Christine, he has done it to . . . But I'll say no more. Of course we – might fly now.'

'No, no; we might not,' said she hastily.

'Very well. But this is hard to bear! "When I looked for good then evil came unto me, and when I waited for light there came darkness." So once said a sorely tried man in the land of Uz,[24] and so say I now! . . . Is he near at this moment?'

She told him how Bellston had gone out for a short walk whilst she broke the news; that he would be in soon.

'And is this meal laid for him, or for me?'

'It was laid for you.'

'And it will be eaten by him?'

'Yes.'

'Christine, are you *sure* that he is come, or have you been sleeping over the fire and dreaming it?'

She pointed to the portmanteau in the corner, with the initials 'J.B.' in white letters.

'Well, goodbye – goodbye! Curse that parson for not marrying us fifteen years ago!'

It is unnecessary to dwell further upon that parting. There are scenes wherein the words spoken do not even approximate to the level of the mental communion between the actors. Suffice it to say that part they did, and quickly; and Nicholas, more dead than alive, went out of the house homewards.

Why had he ever come back? During his absence he had not cared for Christine as he cared now. His last state was worse than his first. He was more than once tempted[25] to descend into the meads instead of keeping along their edge. The Swenn was down there, and he knew of quiet pools in that stream to which death would come easily. One thought, however, kept him from seriously contemplating any desperate act. His affection for her was strongly protective, and in the event of her requiring a friend's support in future troubles there was none but himself left in the world to afford it. So he walked on.

Meanwhile Christine had resigned herself to circumstances. A resolve to continue worthy of her history and of her family lent her heroism and dignity. She called Mrs Wake, and explained to that worthy woman as much of what had occurred as she deemed necessary. Mrs Wake was too amazed to reply; she retreated slowly, her lips parted; till at the door she said with a dry mouth, 'And the beautiful supper, ma'am?'

'Serve it when he comes.'

'When Mr Bellston – yes, ma'am, I will.' She still stood gazing, as if she could hardly take in the order.

'That will do, Mrs Wake. I am much obliged to you for all your kindness.' And Christine was left alone again, and then she wept.

She sat down and waited. That awful silence of the stopped clock began anew, but she did not mind it now. She was listening for a footfall, in a state of mental tensity which almost took away from her the power of motion. It seemed to her that the prescribed hour of her husband's absence must have expired; but she was not sure, and waited on.

Mrs Wake again came in. 'You have not rung for supper —'

'He is not yet come, Mrs Wake. If you want to go to bed, bring in the supper and set it on the table. It will be equally good cold. Leave the door unbarred.'

Mrs Wake did as was suggested, made up the fire, and went away. Shortly afterwards Christine heard her retire to her chamber. But Christine still sat on, and still her husband postponed his entry.

She aroused herself once or twice to make up the fire, but was ignorant how the night was going. Her watch was upstairs and she did not make the effort to go up to consult it. In her seat she continued; and still the supper waited, and still he did not come.

At length she was so nearly persuaded that his visit must have been a dream after all, that she again went over to his portmanteau, felt it and examined it. His it unquestionably was; it was unlocked, and contained only some common articles of wearing apparel. She sighed and sat down again.

Presently she fell into a doze, and when she again became conscious she found that the four candles had burnt into their sockets and gone out. The fire still emitted a feeble shine. Christine did not take the trouble to get more candles, but stirred the fire and sat on.

After a long period she heard a creaking of the chamber floor and stairs at the other end of the house, and knew that the farmer's family were getting up. By-and-by Mrs Wake entered the room, candle in hand, bouncing open the door in her morning manner, obviously without any expectation of finding a person there.

'Lord-a-mercy! What sitting here again, ma'am?'

'Yes, I am sitting here still.'

'You've been there ever since last night?'

'Yes.'

'Then —'

'He's not come.'

'Well, he won't come at this time o' morning,' said the farmer's wife. 'Do 'ee get on to bed, ma'am. You must be scrammed to death!'

It occurred to Christine now that possibly her husband had thought better of obtruding himself upon her company within an hour of revealing his existence to her, and had decided to pay a more formal visit next day. She therefore adopted Mrs Wake's suggestion and retired.

VIII

Nicholas had gone straight home, neither speaking to nor seeing a soul. From that hour a change seemed to come over him. He had ever possessed a full share of self-consciousness; he had been readily piqued, had shown an unusual dread of being personally obtrusive. But now his sense of self, as an individual provoking opinion, appeared to leave him. When, therefore, after a day or two of seclusion, he came forth again, and the few acquaintants he had formed in the town condoled with him on what had happened, and pitied his haggard looks, he did not shrink from their regard as he would have done formerly, but took their sympathy as it would have been accepted by a child.

It reached his ears that Bellston had not reappeared on the evening of his arrival, either at his wife's house or at any hotel in the town or neighbourhood. 'That's a part of his cruelty,' thought Nicholas. And when two or three days had passed, and still no account came to him of Bellston having joined her, he ventured to set out for Swenn-Everard.

Christine was so shaken that she was obliged to receive him as she lay on a sofa, beside the square table which was to have borne their evening feast. She fixed her eyes wistfully upon him, and smiled a sad smile.

'He has not come back?' said Nicholas under his breath.

'He has not.'

Then Nicholas sat beside her, and they talked on general topics merely like saddened old friends. But they could not keep away the subject of Bellston, their voices dropping as it forced its way in. Christine, no less than Nicholas, knowing her husband's character, inferred that, having stopped her game, as he would have phrased it, he was taking things leisurely, and, finding nothing very attractive in her limited mode of living, was meaning to return to her only when he had nothing better to do.

The bolt which laid low their hopes had struck so recently, that they could hardly look each other in the face when speaking that day. But when a week or two had passed, and all the horizon still remained as vacant of Bellston as before, Nicholas and she could talk of the event with calm wonderment. Why had he come, to go again like this?

And then there set in a period of resigned surmise, during which

'So like, so very like, was day to day,'[26]

that to tell of one of them is to tell of all. Nicholas would arrive between three and four in the afternoon, a faint trepidation influencing his walk as he neared her door. He would knock; she would always reply in person, having watched for him from the window. Then he would whisper –

'He has not come back?'

'He has not,' she would say.

Nicholas would enter then, and she being ready bonneted, they would walk into the Sallows together as far as the waterfall, the spot which they had frequently made their place of appointment in their youthful days. A plank bridge, which Bellston had caused to be thrown over the fall during his residence with her in the manor-house, was now again removed, and all was just the same as in Nicholas's time, when he had been accustomed to wade across on the edge of the cascade and come up to her like a merman from the deep. Here on the felled trunk, which still lay rotting in its old place, they would now sit, gazing at the descending sheet of water, with its never-ending sarcastic hiss at their baffled attempts to make themselves one flesh. Returning to the house they would sit down together to tea, after which, and the confidential chat that accompanied it, he walked home by the declining light. This proceeding became as periodic as an astronomical recurrence. Twice a week he came – all through that winter, all through the spring following, through the summer, through the autumn, the next winter, the next year, and the next, till an appreciable span of human life had passed by. Bellston still tarried.

Years and years Nic walked that way, at this interval of three days, from his house in the neighbouring town; and in every instance the aforesaid order of things was customary; and still on his arrival the form of words went on –

'He has not come back?'

'He has not.'

So they grew older. The dim shape of that third one stood continually between them; they could not displace it; neither, on the other hand, could it effectually part them. They were in close communion, yet not indissolubly united; lovers, yet never cured of love. By the time that the fifth year of his visiting had arrived, on about the five-hundredth occasion of his presence at her tea-table, he noticed that the bleaching process which had begun upon his own locks was also spreading to hers. He told her so, and they laughed. Yet she was in good health: a condition of suspense, which would have half-killed a man, had been endured by her without complaint, and even with composure.

One day, when these years of abeyance had numbered seven, they had strolled as usual as far as the waterfall, whose faint roar formed a sort of calling voice sufficient in the circumstances to direct their listlessness. Pausing there, he looked up at her face and said, 'Why should we not try again, Christine? We are legally at liberty to do so now. Nothing venture nothing have.'

But she would not. Perhaps a little primness of idea was by this time ousting the native daring of Christine. 'What he has done once he can do twice,' she said. 'He is not dead, and if we were to marry he would say we had "forced his hand", as he said before, and duly reappear.'

Some years after, when Christine was about fifty, and Nicholas fifty-three, a new trouble of a minor kind arrived. He found an inconvenience in traversing the distance between their two houses, particularly in damp weather, the years he had spent in trying climates abroad having sown the seeds of rheumatism, which made a journey undesirable on inclement days, even in a carriage. He told her of this new difficulty, as he did of everything.

'If you could live nearer,' suggested she.

Unluckily there was no house near. But Nicholas, though not a millionaire, was a man of means; he obtained a small piece of ground on lease at the nearest spot to her home that it could be so obtained, which was on the opposite brink of the Swenn, this river forming the boundary of the Swenn-Everard manor; and here he built a house large enough for his wants. This took time, and when he got into it he found its situation a great comfort to him. He was not more than two hundred yards from her now, and gained a new pleasure in feeling that all sounds which greeted his ears, in the day or in the night, also fell upon hers – the caw of a particular rook, the voice of a neighbouring nightingale, the whistle of a local breeze, or the purl of the fall in the meadows, whose rush was a material rendering of Time's ceaseless scour over themselves, wearing them away without uniting them.

Christine's missing husband was taking shape as a myth among the surrounding residents; but he was still believed in as corporeally imminent by Christine herself, and also, in a milder degree, by Nicholas. For a curious unconsciousness of the long lapse of time since his revelation of himself seemed to affect the pair. There had been no passing events to serve as chronological milestones, and the evening on which she had kept supper waiting for him still loomed out with startling nearness in their retrospects.

In the seventeenth pensive year of this their parallel march towards the common bourne, a labourer came in a hurry one day to Nicholas's house and brought strange tidings. The present owner of Swenn-Everard – a non-resident – had been improving his property in sundry ways, and one of these was by dredging the stream which, in the course of years, had become choked with mud and weeds in its passage through the Sallows. The process necessitated a reconstruction of the waterfall. When the river had been pumped dry for this purpose, the skeleton of a man had been found jammed among the piles supporting the edge of the fall. Every particle of his flesh and clothing had been eaten by fishes or abraded to nothing by the water, but the relics of a gold watch remained, and on the inside of the case was engraved 'J. Bellston: 1838.'[27]

Nicholas, deeply agitated, hastened down to the place and examined the remains attentively, afterwards going across to Christine, and breaking the discovery to her. She would not come to view the skeleton, which lay extended on the grass, not a finger or toe-bone missing, so neatly had the aquatic operators done their work. Conjecture was directed to the question how Bellston had got there; and conjecture alone could give an explanation.

It was supposed that, after calling upon her, he had gone rambling about the grounds, with which he was naturally very familiar, and coming to the fall under the trees had expected to find there the plank by which, during his occupancy of the premises, he had been accustomed to cross into the meads on the other side. Before discovering its removal he had probably overbalanced himself, and was thus precipitated into the cascade, the piles beneath the descending current holding him between them like the prongs of a pitchfork, and effectually preventing the rising of his body, over which the weeds grew. Such was the reasonable supposition concerning the discovery; but proof was never forthcoming.

'To think,' said Nicholas, when the remains had been decently interred, and he was again sitting with Christine – though not beside the waterfall – 'to think how we visited him! How we sat over him, hours and hours, gazing at him, bewailing our fate, when all the time he was ironically hissing at us from the spot, in an unknown tongue, that we could marry if we chose!'

She echoed the sentiment with a sigh.

'You might have married me on the day we had fixed, and there would have been no impediment. You would now have been seventeen years my wife, and we might have had tall sons and daughters.'

'It might have been so,' she murmured.

'Well – is it still better late than never?'

The question was one which had become complicated by the increasing years of each. Their wills were somewhat enfeebled now, their hearts sickened of tender enterprise by hope too long deferred. Having postponed the consideration of their course till a year after the interment of Bellston, each seemed less disposed than formerly to take it up again.

'Is it worth while, after so many years?' she said to him. 'We are fairly happy as we are – perhaps happier than we should be in any other relation, seeing what old people we have grown. The weight is gone from our lives; the shadow no longer divides us: then let us be joyful together as we are, dearest Nic, in the days of our vanity; and

"With mirth and laughter let old wrinkles come!"[28]

He fell in with these views of hers to some extent. But occasionally he ventured to urge her to reconsider the case, though he spoke not with the fervour of his earlier years.

I

A lorn milkmaid[1]

It was an eighty-cow dairy,[2] and the troop of milkers, regular and supernumerary, were all at work; for, though the time of year was as yet but early April, the feed lay entirely in water-meadows and the cows were 'in full pail'. The hour was about six in the evening, and three-fourths of the large, red, rectangular animals having been finished off, there was opportunity for a little conversation.

'He brings home his bride tomorrow, I hear. They've come as far as Anglebury[3] today.'

The voice seemed to proceed from the belly of the cow called Cherry, but the speaker was a milking-woman, whose face was buried in the flank of that motionless beast.

'Has anybody seen her?'[4] said another.

There was a negative response from the first. 'Though they say she's a rosy-cheeked, tisty-tosty little body enough,' she added; and as the milkmaid spoke she turned her face so that she could glance past her cow's tail to the other side of the barton, where a thin, faded woman of thirty milked somewhat apart from the rest.

'Years younger than he, they say,' continued the second, with also a glance of reflectiveness in the same direction.

'How old do you call him, then?'

'Thirty or so.'

'More like forty,' broke in an old milkman near, in a long white pinafore or 'wrapper', and with the brim of his hat tied down, so that he looked like a woman. ' 'A was born before our Great Weir was builded,[5] and I hadn't man's wages when I laved water there.'

The discussion waxed so warm that the purr of the milk-streams became jerky, till a voice from another cow's belly cried with authority, 'Now then, what the Turk do it matter to us about Farmer Lodge's age, or Farmer Lodge's new mis'ess? I shall have to pay him nine pound a year for the rent of every one of these milchers, whatever his age or hers. Get on with your work, or 'twill be dark before we have done. The evening is pinking in a'ready.' This speaker was the dairyman himself, by whom the milkmaids and men were employed.

Nothing more was said publicly about Farmer Lodge's wedding, but the first woman murmured under her cow to her next neighbour, ' 'Tis hard for *she*,' signifying the thin worn milkmaid aforesaid.

'Oh no,' said the second. 'He hasn't spoken to Rhoda Brook[6] for years.'

When the milking was done they washed their pails and hung them on a many-forked stand made of the peeled limb of an oak-tree,[7] set upright in the earth, and resembling a colossal antlered horn. The majority then dispersed in various directions homeward. The thin woman who had not spoken was joined by a boy of twelve or thereabout, and the twain went away up the field also.

Their course lay apart from that of the others, to a lonely spot high above the water-meads, and not far from the border of Egdon Heath, whose dark countenance was visible in the distance as they drew nigh to their home.

'They've just been saying down in barton that your father brings his young wife home from Anglebury tomorrow,' the woman observed. 'I shall want to send you for a few things to market, and you'll be pretty sure to meet 'em.'

'Yes, mother,' said the boy. 'Is father married, then?'

'Yes . . . You can give her a look, and tell me what she's like, if you do see her.'

'Yes, mother.'

'If she's dark or fair, and if she's tall – as tall as I.[8] And if she seems like a woman who has ever worked for a living, or one that has been always well off, and has never done anything, and shows marks of the lady on her, as I expect she do.'

'Yes.'

They crept up the hill in the twilight, and entered the cottage. It was thatched, and built of mud-walls, the surface of which had been washed by many rains into channels and depressions that left none of the original flat face visible; while here and there a rafter showed like a bone protruding through the skin.

She was kneeling down in the chimney-corner, before two pieces of turf laid together with the heather inwards, blowing at the red-hot ashes with her breath till the turves flamed. The radiance lit her pale cheek, and made her dark eyes, that had once been handsome, seem handsome anew. 'Yes,' she resumed, 'see if she is dark or fair, and if you can, notice if her hands are white; if not, see if they look as though she had ever done housework, or are milker's hands like mine.'

The boy again promised, inattentively this time, his mother not observing that he was cutting a notch with his pocket-knife in the beech-backed chair.

II

The young wife

The road from Anglebury to Holmstoke is in general level; but there is one place where a sharp ascent breaks its monotony. Farmers homeward-bound from the former market-town, who trot all the rest of the way, walk their horses up this short incline.

The next evening, while the sun was yet bright, a handsome new gig, with a lemon-coloured body and red wheels, was spinning westward along the level highway at the heels of a powerful mare. The driver was a yeoman in the prime of life, cleanly shaven like an actor, his face being toned to that bluish-vermilion hue which so often graces a thriving farmer's features when returning home after successful dealings in the town. Beside him sat a woman, many years his junior – almost, indeed, a girl. Her face too was fresh in colour, but it was of a totally different quality – soft and evanescent, like the light under a heap of rose-petals.

Few people travelled this way, for it was not a turnpike-road; and the long white riband of gravel that stretched before them was empty, save of one small scarce-moving speck, which presently resolved itself into the figure of a boy, who was creeping on at a snail's pace, and continually looking behind him – the heavy bundle he carried being some excuse for, if not the reason of, his dilatoriness. When the bouncing gig-party slowed at the bottom of the incline above mentioned, the pedestrian was only a few yards in front. Supporting the large bundle by putting one hand on his hip, he turned and looked straight at the farmer's wife as though he would read her through and through, pacing along abreast of the horse.

The low sun was full in her face, rendering every feature, shade, and contour distinct, from the curve of her little nostril to the colour of her eyes. The farmer, though he seemed annoyed at the boy's persistent presence, did not order him to get out of the way; and thus the lad preceded them, his hard gaze never leaving her, till they reached the top of the ascent, when the farmer trotted on with relief in his lineaments – having taken no outward notice of the boy whatever.

'How that poor lad stared at me!' said the young wife.

'Yes, dear; I saw that he did.'

'He is one of the village, I suppose?'

'One of the neighbourhood. I think he lives with his mother a mile or two off.'

'He knows who we are, no doubt?'

'Oh yes. You must expect to be stared at just at first, my pretty Gertrude.'

'I do, – though I think the poor boy may have looked at us in the hope we might relieve him of his heavy load, rather than from curiosity.'

'Oh no,' said her husband off-handedly. 'These country lads will carry a hundredweight once they get it on their backs; besides, his pack had more size than weight in it. Now, then, another mile and I shall be able to show you our house in the distance – if it is not too dark before we get there.' The wheels spun round, and particles flew from their periphery as before, till a white house of ample dimensions revealed itself, with farm-buildings and ricks at the back.

Meanwhile the boy had quickened his pace, and turning up a by-lane some mile and half short of the white farmstead, ascended towards the leaner pastures, and so on to the cottage of his mother.

She had reached home after her day's milking at the outlying dairy, and was washing cabbage at the doorway in the declining light. 'Hold up the net a moment,' she said, without preface, as the boy came up.

He flung down his bundle, held the edge of the cabbage-net, and as she filled its meshes with the dripping leaves she went on, 'Well, did you see her?'

'Yes; quite plain.'

'Is she ladylike?'

'Yes; and more. A lady complete.'

'Is she young?'

'Well, she's growed up, and her ways are quite a woman's.'

'Of course. What colour is her hair and face?'

'Her hair is lightish, and her face as comely as a live doll's.'

'Her eyes, then, are not dark like mine?'

'No – of a bluish turn, and her mouth is very nice and red; and when she smiles, her teeth show white.'

'Is she tall?' said the woman sharply.

'I couldn't see. She was sitting down.'

'Then do you go to Holmstoke church tomorrow morning: she's sure to be there. Go early and notice her walking in, and come home and tell me if she's taller than I.'

'Very well, mother. But why don't you go and see for yourself?'

'*I* go to see her! I wouldn't look up at her if she were to pass my window this instant. She was with Mr Lodge, of course. What did he say or do?'

'Just the same as usual.'

'Took no notice of you?'

'None.'

Next day the mother put a clean shirt on the boy, and started him off for Holmstoke church. He reached the ancient little pile when the door was just being opened, and he was the first to enter. Taking his seat by the font, he watched all the parishioners file in. The well-to-do Farmer Lodge came nearly last; and his young wife, who accompanied him, walked up the aisle with the shyness natural to a modest woman who had appeared thus for the first time. As all other eyes were fixed upon her, the youth's stare was not noticed now.

When he reached home his mother said 'Well?' before he had entered the room.

'She is not tall. She is rather short,' he replied.

'Ah!' said his mother, with satisfaction.

'But she's very pretty – very. In fact, she's lovely.' The youthful freshness of the yeoman's wife had evidently made an impression even on the somewhat hard nature of the boy.

'That's all I want to hear,' said his mother quickly. 'Now, spread the table-cloth. The hare you caught is very tender; but mind that nobody catches you. – You've never told me what sort of hands she had.'

'I have never seen 'em. She never took off her gloves.'

'What did she wear this morning?'

'A white bonnet and a silver-coloured gownd. It whewed and whistled so loud when it rubbed against the pews[9] that the lady coloured up more than ever for very shame at the noise, and pulled it in to keep it from touching; but when she pushed into her seat, it whewed more than ever. Mr Lodge, he seemed pleased, and his waistcoat stuck out, and his great golden seals hung like a lord's; but she seemed to wish her noisy gownd anywhere but on her.'

'Not she! However, that will do now.'

These descriptions of the newly-married couple were continued from time to time by the boy at his mother's request, after any chance encounter he had had with them. But Rhoda Brook, though she might easily have seen young Mrs Lodge for herself by walking a couple of miles, would never attempt an excursion towards the quarter where the farmhouse lay. Neither did she, at the daily milking in the dairyman's yard on Lodge's outlying second farm, ever speak on the subject of the recent marriage. The dairyman, who rented the cows of Lodge, and knew perfectly the tall milkmaid's history, with manly kindliness always kept the gossip in the cow-barton from annoying Rhoda. But the atmosphere thereabout was full of the subject during the first days of Mrs Lodge's arrival; and from her boy's description and the casual words of the other milkers, Rhoda Brook could raise a mental image of the unconscious Mrs Lodge that was realistic as a photograph.[10]

III

A vision

One night, two or three weeks after the bridal return, when the boy was gone to bed, Rhoda sat a long time over the turf ashes that she had raked out in front of her to extinguish them. She contemplated so intently the new wife, as presented to her in her mind's eye over the embers, that she forgot the lapse of time. At last, wearied with her day's work, she too retired.

But the figure which had occupied her so much during this and the previous days was not to be banished at night. For the first time Gertrude Lodge visited the supplanted woman in her dreams. Rhoda Brook dreamed – since her assertion that she really saw, before falling asleep, was not to be believed[11] – that the young wife, in the pale silk dress and white bonnet, but with features shockingly distorted, and wrinkled as by age, was sitting upon her chest as she lay. The pressure of Mrs Lodge's person grew heavier; the blue eyes peered cruelly into her face; and then the figure thrust forward its left hand mockingly, so as to make the wedding-ring it wore glitter in Rhoda's eyes. Maddened mentally, and nearly suffocated by pressure, the sleeper struggled; the incubus, still regarding her, withdrew to the foot of the bed, only, however, to come forward by degrees, resume her seat, and flash her left hand as before.

Gasping for breath, Rhoda, in a last desperate effort, swung out her right hand, seized the confronting spectre by its obtrusive left arm, and whirled it backward to the floor, starting up herself as she did so with a low cry.

'Oh, merciful heaven!' she cried, sitting on the edge of the bed in a cold sweat, 'that was not a dream – she was here!'

She could feel her antagonist's arm within her grasp even now – the very flesh and bone of it, as it seemed. She looked on the floor whither she had whirled the spectre, but there was nothing to be seen.

Rhoda Brook slept no more that night, and when she went milking at the next dawn they noticed how pale and haggard she looked. The milk that she drew quivered into the pail; her hand had not calmed even yet, and still retained the feel of the arm. She came home to breakfast as wearily as if it had been supper-time.

'What was that noise in your chimmer, mother, last night?' said her son. 'You fell off the bed, surely?'

'Did you hear anything fall? At what time?'

'Just when the clock struck two.'

She could not explain, and when the meal was done went silently about her household work, the boy assisting her, for he hated going afield on the farms, and she indulged his reluctance. Between eleven and twelve the garden-gate clicked, and she lifted her eyes to the window. At the bottom of the garden, within the gate, stood the woman of her vision. Rhoda seemed transfixed.

'Ah, she said she would come!' exclaimed the boy, also observing her.

'Said so – when? How does she know us?'

'I have seen and spoken to her. I talked to her yesterday.'

'I told you,' said the mother, flushing indignantly, 'never to speak to anybody in that house, or go near the place.'

'I did not speak to her till she spoke to me. And I did not go near the place. I met her in the road.'

'What did you tell her?'

'Nothing. She said, "Are you the poor boy who had to bring the heavy load from market?" And she looked at my boots, and said they would not keep my feet dry if it came on wet, because they were so cracked. I told her I lived with my mother, and we had enough to do to keep ourselves, and that's how it was; and she said then, "I'll come and bring you some better boots, and see your mother." She gives away things to other folks in the meads besides us.'

Mrs Lodge was by this time close to the door – not in her silk, as Rhoda had seen her in the bed-chamber, but in a morning hat, and gown of common light material, which became her better than silk. On her arm she carried a basket.

The impression remaining from the night's experience was still strong.[12] Brook had almost expected to see the wrinkles, the scorn, and the cruelty on her visitor's face. She would have escaped an interview, had escape been possible. There was, however, no back-door to the cottage, and in an instant the boy had lifted the latch to Mrs Lodge's gentle knock.

'I see I have come to the right house,' said she, glancing at the lad, and smiling. 'But I was not sure till you opened the door.'

The figure and action were those of the phantom; but her voice was so indescribably sweet, her glance so winning, her smile so tender, so unlike that of Rhoda's midnight visitant, that the latter could hardly believe the evidence of her senses. She was truly glad that she had not hidden away in sheer aversion, as she had been inclined to do. In her basket Mrs Lodge brought the pair of boots that she had promised to the boy, and other useful articles.

At these proofs of a kindly feeling towards her and hers, Rhoda's heart reproached her bitterly. This innocent young thing should have her blessing and not her curse. When she left them a light seemed gone from the dwelling. Two days later she came again to know if the boots fitted; and less than a fortnight after that paid Rhoda another call. On this occasion the boy was absent.

'I walk a good deal,' said Mrs Lodge, 'and your house is the nearest outside our own parish. I hope you are well. You don't look quite well.'

Rhoda said she was well enough; and indeed, though the paler of the two, there was more of the strength that endures in her well-defined features and large frame, than in the soft-cheeked young woman before her. The conversation became quite confidential as regarded their powers and weaknesses; and when Mrs Lodge was leaving, Rhoda said, 'I hope you will find this air agree with you, ma'am, and not suffer from the damp of the water-meads.'

The younger one replied that there was not much doubt of it, her general health being usually good. 'Though, now you remind me,' she added, 'I have one little ailment which puzzles me. It is nothing serious, but I cannot make it out.'

She uncovered her left hand and arm; and their outline confronted Rhoda's gaze as the exact original of the limb she had beheld and seized in her dream. Upon the pink round surface of the arm were faint marks of an unhealthy colour, as if produced by a rough grasp.

Rhoda's eyes became riveted on the discolorations; she fancied that she discerned in them the shape of her own four fingers.

'How did it happen?' she said mechanically.

'I cannot tell,' replied Mrs Lodge, shaking her head. 'One night when I was sound asleep, dreaming I was away in some strange place, a pain suddenly shot into my arm there, and was so keen as to awaken me. I must have struck it in the daytime, I suppose, though I don't remember doing so.' She added, laughing, 'I tell my dear husband that it looks just as if he had flown into a rage and struck me there. Oh, I daresay it will soon disappear.'

'Ha, ha! Yes . . . On what night did it come?'

Mrs Lodge considered, and said it would be a fortnight ago on the morrow. 'When I awoke I could not remember where I was,' she added, 'till the clock striking two reminded me.'

She had named the night and the hour of Rhoda's spectral encounter, and Brook felt like a guilty thing. The artless disclosure startled her; she did not reason on the freaks of coincidence; and all the scenery of that ghastly night returned with double vividness to her mind.

'Oh, can it be,' she said to herself, when her visitor had departed, 'that I exercise a malignant power over people against my own will?' She knew that she had been slily called a witch since her fall; but never having understood why that particular stigma had been attached to her, it had passed disregarded. Could this be the explanation, and had such things as this ever happened before?

IV

A suggestion

The summer drew on, and Rhoda Brook almost dreaded to meet Mrs Lodge again, notwithstanding that her feeling for the young wife amounted wellnigh to affection. Something in her own individuality seemed to convict Rhoda of crime. Yet a fatality sometimes would direct the steps of the latter to the outskirts of Holmstoke whenever she left her house for any other purpose than her daily work; and hence it happened that their next encounter was out of doors. Rhoda could not avoid the subject which had so mystified her, and after the first few words she stammered, 'I hope your – arm is well again, ma'am?' She had perceived with consternation that Gertrude Lodge carried her left arm stiffly.

'No; it is not quite well. Indeed it is no better at all; it is rather worse. It pains me dreadfully sometimes.'

'Perhaps you had better go to a doctor, ma'am.'

She replied that she had already seen a doctor. Her husband had insisted upon her going to one. But the surgeon had not seemed to understand the afflicted limb at all; he had told her to bathe it in hot water, and she had bathed it, but the treatment had done no good.

'Will you let me see it?' said the milkwoman.

Mrs Lodge pushed up her sleeve and disclosed the place, which was a few inches above the wrist. As soon as Rhoda Brook saw it, she could hardly preserve her composure. There was nothing of the nature of a wound, but the arm at that point had a shrivelled look, and the outline of the four fingers appeared more distinct than at the former time. Moreover, she fancied that they were imprinted in precisely the relative position of her clutch upon the arm in the trance; the first finger towards Gertrude's wrist, and the fourth towards her elbow.

What the impress resembled seemed to have struck Gertrude herself since their last meeting. 'It looks almost like finger-marks,' she said; adding with a faint laugh, 'my husband says it is as if some witch, or the devil himself, had taken hold of me there, and blasted the flesh.'

Rhoda shivered. 'That's fancy,' she said hurriedly. 'I wouldn't mind it, if I were you.'

'I shouldn't so much mind it,' said the younger, with hesitation, 'if – if I hadn't a notion that it makes my husband – dislike me – no, love me less. Men think so much of personal appearance.'

'Some do – he for one.'

'Yes; and he was very proud of mine, at first.'

'Keep your arm covered from his sight.'

'Ah – he knows the disfigurement is there!' She tried to hide the tears that filled her eyes.

'Well, ma'am, I earnestly hope it will go away soon.'

And so the milkwoman's mind was chained anew to the subject by a horrid sort of spell as she returned home. The sense of having been guilty of an act of malignity increased, affect as she might to ridicule her superstition. In her secret heart Rhoda did not altogether object to a slight diminution of her successor's beauty, by whatever means it had come about; but she did not wish to inflict upon her physical pain. For though this pretty young woman had rendered impossible any reparation which Lodge might have made Rhoda for his past conduct, everything like resentment at the unconscious usurpation had quite passed away from the elder's mind.

If the sweet and kindly Gertrude Lodge only knew of the scene in the bed-chamber, what would she think? Not to inform her of it seemed treachery in the presence of her friendliness; but tell she could not of her own accord – neither could she devise a remedy.

She mused upon the matter the greater part of the night; and the next day, after the morning milking, set out to obtain another glimpse of Gertrude Lodge if she could, being held to her by a gruesome fascination. By watching the house from a distance the milkmaid was presently able to discern the farmer's wife in a ride she was taking alone – probably to join her husband in some distant field. Mrs Lodge perceived her, and cantered in her direction.

'Good morning, Rhoda!' Gertrude said, when she had come up. 'I was going to call.'

Rhoda noticed that Mrs Lodge held the reins with some difficulty.

'I hope – the bad arm,' said Rhoda.

'They tell me there is possibly one way by which I might be able to find out the cause, and so perhaps the cure, of it,' replied the other anxiously. 'It is by going to some clever man over in Egdon Heath. They did not know if he was still alive – and I cannot remember his name at this moment; but they said that you knew more of his movements than anybody else hereabout, and could tell me if he were still to be consulted. Dear me – what was his name? But you know.'

'Not Conjuror Trendle?'[13] said her thin companion, turning pale.

'Trendle – yes. Is he alive?'

'I believe so,' said Rhoda, with reluctance.

'Why do you call him conjuror?'

'Well – they say – they used to say he was a – he had powers other folks have not.'

'Oh, how could my people be so superstitious as to recommend a man of that sort! I thought they meant some medical man. I shall think no more of him.'

Rhoda looked relieved, and Mrs Lodge rode on. The milkwoman had inwardly seen, from the moment she heard of her having been mentioned as a reference for this man, that there must exist a sarcastic feeling among the work-folk that a sorceress would know the where-abouts of the exorcist. They suspected her, then. A short time ago this would have given no concern to a woman of her common-sense. But she had a haunting reason to be superstitious now; and she had been seized with sudden dread that this Conjuror Trendle might name her as the malignant influence which was blasting the fair person of Gertrude,[14] and so lead her friend to hate her for ever, and to treat her as some fiend in human shape.

But all was not over. Two days after, a shadow intruded into the window-pattern thrown on Rhoda Brook's floor by the afternoon sun. The woman opened the door at once, almost breathlessly.

'Are you alone?' said Gertrude. She seemed to be no less harassed and anxious than Brook herself.

'Yes,' said Rhoda.

'The place on my arm seems worse, and troubles me!' the young farmer's wife went on. 'It is so mysterious! I do hope it will not be a permanent blemish. I have again been thinking of what they said about Conjuror Trendle. I don't really believe in such men, but I should not mind just visiting him, from curiosity – though on no account must my husband know. Is it far to where he lives?'

'Yes – five miles,' said Rhoda backwardly. 'In the heart of Egdon.'

'Well, I should have to walk. Could not you go with me to show me the way – say tomorrow afternoon?'

'Oh, not I – that is,' the milkwoman murmured, with a start of dismay. Again the dread seized her that something to do with her fierce act in the dream might be revealed, and her character in the eyes of the most useful friend she had ever had be ruined irretrievably.

Mrs Lodge urged, and Rhoda finally assented, though with much misgiving. Sad as the journey would be to her, she could not conscientiously stand in the way of a possible remedy for her patron's strange affliction. It was agreed that, to escape suspicion of their mystic intent, they should meet at the edge of the heath, at the corner of a plantation which was visible from the spot where they now stood.

V

Conjuror Trendle

By the next afternoon Rhoda would have done anything to escape this inquiry. But she had promised to go. Moreover, there was a horrid fascination at times in becoming instrumental in throwing such possible light on her own character as would reveal her to be something greater in the occult world than she had ever herself suspected.

She started just before the time of day mentioned between them, and half an hour's brisk walking brought her to the south-eastern extension of the Egdon tract of country, where the fir plantation was. A slight figure, cloaked and veiled, was already there. Rhoda recognized, almost with a shudder, that Mrs Lodge bore her left arm in a sling.

They hardly spoke to each other, and immediately set out on their climb into the interior of this solemn country, which stood high above the rich alluvial soil they had left half an hour before. It was a long walk; thick clouds made the atmosphere dark, though it was as yet only early afternoon; and the wind howled dismally over the hills of the heath – not improbably the same heath which had witnessed the agony of the Wessex King Ina, presented to after-ages as Lear.[15] Gertrude Lodge talked most, Rhoda replying with monosyllabic pre-occupation. She had a strange dislike to walking on the side of her companion where hung the afflicted arm, moving round to the other when inadvertently near it. Much heather had been brushed by their feet when they descended upon a cart-track, beside which stood the house of the man they sought.[16]

He did not profess his remedial practices openly, or care anything about their continuance, his direct interests being those of a dealer in furze, turf, 'sharp sand', and other local products. Indeed, he affected not to believe largely in his own powers, and when warts that had been shown him for cure miraculously disappeared – which it must be owned they infallibly did – he would say lightly, 'Oh, I only drink a glass of grog upon 'em – perhaps it's all chance,' and immediately turn the subject.

He was at home when they arrived, having in fact seen them descending into his valley. He was a grey-bearded man, with a reddish face, and he looked singularly at Rhoda the first moment he beheld her. Mrs Lodge told him her errand; and then with words of self-disparagement he examined her arm.

'Medicine can't cure it,' he said promptly. ' 'Tis the work of an enemy.'

Rhoda shrank into herself, and drew back.

'An enemy? What enemy?' asked Mrs Lodge.

He shook his head. 'That's best known to yourself,' he said. 'If you like I can show the person to you, though I shall not myself know who it is. I can do no more; and don't wish to do that.'

She pressed him; on which he told Rhoda to wait outside where she stood, and took Mrs Lodge into the room. It opened immediately from the door; and, as the latter remained ajar, Rhoda Brook could see the proceedings without taking part in them. He brought a tumbler from the dresser, nearly filled it with water, and fetching an egg, prepared it in some private way; after which he broke it on the edge of the glass, so that the white went in and the yolk remained. As it was getting gloomy, he took the glass and its contents to the window, and told Gertrude to watch them closely.[17] They leant over the table together, and the milkwoman could see the opaline hue of the egg-fluid changing form as it sank in the water, but she was not near enough to define the shape that it assumed.

'Do you catch the likeness of any face or figure as you look?' demanded the conjuror of the young woman.

She murmured a reply, in tones so low as to be inaudible to Rhoda, and continued to gaze intently into the glass. Rhoda turned, and walked a few steps away.

343

When Mrs Lodge came out, and her face was met by the light, it appeared exceedingly pale – as pale as Rhoda's – against the sad dun shades of the upland's garniture. Trendle shut the door behind her, and they at once started homeward together. But Rhoda perceived that her companion had quite changed.

'Did he charge much?' she asked tentatively.

'Oh no – nothing. He would not take a farthing,' said Gertrude.

'And what did you see?' inquired Rhoda.

'Nothing I – care to speak of.' The constraint in her manner was remarkable; her face was so rigid as to wear an oldened aspect, faintly suggestive of the face in Rhoda's bed-chamber.

'Was it you who first proposed coming here?' Mrs Lodge suddenly inquired, after a long pause. 'How very odd, if you did!'

'No. But I am not sorry we have come, all things considered,' she replied. For the first time a sense of triumph possessed her, and she did not altogether deplore that the young thing at her side should learn that their lives had been antagonized by other influences than their own.

The subject was no more alluded to during the long and dreary walk home. But in some way or other a story was whispered about the many-dairied Swenn valley that winter that Mrs Lodge's gradual loss of the use of her left arm was owing to her being 'overlooked'[18] by Rhoda Brook. The latter kept her own counsel about the incubus, but her face grew sadder and thinner; and in the spring she and her boy disappeared from the neighbourhood of Holmstoke.

VI

A second attempt

Half a dozen years passed away, and Mr and Mrs Lodge's married experience sank into prosiness, and worse. The farmer was usually gloomy and silent: the woman whom he had wooed for her grace and beauty was contorted and disfigured in the left limb; moreover, she had brought him no child, which rendered it likely that he would be the last of a family who had occupied that valley for some two hundred years. He thought of Rhoda Brook and her son; and feared this might be a judgement from heaven upon him.

The once blithe-hearted and enlightened Gertrude was changing into an irritable, superstitious woman, whose whole time was given to experimenting upon her ailment with every quack remedy she came across. She was honestly attached to her husband, and was ever secretly hoping against hope to win back his heart again by regaining some at least of her personal beauty. Hence it arose that her closet was lined with bottles, packets, and ointment-pots of every description – nay, bunches of mystic herbs, charms, and books of necromancy, which in her schoolgirl time she would have ridiculed as folly.

'Damned if you won't poison yourself with these apothecary messes and witch mixtures some time or other,' said her husband, when his eye chanced to fall upon the multitudinous array.

She did not reply, but turned her sad, soft glance upon him in such heart-swollen reproach that he looked sorry for his words, and added, 'I only meant it for your good, you know, Gertrude.'

'I'll clear out the whole lot, and destroy them,' said she huskily, 'and attempt such remedies no more!'

'You want somebody to cheer you,' he observed. 'I once thought of adopting a boy; but he is too old now. And he is gone away I don't know where.'

She guessed to whom he alluded; for Rhoda Brook's story had in the course of years become known to her; though not a word had ever passed between her husband and herself on the subject. Neither had she ever spoken to him of her visit to Conjuror Trendle, and of what was revealed to her, or she thought was revealed to her, by that solitary heath-man.

She was now five-and-twenty; but she seemed older. 'Six years of marriage, and only a few months of love,' she sometimes whispered to herself. And then she thought of the apparent cause, and said, with a tragic glance at her withering limb, 'If I could only again be as I was when he first saw me!'

She obediently destroyed her nostrums and charms; but there remained a hankering wish to try something else – some other sort of cure altogether. She had never revisited Trendle since she had been conducted to the house of the solitary by Rhoda against her will; but it now suddenly occurred to Gertrude that she would, in a last desperate effort at deliverance from this seeming curse, again seek out the man, if he yet lived. He was entitled to a certain credence, for the indistinct form he had raised in the glass had undoubtedly resembled the only woman in the world who – as she now knew, though not then – could have a reason for bearing her ill-will. The visit should be paid.

This time she went alone, though she nearly got lost on the heath, and roamed a considerable distance out of her way. Trendle's house was reached at last, however: he was not indoors, and instead of waiting at the cottage she went to where his bent figure was pointed out to her at work a long way off. Trendle remembered her, and laying down the handful of furze-roots which he was gathering and throwing into a heap, he offered to accompany her in her homeward direction, as the distance was considerable and the days were short. So they walked together, his head bowed nearly to the earth, and his form of a colour with it.

'You can send away warts and other excrescences, I know,' she said; 'why can't you send away this?' And the arm was uncovered.

'You think too much of my powers!' said Trendle; 'and I am old and weak now, too. No, no; it is too much for me to attempt in my own person. What have ye tried?'

She named to him some of the hundred medicaments and counterspells which she had adopted from time to time. He shook his head.

'Some were good enough,' he said approvingly; 'but not many of them for such as this. This is of the nature of a blight, not of the nature of a wound; and if you ever do throw it off, it will be all at once.'

'If I only could!'

'There is only one chance of doing it known to me. It has never failed in kindred afflictions, – that I can declare. But it is hard to carry out, and especially for a woman.'

'Tell me!' said she.

'You must touch with the limb the neck of a man who's been hanged.'

She started a little at the image he had raised.

'Before he's cold – just after he's cut down,' continued the conjuror impassively.

'How can that do good?'

'It will turn the blood and change the constitution.[19] But, as I say, to do it is hard. You must get into jail, and wait for him when he's brought off the gallows. Lots have done it, though perhaps not such pretty women as you. I used to send dozens for skin complaints. But that was in former times. The last I sent was in '13 – near twenty years ago.'[20]

He had no more to tell her; and, when he had put her into a straight track homeward, turned and left her, refusing all money as at first.

VII

A ride

The communication sank deep into Gertrude's mind. Her nature was rather a timid one; and probably of all remedies that the white wizard could have suggested there was not one which would have filled her with so much aversion as this, not to speak of the immense obstacles in the way of its adoption.

Casterbridge, the county-town, was a dozen or fifteen miles off; and though in those days, when men were executed for horse-stealing, arson, and burglary, an assize seldom passed without a hanging, it was not likely that she could get access to the body of the criminal unaided. And the fear of her husband's anger made her reluctant to breathe a word of Trendle's suggestion to him or to anybody about him.

She did nothing for months, and patiently bore her disfigurement as before. But her woman's nature, craving for renewed love, through the medium of renewed beauty (she was but twenty-five), was ever stimulating her to try what, at any rate, could hardly do her any harm. 'What came by a spell will go by a spell surely,' she would say. Whenever her imagination pictured the act she shrank in terror from the possibility of it: then the words of the conjuror, 'It will turn your blood,' were seen to be capable of a scientific no less than a ghastly interpretation; the mastering desire returned, and urged her on again.

There was at this time but one county paper, and that her husband only occasionally borrowed. But old-fashioned days had old-fashioned means, and news was extensively conveyed by word of mouth from market to market or from fair to fair; so that, whenever such an event as an execution was about to take place, few within a radius of twenty miles were ignorant of the coming sight; and, so far as Holmstoke was concerned, some enthusiasts had been known to walk all the way to Casterbridge and back in one day, solely to witness the spectacle. The next assizes were in March; and when Gertrude Lodge heard that they had been held, she inquired stealthily at the inn as to the result, as soon as she could find opportunity.

She was, however, too late. The time at which the sentences were to be carried out had arrived, and to make the journey and obtain admission at such short notice required at least her husband's assistance. She dared not tell him, for she had found by delicate experiment that these smouldering village beliefs made him furious if mentioned, partly because he half entertained them himself. It was therefore necessary to wait for another opportunity.

Her determination received a fillip from learning that two epileptic children had attended from this very village of Holmstoke many years before with beneficial results, though the experiment had been strongly condemned by the neighbouring clergy. April, May, June passed; and it is no overstatement to say that by the end of the last-named month Gertrude wellnigh longed for the death of a fellow-creature. Instead of her formal prayers each night, her unconscious prayer was, 'O Lord, hang some guilty or innocent person soon!'[21]

This time she made earlier inquiries, and was altogether more systematic in her proceedings. Moreover, the season was summer, between the haymaking and the harvest, and in the leisure thus afforded her husband had been holiday-taking away from home.

The assizes were in July, and she went to the inn as before. There was to be one execution – only one – for arson.

Her greatest problem was not how to get to Casterbridge, but what means she should adopt for obtaining admission to the jail. Though access for such purposes had formerly never been denied, the custom had fallen into desuetude; and in contemplating her possible difficulties, she was again almost driven to fall back upon her husband. But, on sounding him about the assizes, he was so uncommunicative, so more than usually cold, that she did not proceed, and decided that whatever she did she would do alone.

Fortune, obdurate hitherto, showed her unexpected favour. On the Thursday before the Saturday fixed for the execution, Lodge remarked to her that he was going away from home for another day or two on business at a fair, and that he was sorry he could not take her with him.

She exhibited on this occasion so much readiness to stay at home that he looked at her in surprise. Time had been when she would have shown deep disappointment at the loss of such a jaunt. However, he lapsed into his usual taciturnity, and on the day named left Holmstoke.

It was now her turn. She at first had thought of driving, but on reflection held that driving would not do, since it would necessitate her keeping to the turnpike-road, and so increase by tenfold the risk of her ghastly errand being found out. She decided to ride, and avoid the beaten track, notwithstanding that in her husband's stables there was no animal just at present which by any stretch of imagination could be considered a lady's mount, in spite of his promise before marriage to always keep a mare for her. He had, however, many horses, fine ones of their kind; and among the rest was a serviceable creature, an equine Amazon, with a back as broad as a sofa, on which Gertrude had occasionally taken an airing when unwell. This horse she chose.

On Friday afternoon one of the men brought it round. She was dressed, and before going down looked at her shrivelled arm. 'Ah!' she said to it, 'if it had not been for you this terrible ordeal would have been saved me!'

When strapping up the bundle in which she carried a few articles of clothing, she took occasion to say to the servant, 'I take these in case I should not get back tonight from the person I am going to visit. Don't be alarmed if I am not in by ten, and close up the house as usual. I shall be at home tomorrow for certain.' She meant then to privately tell her husband: the deed accomplished was not like the deed projected. He would almost certainly forgive her.

And then the pretty palpitating Gertrude Lodge went from her husband's homestead; but though her goal was Casterbridge she did not take the direct route thither through Stickleford. Her cunning course at first was in precisely the opposite direction. As soon as she was out of sight, however, she turned to the left, by a road which led into Egdon, and on entering the heath wheeled round, and set out in the true course, due westerly. A more private way down the county could not be imagined; and as to direction, she had merely to keep her horse's head to a point a little to the right of the sun. She knew that she would light upon a furze-cutter or cottager of some sort from time to time, from whom she might correct her bearing.

Though the date was comparatively recent, Egdon was much less fragmentary in character than now. The attempts – successful and otherwise – at cultivation on the lower slopes, which intrude and break up the original heath into small detached heaths, had not been carried far: Enclosure Acts had not taken effect,[22] and the banks and fences which now exclude the cattle of those villagers who formerly enjoyed rights of commonage thereon, and the carts of those who had turbary privileges which kept them in firing all the year round, were not erected. Gertrude therefore rode along with no other obstacles than the prickly furze-bushes, the mats of heather, the white water-courses, and the natural steeps and declivities of the ground.

Her horse was sure, if heavy-footed and slow, and though a draught animal, was easy-paced; had it been otherwise, she was not a woman who could have ventured to ride over such a bit of country with a half-dead arm. It was therefore nearly eight o'clock when she drew rein to breathe the mare on the last outlying high point of heath-land towards Casterbridge, previous to leaving Egdon for the cultivated valleys.

She halted before a pond,[23] flanked by the ends of two hedges; a railing ran through the centre of the pond, dividing it in half. Over the railing she saw the low green country; over the green trees the roofs of the town; over the roofs a white flat façade, denoting the entrance to the county jail. On the roof of this front specks were moving about; they seemed to be workmen erecting something. Her flesh crept. She descended slowly, and was soon amid corn-fields and pastures. In another half-hour, when it was almost dusk, Gertrude reached the White Hart, the first inn of the town on that side.

Little surprise was excited by her arrival: farmers' wives rode on horseback then more than they do now; though, for that matter, Mrs Lodge was not imagined to be a wife at all; the inn-keeper supposed her some harum-skarum young woman who had come to attend 'hang-fair'[24] next day. Neither her husband nor herself ever dealt in Casterbridge market, so that she was unknown. While dismounting she beheld a crowd of boys standing at the door of a harness-maker's shop just above the inn, looking inside it with deep interest.

'What is going on there?' she asked of the ostler.

'Making the rope for tomorrow.'

She throbbed responsively, and contracted her arm.

' 'Tis sold by the inch afterwards,' the man continued. 'I could get you a bit, miss, for nothing, if you'd like?'

She hastily repudiated any such wish, all the more from a curious creeping feeling that the condemned wretch's destiny was becoming interwoven with her own; and having engaged a room for the night, sat down to think.

Up to this time she had formed but the vaguest notions about her means of obtaining access to the prison. The words of the cunning-man returned to her mind. He had implied that she should use her beauty, impaired though it was, as a pass-key. In her inexperience she knew little about jail functionaries; she had heard of a high-sheriff and an under-sheriff, but dimly only. She knew, however, that there must be a hangman, and to the hangman she determined to apply.

VIII

A water-side hermit

At this date, and for several years after, there was a hangman to almost every jail. Gertrude found, on inquiry, that the Casterbridge official dwelt in a lonely cottage by a deep slow river flowing under the cliff on which the prison buildings were situate[25] – the stream being the self-same one, though she did not know it, which watered the Stickleford and Holmstoke meads lower down in its course.

Having changed her dress, and before she had eaten or drunk – for she could not take her ease till she had ascertained some particulars – Gertrude pursued her way by a path along the water-side to the cottage indicated. Passing thus the outskirts of the jail, she discerned on the level roof over the gateway three rectangular lines against the sky, where the specks had been moving in her distant view; she recognized what the erection was, and passed quickly on. Another hundred yards brought her to the executioner's house, which a boy pointed out. It stood close to the same stream, and was hard by a weir, the waters of which emitted a steady roar.

While she stood hesitating the door opened, and an old man came forth shading a candle with one hand. Locking the door on the outside, he turned to a flight of wooden steps fixed against the end of the cottage, and began to ascend them, this being evidently the staircase to his bedroom. Gertrude hastened forward, but by the time she reached the foot of the ladder he was at the top. She called to him loudly enough to be heard above the roar of the weir; he looked down and said, 'What d'ye want here?'

'To speak to you a minute.'

The candle-light, such as it was, fell upon her imploring, pale, upturned face, and Davies (as the hangman was called) backed down the ladder. 'I was just going to bed,' he said; ' "Early to bed and early to rise," but I don't mind stopping a minute for such a one as you. Come into house.' He reopened the door, and preceded her to the room within.

The implements of his daily work, which was that of a jobbing gardener, stood in a corner, and seeing probably that she looked rural, he said, 'If you want me to undertake country work I can't come, for I never leave Casterbridge for gentle nor simple – not I. Though sometimes I make others leave,' he added formally.[26]

'Yes, yes! That's it! Tomorrow!'

'Ah! I thought so. Well, what's the matter about that? 'Tis no use to come here about the knot – folks do come continually, but I tell 'em one knot is as merciful as another if ye keep it under the ear. Is the unfortunate man a relation; or, I should say, perhaps' (looking at her dress) 'a person who's been in your employ?'

'No. What time is the execution?'

'The same as usual – twelve o'clock, or as soon after as the London mail-coach gets in. We always wait for that, in case of a reprieve.'[27]

'Oh – a reprieve – I hope not!' she said involuntarily.

'Well, – he, he! – as a matter of business, so do I! But still, if ever a young fellow deserved to be let off, this one does; only just turned eighteen, and only present by chance when the rick was fired. Howsomever, there's not much risk of it, as they are obliged to make an example of him, there having been so much destruction of property that way lately.'

'I mean,' she explained, 'that I want to touch him for a charm, a cure of an affliction, by the advice of a man who has proved the virtue of the remedy.'

'Oh yes, miss! Now I understand. I've had such people come in past years. But it didn't strike me that you looked of a sort to require blood-turning. What's the complaint? The wrong kind for this, I'll be bound.'

'My arm.' She reluctantly showed the withered skin.

'Ah! – 'tis all a-scram!' said the hangman, examining it.

'Yes,' said she.

'Well,' he continued with interest, 'that *is* the class o' subject, I'm bound to admit! I like the look of the place; it is truly as suitable for the cure as any I ever saw. 'Twas a knowing-man that sent 'ee, whoever he was.'

'You can contrive for me all that's necessary?' she said breathlessly.

'You should really have gone to the governor of the jail, and your doctor with 'ee, and given your name and address – that's how it used to be done, if I recollect. Still, perhaps, I can manage it for a trifling fee.'

'Oh, thank you! I would rather do it this way, as I should like it kept private.'

'Lover not to know, eh?'

'No – husband.'

'Aha! Very well. I'll get 'ee a touch of the corpse.'

'Where is it now?' she said, shuddering.

'It? – *he*, you mean; he's living yet. Just inside that little small winder up there in the glum.' He signified the jail on the cliff above.

She thought of her husband and her friends. 'Yes, of course,' she said; 'and how am I to proceed?'

He took her to the door. 'Now, do you be waiting at the little wicket in the wall, that you'll find up there in the lane, not later than one o'clock. I will open it from the inside, as I shan't come home to dinner till he's cut down. Good night. Be punctual; and if you don't want anybody to know 'ee, wear a veil. Ah – once I had such a daughter as you!'

She went away, and climbed the path above, to assure herself that she would be able to find the wicket next day. Its outline was soon visible to her – a narrow opening in the outer wall of the prison precincts. The steep was so great that, having reached the wicket, she stopped a moment to breathe; and, looking back upon the water-side cot, saw the hangman again ascending his outdoor staircase. He entered the loft or chamber to which it led, and in a few minutes extinguished his light.

The town clock struck ten, and she returned to the White Hart as she had come.

IX

A rencounter

It was one o'clock on Saturday. Gertrude Lodge, having been admitted to the jail as above described, was sitting in a waiting-room within the second gate, which stood under a classic archway of ashlar, then comparatively modern, and bearing the inscription, 'COVNTY JAIL: 1793.' This had been the façade she saw from the heath the day before. Near at hand was a passage to the roof on which the gallows stood.

The town was thronged, and the market suspended; but Gertrude had seen scarcely a soul. Having kept her room till the hour of the appointment, she had proceeded to the spot by a way which avoided the open space below the cliff where the spectators had gathered; but she could, even now, hear the multitudinous babble of their voices, out of which rose at intervals the hoarse croak of a single voice, uttering the words, 'Last dying speech and confession!' There had been no reprieve, and the execution was over; but the crowd still waited to see the body taken down.

Soon the persistent girl heard a trampling overhead, then a hand beckoned to her, and, following directions, she went out and crossed the inner paved court beyond the gatehouse, her knees trembling so that she could scarcely walk. One of her arms was out of its sleeve, and only covered by her shawl.

On the spot at which she had now arrived were two trestles, and before she could think of their purpose she heard heavy feet descending stairs somewhere at her back. Turn her head she would not, or could not, and, rigid in this position, she was conscious of a rough coffin passing her shoulder, borne by four men. It was open, and in it lay the body of a young man, wearing the smockfrock of a rustic, and fustian breeches. It had been thrown into the coffin so hastily that the skirt of the smockfrock was hanging over. The burden was temporarily deposited on the trestles.

By this time the young woman's state was such that a grey mist seemed to float before her eyes, on account of which, and the veil she wore, she could scarcely discern anything: it was as though she had nearly died, but was held up by a sort of galvanism.

'Now,' said a voice close at hand, and she was just conscious that it had been addressed to her.

By a last strenuous effort she advanced, at the same time hearing persons approaching behind her. She bared her poor curst arm; and Davies, uncovering the face of the corpse,[28] took Gertrude's hand, and held it so that her arm lay across the dead man's neck, upon a line the colour of an unripe blackberry, which surrounded it.

Gertrude shrieked: 'the turn o' the blood,' predicted by the conjuror, had taken place. But at that moment a second shriek rent the air of the enclosure: it was not Gertrude's, and its effect upon her was to make her start round.

Immediately behind her stood Rhoda Brook, her face drawn, and her eyes red with weeping. Behind Rhoda stood her own husband; his countenance lined, his eyes dim, but without a tear.

'D——n you! what are you doing here?' he said hoarsely.

'Hussy – to come between us and our child now!' cried Rhoda. 'This is the meaning of what Satan showed me in the vision! You are like her at last!' And clutching the bare arm of the younger woman, she pulled her unresistingly back against the wall. Immediately Brook had loosened her hold the fragile young Gertrude slid down against the feet of her husband. When he lifted her up she was unconscious.

The mere sight of the twain had been enough to suggest to her that the dead young man was Rhoda's son. At that time the relatives of an executed convict had the privilege of claiming the body for burial, if they chose to do so; and it was for this purpose that Lodge was awaiting the inquest with Rhoda. He had been summoned by her as soon as the young man was taken in the crime, and at different times since; and he had attended in court during the trial. This was the 'holiday' he had been indulging in of late. The two wretched parents had wished to avoid exposure; and hence had come themselves for the body, a waggon and sheet for its conveyance and covering being in waiting outside.

Gertrude's case was so serious that it was deemed advisable to call to her the surgeon who was at hand. She was taken out of the jail into the town; but she never reached home alive. Her delicate vitality, sapped perhaps by the paralysed arm, collapsed under the double shock that followed the severe strain, physical and mental, to which she had subjected herself during the previous twenty-four hours. Her blood had been 'turned' indeed – too far. Her death took place in the town three days after.

Her husband was never seen in Casterbridge again; once only in the old market-place at Anglebury, which he had so much frequented, and very seldom in public anywhere. Burdened at first with moodiness and remorse, he eventually changed for the better, and appeared as a chastened and thoughtful man.[29] Soon after attending the funeral of his poor young wife he took steps towards giving up the farms in Holmstoke and the adjoining parish, and, having sold every head of his stock, he went away to Port-Bredy,[30] at the other end of the county, living there in solitary lodgings till his death two years later of a painless decline. It was then found that he had bequeathed the whole of his not inconsiderable property to a reformatory for boys, subject to the payment of a small annuity to Rhoda Brook, if she could be found to claim it.

For some time she could not be found; but eventually she reappeared in her old parish, – absolutely refusing, however, to have anything to do with the provision made for her. Her monotonous milking at the dairy was resumed, and followed for many long years, till her form became bent, and her once abundant dark hair white and worn away at the forehead – perhaps by long pressure against the cows. Here, sometimes, those who knew her experiences would stand and observe her, and wonder what sombre thoughts were beating inside that impassive, wrinkled brow, to the rhythm of the alternating milk-streams.

All biblical quotations are taken from the King James version of 1611.

'Destiny and a Blue Cloak'

1. *Maiden Newton ... Weymouth by train*: Maiden Newton is a village not far from Hardy's native Higher Bockhampton, Mellstock in the fiction (though Mellstock does not appear on the 1895–6 map, it is just east of Casterbridge). Weymouth is a seaside town, Budmouth Regis in the fictional Wessex, which appears often in Hardy's works as a place of excitement and temptation; it had become a well-known resort in the early nineteenth century as a result of frequent visits there by King George III and his court during the summer 'season'. While living there from summer 1869 to February 1870, Hardy began his first published novel, *Desperate Remedies*, which features key Weymouth scenes. Train service was extended to Weymouth in 1857 (David St John Thomas, *A Regional History of the Railways of Great Britain, Vol. I: The West Country* (1960; rev. edn., Newton Abbot: David & Charles, 1966), p. 136).

2. *Beaminster*: A small town in north-west Dorset, 'Emminster' in the fictional Wessex, the home of the Clare family in *Tess of the D'Urbervilles* (see 1895–6 map).

3. *Cloton village*: The only fictionally named place in the story; not on the 1895–6 map but thought to be based on Netherbury, just south of Beaminster (see above note). Kay-Robinson notes that Netherbury's old mill 'conforms to the description of "Cloton" mill. The stream does form the boundary of a garden, orchard, and paddock, and does separate the property from the "village high-road". "Heavy-headed" trees still grow near. Only the "little wooden bridge" in its swampy surroundings cannot be found; but there is a stone bridge beside the house' (p. 115).

4. *the true Helen*: In Greek myth, the beautiful daughter of Leda by Zeus and wife of King Menelaus of Sparta. One tradition, going back to the sixth century BC and upon which Euripides based one of his tragedies, has Helen residing safely in Egypt while Zeus and Hera send a phantom resembling her with Paris to Troy, thus causing the Trojan War.

5. *Portland*: A large island, attached to the mainland of Dorset only by a thin causeway, jutting out south-west of Weymouth harbour; Hardy made frequent visits to cousins there during his stay in Weymouth. Fictionalized as the Isle of Slingers, it is the main setting for *The Well-Beloved* (1897). The 1895–6 map uses the actual name 'Portland'.

6. *She altered her mind about staying at Beaminster*: As Pamela Dalziel points out in *The Excluded and Collaborative Stories* ((Oxford: Clarendon, 1992), p. 372), Hardy probably meant Maiden Newton: Frances Lovill had travelled that morning as far as Maiden Newton with Agatha Pollin, and the van carrying all three back to Beaminster left from there.

7. *Macaulay*: Thomas Babington Macaulay (1800–59), Member of Parliament, historian, essayist. In his speech supporting the 1833 bill to renew the charter of the East India Company, Macaulay urged that the British Civil Service in India abolish patronage and choose its members by competitive examination, but the idea did not become law until the 1853 Charter Act, which he strongly supported (*DNB*). Macaulay's emphasis was not, like Winwood's, on the issue of equal opportunity for young British men, but on the usefulness for English imperialist interests, in an anticipated relationship of competition with educated Indians, of the elimination of patronage.

8. *Such a case occurs sometimes, and it occurred then*: Based on Hooper Tolbort, who 'took first place, nationally, in the Oxford Middle Class (or Local) Examinations of 1859 and, three years later, in the competitive examinations for entry into the Indian Civil Service' (*Biography*, 70). He became Deputy Commissioner in the Bengal Civil Service and is mentioned by Hardy as one of his three 'literary friends in Dorchester' during his architectural apprenticeship, whose name 'appeared in *The Times* at the head of the Indian examination list, a wide proportion of marks separating it from the name following. It was in the early days when these lists excited great interest' (*Life*, 37, 168). Tolbort published transliterations of works in Persian and Urdu. Millgate notes that in Winwood's speech above the 'optimistic note of the mid-nineteenth-century success ethic . . . can be heard, although it is perhaps characteristic of Hardy that in the story the passage should be humorously undercut by Winwood's inability to explain what he means by the word "bureaucratic" '. Millgate suggests that this 'wryness in Hardy's story' may have resulted from Hardy's feeling himself during those early years 'very much in the shadow of Tolbort's brilliance' (*Biography*, 71).

9. *Bess its deary-eary heart! it is going to speak to me*: This baby-talk anticipates the sadistic style of address used by Lord Uplandtowers toward his young wife in the 1891 story 'Barbara of the House of Grebe'.

10. *to go to Australia*: Free emigration to Australia (in contrast to the transporta-

tion of convicts) grew considerably after the economic decline in Britain during the late 1840s and the Australian gold rush of the early 1850s; emigration was encouraged by the writings of Charles Dickens, Samuel Solomon (whose pseudonym was Samuel Sidney) and Harriet Martineau. Queensland, where Pollin intends to settle, expanded rapidly after it became a separate colony in 1859, quadrupling its non-Aboriginal population between 1861 and 1871 (Robert Hughes, *The Fatal Shore* (New York: Knopf, 1987), pp. 554–60, 579–80). Hardy's story takes place after the death of Macaulay (Winwood refers to his 'honoured memory') in 1859, and if Winwood's success is contemporaneous with that of Tolbert in 1862, it is now a few years later.

11. *Mr Davids*: Pamela Dalziel suggests that the parson is 'appropriately named in view of the biblical David's unscrupulousness in obtaining Bathsheba' ('Hapless "Destiny": an uncollected story of marginalized lives', *Thomas Hardy Journal* 8 (1992), 46). After seeing Bathsheba bathing, David sleeps with her, arranges to have her husband killed in battle and then marries her; he is punished by the death of their child (2 Samuel 11–12).

12. *who fears God and keeps the commandments*: 'Fear God, and keep his commandments; for this is the whole duty of man' (Ecclesiastes 12.13).

13. *Tell him you'll marry him . . . before that time*: This qualified promise recalls that of Bathsheba Everdene to Boldwood in *Far From the Madding Crowd*. Lovill is like Boldwood in preparing his house for the impending marriage even before it is definite.

14. *a hornpipe*: In the early 1860s, a hornpipe was considered an old-fashioned rustic dance. Hardy recalled in the *Life* that his father 'was good, too, when young, at hornpipes and jigs, and other folk-dances, performing them with all the old movements of leg-crossing and hop, to the delight of the children, till warned by his wife that this fast perishing style might tend to teach them what it was not quite necessary they should be familiar with, the more genteel "country-dance" having superseded the former' (p. 18).

'The Thieves Who Couldn't Help Sneezing'

1. *Vale of Blackmore*: 'Blackmoor Vale' on 1895–6 map; thickly wooded and secluded area north of High Stoy, the setting for 'Interlopers at the Knap' and *The Woodlanders*; birthplace of Tess Durbeyfield.

2. *Can you call up spirits from the vasty deep, young wizard*: In William Shakespeare's *1 Henry IV*, Glendower earnestly tells Hotspur: 'I can call spirits from the vasty deep' (III.i.52). The Baronet imitates the condescending tone of Hotspur, who responds to Glendower's hyperbolic claims with amused scorn. However,

Hubert's ironic reply describes an action that he does carry out. Thus Hubert dissociates himself from the superstitious Glendower and whimsically lays claim to the sort of preternatural power actually possessed by Prospero, who in Shakespeare's *The Tempest* creates a storm in which the elements seem to be battling each other: 'The sky it seems would pour down stinking pitch, / But that the sea, mounting to th' welkin's cheek, / Dashes the fire out' (I.ii.3–5).

3. *trick of throwing the voice – called, I believe, ventriloquism*: The earliest example of this usage for 'ventriloquism' is dated 1737 (which may help to date the story); earlier uses alluded to the phenomenon in witchcraft of speaking from the belly (*OED 2*).

4. *the best scented Scotch*: Scotch snuff is a dry and fine powder (*OED 2*). During the eighteenth century, because the pipe was becoming popular among the lower classes, snuff became the chief choice among the upper classes: see Introduction, p. xxi.

5. *which had been occupied by Queen Elizabeth and King Charles successively*: Elizabeth I reigned 1558–1603 and Charles I 1625–49 (James I came between them). No actual house is known to fit this description, nor is the story precise about its historical setting, except to suggest, with the detail of 'snuff-boxes which were then becoming common', that the time is the eighteenth century (see also note 3 above).

'The Distracted Preacher'

1. *The Distracted Preacher*: 1879 *HW* and 1879 *NQM* have 'The Distracted Young Preacher' (1879 *NQM* has the title in italics).

2. *the Wesleyan minister*: Dating back to the evangelical work of John Wesley inside the Anglican church during the eighteenth century, Wesleyan Methodism had become by the 1830s a separate sect. It appealed to the working classes in the industrial North, but also had influence, as David Hempton has noted, 'in seaports and fishing villages, and in rural areas where squire and parson control was weak' (*Methodism and Politics in British Society 1750–1850* (Stanford: Stanford University Press, 1984), pp. 14–15). The existence of 'trimmers' was also not uncommon (see Valerie Cunningham, *Everywhere Spoken Against: Dissent in the Victorian Novel* (Oxford: Clarendon, 1975), p. 107). Committed to services in a chapel, Methodists favoured the New Testament, with its emphasis on conversion (note that Stockdale quotes the gospels and Paul's letters), and plain ceremonies, including the singing of hymns (hence the references to the denial by Methodists of tutelary saints, their disinclination to use church bells, and Stockdale's confusion over hymns). The law-abiding Stockdale, who anticipates a genteel and stable livelihood after his probation period, represents Wesleyan Methodism when it had become associated with a respectable, teetotal middle class and was often a force of political conservatism. His thoughts about becoming a missionary abroad are also typical; the first Methodist Missionary Society had been founded in 1813.

3. *183–*: 1879 *HW* has '1835'. The time is that of Hardy's oral sources: in 1889, he wrote that 'I have known several [persons], now dead, who shared in the adventurous doings along that part of the coast fifty or sixty years ago' (*Collected Letters*, I, 204). Martin Ray speculates that James Selby, of Broadmayne, Dorset, was one of Hardy's sources and that the story's events are loosely based on the 1830 trial of three smugglers – one of whom was Selby's brother-in-law, James Hewlett – who had attacked a customs officer at Dagger's Grave (p. 56). A few years after 'The Distracted Preacher' was published, Hardy copied down in his 'Facts' Notebook (ff. 163–[166]) the *Dorset County Chronicle* account of the trial. According to Millgate, Hardy also heard smuggling stories from George Nicholls, who 'served as a coast-guard until the late 1850s' and who, with his daughter Eliza, became 'major sources for Hardy's interest in the south Dorset coast and its lively smuggling past' (*Biography*, 84, 85); see 'Fellow-Townsmen', note 13. Small-scale smuggling on the south coast, using luggers rather than armed cutters, was on the increase during the 1830s, just as the Coast Guard was becoming similar to a military force. By the middle of the nineteenth century, the smuggling activity had generally been suppressed.

4. *Nether Mynton*: Not on the 1895–6 map, but six miles southeast of Casterbridge near the seacoast east of Budmouth. 1896 *WT* changes the name to 'Nether Moynton'; the original is Owermoigne, which, according to Lea in 1913, 'was once the home of many a smuggler, and some of the old people living there now can remember taking part in smuggling enterprises' (p. 159). According to Kay-Robinson, '[t]here was never a Methodist chapel in Owermoigne, but up a narrow gravel track on the other side of Holland's Mead Avenue stands an ancient stone thatched house, Chilbury Cottage, where Methodist services were held during the last century' (p. 141).

5. *or when there was a tea*: The tea-meeting was a trademark of Victorian Dissenters; Cunningham calls it a 'diluted version of the Methodist Love-Feast' (*Everywhere Spoken Against*, p. 13).

6. *come*: 'floated' in 1912 *WT*, thus increasing Lizzie's precision and irony.

7. *burning strong*: 1896 *WT* has ' 'nation strong', thus making Lizzy's language more crude.

8. *from which she took mouthfuls . . . lips to the hole*: 1879 *HW* and 1879 *NQM* have 'which she poured on the hole'; the revision is more plausible and suggestive. At various stages of revision, Hardy made Lizzie increasingly unorthodox: in 1879 *HW*, probably earlier than 1879 *NQM*, Lizzie is more naive and seems less emotionally involved in the smuggling.

9. *my cousin Owlett*: The words 'my cousin' did not appear in 1879 *HW* or 1879 *NQM*; this and other changes for 1888 *WT* make Owlett less of a sexual rival. This trend continued in 1912 *WT*, where Lizzie calls him 'Mr Owlett' instead of 'Owlett' (p. 64 and elsewhere). Owlett appears to have been based on James Hewlett (see note 3 and 'owl's light', p. 412). Kathryn King suggests that 'Owlett' combines 'Hewlett' with 'owler', a colloquial term for a smuggler (cited in Ray, 56-7).

10. *exciseman*: 1912 *WT* changes to 'Customs-men' and thereafter replaces 'exciseman' with 'Customs-man' or 'preventive-man'. Hardy wrote to T. H. Tilley in 1911 that these officials 'were not called excisemen' (*Collected Letters*, IV, 186), which is corroborated by *OED 2*, which has examples for 'exciseman' chiefly from the seventeenth and eighteenth centuries, while those for 'preventive-men' span 1827 to 1884.

11. *loud enough to rouse the Seven Sleepers*: A Syrian legend popularized in western literature by Gregory of Tours and Edward Gibbon's third volume of *The History of the Decline and Fall of the Roman Empire* (1781), according to which seven Christian youths of Ephesus hid in a cave during the Decian persecution of AD 250; almost two hundred years later they awoke to find Christianity openly proclaimed.

12. *Already he often said Romans for Corinthians in the pulpit*: Paul's letters to the Romans (on love) and to the Corinthians (on law and punishment).

13. *breeches*: 1879 *HW* and 1879 *NQM* have 'leggings'; the change from these, which cover the ankle to the knee, to 'breeches', which cover the loins and thighs, adds to the sexual connotations of the image and may indirectly invoke the phrase, said of a wife, 'to wear the breeches', that is, to assume the authority of the husband, to rule or to be master – an idea already suggested in the previous paragraph. On p. 59, 'and breeches' does not appear in 1879 *HW* and 1879 *NQM*; 1888 *WT* also added, in the same paragraph, 'which is no harm, as he was my own husband', and 'it is only tucked in' – which again emphasize the sexual suggestiveness of Lizzy's wearing breeches. Hardy also explores the erotic effect of a woman wearing men's clothes in *Jude the Obscure*.

14. *Knollsea*: 1879 *HW* and 1879 *NQM* have 'Swanage', the actual name of the original location, for the fictional 'Knollsea', a seaside village (see 1895– 6 map) also featured in *The Hand of Ethelberta*, a novel Hardy completed in 1876 while boarding there; his landlord was 'an invalided captain of smacks and ketches' who told him 'strange stories of his sea-farings; mostly smuggling stories' (*Life*, 110). At this stage in his career, Hardy seems to have used actual names for narratives that were closely linked to historical events (see Gatrell, 122–3).

15. *Ringsworth . . . Holworth*: 1879 *HW* and 1879 *NQM* have 'Ringstead', an actual place on the sea east of Weymouth from whose summit one can obtain 'a fine bird's-eye view of the country to the north, east, and west' (Lea, 160). Hardy retained the actual name of Holworth. None of these names appears on the 1895–6 map, but they are just east of Budmouth.

16. *Cherbourg*: On the French coast, source for contraband liquor.

17. *were always*: 'had been' in 1879 *HW* and 1879 *NQM*; the revision gives the sense of an ongoing rather than a singular plan.

18. *Lullstead*: 'Lulworth' in 1879 *HW* and 1879 *NQM* and 'Lulwind Cove' in 1912 *WT*; the actual place, just east of Weymouth, is Lulworth Cove, and the Wessex 'Lulwind Cove' (not on the 1895–6 map, but east of Budmouth) is the place where Troy is thought to have drowned in *Far From the Madding Crowd*. 'Lulstead Cove' also appears in *Desperate Remedies*.

19. *Render unto Caesar the things that are Caesar's*: Matthew 22.21; Mark 12.17; Luke 20.25; Christ's answer to the Pharisees about the paying of tax.

20. *If I had only stuck to father's little grocery business, instead of going in for the ministry*: This reveals Stockdale's affiliation with the lower echelons of the merchant class and the difference between a Methodist preacher, who could emerge from the lower-middle classes, and an Anglican minister, who would come from a higher class.

21. *Everybody does who tries it*: 'do' in 1879 *NQM*, but not 1879 *HW*; in this and other instances, Lizzie's use of dialect is strongest in 1879 *NQM*.

22. *Lord's Barrow . . . Chaldon Down*: 'Chaldon' was changed to 'Shaldon' in 1912 *WT*; the original is Chaldon Herring. According to Kay-Robinson, 'Hardy says that the travellers reached Chaldon Down, and then a ravine on the outskirts of "Chaldon". In fact, both Chaldons and the ravine linking them lie between Lord's Barrow and the down, so that Lizzie and the preacher must have come to them in the reverse order' (p. 141). None of these places appears on the 1895–6 map, but they lie near the coast east of Budmouth.

23. *quiet and inoffensive persons*: 1912 *WT* adds 'even though some held heavy sticks' and substitutes in the subsequent paragraph 'Dagger's Grave, near Lulwind Cove' for 'Lullstead', thus emphasizing the violence that could accompany the smuggling, as well as the story's connection with the history of James Hewlett (see note 3).

24. *masons*: 'shoemakers' in 1896 *WT*, perhaps to remove a reference to Hardy's father and to suggest his uncle (see note 31).

25. *an iron bar, which he drove firmly into the soil*: Kay-Robinson notes that by 'the foot of a coomb between White Nothe and Durdle Door there is still to be seen an old wire rope, put in place by fishermen or smugglers, no one knows when, to give access to the beach' (p. 141).

26. *carrying a pair of tubs, one on his back and one on his chest*: Hardy's preface to 1896 *WT*, revised and supplemented in 1912, describes this practice and others; it is worth quoting at length:

Among the many devices for concealing smuggled goods in caves and pits of the earth, that of planting an apple-tree in a tray or box which was placed over the mouth of the pit is, I believe, unique, and it is detailed in 'The Distracted Preacher' precisely as described by an old carrier of 'tubs' – a man who was afterwards in my father's employ for over thirty years. I never gathered from his reminiscences what means were adopted for lifting the tree, which, with its roots, earth, and receptacle, must have been of considerable weight. There is no doubt, however, that the thing was done through many years. My informant often spoke, too, of the horribly suffocating sensation produced by the pair of spirit-tubs slung upon the chest and back, after stumbling with the burden of them for several miles inland over a rough-country and in darkness. He said that though years of his youth and young manhood were spent in this irregular business, his profits from the same, taken all together, did not average the wages he might have earned in a steady employment, whilst the fatigues and risks were excessive.

I may add that the action of this story is founded on certain smuggling exploits that occurred between 1825 and 1830, and were brought to a close in the latter year by the trial of the chief actors at the Assizes before Baron Bolland for their desperate armed resistance to the Custom-house officers during the landing of a cargo of spirits. This happened only a little time after the doings recorded in the narrative, in which some incidents that came out at the trial are also embodied.

In the culminating affray the character called Owlett was badly wounded, and several of the Preventive-men would have lost their lives through being overpowered by the far more numerous body of smugglers, but for the forbearance and manly conduct of the latter. This served them in good stead at their trial, in which the younger Erskine prosecuted, their defence being entrusted to Erle. Baron Bolland's summing up was strongly in their favour, they were merely ordered to enter into their own recognizances for good behaviour and discharged.

This account repeats what Hardy had copied into his 'Facts' Notebook; the carrier of the tubs was presumably James Selby (see notes 3, 9 and 23).

27. *seed*: 'zeed' in 1896 *WT*, thus further emphasizing Owlett's rural roots.

28. *Latimer*: Hardy wrote in 1911 to Edwin Stevens, who performed the role of Latimer for a dramatic version, that 'the character of the Customs-Officer . . .

is given under his real name of Latimer, as told me forty years ago by one of the smugglers in his old age. I believe that I am correct in stating that the Latimer buried in Osmington Churchyard, whose headstone you can see there any day, was the same man, though I have no actual proof of it' (*Collected Letters*, IV, 190). Millgate indicates, however, that the name 'is not visible there now, nor has Latimer's name been traced in the parish registers' (*Biography*, 191).

29. *consecrated bells*: Protestant dissenters did not believe in the blessing of objects and did not use church bells to adorn their services.

30. *Warm'll*: Presumably 'Warmwell Cross' or 'the Cross', featured in Part VII; not on the 1895–6 map, but a point west of Nether Mynton where the roads to Budmouth and Casterbridge part; Lea shows a picture of the 'clumps of trees' at Warmwell Cross, where 'it does not require a very vivid imagination . . . to see in fancy the disappointed excisemen bound to the trees and shouting for help, a performance said to have been really enacted in the eighteen-thirties' (p. 162).

31. *Ballam's*: 'Artnell's' in 1912 *WT*; cf. Hardy's uncle by marriage, John Antell, a shoemaker with intellectual aspirations who may have served as an original for the characterization of Jude Fawley (*Biography*, 347–8). Antell had died in December 1878, not long before Hardy wrote 'The Distracted Preacher'. Ray surmises that 'Hardy made a private association between smuggling liquor and his uncle's alcoholism' (64).

32. *curls a foot long, dangling down the sides of her face, in the fashion of the time*: After 1794, according to the Countess of Wilton in 1846, 'the hair was worn in curls, which were sometimes short, at others long and straggling, falling completely over the face, so that the bright orbs beneath could with difficulty peep out from the ringlets which almost entirely concealed them' (*The Book of Costume: Or Annals of Fashion (1846) by A Lady of Rank*, ed. Pieter Bach (Mendocino, CA: R. L. Shep, 1987), p. 173).

33. *with sadness*: 'with a sigh' in 1879 *HW* and 1879 *NQM*.

34. *swept the streets*: 'scraped the roads' in 1912 *WT*.

35. *trembling*: 'moved' in 1912 *WT*.

36. *with his elbow on the mantelpiece*: Hardy appears to have associated this posture with a person who feels misled or betrayed. His poem 'Standing by the Mantelpiece (H. M. M., 1873)' (1928) – presumably spoken by Horace Moule, his friend who committed suicide in 1873 – is addressed to a lover who has broken off a sexual relationship (see *Biography*, 156).

37. *Come and hear my last sermon on the day before I go*: Possibly an ironic reference to the Rev. Dimmesdale in Nathaniel Hawthorne's *The Scarlet Letter* (1850), another fastidious clergyman who has a forbidden sexual alliance; Dimmesdale gives a final sermon before revealing his identity as an adulterer and the father of an illegitimate child. Hardy had read Hawthorne and made several references to his work.

38. *a midland town*: Signifies that Stockdale has returned 'inland' to the Midlands, an industrial centre.

39. *Bere*: 1896 *WT* has 'Kingsbere' (see 1895–6 map), the Wessex name for Bere Regis, perhaps an oblique allusion to the notorious Tolpuddle martyrs, some of whom came from Bere Regis, who were transported for attempting in 1834 to form a trade union.

40. *able to get about*: 1912 *WT* adds 'Then he was caught, and tried with the others at the assizes; but they all got off.'

41. *their married life*: 1912 *WT* adds the following note:

The ending of this story with the marriage of Lizzy and the minister was almost *de rigueur* in an English magazine at the time of writing. But at this late date, thirty years after, it may not be amiss to give the ending that would have been preferred by the writer to the convention used above. Moreover it corresponds more closely with the true incidents of which the tale is a vague and flickering shadow. Lizzy did not, in fact, marry the minister, but – much to her credit in the author's opinion – stuck to Jim the smuggler, and emigrated with him after their marriage, an expatrial step rather forced upon him by his adventurous antecedents. They both died in Wisconsin between 1850 and 1860.

'Fellow-Townsmen'

1. *But the community . . . and a staple manufacture*: Hardy wrote to Walter Tyndale in 1904, 'Bridport (town & harbour both) is the entire scene of "Fellow Townsmen" ' (*Collected Letters*, III, 147). The town of Bridport (Port Bredy on the 1895–6 map) is west of Weymouth ('Budmouth') on the Dorset coast and has been known since the thirteenth century for its manufacture of rope, twine and nets, originally made with flax grown in the area nearby (Barnet's father was a flax-merchant). Under Henry VIII, according to Lea, 'it was prescribed by royal edict that all the cordage used in the royal navy should be of Bridport manufacture', and the town was later known for its production of hangmen's ropes, from which came the saying 'that So-and-So had been "stabbed with a Bridport dagger" – a polite way of intimating that he had been hanged' (p. 155).

2. *five-and-thirty years ago*: Since first publication was in 1880, the setting for the opening presumably would be about 1845.

3. *a pedestrian . . . overtaken by a phaeton*: This meeting between Downe and Barnet was added for 1888 *WT*. In 1880 *HW* and 1880 *NQM*, Barnet leaves his fashionable house, after slamming the door, and then walks towards Downe's house, where he meets Downe with his wife and daughters.

4. *Château Ringdale*: In 1880 *HW* and 1880 *NQM* this is 'Château Kingdale'; Kay-Robinson notes that ' "Château Ringdale" certainly never existed, but its site is real, and on it there was once a mansion of comparable importance. This was Wanderwell, and it stood on a rise just as did Château Ringdale; even the elm-trees really existed, and the only discrepancy is the Bridport road passes to the west of the rise, not the east' (p. 118). Ray speculates that 'Ringdale' and 'Kingdale' are 'partly' based on 'Knapdale', Alexander Macmillan's house (p. 48 n). The Hardys visited the publisher in 1878, when they also lived in Upper Tooting (*Life*, 124–5), and 'Fellow-Townsmen' was probably written there in 1880.

5. *Black-Bull Hotel*: 1880 *HW* and 1880 *NQM* call it 'Black Swan Hotel'; it is based on Bridport's Bull Hotel (Kay-Robinson, 120).

6. *To preserve peace in the household. I do anything for that; but I don't succeed*: In his relationship with his wife, Barnet has affinities with the speaker of Robert Browning's 'Andrea del Sarto' (1855).

7. *If you only knew everything*: 1880 *HW* and 1880 *NQM* read 'If you had only witnessed what I witnessed this evening'. The revisions make the unhappiness in Barnet's marriage an ongoing process rather than the result of a single discovery.

8. *and he fell upon his knees in the gutter*: 1880 *HW* and 1880 *NQM* locate this scene inside Downe's house and show the lawyer reopening a wound in his infected thumb.

9. *presently sat down to his lonely meal*: 1880 *HW* and 1880 *NQM* do not include this scene.

10. *the Raffaelesque oval of its contour*: In the style of the Renaissance painter Raphael (1483–1520), many of whose portraits feature women with oval faces; since Raphael often painted the Madonna, the image might also be seen to suggest Lucy's virtue.

11. *seeing how often I have held it in past days*: 1880 *HW* and 1880 *NQM* have 'as an old acquaintance' and Lucy's reply is 'I have no right to look upon you in that light.' Similarly Lucy's reproach to Barnet in 1880 *NQM* was for 'ask[ing] such a thing' as to hold her hand. Four paragraphs later, Barnet's reply to the enquiry about Mrs Barnet had been 'For God's sake, don't let us talk of her – for a few minutes at least.'

12. *not to mince matters, to visit a woman I loved. Don't be angry*: Added for 1888 *WT*, as was the phrase, a few sentences later, 'and thought what might have been in my case'.

13. *Miss Savile*: The characterization of Lucy Savile may be broadly based on

Hardy's early relationship, possibly an engagement between 1863 and 1867, with Eliza Bright Nicholls (for details, see *Biography*, 84–5). All of Hardy's works during this period, including 'The Distracted Preacher' and *The Trumpet-Major*, were set on the south Dorset coast, not far from the coast-guard cottages where Eliza lived with her father, George Nicholls, and some of the incidents in 'The Distracted Preacher' derived from his stories. There are many oblique connections between the Hardy/Eliza and the Barnet/Lucy relationship: in both, the woman was forsaken by the man, after which he felt a sense of lost happiness; Eliza's father worked for the coast-guard, while Lucy's was a lieutenant in the navy; 'Savile', read backwards, could be a rough acronym for 'Eliza'; the date of the story's conclusion, 1866 or 1867, is roughly the date of the termination of the relationship between Hardy and Eliza. If the parallel was a recognizable one for Eliza, she may have been responding to the plot of 'Fellow-Townsmen' when she visited Hardy in 1913 after the death of his first wife (see *Biography*, 494). Kathryn King has also suggested that 'Savile' may be a reference to Kegan Paul, editor of the *New Quarterly Magazine*, who helped Hardy in 1878 to secure membership in the exclusive Savile Club (cited in Ray, 42).

14. *Everything was so indefinite . . . said nothing*: This passage had read in 1880 *HW* and 1880 *NQM*: 'You had made me no promises, and I did not feel that you had broken any, nor have I ever accused you of doing so to anybody. I should, indeed, be weak and foolish if I were to accuse you of doing wrong because you saw some woman more after your own heart than I was, and, feeling her more capable than myself of making you happy, married her.' Another speech by Lucy, deleted after the serializations, emphasizes the class differences between the two women, but makes Lucy uncharacteristically bold and insinuating: 'Don't you think you may have offered provocation on your side? Perhaps you may have said in a moment of haste that you married her only for what she possessed, or some such thing? – and nothing would exasperate a woman more than that.'

15. *It is a very common folly of human nature, you know, to think the course you did* not *adopt must have been the best*: Lennart A. Björk links this passage to a quotation in the literary notes from William Shenstone's *Essays on Men and Manners*, printed in Sir Arthur Helps's *Essays Written in the Intervals of Business* (1841): 'We find the scheme which we have chosen answers our expectations but indifferently . . . We therefore repent of our choice, & immediately fancy happiness in the paths which we decline . . . It is not improbable we had been more unhappy . . . had we made a different decision' (*Literary Notebooks*, I, 101).

16. *But I shall never again meet with such a dear girl as you*: 1880 *HW* and 1880 *NQM* have 'Heaven bless you for a dear girl!'

17. *Not poppy nor mandragora*: From Shakespeare's *Othello*; Iago has planted the seeds of jealousy in Othello's mind:

> Not poppy, nor mandragora,
> Nor all the drowsy syrups of the world
> Shall ever medicine thee to that sweet sleep
> Which thou ow'dst yesterday. (III.iii.330–33)

18. *his handsome Xantippe*: The shrewish wife of Socrates.

19. *that* politesse du coeur *which was so natural to her having possibly begun already to work results*: Emily Downe's gestures of kindness are reminiscent of those of Dorothea Brooke in George Eliot's *Middlemarch* (1871–2), especially her attempts to help the cold-hearted and worldly Rosamond Lydgate. See also note 23 below.

20. *like the Libyan bay which sheltered the ship-wrecked Trojans*: In Book I of the *Aeneid*, Aeneas and his comrades escape from a storm to a safe harbour on the Libyan coast, where they are welcomed by Dido, Queen of Carthage; he becomes her lover, but then abandons her for his epic mission.

21. *Her complexion was that seen in the numerous faded portraits by Sir Joshua Reynolds*: Reynolds (1723–92) was President of the Royal Academy from its founding in 1768; typical of paintings from the eighteenth century when women wore powder, the women in his portraits have pale complexions; the images may also be faded because the paint has lost some colour.

22. *an octavo volume of Domestic Medicine*: There are several books entitled *Domestic Medicine*, the best known of which was William Buchan's (1769), which ran to scores of editions and many translations. Buchan emphasized the need for persistence in the treatment of drowning victims, but the quoted passage has not been found; it is possible that Hardy composed it to fit his story, including its ironic parallel with Shakespeare's *Pericles*, in which Thaisa, a beloved wife, is restored to life after being washed ashore in a coffin; Cerimon, the doctor who revives her, observes:

> Death may usurp on nature many hours,
> And yet the fire of life kindle again
> The o'erpressed spirits. (III.ii.84–6)

23. *by merely doing nothing . . . a deliverance for himself as he had never hoped for*: Barnet's situation parallels that of Nicholas Bulstrode in Eliot's *Middlemarch* when the Charlson-like Raffles, who has been blackmailing him, lies ill in his house; Bulstrode succumbs to the temptation of allowing a servant to give Raffles an amount of liquor that he knows might kill him.

24. *Nothing less will do justice to my feelings, and how far short of them that will fall*:

Downe's behaviour recalls Charles Bovary's absurdly extravagant plans for his wife's coffin and tomb in Gustave Flaubert's *Madame Bovary* (1857).

25. *something like an inherited instinct*: As his reading of Darwin, Huxley and others makes clear, Hardy had an ongoing interest in ideas about biological inheritance.

26. *there being at this date no railway within a distance of eighty miles*: The train did not come as far as Bridport until 1857, when it was also extended to Weymouth ('Budmouth'), presumably the 'junction' in section IX (Thomas, *A Regional History of the Railways of Great Britain, Vol. I: The West Country*, pp. 148, 141).

27. *Lucy's new silk dress sweeping with a smart rustle round the base-mouldings of the ancient font*: Recalls Hardy's memory of Julia Augusta Martin as 'the lady he had so admired as a child, when she was the grand dame of the parish in which he was born': 'she revived throbs of tender feeling in him, and brought back to his memory the thrilling "frou-frou" of her four grey silk flounces when she had used to bend over him, and when they brushed against the font as she entered church on Sundays' (*Life*, 104–5). A similar image is used in 'The Withered Arm'. All three instances describe erotic desire for an inaccessible woman.

28. *Barnet's old house was bought by the trustees of the Congregational Baptist body in that town, who pulled down the time-honoured dwelling and built a new chapel on its site*: Kay-Robinson notes that this house was not on South Street, 'but where the Congregational church, built in 1860, stands today, in East Street' (p. 119).

29. *while the church had had such a tremendous practical joke played upon it by some facetious restorer or other as to be scarce recognizable by its dearest old friends*: According to Kay-Robinson, the architect 'whose restoration work in 1860 drew [Hardy's] acid comment was Talbot Bury; and it must be admitted that he left precious little of the original fabric except the "ancient font" ' (p. 119).

30. *greasiness*: 1880 *HW* and 1880 *NQM* have 'shine'.

31. *the world*: 1880 *HW* and 1880 *NQM* have 'I'.

32. *feverish*: 1896 *WT* has 'forced'.

33. *seven*: 1896 *WT* has 'six'.

34. *half-an-hour*: 1880 *HW* and 1880 *NQM* have 'an hour'.

'The Three Strangers'

1. *Fifty years ago*: Based on 1883 first publication, the time is roughly 1833; the narrator later refers, however, to 'March 28, 182 – ', putting the story before 1832, when a man could still be hanged for stealing sheep, and before two notorious uprisings by rural workers in southern England: the Tolpuddle

Riots of the early 1830s and the Captain Swing protests of 1830–31. In 'The Dorsetshire Labourer' (also published in *Longman's Magazine* in 1883), Hardy laments the disappearance of village craftsmen as a class.

2. *a Timon or a Nebuchadnezzar*. Based on sources in Plutarch, Lucian and Shakespeare, Timon of Athens was a notorious misanthrope who exiled himself in the desert; Nebuchadnezzar was a tyrannical king of Babylon during the fifth century BC, described in the Book of Daniel as punished by being 'driven from men', after which he 'did eat grass as oxen, and his body was wet with the dew of heaven, till his hairs were grown like eagles' feathers, and his nails like birds' claws' (4.33).

3. *conceive and meditate of pleasant things*: I have not found a source for this quotation.

4. *Higher Crowstairs*: 'Higher Polenhill' at its first appearance in the manuscript (Ray, 10). Not on the 1895–6 map, presumably a few miles north or northeast of Casterbridge. According to Kay-Robinson, the 'likely site' is

[h]igh on the downs in the broad fork by Charminster . . . It is doubtful whether this cottage ever existed, but the 'hog's-back elevation which dominated this part of the down' can be pinpointed as Hog Hill, south-east of Grimstone Down . . . The lynchets over which the search-party stumbled are on the eastern or Stratton Bottom side; the Bottom itself is the 'grassy, briery, moist defile' where they searched; and there are still several small areas of woodland. Another school of thought places 'Higher Crowstairs' farther east, on Waterston Ridge, where all Hardy's 'requirements' – except the cottage – are also to be found (p. 105).

5. *like the clothyard shafts of Senlac and Crecy*: Senlac is the Sussex hill where the Battle of Hastings (1066) took place; Crécy is a town in Northern France where in 1346 the outnumbered English, under Edward III, won a victory over the French army of King Philip of Valois. In both battles, the British used long-bows with arrows the length of a clothier's yard (36 inches).

6. *like the laughter of the fool*: 'For as the crackling of thorns under a pot, so is the laughter of the fool: this also is vanity' (Ecclesiastes 7.6).

7. *The fiddler was a boy of those parts*: Possibly an allusion to a young Hardy playing the fiddle for 'country-dances, reels, and hornpipes at an agriculturalist's wedding, christening, or Christmas party in a remote dwelling among the fallow fields' (*Life*, 36).

8. *settlement*: 1883 *LM* and 1883a *HW* have 'homestead'.

9. *desirable*: 1883 *LM* and 1883a *HW* have 'comfortable'.

10. *family*: 1883 *LM* and 1883a *HW* have 'large'.

11. *the purest first-year or maiden honey*: The first honey taken from the hive.

12. *waft 'em to a far countree*: 'waft' could serve as a pun: in dialect usage, it is a wraith or supernatural appearance of one whose death is imminent (Wright's); the exclamation point (after 'countree'), like most of the others remaining, was added for 1888 *WT*.

13. *Belshazzar's Feast*: The son of Nebuchadnezzar who was unable to read the cryptic handwriting on the wall at his elaborate feast; only Daniel could decipher the message, a prophecy of the imminent end of Belshazzar's rule (Daniel 5).

14. *Shottsford*: Wessex name for Blandford; 1883 *LM* and 1883a *HW* have Anglebury, further south, the Wessex name for Wareham; Shottsford and Anglebury are both on the 1895–6 map.

15. *cottage under the prison wall*: The Hangman's Cottage, setting for an important scene in 'The Withered Arm', still standing outside Dorchester; Hardy used a photograph of it as the frontispiece of 1912 *WT*.

16. *circulus, cujus centrum diabolus*: Latin for 'a circle, the centre of which is the devil', presumably part of a magic ritual: at a witch's sabbath, the devil remains inside a magic circle dug into the turf; conjurors, when raising spirits, protect themselves by keeping the spirit within a circle (see John Webster, *The Duchess of Malfi* (1623), I.i.411–14; Thomas Dekker and Webster, *Westward Hoe* (1607), IV.ii.7–10). This visual effect was reproduced by the stage directions in the 1911 revision to *The Three Wayfarers*, Hardy's dramatic adaptation: '*They form again for the six-hands round. College Hornpipe.* HANGMAN *tries to get each woman severally as partner: all refuse. At last* HANGMAN *dances in the figure by himself, with an imaginary partner, and pulls out rope*' (quoted in Wilson, 32).

17. *his friend*: 1883 *LM* and 1883a *HW* have 'the stranger'; several paragraphs later, as Sommers and the Hangman shake hands, the word 'heartily' was added for 1888 *WT*, again ironizing their supposed friendship. Revisions in the manuscript had made Sommers ('Summers' after 1896 *WT*) more appealing and the hangman more sinister (see Ray, 9).

18. *in the name of the Father – the Crown, I mane*: The constable begins to utter the Lord's Prayer before shifting to the formula for arresting someone; his ineptitude recalls Dogberry in Shakespeare's *Much Ado about Nothing*.

19. *a matron in the sere and yellow leaf*: Shakespeare's Macbeth soliloquizes about his intimations of futility and decline:

> I have liv'd long enough: my way of life
> Is fall'n into the sear, the yellow leaf . . . (V.iii.22–3)

This final framing of the narrative in the distant past recalls the conclusion of John Keats's 'The Eve of St Agnes' (1820), also set inside a warm dwelling on a stormy night.

'The Romantic Adventures of a Milkmaid'

1. *Where are you going . . . she said*: Omitted after 1883 *G* and 1883b *HW*, the opening lines of a well-known anonymous poem that appears in James Orchard Halliwell's *The Nursery Rhymes of England*, published in seven editions between 1842 and 1870. The remaining lines of this version (1870; London: Bodley Head, 1970) ironically summarize some of the ambivalences in the sexual attraction across class lines between the baron and Margery:

> May I go with you, my pretty maid?
> You're kindly welcome, sir, she said.
> What is your father, my pretty maid?
> My father's a farmer, sir, she said.
> Say, will you marry me, my pretty maid?
> Yes, if you please, kind sir, she said.
> Will you be constant, my pretty maid?
> That I can't promise you, sir, she said.
> Then I won't marry you, my pretty maid!
> Nobody asked you, sir! she said.

2. *the valley of the Swenn*: The first of many topographical references changed for 1913 *CM* when the setting was moved from Dorset to Devon ('South' to 'Lower' Wessex on the 1895–6 map): the Swenn (in some works the Froom, based on the Frome) became the Exe; Casterbridge (Dorchester) became Exonbury (Exeter); Anglebury (Wareham) became 'the town'; Budmouth (Weymouth) became Tivworthy (Tiverton) and, at a later stage, Plymouth; and 'a little cove' with features like those of Lulworth became Idmouth (Sidmouth). Purdy speculates that the shift was made 'possibly to remove the story from the scene of *Tess*', published eight years later (p. 49); and Ray (p. 330) suggests that the shift to Plymouth conforms with the setting of 'The Daemon Lover' (see notes 33 and 61); Simon Gatrell has argued that the pervasive topographical inconsistency in 1883 *G*, which was written before Hardy defined Wessex as a mappable place analogous to the five counties of southern England and linking all of his fictional texts, made too difficult the job of re-organizing the existing topography; instead, Hardy 'threw up his hands and moved ['Romantic Adventures'] off to a part of Wessex uninhabited by other stories' ('Topography in "The Romantic Adventures of a Milkmaid" ', *Thomas Hardy Journal* 3 (1987), 45). The first paragraph in 1913 *CM* explicitly dates the story 'in the eighteen forties' (this is implicit in 1883 *G* and 1883b *HW* when the narrator refers to a forty-year time gap and in the manuscript, which makes it thirty-five years (Ray, 333); see also note 18 below) and parenthetically introduces an ironizing source, the 'testimony' of a land-surveyor described as 'a gentleman with the faintest curve of humour on his lips'.

3. *On her arm she carried a withy basket*: This and other details connected with Margery's visit to her grandmother suggest 'Little Red Riding Hood', while Margery's transformation for the ball recalls 'Cinderella'; both fairy-tales had been well known to British readers since the eighteenth century (Iona and Peter Opie, *The Classic Fairy Tales* (Oxford: Oxford University Press, 1974), pp. 93, 117–21).

4. *She carefully avoided treading on the innumerable earthworms that lay in couples across the path*: 1913 *CM* removes this detail, perhaps to avoid comparison with a similar scene in *Jude the Obscure*. The allusion to the earthworm couples implies, not only a capacity in Margery for sympathy, but also a Darwinian comparison between her situation and that of these small animals.

5. *of the Italian elevation made familiar by the works of Inigo Jones*: Inigo Jones (1573–1652), who twice visited Italy to study its architecture, the founder of the English classical tradition of architecture.

6. *He was quite a different being from any of the men to whom her eyes were accustomed*: 1913 *CM* inserts a sentence to illustrate: 'She had never seen mustachios before, for they were not worn by civilians in Lower Wessex at this date.' The mustache, a sign of the baron's class and cultural differences, provides a contrast with Jim Hayward, who has 'scarcely any beard'. Revisions that emphasize the foreign accent of the baron, including the exclamation 'My Gott', were also added in 1913.

7. *and slipped something into the pocket of his dressing-gown*: 1913 *CM* adds the first of several references to a gun: 'She was almost certain that it was a pistol.' The manuscript had originally been explicit about the baron's suicidal intentions (Ray, 331).

8. *Stickleford Dairy-house*: Stickleford, also the setting of Hardy's 1893 story 'The Fiddler of the Reels', is Tincleton, a village between Dorchester and Wareham (Casterbridge and Anglebury on the 1895–6 map); the topographical shift of 1913 put the dairy-house in 'Silverthorn', based on Silverton, a dairying area in Devon (Kay-Robinson, 205).

9. *I do hope you be not ill, sir*: 1913 *CM* alters 'be' to the grammatically correct 'are', the first of several changes that remove Dorset dialect usage from Margery's speech, perhaps to make her more acceptable to the baron, but also possibly to make her a more credible inhabitant of Devon (Jim's 'do' is revised to 'dew', a dialect pronunciation of Devon). In section XIII, however, when Margery is alone with Jim, 1913 *CM* replaces 'cruel conspiracy' and 'ensnare' with 'footy plot' and 'snare'.

10. *I suffer from sleeplessness. Probably you don't*: The baron's attitude toward Margery, which presumes her natural simplicity in contrast to his sophisticated depression, anticipates Angel Clare with Tess Durbeyfield, but the latter has an intellectual complexity that makes Clare appear imperceptive in a way that the baron does not.

11. *guardian angel*: 1913 *CM* substitutes 'child', emphasizing the emotionalism of the baron. In the subsequent dialogue, 'indescribable folly' becomes 'an act of madness' and the 'peculiar conditions' in which Margery found him become 'ghastly conditions'. She is also made to seem more aware that the baron has been on the brink of suicide. For example, when she says that she will tell no one about what has happened, she is described as 'a little puzzled', but this was deleted for 1913 *CM*, and 'Margery did not know' becomes 'Margery could guess that he had meditated death at his own hand.'

12. *Mount Lodge*: Kay-Robinson believes this is an imaginary place (p. 231), but Gatrell associates it with the 'Cliff Mount', north-east of Tincleton on nineteenth-century Ordnance Survey maps, called Clyffe House in more recent maps ('Topography', p. 39).

13. *I can't interpret no more than Pharoah*: Pharoah cannot interpret his strange dreams and sends for all the wise men and magicians of Egypt to do so; when they fail, Pharoah discovers that the imprisoned Hebrew, Joseph, is the only one who can (Genesis 41).

14. *moved Margery deeply*: 1913 *CM* has 'excited Margery', making her responses to the baron more superficial and adolescent, and he is made more indifferent to Margery's identity, while drawn to her image of rural innocence: when he is surprised to see her, in 1883 *G* he says, 'Ah – Margery!', while 1913 *CM* has him say, in confusion and hesitation, 'Ah my maiden – what is your name – Margery!' The baron of the manuscript is unambiguously virtuous (Ray, 332–3).

15. *proh pudor*: 'for shame' in Latin, used as an exclamation and common in classical texts.

16. *You will promise not to tell, sir*: This question and the baron's answer were deleted for 1913 *CM*, perhaps because the baron does later tell.

17. *Lord Blakemore's*: 1913 *CM* has 'Lord Toneborough's'; the change removes the implicit reference to the 'Vale of Blackmoor', an important setting in *Tess*, and the new name adds to the satirical treatment of the people at the ball.

18. *there is a new dance at Almack's and everywhere else, over which the world has gone crazy*: When Hardy lived in London in 1862, he danced at Willis's Rooms, previously called Almack's Assembly Rooms, in King Street. Built in 1765, Almack's, according to Philip J. S. Richardson, became after 1800 an exclusive place whose dances 'were copied everywhere' (*The Social Dances of the Nineteenth*

Century in England (London: Herbert Jenkins, 1960), pp. 30–31). Hardy claimed that in 1862 'dances had not . . . degenerated to a waltzing step, to be followed by galloping romps to uproarious pieces' (*Life*, 45), but the waltz had been introduced to England by 1812, and the polka was first performed at Almack's in 1844 (Richardson, *Social Dances*, pp. 35, 88). The latter was thought to be of Bohemian origin, but the baron's more general reference to 'an ancient Scythian dance' indicates East European roots and suggests wildness – an idea reinforced by the baron's trendy comment on a world 'gone crazy'. See also Hardy's poem 'Reminiscences of a Dancing Man' (1909), which refers to dancing in 'those crowded rooms',

> Where to the deep Drum-polka's booms
> We hopped in standard style.
> (*Poetical Works*, I, 266, 23–4)

19. *It was a Rubicon in more ways than one*: The stile, as the class barrier between Margery and the baron, is compared to the Rubicon, the stream that limited Caesar's province and which he crossed before his war with Pompey, and thus any boundary by passing which one becomes committed to an enterprise (*OED 2*).

20. *to whose recollections the writer is indebted for the details of this interview*: Deleted for 1913 *CM*, perhaps because it conflicts with the addition of the gentleman surveyor (see note 2).

21. *the lapse of many many years*: 1913 *CM* has 'lingering emotions', which conforms with its emphasis on Margery's continuing fascination with the baron. Similarly, two paragraphs later, 1913 inserts 'at this date' just before 'distinctly' in the assertion that Margery 'was not distinctly in love with the stranger'.

22. *whether the gentleman were a wild olive tree, or not*: In Romans 11.17, the Romans, addressed as pagans who have converted to Christianity, are imaged as the branches of 'a wild olive tree' that were 'grafted in among [the other branches], and with them partakest of the root and fatness of the olive tree'.

23. *A fleeting romance and a possible calamity*: I cannot find a source for this passage, which could be read as a quotation or a cliché.

24. *a cricket-ball*: 1913 *CM* substitutes 'an apple-dumpling', perhaps to intensify the incongruity of the image; see also note 40 below.

25. *Three-Walks-End in Chillington Wood*: Kay-Robinson indexes Chillington Wood as 'imaginary' (p. 231), but Gatrell speculates that the place is 'Hardy's fictional adaptation of the geographical Ilsington Wood a mile and a half or so to the north-west of Cliff Mount along a ridge'. In this case, Three-Walks-End conforms with a 1930 Ordnance Survey map indicating 'that there were at that time three tracks entering Ilsington Wood, and that they converged near the wood's centre' ('Topography', p. 40).

26. *her eyes became moist*: 1913 *CM* has the more sexually suggestive 'her lips became close'.

27. *She walked to the music of innumerable birds*: An ironic variation of Alfred Tennyson's famous onomatopoeic image, from 'Come down, O maid' in *The Princess* (1847), of 'the murmuring of innumerable bees' (VII.207); the song implores the maiden to come down to the valley, where she will find pleasure and love (in contrast to Margery 'trudging her way up the slopes from the vale'). Among the birds' songs in Hardy's story is that of the cuckoo, which is associated with cuckoldry; the implication is that Margery's actions will somehow, at least in retrospect, make her husband a cuckold. Hardy also uses the image at the end of *Under the Greenwood Tree*.

28. *the wooden shell which enshrouded Margery and all her loveliness*: Ironically invokes standard images of the birth of Venus, in which she is seen emerging on a shell from the foam of the sea.

29. *their swarthy steeds*: 1913 *CM* adds 'as they seemed to her', thus making the Gothic effect originate in Margery's mind.

30. *with romantic mop-heads of raven hair*: This detail, among many others, anticipates 'The Fiddler of the Reels', in which a mysterious Gypsy fiddler, called 'Mop' on account of his wild hair, mesmerizes and seduces a country maiden.

31. *He watches like the Angel Gabriel, when all the world is asleep*: John Milton's *Paradise Lost* adapts the Islamic tradition holding that Gabriel presides over Paradise; in Book IV, he sits, 'Chief of th' Angelic Guards, awaiting night', and later rebukes Satan for his 'bold entrance' into the garden, which 'violate[s] sleep' (ll. 550, 882–3). This detail contrasts with other comparisons of the baron to the devil (see note 36).

32. *as immoveable as Rhadamanthus*: The son of Zeus and Europa and one of the judges of the dead, known for his unflinching adherence to principle.

33. *James Hayward*: Hayward's name reflects his role in the story, that of maintaining his right over Margery: according to Barnes, a hayward is a 'warden of the fences or of a common, whose duty it was to see that it was not stocked by those who had no right of common' (p. 70). Ray (p. 330) suggests that the name echoes that of James Harris, the baron-like former lover in the traditional ballad of 'The Daemon Lover', who lures a married woman from her husband and child to his ship (see notes 2 and 61).

34. *All's well that ends well*: An old saying which Shakespeare used as the title of a comedy that ends with a marriage across class boundaries.

35. *a twining honeysuckle*: The image of a twining plant is associated by Hardy in 'Barbara of the House of Grebe' and 'The Fiddler of the Reels' with weak women. The implication here may be that Margery's lack of fidelity undermines Jim's virility.

36. *Anybody would think the d—— had showed you the kingdoms of the world since I saw you last!*: See Matthew 4.8, in which the devil tempts Christ by showing him 'all the kingdoms of the world'. 1913 *CM* prints the word 'devil' and inserts a reply by Margery, 'Perhaps he has!'

37. *a Talleyrand*: Charles-Maurice de Talleyrand (1754–1838), a French statesman and diplomat under Napoleon, the restored Bourbon monarchy and King Louis-Philippe, was noted for his capacity to survive changes in the ruling regime.

38. *It was a British castle or entrenchment*: This is possibly Maiden Castle, a large prehistoric earthwork southwest of Dorchester ('Casterbridge' on the 1895–6 map), but if so, as Gatrell notes, Hardy shifted it 'to a location somewhere to the south of Athelhampton', which is east of 'Weatherbury' ('Topography', 44).

39. *some of them like Pompeian remains*: The ancient Roman city of Pompeii was destroyed by the eruption of Mt Vesuvius in AD 79, but the volcanic lava and ash preserved the remains of the city; after their discovery, the buildings and the artifacts fostered a neoclassical revival in European taste.

40. *the time when God A'mighty christens the little apples*: The feast of St Swithin, a ninth-century Wessex saint, is 15 July; according to Firor, 'Country folk . . . believe that rain upon this day . . . means a plentiful apple crop; in such an event they say that the saint is christening the apples' (p. 130). A dry St Swithin's Day portends no rain for six weeks. The day when Margery is supposed to marry Hayward turns out to be dry, and 'rain had not fallen for weeks'.

41. *a melancholy, emotional character – the Jacques of this forest and stream*: Björk reads this passage as an allusion to Jean Jacques Rousseau (*Literary Notebooks*, I, 308n), but the more likely source is 'melancholy Jacques' in *As You Like It*, whose cynical comments offer a dark contrast with the pastoral Forest of Arden.

42. *down*: 1913 *CM* has the more accurate 'drawn', as did the manuscript (Ray, 334).

43. *It was that of Prospero over the gentle Ariel*: In Shakespeare's *The Tempest*, Ariel is a spirit under the power of the magician Prospero.

44.*fiercely*: 1913 *CM* substitutes 'sternly', perhaps to conform with the comment a few paragraphs later on the baron's 'severity'.

45. *Rook's Gate*: Kay-Robinson indexes Rook's Gate as 'imaginary' (p. 231), but Gatrell suggests that the Dorset original for this place, before the topography was moved to Devon, was Mack's Gate, the house near a turnpike gate close to the land that Hardy leased, roughly at the time when he was writing

'Romantic Adventures', for the construction of his own house, Max Gate ('Topography', pp. 41–2).

46. *Hobbema and his school*: Meindert Hobbema (1638–1709), one of the most important landscapists of the Dutch school, favoured idyllic country scenes.

47. *the cankered heaps of strange-achieved gold*: In Shakespeare's *2 Henry IV*, King Henry speaks bitterly of the efforts fathers make for their sons:

> For this they have engrossed and pil'd up
> The cank'red heaps of strange-achievèd gold. (IV.v.70–71)

48. *to beard the lion in his den*: The Earl of Angus to Marmion, after Marmion has dared to speak his mind to the Earl in the Earl's own hold:

> And dar'st thou then
> To beard the lion in his den,
> the Douglas in his hall?
> (Walter Scott, *Marmion*, VI.xiv.23–5)

49. *an extremely pure and romantic feeling*: 1913 *CM* removes 'pure and', thus emphasizing 'romantic', with all its complicated associations. Hardy may also have wanted to delete any reference to the controversial subtitle of *Tess*: 'A Pure Woman Faithfully Presented by Thomas Hardy'.

50. *a painless sympathy*: In Alfred Tennyson's *In Memoriam* (1850), the speaker imagines the dead Hallam addressing him:

> How is it? Canst thou feel for me
> Some painless sympathy with pain? (LXXXV.88)

51. *or seemed to whisper*: 1913 *CM* deletes this, which with other changes makes the baron's power over Margery more absolute, and in the second paragraph of section XII 'as yet' was added after 'nature' to 'the innocent nature of the acquaintanceship'.

52. *the miniature Pillars of Hercules which formed the mouth of the cove*: The Pillars of Hercules were erected by Hercules (or Heracles) on either side of the Straits of Gibraltar. This mock-epic image, probably an allusion to the cliffs on either side of the entrance to Lulworth Cove, was deleted when the story's location was moved to Devon for 1913 *CM* (as were all references to the steam power of the yacht). The trip to the cove was added in the proofs for 1883 *G* (Ray, 335).

53. *Algiers*: A base for Barbary pirates before its capture by the French in 1830 and associated with ideas of exoticism and violence.

54. *she did not distinctly deny the widow's impeachment*: In 1913 *CM*, 'distinctly' is removed, thus making unambiguous Margery's decision to appear the baron's widow; also, Mrs Peach addresses her as 'dear Baroness' (rather than as 'ma'am'), and Margery does not correct her.

55. *eagerly*: Omitted in 1913 *CM*, which makes Margery less emotional about Hayward. Similarly, in Section XVI, 1913 *CM* replaces 'miserable' with 'indignant' and 'she was crying' with 'her mood'.

56. *Then the dairyman committed the greatest error of his life*: 1913 *CM* has 'Then the dairyman practised the greatest duplicity of his life', perhaps to remove the narrator's judgement about the story's outcome.

57. *This hamlet had once been a populous village*: The full description of Letscombe Cross, with its medieval cross, was deleted for 1913 *CM*, presumably because of the shift in location (the baron makes his promise with his hand on the hilt of Hayward's sword rather than on the cross). Gatrell offers Vera Jesty's speculation that 'as far as the cross, the depopulation and the situation of the London road are concerned, either Pimperne or Tarrant Hinton just north of Blandford Forum fit [the story] reasonably well, and are far enough from Dorchester to be plausibly at the edge of a horse's comfortable endurance. However, they are both much too far from the Frome, and neither is at the junction of a road that leads down to the water-meadows' ('Topography', pp. 44–5).

58. *now gilded and glorious with the dying fires*: 1913 *CM* has 'now black and daemonic against the slanting fires', thus repeating the demonic imagery associated with the baron.

59. *peremptorily*: Removed for 1913 *CM*, making the baron's tone somewhat more ambivalent in response to a scene that is significantly altered. Margery is much less firm about her decision to stay back with Jim: when the baron asks, 'Don't you think you ought to be [at Jim's house]?', the narrator reports that 'She did not answer'; and when the baron comments 'Of course you ought', we are told 'Still she did not speak'. Further on, when the baron asks Margery to come with him, in 1913 *CM* she says that she cannot simply 'Because –.' In 1913 *CM*, Margery also does not implore the baron to 'save' her, but, after seeing 'all contingencies', leans on the baron with 'clasped hands' and 'a bewildered look' in her eyes. The baron's decision to return her to Jim is a result of 'her distracted look', and when he asks her forgiveness, 1913 *CM* has him calling his mistake 'a lover's bad impulse'. The conclusion is also different: the baron 'seemed to feel the awkwardness keenly', and Margery says, 'Of course I forgive you, sir, for I felt for a moment as you did. Will you send my husband to me?'

60. *doubtful*: 1913 *CM* has 'wreckless'; the baron's 'suggestion that they should pursue Jim' is described more cynically as 'the fancied pursuit of Jim', and the baron's 'doubtful sentiments' become 'impassioned sentiments'.

61. *possible*: 1913 *CM* has 'mournful', which makes a return by the baron impossible, and Margery follows her comment that she is 'sorry' for him with an explicit admission: 'Now that he's dead I'll make a confession, Jim, that I have never made to a soul. If he had pressed me – which he did not – to go with him when I was in the carriage that night beside his yacht, I would have gone. And I was disappointed that he did not press me.' When she says that the baron 'would not move me now', 1913 *CM* adds 'It would be so unfair to baby', again recalling 'The Daemon Lover'. Hardy's alternative ending of 1927 parallels even more closely the ballad's closure (see notes 2 and 33).

62. *his 'la jalousie rétrospective,' as George Sand terms it*: 'Retrospective jealousy', quoted from *Elle et Lui*, chapter XII (1859); Hardy was reading George Sand as early as 1873 and took extensive notes on her works (*Literary Notebooks*, I, 300n).

'Interlopers at the Knap'

1. *Holloway Lane*: The 1889 Macmillan one-volume edition of *Wessex Tales* substitutes for the fictional name an actual one: 'Long Ash Lane', the road out of Dorchester to Yeovil (Casterbridge to Ivell on the 1895–6 map). Hardy made topographical changes to the story at every stage of revision (see Ray, 49–54).

2. *This comfortable position was, however, none of his own making*: In this detail, as in many others, Darton resembles the alienated Mr Barnet of 'Fellow-Townsmen'.

3. *Japheth Johns*: Japheth was a son of Noah blessed by his father: 'God shall enlarge Japheth, and he shall dwell in the tents of Shem; and Canaan shall be his servant' (Genesis 9.27), but Hardy's Japheth is turned down by the woman he courts. The name of the happily unmarried Sarah Hall is similarly misapplied: Sarah was the wife of Abraham about whom Yahweh prophesied, 'she shall be a mother of nations; kings of peoples shall be of her' (Genesis 17.16). The story's New Testament allusions are also ironic, e.g. when Sarah is awaiting Darton, she invokes the image of the star followed by the Magi on the night of the nativity; yet Darton, Johns and Enoch are hardly like the biblical Magi, while the poor people found in the stable turn out to be, not Mary and Joseph with the Messiah, but Philip's wife Helena, whose classical name is associated with division and war, and their children.

4. *Hanging and wiving go by destiny*: In Shakespeare's *The Merchant of Venice*, Nerissa, the waiting gentlewoman of Portia, invokes this 'ancient saying' after the Prince of Arragon has chosen the wrong casket and so has lost the hand of Portia (II.ix.82).

5. *one of the Hintocks (several of which lay thereabout)*: In 1884 *EIM*, 'the old-fashioned village of Hintock Abbas'; both are based on Melbury Osmond, the home of Hardy's mother's family and the place where the senior Hardys were married in 1839. Millgate notes that 'Interlopers' is 'partly based upon [Hardy's] father's journey to Melbury Osmond on the eve of the wedding. Family tradition concurs in the insistence upon the bridegroom's hesitancy and in the anecdote about climbing a signpost in order to read it in the dark' (*Biography*, 15). Kay-Robinson identifies 'the Knap' as Manor Cottage, Melbury Osmond, where the large stump of a yew tree can still be seen near the house's former front door (pp. 109–10). The house appears in the poem 'One Who Married above Him' (1925). King associates it with Alexander Macmillan's house 'Knapdale' (cited in Ray, 49; see also 'Fellow-Townsmen', note 4).

6. *the great fireplace*: 1912 *WT* has 'the town of Smokeyhole'; 1896 *WT* had increased the dialect usage of Johns, but Mrs Hall has dialect removed (e.g. 'match for ye' becomes 'match for you', p. 256) for 1888 *WT*, thus making her seem more respectable.

7. *Don't you be such a reforming radical*: It is inappropriate for Enoch, as a farmer's man, to make a joke to the person for whom he works. Johns may be mockingly associating Enoch with those who had supported the Reform Bill of 1832, which extended voting rights to some male property owners.

8. *as if Skrymir the Giant were sleeping there*: In Norse mythology, when Thor finds Skrymir the Giant sleeping, he is unable to wake him, even with three violent blows to his head; the giant outwits the god.

9. *Hintock village-street*: King notes that the 1903 Macmillan edition of *Wessex Tales* has 'King's-Hintock village-street' (cited in Ray, 53); 1912 *WT* adds that this location is 'only a mile or two from King's-Hintock Court, yet quite shut away from that mansion and its precincts'. The revision makes explicit the closeness of the setting to that of *The Woodlanders*, while also emphasizing the distance of the Hall family from a person like Felice Charmond, who inhabited King's-Hintock Court in an early version. This house, the Wessex version of Melbury House, also provides the setting for the elopement in the 1889 story 'The First Countess of Wessex'.

10. *under Bacchic influence*: Bacchus, or Dionysus, was the god of wine and ecstasy.

11. *sinking down confounded*: Added for 1888 *WT*, as were several exclamation points in this dialogue and below. Also, several paragraphs later, 'bitterly' was added to describe Philip's tone.

12. *Verton*: 1896 *WT* makes this Evershead (see the 1895–6 map), the Wessex name for Evershot, and substitutes the 'Sow-and-Acorn' for the 'Dog'. Both are associated with 'The First Countess of Wessex', and the latter appears in *Tess*.

13. *universal custom thereabout to wake the bees . . . whenever a death occurred in the household*: According to Udal, informing bees 'of the death of their master or mistress by tapping upon the hives and announcing it in order to prevent their forsaking the place is a common superstition in Dorsetshire as in other counties' (p. 246).

14. *to the 'Pack-Horse', a roadside inn*: 1896 *WT* makes this the ' "White Horse", at Chalk Newton', and 1912 *WT* adds that it was a 'fine old Elizabethan inn', with a footnote indicating that the inn 'is now pulled down, and its site occupied by a modern one in red brick'. In 'Destiny and a Blue Cloak', this is the inn from which Agatha took the carrier's van.

15. *I'll swing the mallet*: Since a mallet is used in both croquet and polo, this idiom may mean 'I'll take my turn' or 'I'll give this a shot'.

16. *your nice long speeches on mangold-wurzel*: Recalls the reference in the Finale of George Eliot's *Middlemarch* to Fred Vincy's authorship of a work on 'turnips and mangel-wurzel'. Both uses are sardonic.

17. *But if I had 'twould have been all the same*: 1912 *WT* has 'That you believed me capable of refusing you for such a reason does not help your cause.'

'The Waiting Supper'

1. *Squire Everard's lawn . . . fifty years ago*: The Everard family once occupied Stafford House, near Lower Bockhampton (Mellstock in Wessex, east of Casterbridge), which, according to Ray, 'had formerly been known as Frome Everard' (p. 275). The fictional 'Swenn-Everard House' is like the actual Stafford House in having grounds close to a waterfall on a river, the 'Swenn' in this text, the 'Froom' in 1913 *WT*, at which point the house became 'Froom-Everard House'. So Salisbury becomes Melchester; Troyton Inn becomes the Buck's Head in Roy Town, a setting used also in *Far From the Madding Crowd*; Frome becomes Froom (the Frome River, which runs from Evershot (Evershead) through Dorchester (Casterbridge) to Wareham (Anglebury) and Poole (Havenpool)). Kay-Robinson notes that 'the reach between West Stafford and Woodsford' on the Frome River has sinister connotations in Hardy's fiction: it provides the setting for the drownings of Eustacia Vye and Damon Wildeve in *The Return of the Native* and for the suicide attempt of Retty Priddle in *Tess* (pp. 61–2). If the narrator's present is the date of the story's composition in 1887 or its first publication in 1888, then this scene is set in 1837 or 1838; cf. Christine's letter of 13 Oct. 1838. In 1913 *CM*, the letter has the less specific '183 –'.

2. *the tenant-farmers*: After the Enclosure Acts of the late eighteenth and early nineteenth centuries, during which six million acres of British land became privately owned, most farmers rented land, often in the form of a twenty-one-year or three-lifetimes lease, from owners of large properties (Mitchell, 11, 196). Squire Everard – as a member of the 'smaller gentry' and therefore as a landowner, but not a large one – belongs to the class that is quickly being displaced by the 'territorial landlords'. His allegiances would still be to the landowning classes, however, rather than to the new generation of renting farmers represented by Nic and his uncle.

3. *Take me whilst I am in the humour*: Disguised as a man pretending to be a woman, Rosalind in Shakespeare's *As You Like It* playfully says to Orlando, 'Come, woo me, woo me; for now I am in a holiday humour and like enough to consent' (IV.i.68–9). Though Christine self-consciously may be quoting Rosalind, her tone is petulant.

4. *the clandestine marriage of an aunt under circumstances somewhat similar to the present*: Possibly an allusion (though the date would suggest a great- or great-great-aunt) to the secret marriage in 1735 of Elizabeth Strangways-Horners to Stephen Fox, fictionalized by Hardy in 'The First Countess of Wessex'. The plan for a secret marriage also recalls *A Pair of Blue Eyes*.

5. *the bottle-green glass of the old lead quarries*: Glass was given its colour by the fusion in the glass mixture of metallic oxides.

6. *(for he lived in a remote part of the parish)*: 1913 *CM* has '(for he lived aloofly in the next parish)'. Here and elsewhere, as Ray has noted, 'Nic's social relation to Christine is made more independent in 1913 by moving his farm out of her father the Squire's parish and into a neighbouring one. This removes those undertones in the serial of the Poor Man and the Lady theme' (p. 275).

7. *far*: 1913 *CM* has 'months', diminishing the impression that Christine is too young; also, a few paragraphs further, that 'Christine grew passionate' and that she 'painfully reflected' become that 'Christine [was] spurred by opposition' and that she 'reflected'.

8. *Eldhampton Hall*: 1913 *CM* has 'Athelhall', the Wessex name for Athelhampton, close to Puddletown (Weatherbury in the 1895–6 map), a house Hardy knew in his youth. Kay-Robinson notes that the Great Hall 'still has its fine timbered roof and musicians' gallery', as well as its spiral staircase, 'but it does not and never did give access to the gallery' (p. 55).

9. *her husband and children*: Desmond Hawkins was the first to remark that in all versions this female cousin becomes male several paragraphs later: 'Nicholas's cousin and cousin's wife and cousin's children among the rest' (cited in Ray, 277).

10. *the Parthians, and Medes, and dwellers in Mesopotamia*: The Parthians were inhabitants of an ancient kingdom of western Asia; the Medes, known for

their warlike qualities, were taken over by a Parthian king in 152 BC; Mesopotamia was an ancient country between the Tigris and Euphrates Rivers, often called the 'cradle of civilization'. Bellston's point is that he knows more about ancient peoples than about the 'English rustics' before him. His mention of the Parthians may be especially ironic: they were known for the missiles that were discharged backwards by their flying horsemen.

11. *Michaelmas-daisies and chrysanthemums*: Hardy wrote to C. Kegan Paul in January 1888, presumably in response to a question about this story, that chrysanthemums 'were known 40 years ago – I could not swear to 50 – They were mostly pink, & not much like those we see now' (*Collected Letters*, I, 172).

12. *the celebrated Mellstock fiddlers*: These musicians establish a link with *Under the Greenwood Tree*, set during roughly the same period. They could also refer to older members of Hardy's own family, the originals for the Mellstock Quire, who made a practice of performing at various communal events. As John Rabbetts notes, 'images of the Dewy family . . . flicker throughout Hardy's later fiction with a kind of totemic significance' (*From Hardy to Faulkner: Wessex to Yoknapatawpha* (New York: St Martin's Press, 1989), p. 138).

13. *staleness, flatness, or unprofitableness*: Cf. *Hamlet* I.ii. 134–5: 'How weary, stale, flat and unprofitable / Seem to me all the uses of this world!' In this story about procrastination and indecision, another possible reference to *Hamlet* was added for 1913 *CM*.

14. *a young man of Swenn-Everard*: 1913 *CM* changes the location of Long's 'Homeston Farm' to 'Elsenford', whose original, according to Hardy, was either Bhompston or Duddle Farm. In a story about procrastination and indecision, Elsinore, the setting of Shakespeare's *Hamlet*, may also be invoked.

15. *the very twin halves of a perfect whole*: This may be an allusion to Matthew Arnold's 'Too Late' (1852), which focuses on potentially perfect matches that are not consummated:

> Each on his own strict line we move,
> And some find death ere they find love;
> So far apart their lives are thrown
> From the twin soul which halves their own.
> And sometimes, by still harder fate,
> The lovers meet, but meet too late.
> – Thy heart is mine! – *True, true! ah, true!*
> – Then, love, thy hand! – *Ah, no! adieu!*

16. *But as a sensible, new-risen poet says*: Robert Browning had begun publishing during the 1830s, but Christine anachronistically quotes 'The Statue and the Bust' (1855), of which Hardy said, 'there's nothing about procrastination that is not in that poem' (Elliott Felkin, 'Days with Thomas Hardy: from a 1918–1919 diary', *Encounter* 18 (1962), 30). The poem sees the postponement of sexual consummation as a greater 'sin' than the 'vice' of an adulterous relationship (see also n. 28). Hardy also repeats details from George Crabbe's 'The Parting Hour' (1812), in which former lovers, who have been separated for most of their adult lives, sit together in old age awaiting their deaths; from the *Decameron*'s ninth story of the tenth day, in which a woman's first husband arrives on the scene just as she is marrying the second; and from an old *Dorset County Chronicle*, which he had summarized and commented on in his 'Facts' Notebook, begun in 1882:

Long engagemt. Scotch youth & damsel (Elgin) – attachment – 1794. Separated, & marriage forbidden by their relations. Ten years passed; union again nearly achieved, when doomed to disappt. Twenty more years mutually constant, & in uninterrupted correspce. Then married. Wd. it not have been better to wait till death, &c. –

('Facts' Notebook, [82], quoted in Brady, 179–80)

17. *All's well that ends well*: See 'The Romantic Adventures of a Milkmaid', note 34.

18. *I have suffered more in this last half hour than I hope you may suffer all your life*: 1913 *CM* has 'here's a paragraph in the paper hinting at a secret wedding, and I'm blazed if it don't point to you'. As Ray has pointed out, the change makes Everard's motivation plausible: 'In the serial he seems to move too quickly and for no obvious reason from calling Nic a scoundrel to accepting him as a son-in-law' (p. 276). Also in 1913 *CM*, Hardy dropped the 'almost' from 'I almost feel that you must carry out this attempt'.

19. *Parents propose, and ungrateful children dispose*: Ironic variation of the cliché, 'Man proposes, God disposes.'

20. *the gold-fields*: Given the date is roughly 1853, Long is probably referring to the Australian gold rush of the early 1850s.

21. *shining one at each corner like types of the four Evangelists*: May refer to a feature in chapel architecture where each Evangelist occupies one compartment of a four-part vault; may also refer to Revelation 7.1: 'I saw four angels standing on the four corners of the earth.'

22. *without any warning, the clock slowly inclined forward and fell at full length upon the floor*: According to Udal, this 'foretells a death in the family of the owner' (p. 183); he uses this story as his example.

23. *You are early; it is very good of you*: After this statement, 1913 *CM* offers a significantly different scene, in which Bellston's portmanteau and coat are delivered by a messenger, who reports to Christine that her husband's arrival is imminent.

Ray suggests that the later version is the 'more consistent and plausible' because the Bellston who is described as returning in the serial does not seem vindictive in the ways that Christine and Nic presume him to be (p. 274).

24. *So once said a sorely tried man in the land of Uz*: The quotation is from Job 30. 26; this scene anticipates Jude Fawley's identification with the despairing voice of the biblical Job in *Jude the Obscure* (see note 25); similarly, Christine's comment that she has been 'roughly received back into – the right way!' looks forward to Sue Bridehead's grotesque sense of moral correctness when she returns to Phillotson.

25. *His last state was worse than his first. He was more than once tempted*: 1913 *CM* has 'If he had been younger he might have felt tempted'. This revision and others removing the suggestion that Long is truly suicidal were made after the 1895 publication of *Jude the Obscure*, perhaps to distinguish Long's frustration from Jude's despair.

26. *So like, so very like, was day to day*: From William Wordsworth's 'Elegiac Stanzas, Suggested by a Picture of Peele Castle, in a Storm, Painted by Sir George Beaumont' (1807), l. 6, which describes a peaceful time in the past of the speaker, about which he now has a negative judgement:

> Such happiness, wherever it be known
> Is to be pitied; for 'tis surely blind. (ll. 55–6)

27. *J. Bellston: 1838*: See Introduction for later changes to this detail and additions to the final dialogue.

28. *With mirth and laughter let old wrinkles come*: In Shakespeare's *The Merchant of Venice*, Gratiano argues that one should pursue pleasure to the fullest, even in old age:

> Let me play the fool!
> With mirth and laughter let old wrinkles come,
> And let my liver rather heat with wine
> Than my cool heart with mortifying groans.
> Why should a man whose blood is warm within,
> Sit like his grandsire cut in alabaster? (I.i.79–84)

Again the literary text is used to say the opposite of what it purports. This also may be another connection with Browning's 'The Statue and the Bust': while the young Christine quotes Browning's lady to argue that 'The world and its way have a certain worth', she later quotes Gratiano just after he has told the depressed Antonio 'You have too much respect upon the world' (I.i.74). Also incongruous is Christine's use of biblical language to introduce Shakespeare.

'The Withered Arm'

1. *A lorn milkmaid*: Suzanne R. Johnson notes that the section titles, especially this one and 'The young wife', by foregrounding a basic contrast within the story, serve a function similar to that of the 'Phase' titles of *Tess* ('Metamorphosis, desire, and the fantastic in Thomas Hardy's "The Withered Arm" ', *Modern Language Studies* 23 (1993), 138n).

2. *It was an eighty-cow dairy*: As is also true of Talbothays in *Tess*, the size and capitalist structure of this dairy, where the dairyman rents cows from a landowning farmer and 'supernumerary' workers are hired at particular seasons, were not uncommon during the early nineteenth century. See G. E. Fussell, ' "High Farming" in Southwestern England, 1840–1880', *Economic Geography* 24 (1948), 57; and Barbara Kerr, 'The Dorset agricultural labourer, 1750–1850', *Proceedings of the Dorset Natural History and Archaeological Society* 84 (1962), 176.

3. *Anglebury*: The Wessex name for Wareham (see 1895–6 map).

4. *Has anybody seen her*: 1896 *WT* substitutes 'Hav' ' for 'Has'; such revisions increase the sense that the people who work in the dairy use Dorset dialect, and reinforce the contrast between Rhoda Brook and Gertrude Lodge.

5. *before our Great Weir was builded*: According to Kay-Robinson, this is probably Stony or Bovington Weir, near Hethfelton Old Farm, the original for the 'outlying second farm' of Farmer Lodge; though the milkman's reference to forty years earlier would suggest the weir was built in the late eighteenth century, Stony Weir is actually 'medieval in origin' and 'was fully rebuilt . . . in 1749'. Lodge's large white house at Holmstoke is an earlier incarnation of Hethfelton House, located between Bovington and Stokeford. Rhoda's cottage is 'probably up the lane between Stokeford and Stokeford farm' and 'would have been no more than one of those humble cob-and-thatch dwellings effaced as soon as their owners (if not always their occupants) had ceased to have a use for them'. Holmstoke Church is the church of St Mary, now in ruins (pp. 65–8). Holmstoke does not appear on the 1895–6 map of Wessex, but is west of Anglebury. 1888 *BM* reads 'Stickleford', the Wessex name for Tincleton, instead of Holmstoke; this revision removes the geographical irregularity that had been created by the necessity, in order to make Gertrude Lodge's journey to Casterbridge an arduous one, of moving Stickleford to the other side of Egdon Heath. Hardy may also have wanted to remove the allusions to the area of his own birthplace – and, implicitly, to his mother, his source for this narrative – which would have been familiar to the readers of 1888 *WT* (1888 *BM* had been published anonymously).

6. *Rhoda Brook*: 'Rhoda' comes from the Greek word for rose, while 'Brook' suggests running water; both names, with their emphasis on natural beauty, movement and fertility, contrast with the surname of Farmer Lodge, which suggests his grand house. In *Studies*, Hardy recorded three biblical uses of the word 'lodge' (pp. 38, 44). Kay-Robinson also notes that on an estate map of 1828 Hethfelton House is called ' "Heffleton *Lodge*", a rare term in Dorset, inviting speculation as to whether Hardy's choice of "Lodge" for the surname of his chief characters was entirely coincidental' (pp. 65–6, his italics). In any case, the brook/lodge contrast suggests an opposition between the 'natural' (or, in this case, the 'primitive') and the 'civilized'. 'Brook' might also invoke Rhoda's role of drawing together the worlds of Holmstoke and Casterbridge, just as the water in the meads of Holmstoke comes from the 'deep slow river' that runs by the Hangman's Cottage in Casterbridge. (The name Gertrude – a reference to Hamlet's mother – could be read as ironically applied to Mrs Lodge, whose withered limb is associated with her childlessness.)

7. *a many-forked stand made of the peeled limb of an oak-tree*: 1912 *WT* adds 'as usual' after 'made', thus emphasizing the traditional status of the object, even on a farm with a relatively new economic structure. Romey T. Keys suggests that this detail, among others, links Holmstoke with Casterbridge, the place of the story's hanging: the forked stand 'takes the place of the gallows, which receives the briefest of descriptions' ('Hardy's uncanny narrative: a reading of "The Withered Arm" ', *Texas Studies in Literature and Language* 27 (1985), 111).

8. *If she's dark or fair, and if she's tall – as tall as I*: Rhoda is echoing the desperately jealous instructions of Shakespeare's Cleopatra to her servants soon after she has learned from a messenger that Antony has married Octavia. To one she says,

> Go to the fellow, good Alexas, bid him
> Report the feature of Octavia, her years,
> Her inclination; let him not leave out
> The color of her hair. Bring me word quickly.

Cleopatra continues:

> Bid you Alexas
> Bring me word how tall she is.
> (*Antony and Cleopatra*, II.v.111–14, 117–18)

Like Cleopatra, Rhoda is dark and tall, as well as being an outsider to her lover's social world, and is associated with witchcraft; like Octavia, Gertrude is fair and short, as well as being a member of her husband's class (Octavia is Caesar's sister). Hardy copied down in *Studies* (p. 69) many quotations from

Antony and Cleopatra, including part of Cleopatra's interrogation of the messenger after he has seen Octavia:

> What majesty is in her gait? Remember,
> If e'er thou look'st on majesty. (III.iii.17–18)

9. *It whewed and whistled so loud when it rubbed against the pews*: See 'Fellow-Townsmen', note 27.

10. *realistic as a photograph*: The technology of photography dates back only to 1839 in Britain, more than ten years after the date of the story (see note 20). This detail is not anachronistic, however, for it reflects the time of the narrator in 1888, when photography was well established. A similar effect, of a narrator who invokes scientific concepts to describe the story's strangest moments, was added for 1888 *WT*: when Gertrude Lodge first sees the corpse of the nameless young man, 1888 *BM* says 'it was as though she had half-fainted and could not finish'; 1888 *WT* says, 'it was as though she had nearly died, but was held up by a sort of galvanism'.

11. *since her assertion . . . was not to be believed*: 1888 *BM* has 'if' for 'since'. The revision, which only slightly calls into question the certainty of the event, was one of several made by Hardy in response to Leslie Stephen's criticism:

Either I would accept the superstition altogether and make the wizard a genuine performer – with possibly some hint that you tell the story as somebody told it; or I would leave some opening as to the withering of the arm, so that a possibility of explanation might be suggested, though, of course, not too much obtruded . . .

As it is, I don't know where I am. I begin as a believer and end up as a sceptic.

(Stephen to Hardy, 10 Jan. 1888, in *The Life and Letters of Leslie Stephen*, ed. Frederick William Maitland (London: Duckworth, 1906), pp. 393–4)

12. *The impression remaining from the night's experience was still strong*: Norman D. Prentiss suggests that 'impression' is a pun here: 'The dream leaves a mental impression on Rhoda, but it also leaves a physical impression on Gertrude' ('The poetics of interruption in Hardy's poetry and short stories', *Victorian Poetry* 31 (1993), 49).

13. *Conjuror Trendle*: In Dorset tradition, a conjuror (also called a cunning-man, or a white witch) was the seventh son of a seventh son who had special powers, especially to diagnose and treat illnesses. 'Trendle' is a form of the Anglo-Saxon word meaning circle, a mystical symbol in magic (see 'The Three Strangers', note 16), and may also refer to Trendle Hill near Cerne Abbas, upon whose chalk surface is still carved the ancient image of a huge man with an erect penis; Udal reports that the 'Cerne Giant' was often the location of maypole celebrations and fertility rituals (pp. 157–8). Hardy told Lea that Trendle 'is

a composite figure of two or three [conjurors] who used to be heard of'
(*Collected Letters*, III, 264).

14. *the malignant influence which was blasting the fair person of Gertrude*: The association
of blasting with withering suggests that the story's central image may be linked
to Shakespeare's Richard III, who thinks he has been cursed by his brother's
wife and Jane Shore, his brother's former mistress:

> Look how I am bewitch'd; behold mine arm
> Is, like a blasted sapling, wither'd up.
> And this is Edward's wife, that monstrous witch,
> Consorted with that harlot strumpet Shore,
> That by their witchcraft thus have marked me.
>
> (*Richard III*, III.iv.68–72)

In both texts, the withering of the limb has a sexual dimension.

15. *the Wessex King Ina, presented to after-ages as Lear*: King of Wessex at the end
of the seventh century, just after it had been taken over by the West Saxons;
William Camden relates the story of his relationship with his three daughters
to that of King Lear (*Remaines Concerning Britaine* (1606)).

16. *the house of the man they sought*: Lea reported in 1913 that the conjuror's house
had 'fallen into complete decay', though the walls had been standing twenty
years before, and he claimed to have passed the spot 'some years' before, when
he 'inquired of an old rustic who was working near whether he remembered it
when it was occupied, and he replied that a man used to live there who was
"a seventh of a seventh" ' (pp. 151–2).

17. *he took the glass and its contents to the window, and told Gertrude to watch them
closely*: According to Firor, showing the form of an enemy 'assumed by the
white of an egg dissolved in a glass of water', sometimes called 'Scrying the
future', is 'an ancient mode of divination' (p. 88).

18. *overlooked*: Udal offers numerous instances of overlooking in Dorset and
quotes from a *Handbook of Folk-lore*: 'the belief known as the "Evil Eye" is not
a matter of art, magic, or witchcraft, but a supposedly natural power inherent
in certain persons, *whether voluntarily or involuntarily exerted*'. He comments that
sometimes 'an unusually ill-tempered, shrewish, or for any reason particularly
obnoxious old woman . . . would be credited with such a power' (p. 205, my
italics).

19. *It will turn the blood and change the constitution*: According to Udal (p. 207), the
general belief in Dorset was 'that the most effectual way of neutralizing, or of
removing, the baneful influence exerted by the . . . person who was supposed
to be overlooking the sufferer, was to draw blood from the "overlooker" '
(this is evident in the actions of Susan Nunsuch in *The Return of the Native*).

Firor, however, notes that the 'corpse-cure', or touching of the neck of a man who has just been hanged, was another possible way of turning the blood (the idea was to transfer the parting life of the hanged victim to the dead limb of the living person). It was not uncommon, right up to 1900, for a hangman both to allow people to stand near the scaffold in order to touch the corpse and to sell bits of the rope for medicinal use (p. 111). According to Roger Ebbatson, William Calcraft, the Dorchester hangman, 'was in the habit of selling the rope by the inch after a hanging' (' "The Withered Arm" and history', *Critical Survey* 5 (1993), 132).

20. *The last I sent was in '13 – near twenty years ago*: 1912 *WT* changes 'twenty' to 'twelve', thus dating the story's conclusion in 1825 rather than 1833, and setting it, as Ebbatson notes, before the agricultural unrest of the 1830s (' "The Withered Arm" and history', pp. 132–3). In making arson the boy's alleged crime, however, Hardy may have been thinking of the Kenn incendiaries; he copied the description of their 1830 execution from the *Dorset County Chronicle* into his 'Facts' Notebook. Also relevant is a hanging Hardy's father told him about:

My father saw four men hung for *being with* some others who had set fire to a rick. Among them was a stripling of a boy of eighteen. Skinny. Half-starved. So frail, so underfed, that they had to put weights on his feet to break his neck. He had not fired the rick. But with a youth's excitement he had rushed to the scene to see the blaze . . . Nothing my father ever said to me drove the tragedy of Life so deeply into my mind.

(Newman Flower, *Just as It Happened* (London: Cassell, 1950), p. 92)

Many acts of arson were committed in the early 1830s by frustrated farm labourers protesting their appalling conditions and the loss of work resulting from new technology; thus, as Ebbatson comments, Rhoda's son 'attends a rick-fire which might be aimed at his own father' (' "The Withered Arm" and history', pp. 132–3).

21. *Instead of her formal prayers . . . hang some guilty or innocent person soon*: Added for 1888 *WT*, thus intensifying the sense that Gertrude has lost all her former compassion.

22. *Enclosure Acts had not taken effect*: These parliamentary acts, variously passed between 1750 and 1850, turned six million acres of commonly held agricultural land into private property; see also 'The Waiting Supper', note 20.

23. *She halted before a pond*: 1896 *WT* gives the name 'Rushy-pond', the actual place from which, with a telescope, Hardy witnessed a hanging as a boy. In his poem 'At Rushy-pond' (1925), the place embodies the guilty memory of the male speaker, who had ended his relationship with a woman there.

24. *hang-fair*: According to Firor, hanging 'was a public spectacle up to 1868; executions used to take place over the gateway of the county jail, and formed the excuse for a general holiday. The rich paid for choice seats; the tradesmen, farmers, and rustics ate, drank and made merry with a callousness it is difficult to understand today' (pp. 243–4).

25. *a lonely cottage by a deep slow river flowing under the cliff on which the prison buildings were situate*: According to Kay-Robinson, Hangman's Cottage 'is today a very neatly kept private residence. The outside staircase noticed by Gertrude Lodge has been removed ... The wicket in the prison wall, pointed out by the hangman to Gertrude, has so completely disappeared that it is difficult to judge where it was, for the cottage is not really opposite the prison' (pp. 10–11). The mention of a boy pointing out the cottage may be a reference to Hardy's childhood self: Henry Nevinson reports that Hardy showed him 'the railings he used to climb as a boy to watch the hangman having his tea at a cottage in a hollow below on the evening before an execution, and wonder how the man could eat anything so soon before his terrible task' (*Thomas Hardy* (1941; New York: Haskell House, 1972), p. 18).

26. *formally*: 1888 *BM* has 'slyly'; the change diminishes the hangman's tone of black humour, perhaps to distinguish him from the hangman of 'The Three Strangers', also in 1888 *WT*.

27. *We always wait for that, in case of a reprieve*: On 7 Feb. 1879, Hardy made the following note: 'Father says that when there was a hanging at Dorchester in his boyhood it was carried out at one o'clock, it being the custom to wait till the mail-coach came in from London in case of a reprieve' (*Life*, 128).

28. *uncovering the face of the corpse*: This chilling detail was added for 1888 *WT*.

29. *a chastened and thoughtful man*: 1888 *BM* has 'serious-minded' for 'thoughtful'; Hardy had originally sent *Blackwood's* a manuscript in which Lodge is described as having killed himself, but Hardy then sent on this 'improvement' (*Collected Letters*, I, 170).

30. *he went away to Port-Bredy*: The setting of 'Fellow-Townsmen' recalls that story's focus on alienation and exile. 'Fellow-Townsmen' immediately follows 'The Withered Arm' in 1888 *WT* and all subsequent editions of the collection. The Wessex name for Bridport may also serve as a veiled allusion to the 1833 hanging in Dorchester of an arsonist from Bridport (Ebbatson, ' "The Withered Arm" and history', p. 133).

History of the Short Story Collections

Most of Hardy's short stories first appeared in periodicals and then were collected in volumes: *Wessex Tales: Strange, Lively, and Commonplace* (London: Macmillan, 1888); *A Group of Noble Dames* (London: Osgood, McIlvaine, 1891); *Life's Little Ironies: A Set of Tales with Some Colloquial Sketches Entitled A Few Crusted Characters* (London: Osgood, McIlvaine, 1894); and *A Changed Man, The Waiting Supper, and Other Tales, Concluding with The Romantic Adventures of a Milkmaid* (London: Macmillan, 1913).

The 1888 two-volume first edition of *Wessex Tales* contained 'The Three Strangers' (*Longman's Magazine*, March 1883), 'The Withered Arm' (*Blackwood's Edinburgh Magazine*, January 1888), 'Fellow-Townsmen' (*New Quarterly Magazine*, April 1880), 'Interlopers at the Knap' (*English Illustrated Magazine*, May 1884), and 'The Distracted Preacher' (*New Quarterly Magazine*, April 1879). Macmillan also printed a one-volume edition of *Wessex Tales* in 1889. When Hardy reprinted the collection for the 1896 Osgood, McIlvaine edition of his novels, he added a new story, 'An Imaginative Woman' (*Pall Mall Magazine*, April 1894), which he placed first. For the definitive 1912 Wessex Edition of his novels, Hardy then moved 'An Imaginative Woman' to *Life's Little Ironies* and shifted two stories, 'A Tradition of Eighteen Hundred and Four' and 'The Melancholy Hussar of the German Legion', from *Ironies* to *Wessex Tales*.

The 1891 first edition of *A Group of Noble Dames* contained ten stories loosely connected by a storytelling framework in which the narrators were presented as members of the Wessex Field and Antiquarian Club who are confined by stormy weather and pass the time by telling stories about seventeenth- and eighteenth-century Wessex women (some are loosely based on historical figures from John Hutchins's *History and Antiquities of the County of Dorset*[1]). These narratives are 'The

First Countess of Wessex' (*Harper's New Monthly Magazine*, December 1889); 'Barbara of the House of Grebe', 'The Marchioness of Stonehenge', 'Lady Mottisfont', 'The Lady Icenway', 'Squire Petrick's Lady' and 'Anna, Lady Baxby' (all as 'A Group of Noble Dames', *Graphic*, Christmas Number, 1 December 1890); 'The Lady Penelope' (*Longman's Magazine*, January 1890); 'The Duchess of Hamptonshire' ('The Impulsive Lady of Croome Castle', *Light*, April 1878); and 'The Honourable Laura' ('Benighted Travellers', *Bolton Weekly Journal*, December 1881). *A Group of Noble Dames* was reprinted for the 1896 Osgood, McIlvaine edition and the 1912 Wessex Edition.

The 1894 first edition of *Life's Little Ironies* included eight stories: 'The Son's Veto' (*Illustrated London News*, Christmas number, December 1891); 'For Conscience' Sake' (*Fortnightly Review*, March 1891); 'A Tragedy of Two Ambitions' (*Universal Review*, December 1888); 'On the Western Circuit' (*English Illustrated Magazine*, December 1891); 'To Please His Wife' (*Black and White*, June 1891); 'The Melancholy Hussar of the German Legion' (*Bristol Times and Mirror*, January 1890); 'The Fiddler of the Reels' (*Scribner's Magazine*, May 1893); 'A Tradition of Eighteen Hundred and Four' (*Harper's Christmas*, December 1882). The volume concluded with a series of sketches entitled 'A Few Crusted Characters' ('Wessex Folk', *Harper's New Monthly Magazine*, March–June 1891). *Life's Little Ironies* was reprinted for the 1896 Osgood, McIlvaine edition and for the 1912 Wessex Edition of Hardy's novels (see above for changes to its contents).

After Hardy had rearranged the narratives in *Wessex Tales* and *Life's Little Ironies* for the 1912 Wessex Edition, the first three volumes of stories could be seen to have distinctive principles of organization: *Wessex Tales* consisted of stories that imitated traditional regional narratives, all of them set some decades back in the nineteenth century; *A Group of Noble Dames* consisted of stories about aristocratic Wessex women of the seventeenth and eighteenth centuries; *Life's Little Ironies* – like *Jude the Obscure*, published a year later – consisted chiefly of stories with a contemporary setting and context. *A Changed Man*, however, which Hardy assembled in 1913 in conjunction with the 1912 Wessex Edition, simply brought together the remaining uncollected stories, new and old, that Hardy considered worthy of republication;

it does not display, therefore, a discernible pattern in subject matter or technique. The volume contains 'A Changed Man' (*Sphere*, April 1900); 'The Waiting Supper' (*Murray's Magazine*, January and February 1888); 'Alicia's Diary' (*Manchester Weekly Times*, October 1887); 'The Grave by the Handpost' (*St James's Budget*, Christmas Number, November 1897); 'Enter a Dragoon' (*Harper's Monthly Magazine*, December 1900); 'A Tryst at an Ancient Earthwork' (*Detroit Post*, March 1885); 'What the Shepherd Saw' (*Illustrated London News*, Christmas Number, December 1881); 'A Committee-Man of "The Terror"' (*Illustrated London News*, Christmas Number, November 1896); 'Master John Horseleigh, Knight' (*Illustrated London News*, Summer Number, June 1893); 'The Duke's Reappearance' (*Saturday Review*, Christmas Supplement, December 1896); 'A Mere Interlude' (*Bolton Weekly Journal*, October 1885); and 'The Romantic Adventures of a Milkmaid' (*Graphic*, Summer Number, June 1883).

Several stories remained uncollected: 'How I Built Myself a House' (*Chambers's Journal*, March 1865); 'Destiny and a Blue Cloak' (*New York Times*, 4 October 1874); 'The Thieves Who Couldn't Stop Sneezing' (*Father Christmas*, December 1877); 'An Indiscretion in the Life of an Heiress' (*New Quarterly Magazine*, July 1878); 'The Doctor's Legend' (*Independent*, March 1891); 'Our Exploits at West Poley' (*Household*, November 1892–April 1893); and 'Old Mrs Chundle' (unpublished during Hardy's lifetime, MS in the Dorset County Museum). Hardy also collaborated with Florence Henniker in the composition of 'The Spectre of the Real' (*To-Day*, November 1894). This official collaboration, along with two stories by his second wife that were influenced and corrected by Hardy ('Blue Jimmy: The Horse Stealer', published in the 1911 *Cornhill* under the name F. E. Dugdale, and the unpublished 'The Unconquerable'), has been joined with the uncollected stories in the only full scholarly edition of any of Hardy's short fiction: Pamela Dalziel's *Thomas Hardy: The Excluded and Collaborative Stories* (Oxford: Clarendon Press, 1992).

Note

1. Hutchins's *History* dates back to the eighteenth century, but Hardy owned a copy of the four-volume 3rd edition, published 1861–73 (*Biography*, 582n).

Charles Stanley Reinhart's Illustrations for 'The Romantic Adventures of a Milkmaid'

Although most of Hardy's novels featured illustrations in their magazine appearances, this was not generally the case for the stories. The significant exception in this edition is 'The Romantic Adventures of a Milkmaid', whose 1883 publication in the *Graphic* (a single printing for the Summer Number, dated 25 June) was accompanied by four large pen-and-ink pictures drawn by the well-known American painter and illustrator Charles Stanley Reinhart (1844–96); all but the last of these were also used in the *Harper's Weekly* version (published in seven weekly instalments, from 23 June to 4 August). In the British tabloid-sized *Graphic*, the first three drawings were close together (the fourth appeared a few pages after the end of the story) and each covered a full page; the three pictures featured in the American *Harper's* covered all but the bottom sixth of the page at the beginning of the first, second and fourth instalments, and were placed at a right angle to the opening paragraphs of the text. Neither magazine located the pictures near the relevant passages, but the four incidents – Margery finding the Baron contemplating suicide, Margery emerging in her gown from the tree, Margery encountering her angry father after she has failed to show for her wedding and Jim standing in military garb at his kiln – represent visually striking moments in a story that makes prominent use of pictorial images.

Hardy often consulted with the illustrators of his works, but there is no evidence either that he communicated with Reinhart or that he made any comments about the drawings. Although the image of Margery discovering the despondent baron became the frontispiece for the 1913 Harper and Brothers *A Changed Man* (it replaced the photogravure of Maiden Castle used in the Macmillan first edition), the choice for the American publication may have been a result of Reinhart's long association with Harper's rather than Hardy's personal preference: from 1870 to 1877, Reinhart worked exclusively for Harper's, and although he lived in Paris from 1880 to 1891, he continued to do work for the American publisher until 1890. Reinhart also was to contribute three drawings for the December 1889 printing of Hardy's story 'The First Countess of Wessex' in *Harper's New Monthly Magazine*. He had been trained at the Atelier Suisse in Paris and the Royal Academy in Munich and was recognized for his genre paintings in oil and water-colours, as well as for his pen-and-ink drawings. Among the many authors whose works he illustrated are Charles Dickens, Wilkie Collins, Henry Wadsworth Longfellow and Frances Hodgson Burnett. He also provided drawings for three stories by Henry James, who published an essay about his work in *Harper's Weekly* (14 June 1890, later reprinted in *Picture and Text*, 1893). James praised Reinhart for inspiring a 'revival of illustration' in American magazines with his '[a]bundant, intelligent, interpretative work in black and white': 'The story-teller has . . . the comfort with Mr Reinhart that his drawings are constructive and have the air of the actual. He likes to represent character – he rejoices in the specifying touch.'[1]

'Romantic Adventures' was the first of Hardy's works to appear in the *Graphic*, founded in 1869 at the end of a decade famous for its shift from a caricatural to a realistic style of illustration; the *Graphic* was well known for its large plates and customarily included a column on its artists.[2] According to Gleeson White, the magazine was 'the happy hunting-ground for the earliest work of many a popular draughtsman and painter'.[3] *Harper's* played an analogous role in the United States, taking special pride in its engravings: 'This magazine has reconstructed an art which was torpid and languishing, and has given it life and vigor. Today American wood-engravers have no equals.'[4] In this atmosphere of enthusiasm for detailed pen-and-ink illustrations, Reinhart's vivid pictures for 'The Romantic Adventures of a Milkmaid' may well have contributed to its immense popularity in the United States where, to Hardy's chagrin, it was freely pirated.

The attitude bespoke anguish

'I can't get out of this dreadful tree.'

'What be you here for?'

'Jim stopped at the kiln, while Mrs. Peach held the horse'

403

Notes

1. Henry James, 'Charles S. Reinhart', *Picture and Text* (New York: Harper, 1893), pp. 78, 64, 74.
2. Arlene M. Jackson, *Illustration and the Novels of Thomas Hardy* (London: Macmillan, 1981), pp. 94, 28.
3. Gleeson White, *English Illustration, 'The Sixties': 1855–70* (1897; rpt. Bath: Kingsmead Reprints, 1970), p. 93.
4. *The Making of a Great Magazine* (New York: Harper and Brothers, 1889).

GLOSSARY

Abbreviations

adj.   adjective
adv.   adverb
interj.   interjection
phr.   phrase
p.p.   past participle
pron.   pronoun
pr.t.   present tense
sb.   substantive
sb.pl.   substantive plural
vb.   verb

ace, sb.   the smallest possible amount, hair's-breadth (*OED 2*).

all's winter, adv. phr. all this winter (Smith, 90).

Amazon, sb.   one of a fabulous race of female warriors in Scythia (*OED 2*).

anywhen, adv.   at any time, ever; indefinite compound of 'when'; rare in literature but common in southern dialects (*OED 2*). Wright says the word is characteristic of Dorset.

a-scram, adj.   withered (*OED 2*).

assize, sb.   a periodical session held in each county of England for the administration of civil and criminal justice (*OED 2*).

avast, interj.   stop, cease.

back-brand, sb.   the burning or charred log placed at the back of a fireplace (*OED 2*).

backwardness, sb.   shyness (*OED 2*).

bad abed, phr.	sick in bed (Barnes lists 'bad' as Dorset dialect usage for sick or ill).
Baronet, sb.	titled order, the lowest that is hereditary, ranking next below a baron, having precedence of all orders of knighthood, except that of Garter (*OED 2*).
barrow, sb.	grave-mound, tumulus (*OED 2*).
barton, sb.	farmyard (*OED 2*).
bee-burning, sb.	the harvesting of the bee-hive, a process that involved smoking out the bees.
bell-carriage, sb.	the timber framework from which a bell is hung.
bell-hanging, sb.	the activity of installing bell-pulls and bell-wires (*OED 2*).
bell-wire, sb.	the wire by which a bell-pull is connected with a bell (*OED 2*).
black-coated, adj.	specifically defining clerical or professional as distinguished from industrial or commercial occupations (*OED 2*).
black-pudding, sb.	sausage-shaped pudding of blood or suet (*OED 2*).
bleachy, adv.	used in Wiltshire, Dorset and Somersetshire to mean saltish, brackish or pale (Wright).
blood-money, sb.	money paid to a witness who gives evidence leading to the conviction of a person upon a capital charge (*OED 2*).
blower, sb.	plate or sheet of metal fixed before a fire to increase the draught (*OED 2*).
bonhomie, sb.	(French) geniality.
brimstone, sb.	old name for sulphur (*OED 2*).
brink, sb.	border of water, especially when steep (*OED 2*).
broad-arrow, sb.	the arrow-head-shaped mark used by the British Board of Ordnance and placed upon government property (*OED 2*).
brother-law, sb.	dialect for brother-in-law (Wright).
buffer, sb.	slightly contemptuous term for 'fellow' (*OED 2*).
burgess, sb.	inhabitant of a borough; strictly, one possessing

full municipal rights (*OED* 2).

burgher, sb.   archaic word for the citizen of a town (*OED* 2).

by now, phr.   just now.

carrier, sb.   one who undertakes for hire the conveyance of goods and parcels, usually on certain routes, and at fixed times (*OED* 2).

cave, sb.   case for holding spirit bottles (Wright).

chiffonnier, sb.   piece of furniture consisting of a small cupboard with the top made so as to form a sideboard (*OED* 2).

chimmer, sb.   a use for the word in Dorset, Somerset and Devon is 'chamber', an upper room, either in a house or outbuilding (Wright).

chimney-crook, sb.   bar of iron with a hook at its lower end on which to hang pots, having a contrivance of notches by which it can be lengthened or shortened (Wright).

chine hoops, sb.phr.   the two end hoops on a cask, usually much stouter than the others, which cover the 'chine' or projection of the staves (curved pieces of wood forming sides of a cask) beyond the heads (Wright).

clinker, sb.   small hard brick or a hard metallic cinder (Wright).

clitch, sb.   the fork part of the leg or arm (Wright).

coddle, sb.   one who coddles himself or is coddled, hence *mollycoddle* (*OED* 2).

comb-washings, sb.pl.   the last drainings of the honey-comb (Wright).

coped, adj.   having the top or upper surface sloping down on each side like a coping (*OED* 2).

copper, sb.   vessel made of copper, particularly a large boiler for cooking or laundry purposes (*OED* 2).

copyhold, sb.   temporary tenure of a property belonging to a lord, its duration depending on the will of the lord (*OED* 2); compare 'freehold'.

corporation, sb.   the civic authorities of a borough or incorporated town or city (*OED* 2).

couch-heap, sb.	heap of coarse grass roots piled up for burning (Smith, 91).
council-man, sb.	member of a council, especially that of a incorporated town (*OED* 2).
cross, sb.	the point where two paths cross each other; a crossing, cross-way (*OED* 2).
culpet, sb.	culprit.
cunning-man, sb.	wizard or seer; a conjuror (Barnes).
curry-comb, vb.	to rub down with a curry-comb, an instrument for grooming a horse (*OED* 2).
Custom-house, sb.	government office situated at a place of import or export, as a seaport, at which customs are levied on goods imported or exported (*OED* 2).
Daze it, adv.phr.	in Dorset, used imprecatively, like 'damn'; hence also 'be dazed'.
deedy, adj.	dialect for full of deeds or activity; found first in the combination 'ill-deedy' (*OED* 2).
désinvolture, sb.	(French) ease, gracefulness.
dissenter, sb.	one who separates himself from the communion of the established Church of England; in early use included Roman Catholics, but later usually restricted to those legally styled Protestant dissenters.
down, sb.	open high land, especially, in the plural, treeless undulating chalk uplands of southern England used for pasture (*OED* 2).
draught animal, sb.	animal that draws a cart or plough (*OED* 2).
drawlacheting, adj.	walking lazily or slowly (Barnes).
drawn-bonnet, sb.	bonnet made with drawn-work, fancy work in linen done by drawing out threads (*OED* 2).
dress, vb.	to arrange the furrows upon the surface of a millstone (*OED* 2).
dresser, sb.	kitchen sideboard with shelves for dishes.
drong, sb.	narrow way between two hedges or walls, also called a 'drongway' (Barnes).
d'ye tell o't, phr.	do you tell of it (Barnes).

eaves-dropping, sb.	the dripping of water from the eaves of a house (*OED 2*).
en, pron.	objective case-form of 'he', used in Dorset dialect for the 'personal class' of objects (Barnes).
environ, vb.	to surround with hostile intention; to beset; also figurative of circumstances or conditions, especially of dangers, troubles, etc. (*OED 2*).
ewe-lease, sb.	grass field or down stocked with sheep (Wright).
fag, sb.	drudgery (*OED 2*).
fire-grate, sb.	frame of metal bars for holding the fuel in a fireplace or furnace (*OED 2*).
five-light window, sb.phr.	window with five lights, the perpendicular divisions of a mullioned window (*OED 2*).
flat, sb.	floor or storey in a house (*OED 2*).
fleet, vb.	float (Smith, 90).
flick-flack, sb.	perhaps a version of 'flicket-a-flacket', a representation of the sound made by something flapping (*OED 2*).
flue, sb.	smoke-duct in a chimney, hence any hot-air passage (*OED 2*).
footy, adj.	little; insignificant (Barnes).
freehold, sb.	tenure by which a property is held without a specified limit of time (*OED 2*); compare 'copyhold'.
full pail, (to be) in, vb.phr.	said of a cow, to be in full milk (Wright).
furze, sb.	spiny yellow-flowered evergreen shrub growing on European waste lands, also called gorse (*OED 2*); associated iconographically with the 'fallen' or 'ruined' woman.
gie, vb.pr.t.	also *gee*, meaning 'give' (Wright).
gloury, adj.	*OED 2* gives 'glour' as the obsolete form of 'glower', meaning to look angrily or crossly; Wright defines 'glowery' as out of temper, cross, surly; the word might also be connected to the Dorset usage of 'glow, glaw, glawoo', meaning

'To stare; to watch with fixed and wide open
eyes' (Barnes).

glum, sb.	gloom.
gownd, sb.	gown.
grammer, sb.	grandmother (Barnes).
greatcoat, sb.	a large, heavy overcoat; a top-coat (*OED* 2).
grog-blossom, sb.	pimple or redness on nose from intemperance (*OED* 2).
ground-line, sb.	the base upon which a diagram is constructed (*OED* 2).
guinea-gold, sb.	twenty-two-carat gold of which guineas were coined (*OED* 2).
gwine, vb.pr.t.	going
half-mourning, adj.	the second period of mourning, when black was replaced by white, grey or lavender (*OED* 2).
halfpenny-candle, sb.	candle worth no more than a coin of half the value of a penny; 'halfpenny' expresses depreciation, the idea that something is of con-temptible value (*OED* 2).
have up, vb.phr.	(as in 'I'll have 'em up for this') take up or cause to go before a court of justice in answer to a charge (*OED* 2).
hedge-carpenter, sb.	one whose business is to repair fences (*OED* 2).
het, adj.	hot (*OED* 2).
high-day, sb.	festal day (*OED* 2).
hob-and-nob, vb.	drink with; consort with, be on very friendly terms with (Wright).
home-along, adv.	homewards (*OED* 2).
hontish, adj.	proud.
horn, sb.	the side of a lantern, often made of horn (*OED* 2).
horse-pond, sb.	pond for watering and washing horses (*OED* 2).
hoss, sb.	horse (Barnes).
howsomever, adv.	however.
jack, sb.	familiar, half-contemptuous term for an individual, especially in the phrase 'every jack man' (Wright).

jack-o-lent, sb.	scarecrow of old clothes, sometimes stuffed; the name is taken from that of a ragged and lean figure formerly shown in some Lent processions, and betokening the Lent fast (Barnes).
jiggered, vb.p.p.	put out of joint or exhausted (Wright); used as vague substitute for a profane oath or imprecation, especially in asseverations (*OED 2*).
just by now, phr.	'by now' means just now; hence 'just by now' is tautologous (Smith, 90).
keakhorn, sb.	*OED 2* defines a 'keak' as an antiquated term for a cackle; the 'keakhorn' is presumably the throat or gullet.
keeping, sb.	in painting, the maintenance of the proper relation between the representations of nearer and more distant objects in a picture; hence the maintenance of harmony of composition (*OED 2*).
knee-nap, sb.	presumably 'knee-knaps', leathers worn over the knees by thatchers at work (Barnes).
larry, sb.	confused noise, as of a number of people all talking together; a disturbed condition (Wright).
left-handed wife, sb.phr.	the wife in a false marriage; the term comes from a German custom by which the bridegroom gave the left hand in such marriages (*OED 2*).
lint, sb.	refuse of flax plant used as a combustible for tinder (*OED 2*).
lynchet, sb.	a narrow terrace on the escarpment of downs (Wright).
make-up, sb.	cosmetics, especially used for disguise by an actor (*OED 2*).
mangold-wurzel, sb.	kind of beet used for cattle feed (*OED 2*).
Marther, sb.	Martha.
master-workman, sb.	master-man, that is, a person skilled in some art or craft (*OED 2*).
metheglin, sb.	beer made from honey (Wright).
milk-sop, sb.	piece of bread soaked in milk (*OED 2*).

mixen, sb.	place where dung and refuse is laid; also, a heap of dung, earth, compost, etc., used for manure (*OED* 2).
myrmidon, sb.	warlike race of men inhabiting ancient Thessaly, whom, according to the Homeric story, Achilles led to the siege of Troy; also an unscrupulously faithful follower or hireling; chiefly myrmidon of the law, of justice, applied contemptuously to a policeman, bailiff, or other inferior administrative officer of the law (*OED* 2).
nation, adv.	damnation (used as an expletive).
nonconformity, sb.	the principles or practice of Protestant dissent.
'Od drown it all, phr.	'God drown it all'; a variant meaning of drown is to dilute or to spoil liquor by putting in too much water (Wright).
offset, sb.	in surveyor's language, a short distance measured perpendicularly from the main line of measurement (*OED* 2).
Old Tom, sb.phr.	slang for 'gin'.
orchet, sb.	dialect pronunciation for orchard.
overlook, vb.	to look on with the evil eye (Barnes).
over-right, adv.	right over, against, opposite (Barnes).
owl's light, sb.phr.	the dim and uncertain light in which owls go abroad, twilight, dusk (*OED* 2).
parade, sb.	public square or promenade, especially those running along the border of Weymouth harbour.
pa'son, sb.	parson.
pent-roof, sb.	sloping roof, especially as the subsidiary structure attached to the wall of a main building (*OED* 2).
personal, adj.	associated with chattels and chattel interests in land (*OED* 2); see also 'real'.
pink in, vb.phr.	with reference to daylight, to draw in or diminish (*OED* 2).
pinner, sb.	pinafore.
plaster, sb.	curative application consisting of some substance, often mustard, spread upon muslin and capable

of adhering at the temperature of the body (*OED 2*).

politesse du coeur, sb.phr.
(French) heartfelt politeness.

poll, sb.
head (*OED 2*).

potato-grave, sb.
excavation, pit or trench; originally a trench for earthing up potatoes or other roots (*OED 2*).

pourparler, sb.
(French) informal discussion preliminary to negotiation (*OED 2*).

preventive-man, sb.
man belonging to that department of the Customs which is concerned with the prevention of smuggling (*OED 2*).

pride of the morning, sb.phr.
Barnes defines the Dorset phrase 'pride-o'-the-marnen' as 'a foggy mist in the morning, likely to be followed by a warm day'.

rainwater-butt, sb.
cask or barrel for catching rainwater (*OED 2*).

rathe, adv.
soon, early (Barnes).

real, adj.
associated with land and rights attached to the possession of land (*OED 2*); see also 'personal'.

rendlewood, sb.
barked oak (*OED 2*).

riding-officer, sb.
mounted revenue-officer; the last riding-officer died in 1862 (*OED 2*).

rithe, adj.
high, as in 'high living' (Smith, 91).

road-scraping, sb.
presumably what is picked up by a road-scraper, an instrument for scraping dirt, mud, etc., from roads (*OED 2*).

rod in pickle, sb. phr.
punishment ready to be carried out (*OED 2*).

rope-dancer, sb.
performer on a tight-rope (*OED 2*).

rope-walk, sb.
stretch of ground appropriated to the making of ropes (*OED 2*).

Sarer, sb.
Sarah.

scrammed, adj.
paralysed, benumbed with cold (*OED 2*).

sectarian, adj.
confined to a particular sect; bigotedly attached to a particular sect or denomination (*OED 2*).

serpent, sb.
wind instrument, now little used; its wooden tube with several bends gives a powerful note (*OED 2*).

sharp sand, sb. phr.	sand composed of material having sharp points, used in building (*OED* 2).
shepherd's plaid, sb.	woollen cloth with a black and white checked pattern (*OED* 2).
shreds, sb.pl.	strips of cloth used for tying up plants or fruit trees (*OED* 2).
singing-gallery stairs, sb.phr.	stairs leading to balcony used by singers and musicians.
skimmer-cake, sb.	kind of dumpling or cake, especially one made with surplus dough, and boiled on a skimmer (Wright).
skirting, sb.	narrow boarding, edging of wood, slate or cement, etc., placed vertically along the base of the wall (*OED* 2).
slaked, adj.	chemically combined with water (said of lime) (*OED* 2).
small, sb.	weak or watered down liquor (*OED* 2).
smoke-jack, sb.	apparatus for turning a roasting-spit, fixed in a chimney and set in motion by the current of air passing up this (*OED* 2).
spit-and-dab, sb.	plaster, mud or very rough mortar (Wright).
spring-cart, sb.	cart mounted on springs (*OED* 2).
spring-trap, sb.	trap mounted on springs (*OED* 2).
stoor, sb.	Dorset dialect pronunciation for 'stir' (Barnes).
store-cupboard, sb.	storage cupboard (*OED* 2).
stove in, vb.phr.	having a hole from being crushed inwards (*OED* 2).
strake, sb.	section of the iron rim of a cart-wheel (*OED* 2).
stray-line, sb.	submerged or floating line fastened at one end only (*OED* 2).
stripping, sb.	ingot prepared for rolling into plates, or tobacco leaf with the stock and midrib removed (*OED* 2).
swede-lifting, sb.	act of digging up turnips (*OED* 2).
tacker-haired, adj.	with hairs like a tacker, a shoemaker's waxed thread (Smith, 91).
takings, sb.pl.	state of agitation (*OED* 2).

'Talian iron, sb.phr.   Italian iron, for crimping cap-frills (Smith, 91).

teasle, sb.   teasel, plant with prickly leaves and flower-heads (*OED 2*).

teave, vb.   reach about the limbs in struggling wise, like a restless child (Barnes).

three-cunning, adj.   Barnes defines 'three-cunnen' as over-sharp.

tisty-tosty, adj.   softly round, like a child's toss ball of cowslips (Barnes).

tole, vb.   entice or allure (Barnes).

Tophet, sb.   place near Jerusalem used for idolatrous worship and later for depositing refuse, for consumption of which fires were kept burning; hell.

trimmer, sb.   one who trims between opposing parties in politics, etc., hence, one who inclines to each of two opposite sides as interest dictates. *OED 2* gives an example from John Wesley: 'Nor is it possible for all the trimmers between God and the world to elude the consequence.'

trimming, adj.   Barnes defines 'trimmen', an intensive, as meaning 'great of its kind'.

turbary, sb.   the right of digging turf on another's ground; the place where turf or peat is dug (*OED 2*).

Turk, sb.   ' "A turk of a thing" is an intensive expression, meaning a big or formidable one of its kind' (Barnes). A 'Turk for sprees' is presumably someone who is good at drinking and partying.

turn the blood, vb.phr.   in cases of disease, to cause a reaction by means of some great shock (Wright).

up train, sb.phr.   headed north or toward London.

vamp, sb.   sole of a shoe (Barnes).

vell, sb.   fell, hide or skin (Barnes cites 'I can't zee vell or mark o't' as a standard Dorset idiom, a version of 'I can't see hide or hair').

vis-à-vis, sb.   (French) person facing another, especially in some dances (*OED 2*).

vlanker, sb.   big flake of fire (Barnes).

volk, sb.	Dorset pronunciation of 'folk'.
West-of-England cloth, sb.phr.	high-quality woollen broadcloth long associated with the west of the country; *OED 2*'s earliest example is 1843.
whew, vb.	rustle sharply (Smith).
wool, vb.	Dorset pronunciation of 'will'.
zull, sb.	plough, from the Saxon *sulh* or *syl* (Barnes).
zummat, sb.	Dorset pronunciation for 'something'.

READ MORE IN PENGUIN

In every corner of the world, on every subject under the sun, Penguin represents quality and variety – the very best in publishing today.

For complete information about books available from Penguin – including Puffins, Penguin Classics and Arkana – and how to order them, write to us at the appropriate address below. Please note that for copyright reasons the selection of books varies from country to country.

In the United Kingdom: Please write to *Dept. EP, Penguin Books Ltd, Bath Road, Harmondsworth, West Drayton, Middlesex UB7 ODA*

In the United States: Please write to *Consumer Sales, Penguin Putnam Inc., P.O. Box 12289 Dept. B, Newark, New Jersey 07101-5289*. VISA and MasterCard holders call 1-800-788-6262 to order Penguin titles

In Canada: Please write to *Penguin Books Canada Ltd, 10 Alcorn Avenue, Suite 300, Toronto, Ontario M4V 3B2*

In Australia: Please write to *Penguin Books Australia Ltd, P.O. Box 257, Ringwood, Victoria 3134*

In New Zealand: Please write to *Penguin Books (NZ) Ltd, Private Bag 102902, North Shore Mail Centre, Auckland 10*

In India: Please write to *Penguin Books India Pvt Ltd, 11 Community Centre, Panchsheel Park, New Delhi 110017*

In the Netherlands: Please write to *Penguin Books Netherlands bv, Postbus 3507, NL-1001 AH Amsterdam*

In Germany: Please write to *Penguin Books Deutschland GmbH, Metzlerstrasse 26, 60594 Frankfurt am Main*

In Spain: Please write to *Penguin Books S. A., Bravo Murillo 19, 1° B, 28015 Madrid* ·

In Italy: Please write to *Penguin Italia s.r.l., Via Benedetto Croce 2, 20094 Corsico, Milano*

In France: Please write to *Penguin France, Le Carré Wilson, 62 rue Benjamin Baillaud, 31500 Toulouse*

In Japan: Please write to *Penguin Books Japan Ltd, Kaneko Building, 2-3-25 Koraku, Bunkyo-Ku, Tokyo 112*

In South Africa: Please write to *Penguin Books South Africa (Pty) Ltd, Private Bag X14, Parkview, 2122 Johannesburg*

READ MORE IN PENGUIN

THOMAS HARDY

Tess of the D'Urbervilles
'An extraordinarily beautiful book ... Perhaps this is another way of saying that *Tess* is a poetic novel' A. Alvarez

Far From the Madding Crowd
'The novel which announced Hardy's arrival as a great writer' Ronald Blythe

Jude the Obscure
'The characters ... are built up not merely against the background of the huge and now changing Wessex, but out of it. It is this which makes the novel the completion of an oeuvre' C. H. Sisson

The Woodlanders
'In no other novel does Hardy seem more confidently in control of what he has to say, more assured of the tone in which to say it' Ian Gregor

The Return of the Native
'It came to embody more faithfully than any other book the quintessence of all that Wessex already represented in Hardy's mind' George Woodcock

The Mayor of Casterbridge
In depicting a man who overreaches the limits, Hardy once again demonstrates his uncanny psychological grasp and his deeply rooted knowledge of mid-nineteenth-century Dorset.

and

The Trumpet-Major	**The Distracted Preacher**
A Pair of Blue Eyes	**and Other Tales**
Under the Greenwood Tree	**Selected Poetry**
The Hand of Ethelberta	**A Laodicean**
The Pursuit of the Well-Beloved	**Two on a Tower**
and The Well-Beloved	**Desperate Remedies**